TRY A LITTLE TENDERNESS

Also by Joan Jonker

When One Door Closes
Man Of The House
Home Is Where The Heart Is
Stay In Your Own Back Yard
Last Tram To Lime Street
Sweet Rosie O'Grady
The Pride Of Polly Perkins
Sadie Was A Lady
Walking My Baby Back Home

TRY A LITTLE TENDERNESS

Joan Jonker

HEADLINE

First published in 1998
by HEADLINE BOOK PUBLISHING

10 9 8 7 6 5 4 3 2 1

British Library Cataloguing in Publication Data

Jonker, Joan
Try a little tenderness
I. Title
823.9'14[F]

ISBN 0 7472 2267 3

Typeset by Avon Dataset Ltd, Bidford-on-Avon, Warks

Printed and bound in Great Britain by
Mackays of Chatham plc, Chatham, Kent

HEADLINE BOOK PUBLISHING
A division of Hodder Headline PLC
338 Euston Road
London NW1 3BH

To my Down's Syndrome son, Philip, who is the nicest person I know.

He knows not greed or envy, speaks ill of no one and walks away from raised voices. He enjoys life and appreciates everything. With his ever-ready smile he is a joy to know and I love the bones of him. If there were more people like Philip, wouldn't the world be a better place?

A friendly greeting from Joan

Come with me back in time to the mid-1930s and meet the Nightingale family. Stan and Mary and their two daughters, Laura and Jenny. Both girls are beautiful to look at, but as different in nature as chalk and cheese. And meet their friends and neighbours, the Hanleys and the Moynihans. Bring these characters together and you have a recipe for fun and laughter all the way. There may be the odd tear of sadness, because that's life. But mostly the tears rolling down your cheeks will be tears of laughter. I hope you enjoy meeting my new friends.

Chapter One

'I want me skipping-rope back, Laura, yer've had it for ages and it's not fair because it was my birthday present.'

'Oh, stop yer moaning.' Laura Nightingale threw her sister Jenny a dirty look. 'Me mam said yer had to give me a go.'

'Yeah, but she didn't mean yer could keep it all to yerself.' Jenny stamped her foot in indignation at the injustice of it. At twelve years of age, she was eighteen months younger than her sister and always came off worse when it came to sharing. 'When you got a book for yer birthday, yer wouldn't even read me a story from it, never mind let me read it.'

'That's 'cos I didn't want yer to get dirty marks on it.' Laura was skipping with her arms crossed and jumping on one foot. It wasn't often she got the chance to skip with a proper skipping-rope. Usually it was a piece of clothes-line, but this one had real wooden handles painted in a bright red. 'I'll swap yer me book for yer rope.'

'No! The book's all torn now, I don't want it.' Jenny could see her sister had no intention of relinquishing the rope until she got fed up with it. 'I'm going to tell me mam if yer don't give it to me *now*.'

Laura smirked and kept on skipping. 'Go and tell her, I don't care.'

Near to tears, Jenny ran into the house. She found her mother in the kitchen putting some clothes through the mangle. 'Mam, our Laura won't give me back me skipping-rope. I haven't even had a turn, and it's my birthday present.'

Mary Nightingale sighed as she rubbed her wet hands down the front of her pinny. Mother and daughter were as alike as two peas in a pod. Both were slim, with pale golden hair, a fair complexion and vivid blue eyes. They had the same nature, too. Kind, easygoing and with a sense of humour that brought a ready smile to their faces.

'She's a selfish article, our Laura. She thinks the world revolves around her and what she wants.' Mary made her way to the front door. 'It's about time she learned there are other people beside herself.'

When Laura saw her mother, she laughed. 'Went crying to her mammy, did she? She's like a flippin' baby.'

'Give her the rope, Laura, it's her birthday present.'

1

'I'll give it to her in a minute, when I've had a go skipping backwards.' There was a brazen look on Laura's face. 'Just a couple more minutes.'

'Yer heard what I said.' Mary was trying to contain her rising temper. 'Give it to her now or I'll give yer a clip around the ears.'

Still the girl went on skipping as though daring her mother to carry out her threat. 'I said in a minute.'

Mary stepped forward and caught the rope in mid-flight. 'Do as ye're told and hand it over.'

'I won't, not until I'm ready.' When she felt her mother tugging at the rope, Laura gripped it tight and refused to let go. And all the while she had a smirk on her face. With her dark hair, greeny-hazel eyes and swarthy complexion, there was no resemblance between her and the woman with whom she was having a tug of war. And the war wasn't about the rope, it was about her getting her own way, showing who was the boss.

Mary could no longer stand the insolence and delivered a stinging smack to the side of her daughter's face. 'You asked for that, you impudent, selfish madam. Don't yer ever dare answer me back like that again.' She pulled the rope which was now hanging loose and passed it to Jenny. 'Here yer are, sunshine, and don't let her take it off yer again.'

Laura looked stunned as she held a hand to her cheek. 'You just wait until me dad gets in, he'll have something to say about this. Yer'll be sorry.'

'I warned yer dad twelve years ago that he was spoiling yer and making a rod for his own back. The trouble is, he's made one for my back as well. And everybody else that has to put up with yer selfishness and insolence.' With that Mary turned her back and went into the house. She knew there'd be a row when Stan came in, he wouldn't take her side, never did. But there was only so much a mother could take from a child who was out of hand, and she'd taken enough. They had two daughters and they should be treated equally. But they weren't, not by their father. Laura could do no wrong in his eyes, he thought the sun shone out of her backside. She lied herself out of trouble, always laying the blame at her sister's door. If there was a fight, it was always Jenny who started it. If anything went missing, it was Jenny who'd taken it. And Stan fell for it every time, believing her without question.

Mary put her hip to the side of the mangle and pushed it back into the corner of the tiny kitchen of the two-up-two-down house that had been her home since the day she married, fifteen years ago. She loved her husband, and they'd been happy, until favouritism had reared its ugly head and blighted that happiness. She'd tried to reason with Stan when Laura started getting out of hand, but he wouldn't

2

listen. He couldn't see further than the end of his nose where she was concerned. Poor Jenny didn't get a look in. Although she was the youngest, she was the one who was sent to the corner shop for his five Woodbines when Laura didn't feel like going. She was the one sent down the yard for a shovelful of coal because Laura didn't like the cold. Yet she never complained. She did everything she was asked, because from the time she could toddle she realised her sister was more special to her father than she was. But in the last year she'd begun to rebel against the unfairness and was fighting back.

Mary lifted the lid off the pan of stew and sniffed up in appreciation. 'That should put a lining on their tummies.' She spoke aloud to the empty room. 'I'll set the table and then call the girls in.'

She was laying the knives and forks out when her husband came in, his face red with anger. 'Have you just slapped our Laura for nothing?'

'No, I have not slapped our Laura for nothing.' Mary sighed as she shook her head. 'I slapped her for giving me cheek and for not doing as she was told.'

'Yer made a holy show of her in front of the whole street, that's what yer did. And all over a bleedin' skipping-rope.'

Her anger high, Mary's answer was sharp. 'I think yer should get yer facts straight, Stan Nightingale. And yer won't get them straight off that wayward daughter of ours. Huh! In front of the whole street, was it? I didn't see anyone around, but if there was then they'd have heard her giving her mother cheek, the hard-faced little faggot. And the bleedin' skipping-rope ye're talking about was Jenny's birthday present! She wasn't even allowed to get her hands on it because of your darling Laura. Or had yer forgotten it was Jenny's birthday? Mind you, it wouldn't surprise me. There are times when I think yer've forgotten yer've even got another daughter, all the notice yer take of her.'

'Well, I don't want yer hittin' her no more.' Stan hung his peaked cap on the nail behind the kitchen door. 'If there's any telling-off to do, I'll do it.'

He was about to walk away when Mary grabbed his arm and spun him around. 'You tell our Laura off! That's a good one, that is. I've never known yer raise yer voice to her, nor yer hand, more's the pity. A few smacks when she was younger would have put her on the straight and narrow, taught her right from wrong. But it's too late now, she's set in her ways, lying, cheating and bloody selfish. Yer'll live to rue the day, Stan Nightingale, mark my words. She'll bring trouble to this door, and it'll all be your fault.'

Stan, whose dark colouring Laura had inherited, flushed. 'Yer've always had it in for the girl, yer've never had any time for her. But in future, leave me to deal with her.'

3

Once again he made to walk away and Mary pulled him back. 'Let's get this straight, once and for all. She's my daughter as well as yours, and while she's in this house she does as she's told. If she misbehaves and deserves a crack, I'll give her one. If she's good, we'll get on fine and this house will be a happier place. The choice is hers. But I'll tell yer this, Stan, and yer can take it from me that I mean every word of it. I'm fed up to the back teeth of her getting pampered and our Jenny left out in the cold. I won't tolerate it any longer. Either Laura pulls her socks up and behaves in a reasonable manner, or I'll wash me hands of her and she can run riot for all I care. She'd be your responsibility then. And that is only right, because you made her what she is.' She pushed his arm. 'Go and call the girls in for their dinner. Oh, and unless the words stick in yer throat, wish Jenny a Happy Birthday.

They sat down to their meal in silence. But Laura's eyes were going from her mother to her father. She wasn't satisfied that she'd received the sympathy she thought she deserved. 'Is me face red, Dad, where me mam slapped me?'

Stan's eyes were on his plate when Mary answered. 'I can't see any red. But I'll slap yer again if it's a red face yer want.'

'Did yer hear that, Dad? She said she'd slap me again.'

'Get on with yer dinner,' he grunted, 'before it gets cold.'

Mary pursed her lips. She shouldn't say any more to aggravate the situation, it would make her as childish as her daughter. But in the end she couldn't hold it back. Her and Stan had never argued before, not until Laura started to come between them with her shenanigans. 'Don't call me "she" either. They say that "she" is the cat's mother. So if I'm a "she", what does that make you?'

Jenny was feeling miserable, her heart in her boots. She couldn't bear it when there was an atmosphere in the house, and this time she was to blame. She should have let her sister keep the blinking rope – look at the trouble it had caused. She could tell her mam was upset, and she didn't deserve to be. So Jenny tried to make amends. 'Did yer see me skipping-rope. Dad? It's a smasher, all me mates will be green with envy.'

Laura wasn't having that. She was her dad's favourite, not Jenny. 'Seeing as all your mates are green anyway, no one will notice the difference. They're all as thick as two short planks, every one of them.'

Stan raised his head, his knife and fork standing one in each hand like sentinels. 'That's enough of that, there's no need to be sarky. Get on with yer dinner and have less to say.'

Laura's eyes flew open in surprise. Her dad never spoke to her like that. But she knew who had put him up to it – her mother. But she better hadn't say anything now, not while her dad was there. She'd

4

get her own back though, she vowed as she speared a carrot. If her mother thought she was going to be a goody-goody, like their Jenny, then she had another think coming.

As the meal continued in silence, Laura was wrapped up in thoughts of the future. Only another six months and she'd be leaving school and getting herself a job. She was so selfish, all she dreamed of was having her own money and being able to buy the clothes she liked instead of having to wear the drab things her mother bought for her. Never once had it entered her empty head that her mother had to scrimp and scrape every week to buy those clothes. No, all Laura was concerned about was herself. Not for her the pride of handing over her wages every week in the knowledge that they would make life easier for all the family. She'd already made up her mind that she was entitled to keep more for herself in pocket-money than she handed over. After all, she would be the one going to work so why should she hand it over? In her narrow mind there was only one person in her life that she really loved – Laura Nightingale.

Mary was hanging the washing on the line on the Monday morning when a smile crossed her face. Amy Hanley, her neighbour and best friend, was singing at the top of her voice in the next yard. Over the wall came the strains of a song that had been popular a few years ago. Mind you, it had been sung then by Kate Smith, and Amy was certainly not in the same league as the well-known singer. It wasn't that she was tone deaf, she just sounded like someone who had been thrown out of the pub at closing time after her throat had been oiled by half-a-dozen bottles of stout.

> 'When the moon comes over the mountains,
> I'm alone with my memories of you.
> We kissed and said goodbye,
> You cried and so did I,
> Now do you wonder why I'm lonely?'

Mary took a peg from her mouth, and giggling, she shouted, 'Yer missed a verse out there, Amy. What happened to the "rose-covered valley we knew"?'

'Oh, ye're there, are yer? Well, I'm not in the mood for rose-covered valleys today, girl, I want to be alone with me bleedin' memories.'

'What memories are they, Amy? Must be miserable from the sound of yer.'

'I'm always miserable on wash-day, girl. If the sun was shining and I had nowt to do, and me purse had a few bob in it, me memories would be happy ones. Like remembering when my feller used to put

5

his hands around me waist and tell me I was the most beautiful girl in the world, bar none. He hasn't said that for years, girl. Mind you, I haven't had a bleedin' waist for years, either.'

Although there was a brick wall separating them, Mary could see her friend as clearly as if she was standing next to her. She was only five foot, was Amy, and as round as she was tall. Right now her mousy-coloured hair would be covered by a mobcap which would be down to her eyebrows because the elastic had withered, the pocket of her pinny would be bulging with clothes pegs, her stockings would be wrinkled around her ankles and her face would be creased in a smile.

'Another memory keeps coming back to me, girl, but I have a bit of trouble with it 'cos it's faded with age. It was when we were first married, before the kids came along, and my feller was that eager he used to carry me upstairs to the bedroom.' Amy's laugh was so loud they must have been able to hear it in the next street. 'Now it takes him all his time to carry himself up. And the most I get out of him in bed is, "Don't let me oversleep, d'yer hear?".'

'Well, the men are tired after a hard day's work, Amy, yer've got to make allowances for them. The first flush of youth isn't there any more.'

'What the bleedin' hell do they think we do all day? Sit on our ruddy backsides? I'd willingly swap places with my feller and go out to work while he minded the three kids. He wouldn't know what had hit him, having to polish and scrub, wash, iron, get the shopping in, see to the dinners, do the darning . . . I'd give him a week and he'd be pleading for mercy.'

'Some good could come of it, Amy,' Mary chuckled. 'If he was at home all day he could put his feet up for a couple of hours, then he'd have the energy to carry yer up the stairs to bed again.'

'He'd need more than energy to carry me up the stairs now, girl – he'd need a bleedin' hoist. And by the end of all that palaver he'd have lost the urge.' Amy finished pegging the washing on the line and stood back to gaze with satisfaction at the clothes blowing in the wind. They'd be dry in no time and she could start ironing before the two kids came in from school and got under her feet. 'Ay, girl, yer don't happen to have any custard creams in, do yer?'

'I might have a couple, I think. Why? Are yer having visitors?'

'I'm not, girl – you are! I'm inviting meself in for a cup of tea and a chinwag. There's nothing better to chase the blues away than a good old gossip.' Her chubby face did contortions. 'Yer don't need to get yer best china out for me, girl, I'm not a snob.'

'Don't be funny, Amy Hanley, yer know I haven't got no china cups.'

'That's why I said yer didn't need to get them out, girl, I knew yer didn't have none. I didn't want yer rummaging in yer cupboards for something yer haven't got. And don't be coming over all embarrassed when yer give me a cup with a chip in, 'cos like I said, I'm not a snob.'

'Ye're a bloody scream, you are, Amy! Yer invite yerself over without a by-your-leave, then have the nerve to criticise me crockery before yer come. And ye're expecting custard creams into the bargain.'

'Only one, girl, I don't expect no more. And yer'll get yer money's worth, 'cos I can tell by yer voice that yer need cheering up.' Amy raised her voice to a shout. 'You put the kettle on, girl, while I stick the guard in front of the fire.'

'You're well-off having a fire this time of the morning, aren't yer? Has your feller had a win on the gee-gees?'

Back came a whispered, 'Fooling the neighbours, girl, that's all. I bet a pound to a pinch of snuff that nosy Annie Baxter has had her ear to the wall, listening to every word we've said. She'll be round to Lily Farmer's as fast as her skinny legs will carry her. And by the time she's put her own interpretation on our conversation, it'll end up something like this. "Ay, what d'yer think, Lily? Monday morning, and that Amy Hanley's got a fire up the chimney. And yer'll never guess where she got the money from for a bag of coal. What's that yer said, Lily? Oh, yer'll have three guesses . . . okay. No, she didn't get it on tick off the coalman. No, she didn't find a two-bob piece. No, yer silly cow, the bag hadn't fallen off the bleedin' coal-cart. That's yer three guesses, Lily, and I knew yer wouldn't get it in a month of Sundays. Just wait till I tell yer, yer won't believe it. She got it off her feller for letting him carry her upstairs so he could have his wicked way with her. How about that, eh? Dirty pair of buggers".'

On the other side of the yard wall, Mary was in stitches. Amy might not be able to sing like Kate Smith, but her impersonation of the street gossip was perfect. 'That was very good, Amy, yer sounded just like her.'

'If I had false teeth, girl, I could do it better. Yer know how her teeth are always clicking when she talks – well, I can't do that. Still, it's not worth having all me teeth out just to sound as miserable as she does. I'm all for getting things right, but that would be carrying it a bit too far.'

'It's to be hoped she's not listening to yer now, Amy.'

'I couldn't give a sod, girl, and that's the truth. If she wants to listen in to private conversations, then she doesn't deserve to hear anything good about herself.'

'Ye're right there, sunshine. Anyway, I'm going in or the day will be gone before we know it. I'll have a cuppa on the table in ten minutes. Oh, and I won't forget yer custard cream. It won't be a

7

whole one because I could only afford half-a-pound of broken biscuits, but I'll see if I can stick two together for yer, seeing as ye're me best mate.'

'This is more like it, girl!' Amy faced her friend across the table. 'I've always wanted to be a lady of leisure. If someone could trace me family tree, I'm sure they'd find me ancestors were very wealthy. They could even have been of the nobility, 'cos I've always had the feeling that I was cut out for better things.' Her body shook with laughter. 'Don't worry, girl, I won't be expecting yer to curtsy to me. A slight nod of yer head will do.'

'D'yer think one of yer ancestors lost the family wealth through gambling and loose women?' Mary's face was deadpan. 'That could account for yer being reduced to sitting in the living room of a two-up two-down house, eating broken biscuits. It could also account for yer obsession with what goes on in the bedroom.'

Amy laced her chubby fingers and nodded her head. 'Someone's got a lot to answer for, haven't they, girl? Dragging me down from riches to rags.'

'Money doesn't always bring happiness, sunshine.'

'No, I know that, but at least yer can be miserable in comfort. I wouldn't mind the kids running riot if I was stretched out on one of those chaise longue things, with a glass of whisky in one hand and a big box of Cadbury's in the other.'

'We don't do too bad, Amy, we're better off than some in the street. At least Stan and Ben are working, even if they do get a lousy wage. We've always managed to scrape along somehow. And things can only get better with the kids growing up.' Mary topped the cups up and put the cosy back on the teapot. 'Yer've got your John working already, bringing in a few bob, and Eddy will be leaving school in eighteen months, same time as our Jenny. Then yer'll only have Edna at home, and yer won't know yerself. Yer'll be living the life of Riley.'

Amy grinned. 'I wish I knew this Riley feller, he could give me a few tips. I don't know what he's got that nobody else has, but I'd like a bit of it.' Her brows drew together. 'What are yer looking at, girl?'

'Unless I'm seeing things it's starting to rain. Hang on, I'll make sure.' Mary opened the kitchen door and groaned. 'It's only spitting at the moment, but there's a dirty big black cloud overhead so we could be in for a downpour.'

Amy's legs were too short to reach the floor, so she had to shuffle her bottom to the edge of the chair before she could push herself up. 'Damn, blast and bugger it! I was hoping to have the washing dried and ironed before teatime. There's nothing I hate more than wet clothes drippin' on me bleedin' head while I'm seeing to the dinner. The kitchen gets full of condensation and the steam's so thick yer've got to fight yer way through it.' She adopted the stance of a boxer, her shoulders hunched and her clenched fists stabbing the air while her feet danced in time with them. For a small woman carrying a lot of weight she could certainly move. 'Like this, girl, that's how I fight me way through the steam.'

'Yer've got a screw loose, Amy Hanley.' Mary grinned at the woman who never failed to cheer her up. There might be black clouds in the sky, but when her mate smiled, and her pretty face creased, she brought sunshine into the house. 'Yer'll need to be able to fight if Annie Baxter heard yer talking about her. She'll have yer guts for garters.'

'Huh! She's small fry, that one. I wouldn't need to fight *her* – one good puff and she'd be out for the count.'

'What if she's got her mate with her? Lily Farmer's not half big, she'd make two of you.'

'Ay, well, I've got to admit that Lily's a different kettle of fish. But I've got one thing in my favour, I can run faster than her. I might have a screw loose, girl, but I know me limitations and Lily Farmer is definitely outside of them.' Amy pushed the chair under the table and her face took on a thoughtful expression. 'It's funny yer should mention a loose screw, girl, 'cos I think ye're right. Every time I turn me neck sharply, I can feel this thing rattling around in me head. Could that be the loose screw yer were talking about?'

'Amy, I don't want to rush yer, sunshine, but the rain is teeming down. I'm bringing my washing in now before it's wringing sopping wet. If the weather clears I can put it out again when I come back from the shops.'

'I'll come to the shops with yer, girl, keep yer company. What time are yer going?'

'In about twenty minutes.'

'Just enough time for me to spend a penny, give me face a cat's lick and a promise, pull me stockings up and comb me hair. I don't need to cake me face with powder or lipstick, not with my natural beauty.'

'Ta-ra, sunshine, on yer way! I'll see yer later.' Mary left her friend and dashed out into the heavy rain. She sighed as she unpegged the clothes that were a damn sight more wet than when she'd put them out in the first place. Her eyes went to the heavens. 'Please God, take pity on us poor women, we don't do no one no harm.' She could feel the dampness as the rain soaked her dress, but she managed a smile. 'Only with words, God, and we don't really mean half we say. Besides, words don't harm no one.'

Mary turned into the butcher's shop with Amy in her wake. 'Good morning, Wilf, lovely weather for ducks, isn't it?'

9

'I'm happy for the ducks, Mary, but it's bloody awful weather for business.' The butcher feigned horror when his eyes lit on Amy. 'Oh dear, yer've brought the menace with yer. D'yer not think I've got enough problems without blighting me life with Amy Hanley?'

Amy slowly lowered her basket to the floor before placing her hands on her ample hips. 'Any more lip out of you, Wilf Burnett, and I'll take me custom elsewhere. I don't have to stand here and be insulted by the likes of you, yer know. All I've got to do is walk to the butcher's in the next block and let him insult me. He's better at it than you; some of his insults really get yer here.' With a dramatic gesture she placed a hand where she thought her heart was. 'Cut to the quick I've been, several times. In fact, and Mary here can bear me out, I was once that upset I had an attack of the vapours and someone had to hold a bottle of smelling salts to me nose, to bring me round.'

Wilf was shaking with laughter. He was a middle-aged man with thinning sandy hair and twinkling blue eyes. 'Yer mean sal volatile, Amy?'

Amy dropped her pose. 'What's salvotily when it's out?'

'Smelling salts.'

'That's what I said, yer silly bugger! D'yer know what? Yer've talked that much I've forgotten what I've come in for. It's no wonder yer've got no bleedin' customers, yer've probably talked them to bloody death.' She turned to Mary and gave her a broad wink. 'That funeral that's just passed us, I bet the poor sod used to shop here.'

'Well, I'm going to make amends for insulting yer, Amy, by giving yer a little bit of advice,' Wilf said. 'Next time yer do yer drama queen act, try putting yer hand where yer heart is. Yer were miles out.'

'I'll return the favour and give you a bit of advice, Wilf Burnett. You just keep yer eyes off my . . . off my . . . off my thingummybobs. My Ben wouldn't take kindly to yer weighing me up and down the way yer are. It's not your fault, 'cos men are drawn to me like a moth to a flame, but yer've got to be strong and keep yerself under control. I know yer mean well, and to put yer mind at ease, I do know where me heart is. It's well-covered, like, but it's in there somewhere.'

Mary banged on the counter, and when Wilf turned her way, she waggled her fingers. 'Yer do know I'm still here, don't yer? I hate to split you two up, but I would like serving.'

'Ah, she's jealous.' Amy shook her head and pouted her lips. 'I get this with her all the time, Wilf. If a man looks at me with longing in his eyes, she goes into a deep sulk. I feel sorry for her, 'cos she's me bestest mate. But I can't help being desirable, can I? It's not as though I'm a vampire, God forbid.'

When Mary and Wilf doubled up with laughter, Amy looked

surprised. 'Is it a private joke, or can anyone join in?'

Wilf reached for a clean piece of meat cloth and dabbed his eyes before answering. 'Amy, a vampire sucks blood. The word you should have used was vamp, which means a flirt.'

'Go 'way! Well, yer live and learn. I came in here for three-quarters of shin beef and get a lesson in geography and English. Not that I needed the geography lesson 'cos I know where me own bleedin' heart is, but a vampire sucks blood, eh?' Amy curled her fist and rested her chin on it. 'We haven't got none of them living in our street, have we, girl?'

'How about the woman in number seven, sunshine? It looks like bright red lipstick from a distance, but yer never know.'

'I'll weigh the shin beef while you two crucify the poor woman in number seven.' Wilf was reaching into the shop window for a tray of meat when Mary stayed his hand.

'Oh no, you don't! First in, first served, that's how it should be. I'd like a round neck of lamb, please, the leanest yer've got. And will yer chop it into four for us?'

Two more customers came into the shop then, and the friends were soon served and on their way to the greengrocer's. When Mary shopped on her own, she was around the shops in no time. After giving her order in and passing a few pleasant remarks, she was on her way. But shopping with Amy was a different experience altogether.

'Don't be trying to palm me off with a rotten cabbage, Billy Nelson, 'cos I haven't just come over, yer know.'

'What are yer on about, Amy?' Billy scratched his head. He was short and stocky, with a mop of black curly hair and a cheeky grin. 'I'll have yer know that that cabbage was in a field yesterday; it's as fresh as you are.'

'Pull the other one, Billy, it's got bells on. And when the bells start ringing everybody will think it's Sunday and get themselves ready for Mass.'

'Five o'clock this morning I was at the market getting me fruit and veg, Amy. Even the bleedin' birds were still asleep. I'm telling yer, that cabbage is as fresh as yer'll get.'

Mary thought it time to intervene, otherwise they'd be here all day. 'What's wrong with the ruddy cabbage? It looks all right to me.'

'I dunno, girl, I can't put me finger on it but I just don't like the look of it. It might be the shape of the bleedin' thing, or the colour.'

Billy slapped an open palm on his forehead. 'Ah, yer wanted a pink one, did yer, Amy? Or did yer fancy one in pale blue?'

Amy squared her shoulders and pretended to take the huff. 'Ay, Billy Nelson, you get sarky with me and I'll clock yer one. Buying a cabbage is just like buying a hat, yer either like it or yer don't like it.

11

And I'm telling yer now, I don't like that bleedin' cabbage.'

Holding the offending cabbage in the crook of his arm, Billy bent down and took another one out of the wooden box. 'How about this one, yer moaning so-and-so? Is it the right colour and shape for yer? Or would yer like one with a slim waist and a big bust?'

'Nah, we can't have two big busts in the house, we wouldn't be able to pass each other in our small kitchen. That one will do me fine, I've taken a liking to it.' Amy picked a well-worn purse from her basket, asking, 'Did yer say it was a penny, Billy?'

Billy looked forward to Amy's visit, you could always get a laugh out of her. And she didn't get upset if the laugh was at her own expense. Not like some moaning Minnies who came in the shop. 'There's a bloody big sign on the box, Amy, and it says the cabbages are tuppence.'

'Daylight robbery, that's what it is,' Amy said, passing a threepenny bit over. 'Ye're like that Ben Turpin feller who used to waylay people on the highway and rob them.'

Billy threw the coin in the big pocket of his apron and fished out a penny. 'Here's yer change, Amy. And it was Dick Turpin, not Ben.'

'What was Dick Turpin?'

'The highwayman.'

'Oh, it was Dick, was it? Was he Ben's brother?'

'No, Amy, Ben Turpin is a film star.'

'Well, I never!' Amy turned wide eyes on Mary. 'D'yer know what, girl? I've had more education in the last half hour than I had in me nine years at school.'

'I'm afraid yer've had yer last lesson for today, sunshine, 'cos it's time to get home and put the dinner on.' Mary took tight hold of her friend's arm and pulled her through the shop doorway, calling, 'Ta-ra, Billy, we'll leave yer in peace now.'

'Ta-ra, girls, see yer tomorrow.'

Amy was grinning as she moved the basket to her other arm so she could walk on the inside and link her friend. 'I enjoyed, that, girl. We had a good laugh, didn't we? And in case yer haven't noticed, the rain's gone off.'

'It went off twenty minutes ago, sunshine, but you were too busy talking to notice. I'm going to get me stew on, then put me clothes out again. With a bit of luck we'll get them dry this afternoon.'

Amy looked at Mary out of the corner of her eye. 'I heard yer telling your Laura off on Friday night, girl. Had she been giving yer cheek?'

'That's nothing unusual, is it, Amy? She's gone really hard-faced and is always giving me cheek. She went too far on Friday, though, and I slapped her face.'

'She is cheeky, I'll grant yer that. Not only to you, either.' Amy wanted to say more, but bit on her tongue. She could tell Mary a lot about that eldest daughter of hers, so could many of the neighbours in the street. But everybody kept quiet because, apart from Laura, the Nightingales were well-liked and respected. 'Never mind, she'll change when she starts work. It'll be a case of having to, 'cos if she gets a job in a factory none of the women will take any lip from her.'

'I hope ye're right, Amy, because I do worry about her.'

'Of course I'm right.' Amy squeezed her arm. 'Vampires are always right, aren't they?'

Chapter Two

Mary sat one side of the hearth sewing a seam that had come undone in Jenny's gymslip, while Stan sat facing her, reading the evening paper. It was the best time of the day for Mary, when the girls were in bed and she and her husband could discuss the events of the day, or sit in companionable silence. At the moment the only sounds in the room were the rustle of newspaper when Stan turned a page, the ticking of the clock and an occasional spurt from one of the coals.

With a sigh of contentment, Mary sewed the last stitch and snapped the cotton between her teeth. 'That's one job done, thank goodness. With a bit of luck Jenny will get a few more months' wear out of it.' She rubbed her eyes with the heel of her hands. 'I'll leave your socks until tomorrow, it's hopeless trying to sew in this light.'

Stan looked over the top of the paper. 'I think the gas is going, love, it's taking me all me time to read. Yer'd best put a penny in the meter before it goes altogether and we're left in the dark.'

'I can remember the time when yer'd have been glad to sit in the dark.' Mary grinned. 'Stealing kisses when me mam and dad had gone to bed.'

Stan lowered the paper to his lap. 'That brings back a few memories. I used to dread the sound of yer mam knocking on the floor with her shoe.' He chuckled. 'If she didn't hear me leave right away, she used to bang so hard I expected the ceiling to cave in on us. I got the distinct impression she didn't trust me.'

'All mothers are like that with their daughters. I used to call her for everything, saying she was treating me like a child. Now I've got daughters of me own, I understand why she was so protective. I'll always regret not telling her that she'd been a good mother and I loved her dearly. The trouble is, yer think yer've got plenty of time to say all these things; yer don't expect yer mam to die at fifty-two.'

'Yer mam didn't need telling, pet, she knew yer loved her.'

'She probably thought me dad loved her, as well. Yer would after being married for nearly thirty years, wouldn't yer? I thought he doted on her, they always seemed so happy.' Mary gave a deep sigh. 'But he couldn't have loved her that much, could he? Not to have married again six months after she died. And to a girl only half his age. A man of fifty-five, trying to act as young as the girl he'd wed. I'll never forget the first night he brought her here and she was all over him. She seemed to be flaunting him, as though to say "Look what I've got". I didn't know where to put meself, and me older than her. He didn't take long to forget me mam, and I don't think I'll ever forgive him for that.'

'Yeah, I've got to say it was the biggest surprise I've ever had in me life. If she'd been older I might have understood him marrying for companionship, but she's a fly turn, just out for a good time. I've seen them a few times down Walton Road, and a stranger seeing them would take them for father and daughter until they saw the antics out of them. Stupid bugger, that's all I can say.'

'I often wonder what me mam's old neighbours make of it. Especially the woman next door, Monica Platt. Her and me mam were real good mates. All the years they lived next door to each other never a cross word passed between them. And me dad used to be friendly with her husband, Phil – they used to go to the pub together a couple of times a week. I bet they're not so friendly now he's married a slip of a girl. They probably think he's lost the run of his senses, and they wouldn't be far wrong.'

The gas-light started to flicker and Mary jumped to her feet. 'I'd better feed the meter while I can still see it, save me fumbling around in the dark.'

'Here yer are, I've got a penny in me pocket.'

'No, I've got me week's supply on the kitchen shelf.' Mary reached up to where she kept the pennies, and as her hand covered the one at the top of the pile, a frown crossed her face. She lifted them all down and her frown deepened when she counted them. She'd put six there when she'd got back from the shops, she was certain of that, and now there were only four. When one had gone missing last week she'd put it down to a mistake on her part and thought no more of it. But she hadn't made a mistake today, that was definite.

Mary bent down and pressed a penny into the meter slot, then she turned the knob and waited for the coin to drop. Someone had taken two pennies and it wasn't something you could just brush aside. But if she mentioned it to Stan now, it would only cause trouble and spoil the closeness there'd been between them. He hadn't taken them, that was a cert, so that left the two girls. She'd have a word with them in the morning – try to sort it out without involving her husband. And she pushed aside the thought that there was no need to have a word with both of them because, God forgive her, she knew which one would be the thief.

Stan folded the paper up when Mary came back into the room. 'How about a cup of tea and then an early night in bed, love?' There was that special look in his hazel eyes which never failed to set Mary's pulses racing. 'It's yer own fault for reminding me of the days when we were courting.'

'You cheeky beggar!' Mary didn't need to put a smile on her face, it came of its own free will. She'd sort out the problem of the missing pennies tomorrow, and make sure it didn't happen again. But tonight belonged to her and Stan. 'I've a good mind to tell yer I've got a headache, that would dampen yer passion.' She huffed. 'Reminding indeed! That's an insult, that is. I'm going to have to ask Amy for some tips, see where I'm going wrong. She said every time Ben looks at her his eyes fill with desire for her voluptuous body.'

'She's a corker, she is.' Stan laughed. 'She's got a voluptuous body all right, yer could lose yerself in it.'

'I'll put the kettle on while you dream of Amy's body. When I see her tomorrow I'll tell her what yer said and she'll be over the moon.'

'Ooh, don't tell her, love, I'd never hear the end of it. She'd be waiting for me coming home from work and she'd make a holy show of me in the street.'

'Be a coward and come in the back way, then.' Mary was chuckling as she walked through to the kitchen. 'By dinnertime tomorrow, Wilf the butcher, Billy the greengrocer and Greg from the Maypole will all know that yer fancy her.' She popped her head around the door. 'Of course, if yer treat me right I promise not to tell her.'

'That's blackmail, that is.'

'Yeah, I know. Isn't it lovely? I've got yer in me clutches now, so behave yerself.' She gave him a broad wink. 'No, on second thoughts, I don't want yer to behave yerself.'

'I've no intention of behaving meself, love, not tonight.'

'That's all right, then. I'll see if I've got a Beechams Powder in the house, just in case I feel a headache coming on.'

Mary carried a plate of toast through the next morning and placed it on the table. The two girls were sitting next to each other and Mary stood opposite, her knuckles white as she leaned her weight on the table. Since Stan had left for work she'd been rehearsing in her mind how she would broach the subject. But there was no nice way of doing it, so she gazed from one to the other, and said, 'There's two pennies missing from me gas money. Who knows anything about it?'

Laura's reply came quickly. 'Don't look at me, I don't know nothing about it.'

Jenny looked puzzled. 'What d'yer mean, Mam, two pennies have gone missing?'

'Just what I said, sunshine. I put six pennies on the shelf when I came back from the shops, but when I went to get one for the meter last night, there were only four there. And they couldn't have walked away by themselves.'

17

Laura bit off a piece of toast and talked through a mouthful of the crispy golden bread. 'Me dad must have taken them for his fare. Ask him when he comes home.'

'And shall I ask him if he took the one that went missing last week? No, yer can leave yer dad out of this, he didn't take them. So I want to know what you two know about it?'

Jenny's head was bent over her plate and her voice was low. 'I didn't take them, Mam. That would be stealing.'

'Ooh, listen to Miss Goody Two-shoes,' Laura mocked. 'Never does nothing wrong.'

'Less of that, Laura.' Mary's voice was sharp. 'Your sister's said she didn't take them, so what have you got to say for yerself?'

'I didn't take yer rotten pennies.' Laura chewed on the last bit of toast, a bold look in her green eyes. 'They must have dropped off the shelf and fallen behind the cupboard.' She licked her fingers before pushing her chair back. 'Or yer could have been mistaken and only put four there in the first place. Anyway, it's time we were on our way to school if we don't want to get the cane for being late.'

'Sit down,' Mary said, her face set. 'Neither of yer leaves this house until we find out what happened to those pennies. I'm not so well off I can afford to lose them, but that's not the real issue. If there's a thief in this house I want to know who it is.'

Laura laughed. 'Don't be stupid! Yer can't keep us off school, me dad would go hairless if yer did that.'

Mary leaned forward so her face was on a level with her daughter's. 'Don't you ever dare call me stupid or I'll give yer the hiding of yer life. If I say yer not going to school, then that's the end of the matter. And don't threaten me with telling your father, because yer won't need to, I'll do it meself.'

'Mam, we will get into trouble if we don't go to school,' Jenny said. 'We'll get six strokes of the cane and be behind with our lessons.'

'No, yer won't get the cane because I'll give yer a note to take in. But neither of yer leave here until the matter is settled. If a thief gets away with it once, they'll steal again, and I'll not entertain it in this house.'

Jenny was near to tears. She enjoyed school and was an eager pupil. If she missed a day she'd be behind her friends. 'That's not fair, Mam, 'cos I haven't done nothing wrong. I haven't got the pennies and keeping me off won't help yer find them.'

'Oh, shut yer face,' Laura said, giving her sister a sharp dig in the ribs. 'Ye're a proper whinger, you are.'

'I'd rather be a whinger than a thief.' Jenny had put up with a lot over the years, taken the blame too often for her sister's misdeeds. She'd tolerated it for a quiet life, but having to miss school was the last straw. 'I think me mam's two pennies are in yer shoe. I saw yer messing around when I was getting dressed but thought nothing of it.'

Before Mary realised what was happening, Laura had grabbed locks of her sister's long golden hair in both hands and was pulling hard, a vicious look on her face. 'You rotten liar! I haven't got nothing in me shoes.'

Jenny was wincing with pain as she pleaded, 'Let go, ye're hurting me.'

Mary rounded the table and took hold of a handful of Laura's dark hair. 'Let go, or I'll give yer a dose of yer own medicine.' The threat didn't work, but a sharp tug did. 'Now stop this fighting right away, d'yer hear me? Sit up straight in yer chairs and behave yerselves.'

Mary sighed as she gazed down at her daughters. Was she going too far? Making a mountain out of a molehill? No, she told herself, she couldn't just let it go. It was one penny last week, two pennies today, what would she do when it came to sixpences – let that go as well?

'Laura, have you got the money?'

'No, I haven't! She's a liar, trying to get me into trouble.'

Jenny's face was white. 'I might be wrong, Mam.'

'Right, well you go off to school now, sunshine, and Laura will follow in five minutes. I'm not having the two of yer fighting in the street. If yer run all the way, yer'll make it in time.'

Jenny grabbed her coat off the hook behind the door and was out of the house like greased lightning. She knew her sister would have it in for her, but if Laura hit her she wouldn't just stand there like she usually did, she'd fight back this time.

Mary waited until she heard the front door close, then sighed. 'I'll ask yer again, Laura. Have yer got the money in yer shoe?'

'No, I haven't, so there!' Laura tossed her hair. 'I told yer that once, so why ask?'

'In that case, yer won't mind taking yer shoes off for me.'

'Oh yes, I would mind! I'm going to tell me dad on yer, he'll have something to say.'

'If I were you I wouldn't mention it to yer dad, he'd be so disappointed in yer. If yer've got the money, hand it over and we'll say no more about it. I won't tell yer dad or Jenny, or anyone. Unless it happens again, and then I will shout my mouth off.'

Laura glared. All this for two lousy pennies. But she could tell by the set of her mother's jaw that she meant every word she said. 'Oh, all right.' She bent down and took a shoe off then emptied it over the table. The two coins rolled towards Mary, who stopped them with her hand. 'I wouldn't have to pinch if yer gave us enough pocket-money.'

Mary felt no anger, only sadness. 'We give you as much pocket-money as we can afford. I have to rob Peter to pay Paul every week, but you wouldn't understand that. Well, yer might understand, but yer wouldn't care. All yer think about, Laura, is yerself. I've always known yer were selfish, but I never dreamt yer would stoop to stealing from yer own mother. I won't tell yer dad about this because it would kill him. So I'll give yer one more chance. But a word of warning . . . nobody likes a liar or a thief and yer could end up without a friend in the world.'

Laura bent to put her shoe back on. 'Yer won't tell anyone, will yer?'

Mary sighed and shook her head. 'No, not this time. But do it again, sunshine, and I'll be the one who goes running to yer dad.' She waited until her daughter straightened up and held out her arms. 'Come and give us a kiss and say ye're sorry, and promise me faithfully yer'll never do it again. Yer see, Laura, if anyone found out, they'd never trust yer again, and yer don't want that, do yer?'

When Laura walked into her mother's arms, sobbing that she definitely wouldn't do it again, the tears she shed were not of shame or remorse. They were tears of relief that her father wasn't going to find out, and regret that she'd been caught. And there was a certain amount of self-pity as she told herself she was stupid to have taken the two pennies. If only she'd been satisfied with one, like last week, her mother probably wouldn't have noticed.

'Come on, now, sunshine, wipe yer eyes and get going. If yer run like the wind yer might just make it before the bell goes and the gates are closed.'

Mary's heart was heavy as she watched her daughter running down the street. She'd keep her promise and not mention the matter to a living soul. But as she closed the front door, she let out a deep sigh. She wanted to believe Laura when she promised not to do it again, but try as she might, Mary couldn't help feeling that the tears and promises were an act put on to get her out of trouble. And she doubted that her daughter meant a word of what she'd said.

Gasping for breath, Laura slipped through the school gate just as it was being closed by Mr Johnston, one of the teachers from the boys' school. The two schools were housed in the same building, but the two sexes never mixed. Even the playground was divided by high iron railings.

'Leave the house earlier in future, or you'll be locked out.' Mr Johnston's voice was stern, his eyes angry. 'All the children are in assembly now, so wait in the corridor until prayers are over, then report to Miss Harrison's office.'

Laura gaped. You only reported to the headmistress's office if you were going to get the cane. 'I couldn't help being a bit late, Mr Johnston, it wasn't my fault. Me mam's not feeling well and sent me on a message to the corner shop.' The lies dripped off her tongue. 'And I ran all the way, honest. I ran that fast I've got a pain in me chest.'

'You have missed assembly and Miss Harrison will want to know why.' The giant key to the school gate was tapped on the palm of the teacher's open hand. 'I suggest you make your excuses to her and she will judge whether you deserve to be punished or not.'

He walked ahead of Laura through the double doors, and without a backward glance he turned sharp left towards the ever-locked door which separated the two schools. The girl was so angry she felt like pulling tongues behind his back, but thought better of it. She was in enough trouble without asking for more. With a bit of luck the headmistress might believe her story about being sent to the shops, especially if she offered to bring a note in tomorrow from home.

The corridors were empty and quiet with everyone in assembly, and as Laura stood outside Miss Harrison's office the silence played on her nerves. The headmistress was very strict and feared by all the children. A smile on her face was a rare sight indeed. It wasn't going to be easy to pull the wool over her eyes, but she could only try. Getting six strokes of the cane off a woman who looked as though she thoroughly enjoyed inflicting pain, was no laughing matter.

Laura didn't lay any of the blame for her predicament at her own door. If their Jenny hadn't snitched on her she wouldn't be standing here now, shivering with apprehension. Her mother would never have dreamt of looking in her shoe for the missing pennies if her sister hadn't put the idea into her head. Well, she'd be sorry she hadn't kept her mouth shut by the time Laura had finished with her. She'd get her in the playground when they had their mid-morning break and Miss Goody Two-shoes would regret clatting on her.

The double doors of the assembly hall burst open and a stream of girls rushed out, chattering as they headed for their classrooms. Some of them sneered behind their hands when they saw Laura, who was unpopular with most of the girls because she was always bullying the younger children and causing trouble. Two of her mates stopped, curious to know what she'd done to warrant a visit to the dreaded office, but she hissed that she'd tell them later. Her eyes were peeled for sight of her sister, and when Jenny passed, Laura bared her teeth in a snarl. 'I'll get you for this, just see if I don't.'

Jenny shrugged her shoulders and walked on. Another time she might have been frightened by her sister's threat, but not now. She wasn't sorry for what she'd done, and she'd do it again if need be. Laura had played some dirty tricks in her life but stealing from her

21

own mother was a terrible thing to do. Especially when their mam had a struggle every week to make ends meet.

Laura stood to attention when the headmistress strode towards her, her figure squat and her walk manly. One look at the severe expression on the plain face told the girl she could expect no sympathy from that quarter. 'Good morning, Miss Harrison.'

Ignoring the greeting, the headmistress turned the handle on the office door and pushed it open. Her face only an inch away from the terrified girl, she barked, 'Enter.'

Laura nearly jumped out of her skin. And as she entered the office, tears welled up in her eyes and she allowed them to flow freely down her cheeks.

'Stop that snivelling, girl!' Miss Harrison sat down at the far side of the desk and with the end of her pencil, began a rhythmic tapping on the wooden top. 'Mr Johnston tells me you were late for school.'

Laura made no attempt to stem the flow of tears. She needed all the help she could get right now. 'I got in before the gate closed, Miss Harrison. And it wasn't my fault. I was ready for school in time but me mam's not well and she sent me on a message for her. She was going to write me a note, explaining, but I would have been worse late.'

'Worse late, Nightingale!' The dark grey eyebrows nearly touched the matching grey hairline. 'Your grammar is atrocious! Have you learned nothing in your nine years of schooling?'

'I'm sorry, Miss.'

'Being sorry won't get you a job when you leave school, my girl. Now stop that blabbering and listen to me. You will bring a note from your mother in the morning, and if I'm convinced that you haven't written it yourself, you'll be excused punishment for being late. But you will be punished for your treatment of the English language. You will stay in the classroom during playtime this morning and this afternoon, and you will write out fifty sentences, each sentence containing one of these words.' Miss Harrison reached for a pad lying on the side of her desk and began to write quickly. Then she tore the page off and held it out. 'Read them to me and tell me if you understand their meaning.'

Laura stared down at the paper and read the words aloud. 'Late, later, latest, lately and lateness.' She looked up and kept her face a picture of innocence, even though she was seething inside. Fifty sentences meant twenty-five this morning and the same in the afternoon. She'd never do that many in fifteen minutes. And she wasn't good at English, she'd make all sorts of mistakes with no one to copy off. But their Jenny could do it, she was always top of the class in English. 'If I don't get them all done, Miss, can I take them home and finish them there?'

'If you put your mind to it, Nightingale, instead of staring out of the window, you should have no trouble writing short sentences in a matter of seconds. How about, "I was late today"? Or have you forgotten the reason you are standing in my office? Now, away to your classroom and I'll expect you to report back here at half-past three with the finished work, all neat and tidy and without any spelling errors.' She waved a dismissive hand. 'Now, go.'

Laura forced herself to turn slowly and leave the room, closing the door quietly behind her. Once in the corridor, though, she gave vent to her anger. Her fists clenched, she swore vengeance on her sister. It was through Jenny she was going to miss playtime and be a laughing stock in the classroom. She knew most of the girls disliked her and would get great pleasure out of seeing her humiliated. Well, they'd be in for a bigger treat tomorrow because there was no way she could do fifty sentences, let alone without a spelling error. And that would earn her the wrath of Miss Harrison and six strokes of the cane.

But luck was on Laura's side when she got to her classroom and found herself sitting next to one of the cleverest girls in the class. She never had a kind word for the girl usually, always skitting her for being a brainbox. The task the headmistress had set would be no problem to this girl, a fact Laura's crafty mind was quick to work out. So as she lifted the lid of her desk she gave her a bright smile. 'Hello, Helen.'

Helen's brown eyes were suspicious. 'What have you been up to?'

Laura made sure the teacher's back was towards them before she answered. 'Nothing. I was late getting in and I've got to bring a note tomorrow from me mam to say why.' She closed the lid of the desk and slid the piece of paper across. 'Could you write fifty short sentences using one of those words in each?'

Helen fingered the paper. 'Of course I could, easy.'

'I bet yer couldn't do it in half-an-hour.'

The girl's smile was smug. 'I could, but then I'm not a dunce like you.'

Laura bit on her tongue. 'Go on, show us then. I bet yer any money yer can't do it.'

The teacher, Miss Baldwin, had been chalking on the blackboard and she now turned to face the class. 'These are your sums for today. Copy them into your book and I want them completed and on my desk before the bell goes.'

Helen dutifully opened her exercise book and began to copy the sums in her neat writing. There were never any dirty fingermarks on her pages, nor any altered figures. She turned her head when Laura poked her on the arm. 'Don't be stupid, I can't do them now.'

'Yer'll be finished with the sums before anyone else, so yer could do a few sentences. Just to prove to me that yer can do it.'

Casting doubt on her ability was something Helen wouldn't tolerate. She finished her sums before Laura was halfway through hers, then, keeping a watchful eye on the teacher, she tore a page from the middle of her exercise book. After checking the words on the piece of paper Laura had put in front of her, she began to write. And when the bell went to announce the morning break, she slid the sheet of paper across to Laura with a supercilious grin on her face. 'There you are, twenty-five sentences. You could never do that, ye're too thick.'

Laura smiled as she gazed down at the neatly written sentences. Once she had copied them into her exercise book, she was halfway there. And now Helen had given her an idea of what to write, all she had to do for the next twenty-five was to alter each sentence a little. Her troubles were over, and for that she'd let Helen get away with saying she was thick. Although, when you came to think about it, it was Helen who was thick for walking into her trap. 'That's great, that is. Yer are clever, Helen.'

The girls lined up to put their books on the teacher's desk, then hurried out, eager to be away from the eagle eye of Miss Baldwin. Laura stayed at her desk waiting for the classroom to empty, and when one of her friends stopped to ask if she was coming, she explained that she'd been given lines to do by the headmistress and warned her not to let on to any of the other girls. Helen need never know she'd been duped because the lesson after playtime was history, and that was taken by Miss Hawkins in a different classroom. And the chances of sitting next to Helen again were remote, Laura would make sure of that.

History and geography were Laura's worst subjects. They didn't interest her and she could see no sense in them. After all, what good did it do you to know that the Battle of Hastings was fought in 1066? How many times in her life was she going to be asked that? No, when she left school in a couple of months she'd be too busy going out with boys, to the pictures or dancing, to give a thought to the likes of Henry VIII and all his blinking wives.

When Mary answered the knock on the door her eyes flew open in surprise. 'Dad! I never expected to see you! Aren't yer at work today?'

Joe Steadman took his cap off and ran his fingers nervously back and forth along the stiffened peak. 'Yeah, I'm working near here and thought I'd nip along and see yer in me dinner hour.'

Mary opened the door wider and waved a hand. 'Come on in, don't be standing on me step or the neighbours will think ye're the club-man and I owe yer money.' She closed the door behind him and bustled through to the kitchen. 'I'll put the kettle on and make yer a sandwich. It won't be much, mind, 'cos I haven't got much in.'

'There's no need, lass, I've got me carry-out with me. But a cup of tea would go down a real treat.' Joe took a small parcel from his pocket before sitting down. He gazed around the room, noting everything was neat and tidy, and spotlessly clean. He closed his eyes as a feeling of sadness descended on him. It must be nearly a year since he'd been in this house. His marrying Celia so soon after his wife died had caused a rift between him and his daughter which he bitterly regretted. She was his own flesh and blood, and he missed her so much, and Stan and the two girls. He wouldn't have stayed away so long, but he knew the sight of him and his young wife upset and embarrassed Mary and he thought it was for the best. But his longing to see her had grown stronger over the months and today he could no longer resist that longing. He hadn't been sure of the reception he'd get, but at least she hadn't closed the door in his face.

In the kitchen Mary lit the gas-ring under the kettle then leaned against the sink to sort her thoughts out. She'd called her father all the names under the sun since her mam died, but when she saw him standing on her step, looking like a little boy who was hoping the person opening the door would be glad to see him, her heart went out to him. He was her dad and she still loved him. Although she'd never admitted it, for the last year there'd been a void in her life without him. She would never change her view that what he did was wrong, but she still had fond memories of the man who used to tickle her tummy to make her laugh, gave her piggy-backs and took her to the swings in the park. She remembered how full of fun he always was and how happy their home had been.

The kettle gave out a piercing whistle and she turned the gas off before reaching for a cloth to wrap around the hot handle. 'Won't be long now, Dad. I'll just let it brew for a few minutes because I know yer like yer tea strong enough to stand a spoon up in.'

'Don't worry, lass, I'll drink it as it comes.'

He was sitting in Stan's chair when Mary carried two steaming cups through, and she tutted. 'Why don't yer sit at the table and I'll give yer a plate to put yer sandwiches on? Anyone would think we were poverty-stricken if they saw yer eating from the paper.' She pulled a chair out and sat down. 'Come on, sit at the table in a proper manner.'

'I haven't got long, lass, we only get an hour for dinner.' He lowered his eyes to the plate. 'I just wanted to see yer and make sure yer were all right. It's been over a year now, and I have missed yer.'

'Yeah, it's been too long, Dad.' Mary frowned as she watched him transfer the sandwiches from the paper to the plate. 'In the name of

God, Dad, what d'yer call them? They don't look very appetising, and there's not enough there to feed a bird.'

Joe Steadman flushed and averted his eyes. 'I made them meself and I'm not very good at it.' He lifted his head and attempted a smile. 'I've never been house-trained, yer see.'

'Yer don't need to be house-trained when yer've got a wife to look after yer.' Mary studied his face and it suddenly struck her that he was a lot thinner than he'd ever been. And there were a lot more lines on his face, adding years to his appearance. 'Doesn't she get out of bed to see to yer breakfast and carry-out?'

'It's not worth her getting up for that, I can manage meself.'

'Yer've lost a lot of weight, Dad. It seems to me she doesn't feed yer proper.'

'She does her best, but she's only young and yer can't expect miracles.'

'Miracles! A pan of scouse isn't a miracle, Dad! Even our Laura and Jenny could make a really good stew if it came to the push. They help me at the weekend making the dinner and they're not bad little cooks for their age. And they're only schoolkids, Dad – a lot younger than the one you married. If they can do it, why can't she?'

'She wasn't used to housework and she's still learning.' Joe couldn't hold back the sigh that escaped. 'She'll be all right, given time.'

One part of Mary's mind was telling her to mind her own business, another was reminding her that Joe was her father – and he had certainly gone down the nick since she last saw him. She couldn't just ignore it. 'So, while she's learning, playing mothers and fathers, like, you're going to starve to death? Buck yer ideas up, Dad, and be firm with her. Otherwise she'll act the fool for the rest of her life. She's a grown woman, for crying out loud, not a ruddy chit of a girl. She wanted to get married and be a housewife, so for heaven's sake make her get on with it.'

Twelve months ago, Joe would have risen to his new wife's defence, but not now, he was too weary. 'I've tried, lass, but talking to her is like water off a duck's back. She's still a child, never quite grown up. And I'm beginning to think she never will.'

'She never will, unless yer put yer foot down with her!' Mary sighed with frustration. 'My God, she knew a soft touch when she saw one.' She knew she was walking on eggshells, but she couldn't keep the words back. 'Does she keep yer house like me mam used to?'

'She does her best.' Joe pushed the plate away and leaned his elbows on the table. 'I'll have to be more firm with her, that's all.'

At that moment, Mary knew in her heart that her father rued the day when he'd married the young Celia. She'd chased after him, flattered him and made him feel young again. Their honeymoon had been a whirl of pubs, pictures and dances, and had lasted three months. After that, Celia didn't bother putting up a pretence and allowed her real self to surface. Her real self being lazy, brazen and man-mad.

'Well, that's your business, Dad. I won't say any more except don't be daft with her. It's no good our falling out the first time we meet in twelve months.' Mary laced her fingers and rested her chin on them. 'Yer said yer were working near here, where exactly is that?'

Joe was a plumber and had been with the same firm since he left school. 'We're working on a school in Bedford Road, laying some new pipes and putting in a couple of wash-basins. It's not a big job, we'll be finished this week.'

Mary glanced at the clock. 'It's a good ten-minute walk, Dad, yer'd better watch the time.'

'Yeah, I'll just have another half a cup of tea, then I'll be off.'

As she poured the tea, Mary asked, 'Why don't yer come tomorrow dinnertime and I'll have something ready for yer? It won't be a banquet, but even egg on toast would be better than those ruddy sandwiches yer've just had.' She smiled across the table. 'Anyway, I'd like to see yer again.'

Joe's face showed his pleasure. 'As long as yer don't mind. I don't want to put yer out, be any bother.'

'No bother at all. Just wait until I tell Stan and the girls yer've been, they'll be dead jealous they didn't get to see yer.'

'I'll call in one night and see them.' Joe saw his daughter's eyes cloud over and was quick to put her mind at rest. 'Celia goes out with a mate sometimes. I'll come on one of the nights she's going out.'

When Mary was seeing him out, Joe bent to kiss her cheek. 'I was worried about coming, but I'm glad I did. We've broken the ice, now, haven't we, lass?'

'Yes, Dad, we've broken the ice and it'll stay broken.' She felt quite emotional as she gave him a big hug. 'I'll see yer tomorrow. Ta-ra.'

'You're late.' Mary turned the tap off when Laura came through to the kitchen. 'Our Jenny got home ages ago.'

'I had to go to Miss Harrison's office after classes and she kept me waiting in the corridor for about ten minutes. I got into trouble for being late and she gave me lines to do during playtime. And on top of that she wants you to give me a note to take in tomorrow. I told her I had to go on a message for yer. It was dead unfair, though, 'cos I got through the gate before Mr Johnston had closed it. He could have let me off but he's too miserable. I'll be glad when I leave school, I hate it.'

Knowing her daughter's writing was terrible and she couldn't spell for toffee, Mary was apprehensive when she asked, 'And these lines yer had to do, did Miss Harrison check them before yer left?'

Laura tossed her head and looked really superior. 'She checked them all right, with a blinking fine-tooth comb. I felt like asking her if she wanted a magnifying glass. But she couldn't find any mistakes and I felt like pulling faces at her.'

'Yer did well, sunshine, not to make any mistakes. But if she wants a note off me, explaining why yer were late, why did she give yer lines to do?'

'Because she likes to throw her weight around, that's why.' Laura decided her best policy would be to make herself scarce before awkward questions started to be asked. 'I'm going out to see Cynthia, but I'll only be in the street if yer want me.' She was smiling as she walked away with a jaunty air, feeling very proud of herself as she remembered the look of suspicion on the headmistress's face as she tried to find fault with her work. But she couldn't because it was faultless. And that was all down to good old 'brainbox' Helen. She was as dull as ditchwater, but she had come in useful today. Without her, Laura would have been in real trouble and her hands would now be stinging from six strokes of the cane.

Laura saw her friend, Cynthia, coming towards her and waved. In a couple of months she'd never have to worry about the cane again; she'd be a working girl who could buy her own clothes, go to the pictures if she wanted, stay out late and go with boys.

Chapter Three

Mary sat at the table with her Christmas club cards spread out before her. She'd been adding up how much she'd paid into each and there was a smile of pleasure on her face because she was better off than she thought she was. There was enough in the greengrocer's to pay for the potatoes, the vegetables and fruit, and what she had in the butcher's should cover her for a small turkey and a chicken. She had been hoping to buy a Christmas tree this year, but it wouldn't run to it. Next year, though, with a few bob coming in from Laura they'd definitely have a tree, and all the trimmings.

She saw a shadow pass the back window and the next minute Amy's face was pressed against the glass pane, her nose squashed flat like a prize-fighter's. Mary lowered her head pretending she hadn't seen, and feigned interest in the cards while chuckling to herself. But two seconds later she regretted her action when Amy's knock on the window was so hard it seemed that not only was the glass pane in danger of coming in, but the whole window frame with it. She sprang to her feet, telling herself it served her right for trying to play a prank on her neighbour.

'Good God, Amy, yer almost put the flamin' window in!' Mary held the back door open and her friend hurried past, rubbing her arms briskly to warm them up. 'Apart from making me nearly jump out of me skin.'

'It's too cold to hang about outside, girl, it's bleedin' freezing. If I was a monkey I'd have had me you know whats frozen off by now.'

'Get over by the fire, then, and let me close this door to keep the draught out.'

'Blimey, girl, do yer call this a fire? I'd get more heat if yer breathed on me.'

'Ye're lucky I've got a fire at all, yer moaning so-and-so. I'm trying to save coal so we can have a bit extra for over the Christmas holidays. Anyway, if you've got a fire roaring up the chimney, why didn't yer stay in yer own house?'

' 'Cos it's like the frozen wastes of Siberia in there, girl, that's why. Yer see, I haven't got no fire at all, that's why I came in here to get a warm and scrounge a cup of tea.'

Mary's blue eyes were laughing as she pointed a finger. 'Yer might not have any fire, Mrs Woman, but yer've got plenty of cheek to make up for it. The nerve of yer, telling me ye're saving yer coal and tea, then having the brass neck to moan at me because me fire's low! I suppose yer'd like me to put a shovelful of coal on the fire before I make yer a cup of tea, would yer? And while ye're at it, why not go the whole hog and ask me for a round of toast to go with it?'

'That's neighbourly of yer, girl, I must say.' Amy folded her chubby arms across her tummy so her friend couldn't see it shaking with laughter. Adopting an innocent expression and adding a plaintive catch to her voice, she asked, 'I don't suppose yer've got an egg yer could put on the toast, have yer? Now that would be what I call real neighbourly.'

'Sod off, Amy Hanley! I'm beginning to think I can't afford you for a friend, yer friendship is costing me too much money.'

'Bloody hell, girl, yer get yer money's worth out of me. For a lousy cup of tea and round of toast, yer'll get all the gossip of the neighbourhood. I've a good mind to take me business elsewhere, where I'm appreciated.'

'Like yer neighbour on the other side, I suppose, the nosy Annie Baxter?'

'That's a thought, girl. I'd definitely get a poached egg on me toast if I went to her with the juicy gossip I've got in my possession.' Amy's lips were pursed as she nodded her head. 'Hot off the presses, it is. Hasn't had time to get around the street yet.'

Mary pulled out a chair. 'Yer've got me curious, now, sunshine, so sit yerself down and tell us what this hot news is.'

'Uh, uh! Ye're not soft, are yer, girl? Not a word passes me lips until me tea and toast is on the table in front of me. I want to see what I'm getting for me information. And if I think yer've been skinny with the margarine, I'll only tell yer half the story. I'll leave the best bit out.'

'Ye're a hard woman to do business with, Amy Hanley, and I'm a ruddy fool for falling for it.' Mary clicked her tongue on the roof of her mouth and rolled her eyes towards the ceiling. 'I'll make a pot of tea, and do yer a round of toast, but this gossip better be good. Something like Elsie Blackburn's husband catching her in bed with the milkman. Now that wouldn't be news, but it would be gossip.'

Amy's brows drew together. 'What d'yer mean? I know everything what goes on in this street and I've never heard that about Elsie Blackburn. How come you know about it and I don't?'

'How come I know what, sunshine?'

'About Elsie Blackburn.'

'What about Elsie Blackburn?'

'So help me, I'll strangle yer in a minute, Mary Nightingale. Yer know damn well what I'm talking about – her husband catching her in bed with the milkman.'

Mary let her mouth gape in feigned horror. 'He didn't, did he? Ooh, he wouldn't like that, would he? Did he give her and the milkman a good hiding?'

Amy's face was set for a few seconds, then her infectious laughter filled the room. 'Yer had me going for a while, there, girl. I thought to meself, aye aye, she must be pinching me job off me 'cos her gossip's better than mine. Me own common sense should have told me yer were having me on. I mean, the state of Elsie! A feller would have to be blind to go with Elsie, and the milkman's not blind. He's flat-footed, got a squint in one eye and yer can count the hairs on his head, but blind he ain't.'

'May God forgive us, Amy Hanley, for talking about them like that. Elsie's a nice woman, wouldn't say boo to a goose, and the milkman, Harry, is a decent bloke and a happily married man. Neither of them are bad-looking, either! Anyone would think we were Jean Harlow lookalikes, to hear us talk.'

'It's only in fun, girl, we're not doing no one any harm. I know I don't look like Jean Harlow because I haven't got blonde hair.' Amy pinched on her bottom lip, her eyes narrowed in thought. 'No, I'd say I'm more yer Joan Bennett type – slim, sultry and dark-haired.'

Mary grinned. 'I'll go and put the kettle on and leave yer to yer wishful thinking. Yer've got such a vivid imagination, sunshine, can't yer imagine Joan Bennett sitting at the table in her big Hollywood mansion, saying, "I'm a dead ringer for that Amy Hanley what lives in Liverpool. I'm lucky she doesn't live in Hollywood, or she'd be pinching me job off me".'

Amy waited until her friend had filled the kettle and lit the gas-ring before calling through to the kitchen. 'Many a true word is spoken in jest, girl, remember that. One of these days I will catch the eye of one of them talent scouts, then I'll be on me way up in the world. The new sex siren, that's what they'll call me. But I won't let it go to me head, girl, I'll always remember me friends. Yer'll always be welcome in my mansion, and there'll always be a cup of tea and a round of toast for yer.'

Mary popped her head around the door. 'D'yer mean I've got to wait until ye're a film star before I get a cup of tea off yer?'

Amy's face took on what she thought was a haughty expression. 'Sarcasm does not become you, Mary Nightingale. And have you forgotten that cup of tea you had in my house last Pancake Tuesday?'

'I most certainly have not! It was such a red-letter day, I made a note of it.' Mary gave a low cry. 'Ooh, I've forgotten yer flippin' toast – it'll be burnt to a cinder.'

'Put plenty of marge on it, girl, and I won't notice.' Amy picked up one of the cards lying on the table. 'Counting yer club money, were yer, girl?'

'Yeah.' Mary put a plate down in front of her neighbour and hurried back for the two cups of tea. 'I've done better than I thought and I'm dead pleased with meself.'

'That's what I came in for, to talk about Christmas, but yer put me off me stroke talking about Elsie Blackburn. A right bit of useless information, that was.'

'You cheeky beggar! Yer came in here to do a deal, that's what. A cup of tea and a round of toast in exchange for the latest gossip. I've kept my part of the bargain, so start talking, sunshine, and make it good.'

Amy folded the round of toast and took a big bite. She grinned as she chewed, her short legs swinging backwards under the chair. 'I did that so yer couldn't take it back off me if yer thought what I've got to tell yer wasn't worth it.'

'It's such a long time ago, Amy, I've lost interest, anyway.'

'I know how yer feel, girl, 'cos I've lost interest meself. I thought it was funny when I first heard it, but now it's as stale as this piece of bread.' When Mary's mouth opened to protest, Amy raised her hand. 'Only kidding, girl, don't get yer knickers in a twist. I'll tell yer quick, then we can talk about me plans for Christmas.' She finished the last of the toast and licked her fingers. 'Sammy Cooper staggered home last night, dead drunk. And Aggie did no more than hit him over the head with a rolling pin. I believe he's gone to work this morning with a lump on his head as big as an egg.' Amy's tummy rumbled with laughter. 'The part that tickled me was, he couldn't remember anything and asked Aggie if he'd fallen out of bed. She told him she didn't know because she was sound asleep, but if he had fallen he must have picked himself up again because she certainly didn't.'

'Ah, she shouldn't have done that, the poor man hardly ever goes out. She's twice the size of him, too, she could have killed him.'

'Don't worry, she won't do it again. Frightened the life out of herself, she did. And to make it up to him, she's giving him his favourite meal – liver and onions. The silly cow doesn't realise he'll twig something's up. He'll be sitting at the table wondering how he came by this ruddy big lump, and she'll put a plate of liver and onions in front of him. That's never been known on a Tuesday night before, so he's bound to put two and two together. And if he does we can expect to see Aggie with a black eye tomorrow.' Amy rested her elbows on the table. 'Now that's out of the way, let's get down to business. How about us having a party on Christmas night? We could go halfy-halfy with the food and it wouldn't cost that much. We've never had a real knees-up, jars out party, on account of the kids. But they're old enough now, so let's have a bit of fun and enjoy ourselves.'

'I won't have any money to spare, Amy, I've only got what's in me clubs.'

'That's all yer'd need, girl! We could do some turkey sandwiches, make a jelly and blancmange and bake some fairy cakes. Yer don't need a lot of food to enjoy yerself, just some good company.'

Mary's face lit up. 'Yeah, ye're right, sunshine, let's go for it. We'll share what we've got and I'll give yer a hand with the table and everything.'

Amy curled a fist and rested her chin on it. 'How d'yer mean, girl, yer'll give me a hand? I thought we were having the party here?'

Mary gasped. 'Amy Hanley, even by your standards, that's bare-faced cheek, that is. It was your idea to have a party, I wouldn't have thought of it.'

'Ah well, yer see, girl, the idea was my contribution to the party. Your contribution is to have the jollification in your house. Now yer can't say that's not fair, can yer? Without me, there wouldn't have been no party.'

'I'm speechless! Why can't we have it in *your* house? They're exactly the same size, it's not as though I've got more room.'

'No, yer haven't got more room, girl, I'll grant yer that. What yer have got, though, is more nous. Ye're very good at arranging things, doing them proper, like.'

'Don't you be buttering me up, Amy Hanley, I know when I'm being taken for a sucker. How soft you are! Let's have a knees-up, jars out party, yer said. Let's have some fun and enjoy ourselves. And soft girl here fell for it! I must want me bumps feeling for listening to yer.'

Her face as innocent as a baby's, Amy asked, 'So it's all settled, is it, girl? Christmas night at the Nightingales'? Ay, hasn't that got a nice ring to it? Christmas night at the Nightingales'. It sounds proper posh. Just wait until I tell my Ben he's been invited to a party, he'll be over the moon. I'll have to make sure I get his suit out of the pawnshop so he'll look the part.'

'Just hang on a minute, sunshine! I don't remember agreeing to it.'

'Of course yer agreed to it, girl. Yer just weren't listening to yerself when yer said it. And I'll say here and now, with me hand on me heart, that I think it's real magam . . . er, manig . . . er, real good of yer.'

'What yer were trying to say, sunshine, is that it's magnanimous of me.'

'There yer are, yer see, you think ye're that as well! And that's another reason why yer make a better hostess than me – yer know all the big words.'

'For the life of me, sunshine, I can't see what big words have got to do with a party.'

'Well, it's like this, yer see, girl. They say God made everybody good at something. To you He gave the gift of words, to me He gave the gift of craftiness. And they'll both come in useful at our party. When you're handing the plates of sandwiches around, all yer've got to do is throw in a few of those big words and they'll be that flabbergasted they won't notice the sandwiches are brawn, and not turkey.'

Mary couldn't hold out any longer and she shook with laughter. What could you do with someone who had an answer for everything? With tears running down her cheeks, she answered herself. You could have a party for her, that's what.

The knock on the front door had Mary pushing her chair back as she wiped her eyes. 'Who on earth can this be?'

'Unfortunately, girl, God didn't give me the gift of seeing through walls, so I'm afraid the only way yer'll find out is to open the bleedin' door.'

When Mary saw who her visitor was, her smile widened. 'Hello, Molly, get yerself inside out of the cold.'

'It's yerself, then, Mary? Sure, haven't I been knocking so long I was beginning to think there was no one at home.' It was ten years since Molly Moynihan left the shores of Ireland but the lovely lilting accent was as strong as ever. She was a tall woman, well built, with a shock of light gingery hair, pale blue eyes and a face that was never far from a smile. As she stepped into the hall she peered down at Mary, concern in her blue eyes. 'Have yer been crying, me darlin'?'

'I'm having an attack of hysterics, Molly, which means I don't know whether to laugh or cry.' Mary winked at the woman who had lived in the house opposite for ten years and was a good friend. 'And as yer might know, it's me mate what's brought about this state of affairs. She's in there now, but take my advice and don't mention the word Christmas if yer know what's good for yer.'

Amy's voice came through to them. 'Ay, I heard that! Don't you be blackening my name, Mary Nightingale, or I'll have yer up for slander.'

Molly was laughing as Mary pushed her into the living room. 'Oh, it's yerself, Amy Hanley. And what mischief has the good Lord allowed yer to be up to now?'

Amy spread out her hands, a real hard-done by look on her face. 'I can't believe anyone can be as ungrateful as this one. I did her a big favour by sharing me great knowledge and experience with her, and do I get any thanks in return? Do I heckerslike! A load of abuse, that's what I get. I tell yer what, Molly, it puts yer off helping people. They take yer kindness and throw it back in yer face.'

'Me heart bleeds for yer, so it does.' Molly pulled out a chair and sat facing Amy. 'And it's surprised I am that yer best friend doesn't appreciate yer kindness. What was it yer were offering that she threw back in yer face?'

'Don't ask, Molly, or yer'll live to regret it.' Mary got in quickly before her friend. 'I'll tell yer how crafty this one is. She's sitting there looking all angelic, as though butter wouldn't melt in her mouth, but behind that mask she's dead devious. I'll tell yer the story, word for word, and yer can judge for yerself. It started off with her coming in to scrounge a cup of tea and get a warm by my fire because she's too mean to have one of her own . . .'

Molly and Amy leaned their elbows on the table and waited to be entertained. They knew how good Mary was at imitating her neighbour, she had the voice and facial expressions off to perfection. And they weren't disappointed. Their giggles turned to chuckles, and then loud guffaws as Mary took them from the round of toast to Elsie Blackburn and the milkman, Sammy Cooper with the lump on his head and the meal of liver and onions his wife was going to set before him as a peace offering. But when it came to the Christmas party, and how Amy had skilfully worked it around so that Mary, thinking she was being invited as a guest to the Hanleys', was inveigled into becoming the hostess, the Irishwoman was banging the table as she rocked back and forth with laughter. 'Holy Mother of God, Amy Hanley, is there no end to yer trickery?'

Amy was sitting back with her arms folded, looking extremely pleased with herself. She found Mary's version of events very funny, and thought she herself came out of it very well. 'I didn't trick her, Molly Moynihan, she walked straight into it. She'd fall for the cat, she's that gullital.'

Mary spluttered. 'Yer mean I'm gullible, yer daft nit, not gullital.'

'There yer are, Molly, she admits I'm right. Now yer can't argue with that, yer heard it with yer own ears.' Amy tilted her head and narrowed her eyes. 'By the way, Molly, just out of curiosity, like, is your room any bigger than this?'

'Oh, I'm wise to yer, Amy Hanley, so I am. Yer'll not be catching me out so easy, indeed yer'll not.'

Amy sighed as she gazed at Mary. 'I'm sorry, girl, but yer can't say I didn't do me level best for yer. It looks as though you're stuck with having the party, like it or not.' She turned to Molly. 'Seeing as ye're too miserable to have the party at your house, how would yer like to come to our party? And Seamus, of course, and your Mick.'

Mary dropped her head in her hands and groaned. More often than not Amy's jokes turned into reality. 'What about Annie Baxter and her husband, Amy? And, of course, yer could ask Lily Farmer and her feller.'

'Nah, I can't stand them two, they get on me bleedin' nerves. And after what yer've told me about the antics of Elsie Blackburn and the

35

milkman, I wouldn't associate meself with the likes of them. If yer invite any of them, girl, then even though it would grieve me, I'd have to turn down yer kind invitation.'

Molly chuckled. 'Oh, it's invitation only, is it?'

'I haven't even said I'll have a party yet!' Mary shook a fist in Amy's face. 'All this started because yer were too mean to light a flaming fire! I should have told yer to sling yer hook and I'd have been spared all this.'

'Then yer'd better make it plain, me darlin',' Molly patted her arm, 'before yer friend here invites the whole street.'

'I wouldn't invite the whole street, I'm not that daft.' Amy bit on her bottom lip to try and stop a smile appearing. 'Half the street, perhaps.'

'What would yer do with her?' Mary spread her hands and shrugged her shoulders. 'Okay, I give in. The Hanleys and the Moynihans are invited to a friendly get-together on Christmas night. But yer'll have to help out with the food, otherwise I won't be able to afford it.'

Amy beamed at Molly. 'There yer are! I bet when yer knocked on the door yer didn't expect to get an invite to a party, did yer?' She eyed the Irishwoman with curiosity. 'By the way, what *did* yer knock for?'

'Amy!' Mary blushed with embarrassment. 'Yer'll get me hung one of these days, yer cheeky article. What's it got to do with you why Molly knocked?'

'Yer don't have any secrets from me, do yer, girl?'

'I should be that lucky! You wouldn't let me have any secrets.'

'In that case, Molly may as well tell me what she's come for, save me shouting over the wall to yer later.'

'Well, now, I'd hate yer to have to stand on a bucket to see over the wall, that I would. Sure, I'd never forgive meself if yer fell off and broke a leg.' Molly was glad she had come, the last half-hour had brightened up her day. She had no family here to visit, they were all back in Ireland, so she was grateful that she'd been able to make friends with her neighbours. Life would have been very lonely without them. Particularly these two, who were guaranteed to put a smile on the most miserable of faces. 'A secret is something yer don't want anyone else to know about, but I don't think an ounce of Golden Virginia comes into that category, do you? Seamus asked me to get it for him, but I don't need to go to the shops for anything so I came to see if Mary would get it if she's going out. It's lazy I'm getting in me old age, and that's the truth of it.'

'Yes, I'll get it for yer. I've got to run to the shops, so it's no bother. That's if I can ever get rid of me mate, here.'

Amy shuffled her bottom to the edge of her chair. 'Ye're getting rid of me right now, but not for long. I'm going home to get me coat, then I'm coming to the shops with yer.' She linked her arm through Molly's. 'I'll take yer out with me so yer can't talk about me. Never mind about paying her for the baccy now, yer can see her later.'

Laura rushed in from school that night, her face flushed with excitement. 'Mam, we're all being allowed time off tomorrow to go to the Labour Exchange. Teacher said they give us a card and tell us where to go for a job. If there's any jobs going, we can go for an interview the day after.' She took a deep breath and let her heartbeat slow down. 'Wouldn't it be the gear if I got a job to start after Christmas?'

'It certainly would!' Mary took her hands out of the soapy water and shook them before leaning against the sink. She was pleased for her daughter and privately hoping that getting a job would be the makings of her. 'You'll have to look clean and smart tomorrow, then. I'll press yer gymslip tonight and you can give yer shoes a good polish. Appearances are very important, sunshine, as are first impressions. If yer look scruffy then yer don't stand much chance.'

'We're not going for interviews tomorrow, Mam, only to the Labour Exchange.'

'Yes, I know that, sunshine, but they're the ones who separate the wheat from the chaff. They know what the employers are looking for, and they'll give out cards for interviews accordingly.' Mary wasn't worried about her daughter's appearance, she knew she could stand up against anybody. She was a pretty girl, with a nice slim figure, rich dark hair, finely arched eyebrows, full lips and wide eyes that were constantly changing from hazel to green. Dressed properly she stood as good a chance as any of the other girls. It was her attitude that worried Mary. She was far too self-assured for her age and too fond of answering back. 'Just be pleasant and polite, Laura, and yer'll do fine.'

Laura's hair swung across her face as she shook her head, her green eyes flashing. 'I'm not a kid, yer know, Mam. I do know how to behave meself.'

'It's important yer remember that tomorrow, sunshine, if yer want to get a job.'

Laura tossed her head again as she flounced out of the room. 'I'm going to Cynthia's.'

Mary sighed as she turned and plunged her hands into the water where she'd been washing some socks and knickers. Her daughter wouldn't take criticism, she flew off the handle for the least thing. She was in for a rude awakening when she started work, for no boss would tolerate her high-handed attitude.

Mary rinsed the clothes through and wrung the wet out of them before folding them and placing them on the draining board. It was too late to hang them out now, she'd do it first thing in the morning, weather permitting. She lowered the gas-rings under the pans on the stove, then popped her head around the door to glance at the clock on the mantelpiece. It was a quarter of an hour before Stan was due in, she might as well put her feet up for a few minutes. It was then her eye caught the glint of gold paper on the sideboard and her hand went to her mouth. 'Oh Lord, I forgot to take the baccy over to Molly. I'd better go now before I start putting the dinner out.'

Molly saw her neighbour crossing the cobbled street and when she opened the door she had the exact money in her hand. 'It's an angel, yer are, me darlin'. When yer want the favour returning, all yer have to do is shout out.'

Mary passed the tobacco over and took the money. 'It was no bother, Molly, I had to go out anyway. Besides, shopping with Amy is as good entertainment as yer'll get anywhere. Every shop we go in, she causes mayhem. Honestly, she never ceases to amaze me, the things she comes out with. I'm pretty quick on the uptake, and I think I've got a sense of humour, but she leaves me standing.'

'Sure, she's on her own when it comes to humour, and that's a fact. And she's a heart as big as a week, I'll say that for her.' Molly leaned against the door jamb and folded her arms. 'But don't be talked into having a party on Christmas night, me darlin', 'cos that's taking a joke a bit too far.'

'Oh, I'm not that soft, Molly, believe me. I'll admit I wouldn't have thought of it only for Amy sowing the seed, but I'm quite taken with the idea now. It won't be a lavish affair, and yer'll all have to muck in with the food, but it would be nice for the three families to get together for a few hours, don't yer think?'

'It would be grand, me darlin', and I mean that sincerely. But, sure, I'd be happy to invite yer over here, save you the bother.'

Mary shook her head. 'No, it's all arranged now, Molly.' She grinned. 'Another of Amy's bright ideas was that I should send invitations out and do the job properly. Actually, her exact words were, "Show them yer were brought up, girl, and not dragged up." But I'll settle for asking yer by word of mouth. Seven o'clock, Christmas night, at the Nightingales'.'

Molly straightened up, a wide smile on her face. 'Will yer look at these two fine-looking men coming down the street. The two finest specimens of manhood ye're likely to see in the whole of Liverpool.'

Mary followed her neighbour's eyes and saw Seamus Moynihan, with his son Mick, walking down the street. And as Molly had said, they were fine-looking men. Seamus was taller and broader than his sixteen-year-old son, but both were as handsome as they come. They would stand out in any crowd, with their raven black hair, deep blue eyes, strong white teeth and dimpled cheeks.

'Good evening to yer, Mary.' Seamus swept off his cap with a flourish. 'Sure I hope the Good Lord is looking after yer, keeping yer fit and well.'

'Hello, Seamus, and you, Mick. I'm fine, thank you. On top of the world, as yer might say in Ireland.'

'Yer can thank Mary for getting yer baccy for yer, Seamus Moynihan. I wasn't in the mood for shopping, so Mary was kind enough to oblige. If it hadn't been for her yer'd have been puffing on an empty pipe all night, and with the divil's own temper in yer.'

When Mick laughed, Mary thought what a handsome lad he was. He'd be breaking many a girl's heart in years to come. 'Take no notice, Mrs Nightingale, me dad isn't allowed to have a temper.' He'd been six years old when his parents brought him to England and, although there was still a trace of his Irish accent, it was now mixed with the Liverpool twang. 'There's only one boss in our house, and although I won't tell yer who it is, I will tell yer that it's not me or me dad.'

Molly shook an admonishing finger, but there was love and laughter in her eyes. 'It's not too old for a spanking, yer are, Mick Moynihan, and don't yer be forgetting that.'

'Not too old, Mam, but I think yer'd have a job putting me across yer knees. Yer see, yer'd need yer two hands to stop me from slipping off.'

Mary saw Stan's familiar figure turn the corner of the street and she laid a hand on Molly's arm. 'Ay out, here's my feller. I'll see yer tomorrow, sunshine. Ta-ra Seamus, ta-ra Mick.' She couldn't resist patting the boy's cheek. 'If I was twenty years younger, sunshine, I'd be running after yer.'

'If yer were twenty years younger, Mrs Nightingale,' he called after her, 'yer wouldn't have to run fast, I'd be letting yer catch me.'

'I'm going to be stuck for money,' Mary told her friend as they sat facing each other across the table. 'I'm all right for food, but it's the presents. The two girls want clothes, and Stan could do with a new shirt and pullover. The few bob I'll have isn't going to run to it.'

'Do what I'm doing,' Amy said, her hands curled around the cup. 'Get a cheque off yer club woman. I'm just as broke as you are, so it's a case of having to.' Her chubby face creased in a smile. 'I'll be cursing the poor woman every week when she's due, hoping she falls and breaks a leg before she gets to our house.' She saw Mary shaking her head and chuckled. 'Yer know I don't really hope she breaks a leg, I'm not that wicked. Just a sprained ankle would do, that would be enough to keep her off work.'

'Amy Hanley, I don't know how you sleep at night. God will pay yer back one day, you just mark my words.'

'Nah, He wouldn't do that. Yer see, girl, God's got a good sense of humour, which is more than can be said for you.'

'I've got a sense of humour, sunshine, but it isn't warped, like yours is. Anyway, I think I'll take yer advice and ask the club woman for a two-pound cheque. That would save me scrimping and scraping. And with our Laura passing that interview for a job at Ogdens, I'll be able to afford to pay an extra bob a week.'

'I bet she was over the moon, was she?'

'Like a dog with two tails. Honestly, she never stopped talking. Anyone would think she was the only one ever to get a job. And what she's going to do with her pocket-money is no one's business. Talk about breaking eggs with a big stick, isn't in it.'

'I know someone who used to work there, and she said the money wasn't bad and they were a good firm to work for. She was on packing the cigarettes, and she said they got so many for nothing each week. So your Stan could come up lucky.' Amy put the cup down on the saucer and wiped the back of her hand across her mouth. 'It's to be hoped your Laura doesn't start smoking, though, girl. I can't stand to see a woman with a fag hanging out of the side of her mouth. Always reminds me of a gangster's moll.'

'Yeah, I think they look as common as muck.'

'My grandma used to smoke a clay pipe, mind. I was only little, but I can remember her as plain as day. She used to shuffle to the corner pub every night, with a jug hidden under her shawl for a pint of stout. And she'd sit in her rocking chair, as happy as Larry, puffing at this clay pipe and drinking her stout. Deaf as a doorpost she was, couldn't hear a word yer said to her. Yer could tell her someone had died, and she'd laugh her bleedin' head off. Didn't do her no harm either, 'cos she lived until she was ninety.'

'There yer are, yer see, a warped sense of humour runs in your family.' Mary stood up and reached for the cups. 'Let's get down to the shops before they close for dinner. I want to get all the ironing done this afternoon, that'll be one thing off me mind.'

'I'm ready, girl, I brought me coat with me. I don't want much shopping, so I can put me things in your basket.'

Mary came back from putting the cups in the kitchen. 'Yer may have a warped sense of humour, sunshine, and yer may be wicked, but no one could ever say yer were daft. Use my basket indeed, and let me do the carrying.'

'For crying out loud, girl, I only want a couple of things from the Maypole. It's not as if I'd asked yer to get me a hundredweight of bleedin' coal.'

'Shut yer face, Amy Hanley, and let's get cracking. And do us a favour, try and behave yerself.'

Their first stop was the Maypole. A young girl assistant came over, smiling. 'What can I get for yer?'

'Nothing against you, girl, but I want to see the manager,' Amy said, pulling herself to her full height and thrusting her bosom forward. 'I have a complaint to make.'

Mary grabbed her arm. 'Amy, for heaven's sake, don't be making a scene.'

'Me! Make a scene! Now as if I would.'

The manager, Greg, came in answer to the young assistant's call. 'Good morning, ladies, can I help yer?'

Amy's face was so serious, no one would guess the laughter that was going on inside of her. 'I've got a bone to pick with you. Well, I don't know whether bone's the right word to use. Do bluebottles have bones?'

Greg looked to Mary for guidance, but as she was as wise as he was, she could only shrug her shoulders. 'Why do you ask, Mrs Hanley?'

' 'Cos the half of margarine I got off yer yesterday had a ruddy big bluebottle in the middle of it. Fair made me sick, it did.'

Mary stepped back so she was standing behind her friend, and she shook her head at the bewildered manager. 'She's pulling yer leg,' she mouthed.

'I'm sorry about that, Mrs Hanley.' Greg kept his face straight. 'But you can rest assured I did not charge yer for the bluebottle.'

'I never said yer did, did I? No, I'm a fair-minded woman, and I only want what's due to me. What I'm asking for is me money back for the margarine the bleedin' bluebottle ate.' The shoulders were stiffened and the jaw set. 'I can't afford to be feeding no ruddy bluebottles, and yer should have seen the ruddy big hole in the margarine, yer wouldn't believe it.'

'Yer should have brought it back, Mrs Hanley.'

'Brought what back – the hole? Oh, I couldn't do that! Yer see, I used the hole for me husband's carry-out.'

All the staff and customers were listening by this time. Amy was noted in the neighbourhood for pulling people's legs, and if there was free entertainment going, they wanted some.

'Well, you should have brought the bluebottle back. At least that would have been some proof that what ye're saying is true.'

'Ah, I couldn't bring that back.' Amy's eyes went around her audience. 'Yer'll all cry yer eyes out when yer hear this, it's that sad. Yer see, poor Bluey died from over-eating. Near broke me heart it did, to see him on his back, his little legs waving about until the end finally came. I put him in a matchbox, but I haven't buried him yet because yer can't have a burial without flowers. So to give him a decent send-off, I'm here to collect for a wreath for him – and I know yer'll all be generous. Especially you, Greg, because it's your fault he's dead. If you hadn't been careless enough to let him fly on my margarine, the poor bugger would be still alive. He'd be sitting in

41

your window right now, flying from the brawn to the bacon, really enjoying himself with his sister. She's sitting on yer boiled ham right now, using it as a lavvy, and wondering where he is.'

The Maypole was usually a very quiet shop, except when Amy Hanley was in it.

Chapter Four

'Ay, isn't this the gear, girl?' Amy's round face beamed. 'All the food and presents in, and nowt to do but sit back and enjoy ourselves.'

'You're looking on the bright side, aren't yer?' Mary had finished wrapping the dress she'd bought Laura for Christmas and was tying the parcel with green string. 'What about preparing all the spuds and veg, cooking the turkey, making the stuffing and gravy? There's stacks of jobs to do yet, and I'm going to start on them as soon as yer've gone, save standing in the kitchen all night.' She patted the stack of presents and smiled with pleasure. 'That's them seen to. I just hope they like them.'

'Of course they will! And as I was saying to meself as I was wrapping mine, it's too bleedin' bad if they don't like them. Yer can only do so much with the money yer've got, and we've both done that, girl. I mean, me and God are the best of friends, but even He draws the line at performing miracles for me.'

'He performed one for me last night,' Mary said. 'I nearly died when Seamus knocked at the door to say he was getting their Christmas tree today off some bloke he knows who works at the market, and that he'd cadge one off him for us. It's years since we had a tree, but I've still got some decorations upstairs I can use. Apart from brightening the place up, it'll be nice to come down in the morning to see the presents hanging from it.'

'Don't try and hang that pullover of Stan's on it, it's so heavy it'll pull the bleedin' tree over, then yer'll have a right mess.'

'Credit me with some sense, sunshine, I ain't exactly brainless. Anything too heavy, I'll put underneath it.' Mary picked the parcels up and put them on the sideboard. 'They can stay there until the tree comes. Molly is expecting her men home about three o'clock and she said she'll send Mick over as soon as they arrive. That gives me time to prepare tomorrow's dinner and get this place dusted. The girls are really excited, they can't wait to help me decorate it.'

'How is your Laura these days? Still playing yer up, is she?'

'I'm hoping that when she starts work she'll have some of the insolence knocked out of her. She's far too forward for her age.'

Amy lowered her eyes. She'd seen Laura in the entry last night, kissing a boy from the top of the street. And it was the girl who was doing the kissing. It wasn't the first time she'd caught her at it either, and each time it was with a different boy. Other women had witnessed it too, and many tongues had wagged. One woman had seen Laura take her son's hand and lead him into a side entry that ran through to the next street. She'd done no more than chase after them, boxed her son's ears in front of the girl and told him if it happened again she'd get his father to take his belt to him. According to the woman, Laura hadn't run away or shown fear at being caught. Even the threat of her mother being told didn't make her turn a hair. She'd just stood by and brazened it out.

Amy sighed silently. Laura Nightingale was more than forward, but how did you tell her mother that when she was your best friend? And not only your best friend, but a thoroughly nice person who deserved better from her eldest daughter. 'I agree with yer, girl, she is a hard-clock if ever there was one. In her case a few smacks when she was younger wouldn't have gone amiss, instead of being spoiled rotten.'

'Stan's to blame for that, he can't see any wrong in her. Mind you, I've seen him taking more notice lately and I think the penny has finally dropped. Let's hope it's not too late, or she'll never have any decent friends.'

'She hasn't got any now, girl! That Cynthia is a real hard-faced article, as tough as old rope. She treats her mother like a piece of dirt, but like your Laura, she's as nice as pie to her father. They're two of a kind and it would be a good thing if they were split up.'

'I know, I've never liked that girl. Laura wanted to ask her to the party but I put my foot down over that.'

Amy laid her arms flat on the table. 'I've been meaning to ask yer, girl, have yer invited yer dad and his wife?'

Mary shook her head. 'I've had sleepless nights over that. He's me dad, I love him and we're getting on fine together now. But seeing him with her would spoil the whole thing for me. Just put yerself in my shoes, Amy, and see how you'd like it. She's younger than me, hasn't got an ounce of sense in her head and I know she doesn't look after him properly. To invite her here and be nice to her would be hypocritical. I can't, and won't do it.'

'I'm not blaming yer, girl, I'd probably feel the same in your place. But it's such a shame 'cos I've always liked your dad. And it's sad that he won't see his grandchildren over Christmas. Sad for them, as well.'

'He will see them, sunshine, he's coming in the morning with presents for them. And I've got socks and hankies for them to give him.'

Amy looked puzzled. 'How can he come in the morning? There's no trams or buses running on Christmas Day.'

'He said he'll walk. I was honest with him, told him about the party and the way I feel. He said he understood but he wasn't going to miss seeing us tomorrow, so he's decided to use shanks's pony. He'll do it in half an hour, he said.'

Amy sniffed up. 'It's sad, that is. I'll be crying in a minute.'

'If yer do, it'll be in yer own house. I want yer to be a good girl and go home, so I can start on the spuds.'

Amy's bottom shuffled to the edge of the chair. 'Bleedin' marvellous, isn't it, when yer best friend tells yer to bugger off. I mean, even though yer said it nicely, it still means the same, doesn't it? So I'll do as yer ask and take me body elsewhere. But before I go, what about tomorrow? Are we all sorted out?'

'Yeah. Molly's making a jelly and a dish of trifle, you're making two dozen fairy cakes and I'm doing the sandwiches. If yer'll bring them in about six, I can get the table set for seven o'clock.'

Amy swayed towards the door. 'D'yer want any help making the sandwiches?'

'No, I've got the girls to help me.' Mary put her arms around her friend and hugged her tight. 'A Merry Christmas, sunshine.'

Amy hugged her back. 'And you too, girl. And you too.'

Mary sat back and watched the girls decorating the tree. 'It looks nice, doesn't it, love? I'm really grateful to Seamus.'

Stan returned her smile. 'Yeah, it looks great. It's a good one, too, nice thick branches. Did yer say he got it for nothing?'

'That's what he told me. Off some feller he knows at the market.' Mary was pleased to see her two daughters laughing as they hung the strips of red and green bunting on the tree. It was a rare sight to see Laura being friendly and close to her sister. 'You can spread the big presents out underneath now, and hang the small ones on the branches.'

The girls elbowed each other out of the way to be first at the sideboard. As usual, Jenny gave way to her sister and let her take the big presents. 'This is for you, Dad,' Laura said, balancing the parcel on her hand. 'It's not half heavy.'

'D'yer think it could be two bricks?' Stan laughed. 'They'd be handy to put in the oven to warm, and I could take them to bed with me to put me feet on.'

'This one's for me.' Laura fingered the parcel before looking at her mother. 'I hope it's not one of those frumpy, old-fashioned dresses yer usually buy me.'

In a split second, Stan saw the pleasure leave his wife's face and Jenny's happy smile turn to sadness. 'Don't you dare talk to yer mam like that.' His voice was sharp. 'Now say ye're sorry, go on.'

'I didn't mean nothing, Dad, it was only a joke.'

45

'I didn't think it was funny, Laura, so do as ye're told and apologise.'

'I'm sorry.' The words were said with ill-grace as Laura shrugged her shoulders and turned back to the tree. 'It was only a flippin' joke.'

When Mary saw Stan's face redden and his hands grip the arms of the chair, she touched his lightly. 'Leave it be, love, we don't want any rows, tonight of all nights.'

'If you say so, love.' He took her hand and held it in his. 'But she is getting too big for her boots and I should have listened to yer years ago.'

Mary was up very early the next morning and her first task was to spoon the stuffing into the turkey before putting it in the oven on a low light to cook slowly. Then she set about cleaning the grate and lighting a fire. Soon the coals were burning brightly and she put a kettle on the hob ready to make a pot of tea. There was no sound from upstairs so she sat in Stan's armchair enjoying the peace of the house. The tree looked lovely, and with the presents spread out beneath its branches it gave the room a real festive air. She'd done a lot of moaning in the last week with the extra work and worrying about whether she was going to be able to eke her money out. But right now she felt it had been well worth it. A spark from a coal hissed as it spurted out, bringing Mary to her feet to stamp it out before it had time to singe the hearthrug. Not that another scorch-mark would be noticed, the poor mat had put up with a lot of wear over the years. It had been made from bits of old clothes, and she remembered how her mother had sat with her many a night pegging the strips of cloth through the canvas.

Mary shook herself to chase away the sadness. This was a day for happiness and she didn't want the family to come down and see her looking miserable. She hugged herself as she gazed into the dancing flames. There was a lot to look forward to, with her dad coming this morning and then the party tonight. She had never had a party before, but she was going to take Amy's advice and not worry. So what if her friend's fairy cakes did turn out as hard as rocks, or Molly's jelly hadn't set properly? The world wouldn't come to an end, they would still enjoy themselves.

She was so wrapped up in her thoughts, Mary didn't hear the stairs creaking and jumped when her two daughters burst into the room, chorusing, 'Merry Christmas, Mam.'

'Oh, I must have been miles away, I didn't hear a sound.' Mary hugged and kissed each of them. 'Merry Christmas, sunshine, and I hope yer both like what Father Christmas brought for yer.'

Laura's face was eager. 'Can we open our presents now?'

'Not until yer dad's up, I don't want him to miss any of the fun. Give him a shout while I see to a pot of tea.'

When Stan came down he was carrying a parcel which he put with the others under the tree. He grinned at his wife. 'That's for you, love. I hid it under the bed last night.'

Mary clapped her hands together. 'Ooh, what is it?'

'Yer'll find out soon enough, just be patient. And if yer don't like it yer can tell yer mate off, because she got it for me.'

'Oh dear, in that case it'll be a joke. When I open it, it'll probably blow up in me face.'

Stan's head dropped back and he gave a hearty chuckle. 'Fancy thinking that about yer best mate! I admit I had doubts meself about asking her to get yer something, but I think she's done yer proud.'

'Dad, can I open my presents now?' Laura asked. 'I can't wait.'

'Just hold yer horses, sunshine.' Mary pushed Stan gently down on to the couch, then handed him a cup of tea. 'Me and yer dad will sit and watch. I think the youngest should go first, so let Jenny open hers.'

Jenny opened the small parcel first, and much to Laura's annoyance, insisted upon trying the woollen gloves on. Then she laid them to one side and ripped open the large parcel. Her shriek of delight as she held the dress up brought a glow to Mary's heart. The dress was deep blue with a round collar, long sleeves and belted waist. It was in a heavy cotton, suitable for wear in any weather. The style was plain, but it was the simplicity that made it attractive. 'Oh, it's lovely.' Jenny held the dress close to her chest as she bent and kissed her parents. 'Thank you, Mam and Dad. Can I wear it today?'

'Of course yer can,' Mary said. 'Yer can get all dolled up for yer grandad coming. He won't know yer, think he's come to the wrong house.'

'I'm opening mine now.' Laura's face was set with impatience. But when the small parcel revealed her first pair of grown-up long rayon stockings, she jumped for joy. 'Just what I wanted. I'm over the moon, Mam, they're brilliant! I was frightened I'd have to go to work in me school socks.'

'I hope yer like yer other present as much.' Mary had her doubts. She'd spent a long time choosing a dress for her eldest daughter, trying to find a style that was neither too young, nor too old. And it was with apprehension she watched her daughter undo the parcel. But when she saw Laura's face, she knew her fears were groundless.

The girl was lost for words when she held up the cherry-red dress. She gazed with open mouth at the sweetheart neck, the long sleeves and the full flared skirt. 'It's beautiful! It's the most beautiful dress I've ever seen. I bet Cynthia doesn't get anything as nice as this.' She twirled round, holding the dress to her. 'I'm going to put it on right now.'

47

'Excuse me, young lady,' Stan said. 'Have you lost yer manners? Don't yer ever thank anyone when they give yer a present?'

'I'm sorry, Mam, I'm just that excited.' The tone of her voice and the offhand peck on her mother's cheek made it clear Laura's heart wasn't in it. She was doing what she was told to do, but her mind was elsewhere. 'I'm going upstairs! I can't wait to see what me dress looks like on.'

Jenny stepped into her sister's path, barring her exit. 'Aren't yer going to wait and see what me mam and dad got for Christmas?'

Laura looked surprised by the question. 'No, I want to go and try me dress on. Anyway, I know what me dad's got so there's no point.'

Laura tried to sidestep her sister but Jenny anticipated the movement and stood her ground. She knew how her mother had struggled to buy those clothes and she thought the least her sister could do was show some gratitude and not be so selfish. 'Me mam knew what we were getting because she was the one who had to find the money for them. But it didn't stop her from being interested enough to want to see our faces when we opened the presents. You're not the only one in the house, yer know, Laura.'

'Oh, you get on my wick, you do.' Laura tried to push her sister aside. 'Get out of me way and mind yer own business.'

Stan was rising from his chair to intervene when Mary gripped his arm and motioned for him to stay out of it. 'Let her go, Jenny, there's a good girl. Yer can't make anyone be interested if they don't want to be.'

Laura sneered into her sister's face before flouncing out of the room, leaving Jenny shaking her head. She always had a vision of families being close on Christmas morning, laughing and joking as they shared the pleasure of presents given and received. But looking back, Laura had always been the first to rip open her presents. They'd been mostly toys when they were younger, and her sister would sit at the table with them and not even throw a glance to see what the others had got. 'She's dead mean, Mam.'

'I know, sunshine, but that's her problem, and her loss. Now, you can go in the kitchen if yer like, and try your dress on.'

Jenny shook her head as she sat down. 'No, I want to see what you and me dad have got. I don't want to miss anything.'

'Then you can give them out, love.' Stan was realising he had a lot of ground to make up with his youngest daughter. He'd spoilt Laura by always putting her first, and he could see now that he hadn't done her any favours. If he hadn't given in to her every whim, she might have grown up to be as good and caring as Jenny. 'Yer mam can go first, then we can have a laugh if Amy has set a booby trap.'

'I'll kill her if she has,' Mary said, taking the parcel. 'This is one day of the year when I can do without me mate's practical jokes.'

She was tearing at the paper as she spoke. 'She's probably wrapped a dead mouse in an old towel, or something.'

'In that case, I want me money back,' Stan said, watching his wife's face closely. 'She's not diddling me.'

The only sound from Mary was a gasp, as she stared down at the neatly folded, deep blue fleecy dressing gown. Then came a long drawn-out sigh. 'Oh Stan, it's lovely. But how could yer afford it? I hope yer haven't gone into debt.'

'That's the last thing I'd do, love. Yer know how I feel about borrowing money. Once yer get into debt yer never get out of it. No, I was determined that this year I'd get yer a decent present. It's always you buying for others, never getting much back for yerself.' Stan took her hand and smiled into her face. 'So, since September, I've only been buying ten Woodbines a day, instead of me usual twenty. And the odd times I do go to the pub, I've only been having a half, instead of a pint. I've put the money away each week religiously, and it soon mounted up. I feel dead chuffed with meself – even gave meself a pat on the back.'

'Oh Stan, it's beautiful and I do love yer.' There were tears in Mary's eyes. 'But yer shouldn't have skinted yerself, I know how much yer enjoy yer ciggies.'

'It hasn't done me no harm, love, and I won't be going back to me twenty fags a day. Instead, we'll go to the pictures more than once every blue moon. The girls are old enough to be left on their own now, and it's about time you and me got out a bit more.'

Jenny was watching them with her head tilted and a smile on her face. Seeing her parents like this brought a warm glow to her heart. 'Mam, will yer show us yer dressing gown now, please? I can only see the colour of it from here.'

'I'll do better than that, sunshine, I'll model it for yer.' Mary felt happier than she had for a long time. Fancy her Stan going without his cigarettes so he could buy her a present. He had to be the best husband in the world. She stood up and passed the gown to Jenny. 'You undo the buttons, sunshine, while I give yer dad a big kiss.' She sat on Stan's knee and put her arms around his neck. Her first kiss was soft and gentle. 'That's because I love yer.' Then she kissed him with passion. 'And that's for being so nice I couldn't help but love yer.'

Jenny coughed gently. 'When you two soppy beggars have finished, can I see me mam in her new dressing gown?'

Mary sprang to her feet, laughing. 'Yeah, all good things must come to an end. If we don't put a move on, me dad will be here before we've had any breakfast.'

With her arms spread, Mary was doing a twirl when Laura came in. 'Ooh I say, the state of you and the price of fish.' She eyed the

49

dressing gown with envy. 'I'll be borrowing that for when I have to get up early to go to work.'

'Like hell you will.' Mary held her daughter's eyes. 'This is the first thing I've had in the last twelve years that hasn't been bought second-hand from a stall in the market, or on a Sturla's cheque. So you will keep your hands off it. Understood?'

Laura pulled a face and shrugged her shoulders. 'Okay, keep yer flippin' hair on. Anyway, isn't anyone going to say they like me dress?' Not realising her appearance and attitude had put a damper on a happy scene, she appealed to her father first, expecting to be heaped with praise. 'It suits me, doesn't it, Dad?'

'Yeah, it's a nice dress.'

'It does suit yer,' Jenny said, feeling guilty for the bad thoughts she was having about her sister. 'It's a lovely colour.'

'It looks a treat on yer, sunshine,' Mary said, determined that nothing or no one was going to spoil this day. 'Turn around and let's see it properly.' The dress fitted Laura to perfection and the colour complemented her dark complexion and black hair. She was a pretty girl, there were no two ways about it. And as she grew older and her figure filled out, she had the makings of a very attractive woman. Her eyes were her outstanding feature, but somehow her smile never reached them. 'Yes, I don't think yer could have got anything to suit yer better.'

'Excuse me,' Stan said, 'but didn't Father Christmas bring me any toys?'

'Ah, you poor thing!' Jenny picked up his presents and placed them on his knee. 'We saved the best till the last.'

Laura was bored stiff having to sit and pretend to be excited about a flipping shirt and pullover, it was all so childish. But she knew she'd blotted her copybook and went out of her way to join in the enjoyment. But while she was laughing, her mind was on the party tonight. How she'd swank in front of John, the boy from next door, and Mick from across the street. They wouldn't half get their eyes open when they saw her in her new dress.

Stan opened the door to his father-in-law and quickly stepped aside to let him pass. 'Come in, Joe, yer must be freezing walking all that way.'

'I'm all right. I set meself a fair pace and soon got warm.' Joe took a glove off and extended his hand. 'Compliments of the season, Stan.'

'Same to you.' Stan opened the living-room door. 'Here he is, the man himself.'

Mary dashed forward to be first to her father. She took his face in her hands and rained kisses on him. 'A Merry Christmas, Dad, and may you be granted everything yer wish for.'

'And the same to you, sweetheart.'

There was a trace of sadness in Joe's eyes and Mary knew he was remembering the other Christmases when her mam was alive. There'd been so much love and warmth then, he was bound to miss it. 'Take yer coat off and get by the fire.'

But the two girls claimed him first. Hanging on to his arms, they stood on tiptoe to kiss him. 'It's lovely to see yer, Grandad,' Jenny said, her face aglow. 'We're never in when yer come to see me mam.'

'I won't stay away so long again, lass, I promise.' There was affection in his eyes as he patted her arm. How proud he and Ada had been when these two grandchildren came along, and how they'd doted on them. 'I'll call in on a Saturday afternoon on me way home from work.'

Laura moved away from him and spread her arms wide. 'How d'yer like me new dress, Grandad, isn't it lovely?'

'Not as lovely as the girl wearing it. And I see that Jenny is also looking very glamorous in her new finery. I'm lucky to be blessed with two of the most beautiful granddaughters yer'd see in a month of Sundays.'

Laura was eyeing the parcel tucked under his arm but for once was wise enough not to ask what he'd brought for them. Instead, she enquired, 'Where's Celia? Why hasn't she come with yer?'

'She's at home seeing to the Christmas dinner.' Joe had prepared himself for this question. 'But she sends her best wishes.'

'Ah,' Laura pouted, 'I wanted her to see me new dress. Can yer bring her tomorrow?'

'I'm sorry, queen, but we've arranged to go somewhere tomorrow.'

'That's enough now,' Stan waved the two girls away. 'Let the poor man come up for air, will yer? Take yer coat off, Joe, and sit down by the fire. Mary's making yer a cup of tea, she'll not be long.'

Joe put the parcel on the chair while he took his coat off. 'The tree looks grand, and there's a delicious smell coming from the kitchen.'

When he was seated, Jenny squatted on the floor at the side of his chair. 'Me and Laura decorated the tree, Grandad. And it's the turkey yer can smell. Me mam was up very early to get it in the oven, and she had the fire lit and everything before we got up.'

'Yer've got a good mother, sweetheart, I hope yer appreciate her.'

'Oh I do, Grandad, she's the best mother in the whole world.' Jenny drew her legs up to her chin and wrapped her arms around them. Her pretty face was animated as she asked, 'Tell us what you got off Father Christmas.'

'I haven't opened me presents yet. I thought I'd leave them until I got back and open them before I have me turkey dinner.' Joe was lying through his teeth. His wife had gone out with one of her mates last night and hadn't come home until the early hours. He'd pretended to be asleep because he was too weary for any more arguments. God knows, he'd tried everything he could to make her see that as a married woman she had a responsibility to her husband and home. But it was a waste of time; she'd never change because she didn't want to. There was no Christmas tree in their house, and no smell of turkey coming from the kitchen – because his wife was still in bed when he left and would probably still be there when he got home.

'Here yer are, Dad, get this down yer, it'll warm the cockles of yer heart.' There was a wide smile on Mary's face when she passed him the cup of tea, but deep down there was an anger building up. She'd been listening to the conversation as she stood in the kitchen waiting for the kettle to boil, and knew with a certainty she couldn't explain, that her father was telling lies. There were no presents, she'd bet any money on that, and there probably wouldn't even be a Christmas dinner. 'The girls have got yer a couple of presents, Dad, but they're not very exciting, I'm afraid.'

Joe balanced his cup on the arm of the chair before reaching for the parcel at his side. 'These are not very exciting either, lass, but it's the thought that counts.'

Mary opened the brown paper parcel to find four smaller ones inside. They were badly wrapped and Mary told herself there was no woman's touch here, her dad had wrapped them himself. This fuelled her anger further. How dare this woman marry her father and then treat him so badly? He was a good man, he deserved better than this. Of course he should never have married the girl, he should have had the sense to see the pitfalls that lay ahead, Mary would never change her mind about that. But neither would she stand by and see the father she loved neglected and humiliated. Her mam would want her to look out for him, see he was well cared for.

Mary and the two girls were given underskirts and they were delighted. Mary's was blue, Laura's pink and Jenny's in a pale lemon. They were in rayon, and each had an inset of white lace in the front. Stan was given a packet of twenty Capstan Full Strength and he lost no time in lighting up. These were a luxury to a man who could only afford Woodbines, and there was a look of contentment on his face as he sat back, crossed his legs and drew on the cigarette before making smoke rings in the air.

When Joe had opened his presents and expressed pleasure in the socks and hankies the girls gave to him, Laura and Jenny went upstairs, eager to put on their new underskirts. 'They're over the moon, Dad, yer couldn't have bought anything to please them more.' Mary walked to the sideboard, and with her back to her father, she asked casually, 'Our dinner's nearly ready. Why don't yer stop and have a bite with us? The long walk back would give yer an appetite for another one when yer get home.'

52

'Yeah, why don't yer do that, Joe?' Stan asked, knowing how his wife's mind was working. 'Ye're more than welcome, yer know that.'

'I know that, Stan, and I'm beholden to both of yer.' There was nothing Joe would have liked more than to stay in this warm, cosy room, surrounded by those he loved and who loved him in return. But he was too proud a man to give even a hint of the bleakness of his life. 'Still, I think it's only fair I go home. I'll rest me legs for half an hour, then make tracks.'

Mary came to perch on the arm of his chair. 'Tell yer what, Dad, I'll save some turkey and have a nice dinner ready for yer the day after tomorrow, when ye're back at work.' She put an arm across his shoulders and kissed his temple. 'You and me will have a Christmas dinner all on our own, eh?'

Chapter Five

Jenny stood in the middle of the kitchen, her blue eyes wide and her hands clasped together under her chin. 'All this food, Mam, I've never seen so much in all me life. It looks so tempting me mouth is watering.'

'I didn't expect so much,' Mary said. 'Amy and Molly have excelled themselves.' The draining board was filled with plates of sandwiches and cakes, and the stove had been covered by a piece of wood to make space for the jelly creams, trifles, and biscuits. And under the sink stood the crate of stout that Seamus had brought over, the bottle of port that had been Ben's contribution, and bottles of lemonade that Mary had bought. 'It does look nice, doesn't it? Even yer Auntie Amy's fairy cakes have turned out all right. And, God love her, nobody is more surprised than she is.'

Jenny put her arms around her mother's waist and hugged her tight. 'It's been a lovely day, hasn't it, Mam?'

'It has, sunshine, it really has. If every day was like today, yer wouldn't hear me complaining. All we need is for the party to go down well and I'll go to bed tonight and sleep the sleep of the just.'

Stan came to stand at the kitchen door, and seeing his wife and Jenny holding each other close, he thought his youngest daughter was growing more like Mary every day. Both had a peaches and cream complexion, an abundance of golden hair, wide blue eyes, tip-tilted noses and mouths that were made for turning upwards into a smile. Jenny was almost as tall as her mother, too, there were only a few inches in it. Funny how he'd never noticed all this before. His daughter was twelve and a half years old and it was as if he was really seeing her for the first time.

Mary caught his eye. 'Are you spying on us, Stan Nightingale? Making sure we're not helping ourselves to the goodies?'

'No, I just heard yer saying that yer hope the party goes down well. I don't know what ye're worrying about, not when Amy and Molly will be here. Amy could entertain us all night on her own, never mind with Molly to help her. If we're not careful, between the two of them they could bring the house down.'

'Aye, well, we'll soon know, they'll be here in half an hour. And our Laura hasn't come back from Cynthia's yet, the little faggot. She

55

always does a bunk when she knows there's work to be done.'

'I'll go down for her, Mam, while you get yerself ready.' Jenny walked through to the living room, saying over her shoulder, 'I'll drag her back if I have to.'

Amy and Ben arrived first, with their son, John. With them they brought the two extra dining chairs needed to seat everyone. 'Are yer all right, girl?' Amy asked, a big grin on her face. 'Have yer got everything under control?'

Mary laughed as she took her coat and handed it to Jenny to take upstairs. 'I did have, sunshine, but you'll soon alter that, won't yer?' She waited until her neighbour had settled on one of the wooden chairs before asking, 'Are you sure your Eddy and Edna are all right to be left on their own? I feel lousy leaving them out.'

'Oh, stop yer worrying, girl, they'll be fine. If anything untoward happens, all they've got to do is knock on the bleedin' wall. It's not as though I'm spending Christmas night on the other side of the world.'

'There's a knock, love,' Stan said. 'I'll answer it, it'll be the Moynihans.'

The room became alive then as hands were shaken and compliments of the season were exchanged. And while Molly was chatting to Amy, Seamus took Stan's elbow and ushered him out to the kitchen. He took a half bottle of whisky from his pocket and pushed it into Stan's hand. 'It's a Christmas box from me boss, God bless him, so you and Ben, and meself, can toast the dear man for having a heart of gold.'

Stan chuckled. 'I'm not used to the hard stuff, Seamus. One glass and I'd be as drunk as a lord.'

'Begorrah, is that right, now? Then I'll be after helping yer, so I will. Add a little drop of water to it, just until yer get the taste, then yer'll be fine. It's a sacrilege, I have to tell yer, to add water to a fine whisky, but I don't think yer'll be making a habit of it.'

Mary came into the kitchen and eyed the men with suspicion. 'Oh aye, what are you two being so secretive about?'

'A glass of whisky isn't a secret, Mary, me darlin', it's the nectar of the gods.'

'I'll have less of yer blarney, Seamus Moynihan. And I'll thank yer not to be teaching me husband any bad habits.'

'Well, it's sorry I am about that, Mary. Yer leave me with no alternative but to drink the whole bottle meself.'

'And have yer giving this house a bad name by rolling out of here blind drunk, singing at the top of yer voice? Not on your life, Seamus Moynihan, yer can just share that bottle with my husband and Ben Hanley.'

Stan wrapped his arms around her. 'Ye're as pretty as a picture, Mary Nightingale, and I love the bones of yer.'

Seamus clapped his hands together. 'Will yer just listen to the man, and not a drop has passed his lips yet.'

'Ay, you lot!' Amy's loud voice boomed. 'Get yerselves in here pronto, and let's get the bleedin' show on the road.'

Mary popped her head into the living room. 'Don't yer want to eat first?'

Amy's legs were six inches short of reaching the floor and she was swinging them back and forth. 'No, I don't want nothing to eat. I want a glass of sherry in this hand, and a glass of stout in this one. After that I'll give yer a song. Then I'll have another sherry and bottle of stout, and I'll give yer two songs and throw a dance in for free.'

Ben groaned loudly. 'For heaven's sake, take pity on me and don't let me wife get to the third sherry and stout. That's when she's just had enough to want to do the dance of the seven veils.'

'Ooh, ay, yeah!' Amy turned to her husband and thumped him so hard on the arm he nearly fell off the chair. 'That's me speciality, that is, when I do me Salome act. Yer'll think there's something wrong with yer eyes when yer see me belly dance.' She gazed at Mary with wide innocent eyes. 'Yer don't happen to have seven veils, do yer, girl?' Then she grimaced and shook her head. 'Of course yer haven't, what a silly question. How about seven scarves?'

Her son, John, was standing with Mick Moynihan and they both had wide grins on their faces. 'Being optimistic, aren't yer, Mam? Wouldn't seven tablecloths be more like it?'

She smiled sweetly. 'Another crack like that, son, and we won't be talking tablecloths we'll be talking sheets. The kind they have in hospitals.'

John held his tummy while he doubled up with laughter. 'One of these days I'll get the better of you, Mam.'

Mick tapped him on the shoulder. 'I wouldn't hold yer breath, John, 'cos yer've not got a snowball's chance of ever getting the better of yer mam.' His white teeth gleamed and his dimples deepened. 'Unless yer catch her when she's asleep.'

Amy preened as she gazed at Molly. 'That's a very clever son yer have, Mrs Moynihan. I don't suppose yer'd think of doing a swap, would yer? I'm in a generous mood now I've got me sherry and me stout, so I'll strike a bargain with yer. My three kids for your one. Now yer wouldn't get a better bargain than that even at Paddy's Market.'

Seamus had been helping Stan serve the drinks, now he stopped in front of Amy and bent until his face was on a level with hers. 'Yer'll not have much luck there, me darlin'. Sure isn't Mick the

57

apple of his mother's eye? There's only one thing I can think of that she'd swap him for, and that's the key to the kingdom of heaven.' He looked up at the ceiling, closed his eyes and roared with laughter. 'And with the key there'd have to be a ticket for a seat at the side of the Good Lord Himself.'

'I could get yer the key, that's no problem, 'cos I know a feller what makes keys.' Amy's pursed lips gave her face an earnest look. 'But I couldn't get a ticket 'cos I don't know no one what knows Saint Peter. He's the one what guards the Pearly Gates, and I've heard he's red hot on not letting anyone through unless they've got a ticket.' She gave a deep sigh. 'Oh well, it looks as though I'm stuck with the three kids.'

'Never mind, love,' Ben said. 'Look on the bright side, it could be worse. We could have had six kids.'

'Where d'yer get the "we" from, Ben Hanley? You didn't have no kids – I had that bleedin' pleasure.' Amy handed her glasses to Jenny to hold before turning to Molly. With her arms folded and her bosom hitched almost to her chin, she said, 'Did yer hear that, Molly? Men are not soft, are they? While we're in bed, riddled with pain, they go down to the pub to wet the baby's head! Did yer ever hear the likes of it? Propping the bar up, they are, their chests sticking out a mile because they've proved what a clever man they are! Huh! I bet a bleedin' tanner that if it was the men who had the babies, we wouldn't have got any further than our John. And I'll also bet that we wouldn't be here tonight, because although our John's fourteen, Ben would still be in bed recuperating.'

'Sure, men are funny creatures, so they are,' Molly grinned. 'Hasn't Seamus Moynihan been wetting the baby's head every night since Mick was born – sixteen years ago.'

Ben tapped his wife on the shoulder. 'Ye're wasting valuable drinking time, love, so come on, get it down yer.'

True to form, Amy was the first to sing. Her rendition of 'Daisy–Daisy' had them not knowing whether to laugh or sing. She always mimed to her songs, her facial expressions and her hands making exaggerated moves to suit the words. It was difficult for those watching to join in the singing while laughing their heads off. And at the end of the song she got a rousing cheer which she accepted by bowing graciously.

Then Seamus and Molly sang a duet, 'When Irish Eyes Are Smiling', and they surprised everyone with their clear, strong voices. They also showed the strength of their love for each other by holding hands and facing each other as they sang, their devotion clear for everyone to see. They refused pleas for an encore, saying they'd sing later when they had a few more drinks down them.

The Moynihans' double act put poor Ben in the dog-house. 'Ay, you, light of my life,' Amy said, 'why don't you sing with me and hold my hand? Got no bleedin' romance in yer, that's why. Jeanette MacDonald's got Nelson Eddy, Molly's got Seamus, but if I want a partner I'll have to buy a singing canary.'

Jenny was sitting on the floor by her mam and dad. This was her first grown-up party and she was having the time of her life. She knew Auntie Amy was always telling jokes and making people laugh, but she'd never seen her in such good form. And the Moynihans were just as funny; there'd never been a dull moment since they'd arrived.

Laura meanwhile was standing near to John and Mick. She was disappointed because not one person had told her she looked nice in her new dress. But then, apart from the two lads, all the others were old fogeys and wouldn't know what was nice and what wasn't.

'I think we'll have a break for eats now,' Mary said, her heart light now the party was going so well. 'Come on, Laura and Jenny, give me a hand to pass the plates around.'

Laura pulled a face at the two lads. 'I hope no one spills anything on me new dress.' She half turned, then asked, 'D'yer like me new dress?'

John shrugged his shoulders. What did he know about girls' dresses? 'Yeah, it's nice.'

'Lovely colour,' Mick said with a smile. 'It suits yer.'

It amazed Mary how quickly the piled-high plates were emptied. 'I thought we had enough food to feed an army,' she told her husband, 'but it's nearly all gone.'

Stan grinned. 'Drink always makes yer peckish.' He put his arms around her waist and held her close. 'I told yer not to worry, didn't I? Everyone's having a whale of a time.'

Her eyes went to the door. 'Let me go, yer daft nit, before someone comes out.'

'It isn't a crime to cuddle yer wife, love.'

'Still, and all, behave yerself and see to the drinks.'

There was a lot of chattering going on when Amy happened to see her son going into the kitchen with his empty plate. Then she saw Laura follow him out. She was off her chair like a shot. 'Excuse me, folks, but I'll have to get meself a glass of water because me throat's so dry I could spit feathers.'

When Amy reached the kitchen door she saw Laura standing in front of her son, who was blushing to the roots of his hair. And she heard the girl say, 'Me grandad said I look beautiful in me new dress, John. Do you think I look beautiful?'

Amy bustled in. Her face was smiling, but her eyes weren't. 'Is yer grandad's eyesight failing, girl? Poor old bugger.' She watched Laura toss her head and flounce out of the kitchen, then turned to her son

59

who was looking relieved. 'Do yerself a favour, John, and keep well away from her. She's one hard-faced little madam.'

'It's her house, Mam. I could hardly tell her to scram.'

Amy smiled at the son who had inherited her sense of fun. 'Come and sit on me knee, yer'll be safe there.'

John returned the smile of the mother he adored. She never complained, was always bright and cheerful. 'Did yer bring me dummy with yer?'

It was one o'clock in the morning when Mary and Stan stood at the door seeing their friends out. They'd all had a wonderful time and were loud in their praises. Mary was worried about the noise they were making but Stan whispered, 'Don't worry, it's the first party we've ever had. And Christmas comes but once a year.'

'Ay, girl,' Amy said, her voice loud and slurred, 'what about New Year's night? Are we being invited again?'

'Sod off, Amy Hanley, and go home. You can have the next party.'

'Charming, that is,' Amy chuckled as Ben led her away. 'And, God help me, she's supposed to be me best mate.'

Seamus shouted from across the street: 'New Year's night in the Moynihans'. How does that suit yer?'

Mary grinned as she was closing the door and heard Amy call back, 'I always knew yer were a man after me own heart, Seamus. Invitation accepted with thanks.'

Mary stood at the bottom of the stairs and shouted, 'If yer don't put a move on, Laura, yer'll be late for yer first day at work.'

'For heaven's sake, keep yer hair on.' Laura appeared on the landing. 'I've got plenty of time yet.'

'You're supposed to start work the same time as yer dad, and he's nearly ready to leave.' Mary sighed. If she had to go through this every morning to get her daughter out of bed, she'd be a bundle of nerves after the first week. 'You haven't even had yer breakfast yet.'

Laura came down the stairs slowly, as though she had all the time in the world. 'It won't take me long to have a swill and eat me breakfast. I don't know what ye're getting yerself all het up for.'

'Neither do I, sunshine.' Mary walked through to the living room. 'In future I'll call yer once and yer can please yerself. If ye're late for work and lose yer job, then it'll be yer own fault.'

Stan was putting his coat on, but his daughter didn't even glance his way. She saw the plate of toast ready for her and the pot of tea in front of her cup and saucer. 'Pour me tea out while I get washed.'

Mary looked at her husband, sighed and shrugged her shoulders. 'She's going to be a real bundle of joy every morning.'

Stan walked to the kitchen door. 'Your mother is not yer servant – pour yer own tea out.'

Laura had her hands in a bowl of water, her face sulky. 'I'm going to work now, same as you, so why can't she pour me tea out? She waits on you.'

'A servant or waitress waits on people, and your mother is neither of those. Yer should have got up when yer were first called, same as I do, instead of leaving it until the last minute. If yer think yer can carry on like this every morning, then yer've got another think coming. In future yer either come down when called, or do without breakfast.' Stan picked up the tin with his carry-out in before kissing his wife's cheek. 'If she gives yer any lip, let me know and I'll deal with her tonight.'

'Me voice is hoarse with calling her, Stan, so she's on her own now. She can just get on with it. I'm going upstairs to wake our Jenny.'

There was no need to wake Jenny, she'd been wide awake since the shouting started. The two sisters shared a bed and she'd given Laura a few digs in the ribs to try and get her to move but all she got for her efforts were a few digs back from a very angry sister. She sat up in bed with a smile on her face. 'I'm getting up now, Mam. I was just waiting until the coast was clear. There was enough racket going on to wake the dead.'

They heard the slam of the front door and Mary hurried through to the front bedroom. She lifted the net curtains to see Laura running up the street eating a piece. What a good start to her working life! You would expect her to be excited and eager about her first day at work, not running hell for leather up the street with a piece of toast in her hand a very strong possibility of being late. Mary recalled the first day she started work, and the memory brought a smile to her face. She'd been so frightened of being late she'd arrived at the gates of the factory half an hour early!

Mary let the curtains fall back into place and made her way downstairs. She'd make a fresh pot of tea and sit at the table for ten minutes while Jenny had her breakfast. That should calm her nerves before she started on the housework. But she hoped this morning's shenanigans weren't a sign of things to come. She couldn't cope with it.

Mary was cleaning her teeth at the kitchen sink when something hit one of the panes of glass in the window and frightened the life out of her. She cupped one of her hands under the tap, filled it with water and rinsed her mouth out. Reaching for the towel hanging on a nail on the door, she told herself one of the slates must have fallen off the roof and she'd have to see the landlord to have it fixed. Otherwise, if they had a downpour, the rain could come into one of the bedrooms. She put the towel back on the nail, and as she lifted the door latch she muttered, 'This is turning into a right miserable day.'

'Is that you, girl?' Amy's voice came floating over the wall. 'I've been shouting me bleedin' head off for ages. I was beginning to think yer'd gone and died on me.'

Mary screwed up her eyes as she stepped down into the yard. 'Yer wouldn't by any chance have been daft enough to throw something at the window, would yer?'

There was silence for a few seconds, then Amy shouted, 'I cannot tell a lie, girl, 'cos God always pays me back when I tell a lie. So, yes, I did throw something at yer window . . . a feather.'

'A feather!' Mary put a hand over her mouth and willed herself not to laugh. After all, it could have ended up with her having to fork out for a pane of glass. 'From the sound it made, I can only assume you were attached to the feather?'

'Nah, I'm not that daft, girl, 'cos I'd have hurt meself. It was a brick.'

'A brick! Well, now I've heard it all. And who, pray, was going to pay for a new window if yer'd broken it?'

'It wasn't a whole brick, yer soft article, only a little piece of one. And I gave it a good talking to before I threw it. I said if it broke me mate's window I'd come around there and crush it under me feet.'

'Amy Hanley, the older yer get, the worse yer get.'

'Well, I was worried about yer, girl! I shouted and shouted, but yer didn't answer. If I never move from this spot, I really thought yer'd fell off yer perch. D'yer know what I said to meself? I said, "I bet that inconsiderate cow has gone and died on me. It's just the sort of thing she would do when I want to borrow a cup of sugar. The only one she ever thinks about is herself." That's what I said, girl, cross my heart.'

'Well, I'm sorry to disappoint yer, sunshine, but I am still alive and kicking. I might not be the happiest person in the world, but I am still breathing.'

'What's the matter, girl, why aren't yer happy?'

'Oh, I dunno. Monday morning blues, I suppose.'

'Are we going to the shops?'

'Yes, I've only got to comb me hair then I'm ready.' Mary undid the ties of her wraparound pinny. 'I've got to get something in for the dinner, there's no turkey or chicken left.'

'Same here, girl. Me cupboard's as bare as Old Mother Hubbard's. I'll give yer a knock in five minutes.'

'Just a light tap will do, Amy, don't put the door in.' As she stepped into the kitchen, Mary could hear her friend chuckling and suddenly her gloom lifted. Half an hour in Amy's company and she'd be as right as rain. Ready for anything.

Arm-in-arm they entered the butcher's shop to be met by Wilf's smiling face. 'Thank God for that,' he said, 'I've only had two customers so far this morning.'

'What d'yer expect after Christmas?' Amy was eyeing the rabbits hanging on a hook from the ceiling. 'Most folk will be eating the leftovers for a few days. It's only greedy buggers like me and me mate here what have been eaten out of house and home.'

'I'll have three-quarters of stewing beef, Wilf,' Mary said. 'It's easier to make a pan of stew than anything else.'

'Ay, girl.' Amy gave her a dig before pointing upwards. 'How about getting one of those rabbits between us? It's a while since we had rabbit.'

'But they're not skinned yet.'

'That won't take me long.' Wilf took a long pole and lifted down two rabbits which were tied together. 'Yer can hang on until I do it, or yer can get the rest of yer shopping done.'

'We'll get our shopping done.' Mary linked her friend's arm. 'When yer've skinned it, Wilf, will yer cut it in half down the middle, so there's no arguing over one getting more than the other? Otherwise me mate will have the tape measure out when we get home. We'll be back in twenty minutes, unless Amy starts gabbing to someone.'

'Just hold yer horses, girl.' Amy gazed down at the two rabbits lying on the counter. Then she pointed to one. 'I don't want that one.'

Mary tugged on her arm. 'For crying out loud, Amy, they're both the same!'

'They're not, girl, just look at them. That one's cock-eyed.'

Wilf pushed his straw hat to the back of his head. 'Amy, when yer come back it'll be decapitated. Yer won't see the eyes because it won't have no head.'

'Ah, yer won't hurt it, will yer?'

'Amy, the bleedin' rabbit is as dead as a dodo.'

'I know, Wilf, and I won't say keep yer hair on 'cos yer haven't got that much to keep on. But yer see, me saying it was cross-eyed was just an excuse. The truth is, it reminds me of my feller.'

Mary gasped. 'Amy Hanley, how can yer say such a thing?'

Amy turned wide eyes on her friend. 'Yer haven't seen my feller in bed, fast asleep, have yer, girl?'

'I should hope not!'

'Well, yer don't need to now, 'cos I'm telling yer, that's what he looks like . . . except the rabbit's better-looking.'

Mary slipped her arm from her friend's and put two hands on her ample waist. 'Out, Amy Hanley.' She pushed the reluctant woman towards the door, calling over her shoulder, 'Twenty minutes, Wilf. And if I'm on me own, yer'll know I've pushed this one under a tram.'

'That won't do yer no good, Mary, she'd only buckle the wheels.'

Laura was in a very happy frame of mind when she came in from work. She never stopped talking as they were eating their meal, her eyes shining and her arms waving. 'It's the gear, Dad, and the women are smashing. Dead friendly, they are.'

Stan was happy to see the change in his daughter. This was how she should be. How he wanted her to be. 'What exactly do yer do, love?'

'The cigarettes are in packets when they come to our bench, and we have to put them in cardboard boxes. There's a supervisor keeping an eye on us all the time to make sure we pack them properly. Her name's Miss Birch and she's got the eyes of an eagle, but she's nice. And as long as we get on with our work we can talk as much as we like.'

'Don't tell yer Auntie Amy that,' Mary laughed, 'or she'll be applying for a job. She'd be in her apple-cart getting paid for talking.'

'She wouldn't be able to work there, 'cos ye're on the go all the time and she's too fat.' Laura was looking down at her plate and missed her mother's expression change. 'Besides, she isn't me real auntie.'

'I'm sure Mrs Hanley is delighted she's not yer real auntie.' Mary wasn't going to sit and listen to her best friend being run down by her own daughter. 'And as for being too fat, she'd run circles round you, any day of the week.'

Laura smirked. 'Aye, in her sleep.'

'That's quite enough now, Laura. Yer'd be advised to keep a civil tongue in yer head.' Why does she have to go and spoil things, Stan asked himself as his heart plummeted. 'Amy Hanley is one of our best friends and yer'd travel a long way to find a nicer woman.'

'Yeah, she's all right, I suppose.' Laura pushed her plate away and swivelled sideways on her chair. 'I'm going up to Cynthia's to see how she got on in her job.'

'Stay right where you are,' Stan ordered. 'It's bad manners to leave the table until everyone has finished eating, and yer mam hasn't finished. And before yer buzz off out, yer can help with the washing up.'

'Ah, ay, Dad! I've been on me feet all day. Let our Jenny help to wash up.'

'Oh, I suppose yer think yer mam's been lounging on the couch all day reading, do yer? I wonder who made the beds, cleaned up, did the washing, and after that went to the shops and came home and made the dinner? D'yer think a fairy with a magic wand did all that?'

'I'll do the dishes, Dad,' Jenny said, hoping to calm things down. 'It won't take me long and I don't mind, honest.'

'Let her go up to her mates, if that's what she wants.' Mary nodded her head in Laura's direction as she collected the dirty plates. 'The mood she's in, she wouldn't wash them properly, anyway. Me and Jenny will see to them.'

Laura didn't wait to hear what her father had to say, she was off the chair and out of the door like a flash of lightning. 'Yer should have made her stay, love. Yer told me off for spoiling her and now you're giving in to her.'

'I'm not spoiling her, Stan, just fed up with her. If she can't see for herself how selfish she is, then there's no use making her do anything against her will because it would be done grudgingly.' Mary smiled at Jenny. 'Come on, sunshine, you and me will have them done in no time.'

'I don't need you to help me, Mam, I'll do them on me own. You sit down and tell me dad about Auntie Amy and the rabbits.' Jenny took the plates from her mother. 'Go on, give him a good laugh.'

Stan was laughing already. 'What's she been up to now?'

'Don't you ever repeat to Ben what I'm going to tell yer.' Mary sat down, rested her elbows on the table and laced her fingers. And while she told the tale, she giggled at the memory of Amy's face, while Stan roared his head off.

'She's a caution, she is,' he said, wiping his eyes. 'Ben wouldn't be upset over that, he'd be the first to see the joke.'

'That's not all she got up to today. She had Billy Nelson pulling his hair out.'

Jenny came running in, water dripping from her hands. 'Yer didn't tell me about that, Mam, so the dishes can wait for a few minutes. Go on, tell us.'

'Well, I'd been served and Amy asked for five pound of potatoes. She stood there and watched Billy weighing them out, and never said a dickie-bird. Then, when he was emptying them into a piece of newspaper she pointed, and said, "Yer can take those little ones out, I don't want them. Me knife's a bleedin' big thing, like what the butcher has, how d'yer expect me to peel those fiddling little things with it? Anyway, by the time they're peeled there'll be nothing left of them. Me hand will be cut to ribbons, blood running down me pinny and making a pool on the kitchen floor, and the only thing in me hand will be fresh air, the bleedin' potato will have vanished".'

Mary's shoulders were shaking. 'I can see Billy's face now. He didn't know whether to laugh or throw the potatoes at her. But he kept his cool, and asked, in a very quiet voice, "Amy, why didn't yer ask for big ones?" And yer know how she squares her shoulders when she gets in a huff – well, she did that, then looking like a little angel, she said, "I've kept this secret for years, Billy, but now I'm going to open me heart to yer. I know yer fancy me, 'cos I can see it in yer eyes every time yer look at me. And I want yer to know that I feel the same way about you. Nothing can come of it, lad, because we're both married, so yer'll have to control yer emotions. But that doesn't mean we can't love each other from afar, does it?" '

Stan reached into his pocket for a hankie to wipe his eyes. 'She's a corker, all right. What happened next?'

'There was no sign of a smile on Billy's face when he asked, "What's all that got to do with potatoes? Or am I missing something?" And with a hand on her heart, me mate says, "It bought me an extra five minutes in yer company. I'll dream of yer tonight in bed and go over every precious word yer've spoken. I'll even dream of yer picking those fiddling little potatoes out and replacing them with decent-sized ones. And, my secret love, I'd be grateful if yer'd put a bleedin' move on 'cos I haven't got all day to stand here listening to you yapping. They say women can talk, but by God, they've got nothing on you".'

Mary stretched out an arm. 'Lend me that hankie, love.' She shook her head as she conjured up the scene in her mind. 'Billy's face was a picture, I can tell yer. He said, "I haven't spoken a dozen flippin' words! It's you what's done all the yapping." And me mate just grinned at him. "That's why I love yer," she said. "I've always fancied the strong and silent type. Yer remind me of Gary Cooper, except yer haven't got no horse".'

'How does Auntie Amy think of all these things?' Jenny asked. 'She's not just funny sometimes, she's funny all the time.'

'Ah, but Billy had an answer for her. He said, "What d'yer mean I haven't got no horse? How d'yer think I got these bow legs? I certainly didn't get them sitting on a twenty-two tram. No, I got them riding the range on me faithful steed, Silver".'

'Did Amy appreciate the joke?' Stan asked. 'I bet she laughed her head off.'

'Oh, she did more than that, did Amy Hanley. Yer know what she's like for having the last word. She gave me a dig in the ribs, and said, "We've seen his horse, girl. It's the one what pulls our coalman's cart. It's a dirty beggar, Billy Nelson, yer should train him proper. Every time he stops outside our door he decides he wants to go to the lavvy. I wouldn't mind so much if we had rose bushes to put it on, but the ruddy horse can see we haven't. Why doesn't he wait until he's outside a house with a garden?" '

'These shopkeepers don't take her serious, do they?' Stan asked.

'I mean, they must know every time she opens her mouth she's having them on.'

'Of course they know she's having them on! They look forward to her coming because they know they'll get a laugh. And they're as quick off the mark as she is. As we were leaving the shop, Billy shouted after her, "Why don't yer put a sign up outside yer house, Amy, saying USE OF TOILET 1d? Yer could make yerself a few coppers, 'cos lots of people get caught short when they're out, not only horses". With that me mate marches back into the shop, shakes a fist at Billy, and says, "Not bleedin' likely! Me first customer would be that nosy cow from next door, Annie Baxter. She's been trying to get into my house for the last ten years. Then she'd tell her mate, Lily Farmer, and before long there'd be a queue a mile long outside me house. Nah, that's a stupid idea, Billy Nelson. In fact, it's fair put me off yer. My feller's got more brains than you have. He'd be smart enough to up the price to tuppence if they wanted paper thrown in".'

Jenny was smiling as she went back to finish off the dishes. She could hear her parents laughing and felt a warm glow spread through her body. Now she was getting older she was allowed to stay up later and she was seeing more of her dad. They were getting to know each other and were closer than they'd ever been. She knew Laura had always been his favourite, but perhaps that was only natural as she was the firstborn and that made her special.

They were sitting around the fire when Laura came in, and as soon as Mary saw her daughter's face as she sat on the arm of Stan's chair, she knew she was after something. And it wasn't long before she was proved right.

'Dad, can I go up to Cynthia's on New Year's Eve? She can't go to the Moynihans' so there won't be much fun for her with just her mam and dad.' Laura neglected to say that her friend had invited two lads she'd met in work. 'Go on, say I can.'

Stan looked at Mary and raised his brows. 'What d'yer think, love?'

'I don't mind, as long as we know where she is.'

'I'll only be in Cynthia's, honest! She is me mate, and we can keep each other company.' Laura twisted a lock of her dark hair around her finger then let it spring back into place. 'Me and Cynthia have been talking about next week, when we get our first week's wages. How much will I have to give me mam out of me wage-packet, Dad?'

Mary opened her mouth, then decided not to voice an opinion until she'd heard what her husband had to say.

'Yer've got it the wrong way round, Laura,' Stan said. 'You hand yer mam yer wage-packet and she gives you pocket-money back.'

Laura's eyes flashed. 'That's not fair! They're my wages, I have to work for them.'

'I pass my packet over to yer mam, and you'll do the same. She's the one who has to run the house and that's the way it should be.' Stan's voice was stern. 'So let's have no argument over it.'

'I don't see why I should hand me packet over, not when I've worked for the money,' Laura said, her face sullen as she put an arm around her father's neck. 'Cynthia's not handing hers over, Dad. She'll be getting seven and six a week, same as me, and she's giving her mam four shillings out of it.'

'That's very big of her, I must say!' Mary laced her fingers together and pressed tight to remind herself to keep her temper under control. 'But I wonder how much say her mother had in it? From what I've heard, the poor woman doesn't have a say in anything, she's treated like a skivvy.'

'Forget Cynthia, and her mother. What goes on in this house has nothing to do with them.' Stan moved Laura's arm away from his neck. She was trying to worm her way into his good books but he wasn't being soft-soaped, not this time. 'Me and yer mam will decide how much pocket-money yer get, not you, or yer mate Cynthia.'

Jenny stood up and stretched her arms. She didn't want to hear any more arguments, nor see her mother get upset. 'I'm going to bed, Mam, I'm dead tired.'

'I'll come with yer, sunshine, I'm tired meself.' Mary stood at the door and gave Stan a look that said he could sort this out. Then, as she climbed the stairs behind Jenny, she could feel tears stinging her eyes. She'd always done the best she could for her girls, gone without things herself so they always went to school looking neat and tidy. She hadn't minded wearing second-hand clothes from the market, as long as her daughters were all right. And it hurt her to think that now life could be a little easier with Laura's money coming in, every penny she got would be begrudged to her.

Standing on the tiny landing, Jenny put her arms around her mother. 'Good night and God bless, Mam. And don't worry about our Laura, she doesn't always mean what she says. She acts tough, but she's not, really.'

Mary managed a smile. 'I hope not, sunshine, because sometimes she sounds as tough as an old pair of leather boots.' She kissed her daughter's cheek. 'Good night and God bless, sunshine. We've got the party to look forward to – that should cheer us up.'

Seamus Moynihan was very well organised. Five minutes after the Nightingales and Hanleys arrived, they were sitting with glasses in their hands, and within half an hour the party was in full swing. They all joined in as Seamus and Molly sang 'Danny Boy', then came the 'Bonnie, Bonnie Banks O'Loch Lomond', followed with gusto by 'She's A Lassie From Lancashire'.

Then a halt was called to refill the glasses. And while the men were busy pouring, Mary crossed the room to where Amy was sitting, her legs dangling six inches from the floor. 'I've been watching you, sunshine, and I'm getting worried.'

'Why's that, girl? There's no need to worry about me, I'm having the time of me life.'

'I know yer too well, Amy Hanley, and I think ye're up to something.'

'Me? Up to something? I'm sitting here minding me own business, girl, and I've got nothing to get up to.'

'Ye're too quiet for my liking. It's never been known for you to refuse to sing, so unless ye're sickening for something, I smell dirty work at the crossroads.'

'Nah, I'm not sickening for anything, girl, I'll give a turn when I've had a few more bottles of stout. Yer'll soon see there's nowt wrong with me.'

Two bottles of stout later, Amy said she'd give them a turn. 'But I'm going to do it proper, like they do at the Metropole. Seamus can introduce me and I'll make my grand entrance from the kitchen.' With her hips swaying, she tapped a finger on Seamus's chin as she passed him, fluttered her eyelashes and in her best Mae West voice, drawled, 'I'll give a shout when I'm ready, big boy, and make it good.'

Seamus thought it was hilarious, and when Amy called, he threw an arm out towards the kitchen door. 'Put your hands together for Kirkdale's own, the one and only – *Amy Hanley!*'

The applause was loud as the door opened slowly. Then, apart from gasps, everything went quiet as a chubby bare leg, with a fancy blue satin garter above the knee, began to kick in and out. Ben closed his eyes and groaned. 'What's that flippin' wife of mine up to now?'

'I knew it!' Mary said. 'I knew she had something up her sleeve.'

Then a chubby hand appeared and moved seductively up and down the door. There wasn't a sound in the room, apart from Ben's, 'So help me, I'll kill her.'

'I hope ye're all ready for this.' Amy's voice preceded her entrance, which knocked everyone for six. She'd cut an old dress up, hacking the sleeves out, making a high neck into a low round one, and cut the hem-line to mid-thigh. And around the bottom she'd sewn a blue silk fringe which danced as she began to Charleston. And every ounce of her fat danced with the fringe. She didn't know the words to the song, so as she kicked her heels backwards and swung her arms, she kept repeating, 'Do the Charleston . . . doh-doh-dee-oh-doh.'

Within a split second, the tune changed and so did Amy's movements. With her arms outstretched she began to shake her shoulders and hips, and to whistles and cheers, she made her way across the room to stand in front of Ben, who looked as though he'd been struck by lightning. 'If I Could Shimmy Like My Sister Kate' she warbled . . . and as she sang, Amy put her all into the dance that had been the craze when she was younger. And as everyone was to say later, they'd never seen a better shimmy.

Ben looked up into eyes that were dancing with devilment, and he grinned. 'Yer could always shimmy better than yer sister Kate.'

The dancing stopped and Amy put her hands on her hips. 'I haven't got no bleedin' sister called Kate.'

'I know yer haven't, love, that's why yer've got to be better than her. Stands to sense, that, doesn't it?'

Amy cut such a comical figure in a dress that showed her figure in all its glory, that everyone was in stitches. Mary and Molly cried tears of laughter into each other's shoulders, Mick and John were doubled up, and Jenny's pretty face was alive. She'd been embarrassed at first at Auntie Amy showing off so much of her body, but oh dear, she was really so funny you couldn't help but laugh.

Seamus bent down to whisper in Stan's ear, and grinning like two schoolboys, they stole up behind Amy. Before she realised what was happening, they'd each put a hand under her armpits, then their other hand went behind her knees and they scooped her up. They lifted her as high as they could, with Seamus saying, 'Here she is, folks, the lovely and very talented, Amy Hanley.'

'Sod off, Seamus Moynihan, yer silly bugger,' Amy called from her great height. 'Yer nearly knocked me bleedin' head off on the gas-light.'

John looked at his mother, and laughing so much he could hardly get his words out, he said, 'Ay, Mam, I don't think the flappers used to wear blue fleecy-lined bloomers.'

'More fool them, son.' Amy looked down to see she wasn't showing anything she shouldn't, otherwise she wouldn't half get it off Ben when they got home. 'Now we know why they were always shimmying and shaking – it was to keep themselves warm. Fancy using all that energy when all they needed was a pair of fleecy-lined bloomers.'

'Ye're right there, Mrs Hanley.' Mick's dimples deepened. 'A pair of those would have kept them warm up to their chins.'

Amy patted the two men on the head. 'Yer can let me down now, boys, and I'll make meself presentable. And as it's eleven o'clock I think it's time the guests were offered something to eat. We can start the party again when the clock strikes midnight.'

It was a quarter past eleven when a knock came on the door and Mick put his plate down on the sideboard. 'I'll go, Mam.'

The chattering stopped when Laura walked into the room. She didn't look as sure of herself as usual, and her laugh was nervous. 'I thought I'd see how yer were getting on. Is that all right, Mrs Moynihan?'

'Of course it is, child. Get the girl a plate, Mick, and she can help herself to whatever she wants to eat.'

'What got into you?' Stan asked. 'I thought yer wanted to be with yer friend.'

'Cynthia's mam wasn't feeling well and went to bed early.' That was true, but the real reason for Laura's early departure was that the two boys hadn't turned up and she had no intention of sitting listening to her mate's dad prattling on about his work. Not when she knew there was a party going on just up the street. And that there'd be two boys there. 'It wasn't worth staying because we couldn't have celebrated the New Year, not with her in bed and us frightened to make a noise.'

There'd been very few words exchanged between Mary and her daughter since the night Stan had put his foot down and said Laura must turn up five shillings towards the housekeeping and pay her own tramfares to work out of the remaining half-a-crown. The girl seemed to put the blame on her mother and had sulked ever since. But she looked so ill at ease with all eyes on her, Mary's motherly instinct came to the fore. 'Get yerself something to eat, sunshine, then come and sit on the floor next to Jenny.'

Seamus Moynihan hadn't stinted on the drinks, and his wife certainly hadn't stinted on the food. Molly had refused help from her neighbours, saying that she had more money coming into the house, and fewer mouths to feed. So it was a heavily laden table that Laura stood in front of. 'Ooh, I don't know where to start, there's so much,' she told Mick, who was being very gentlemanly and holding the plate for her to fill.

'Pick what takes yer fancy, then yer can always come back for more.'

His attention put Laura in a very happy frame of mind, and when she squatted on the floor beside her sister there was a genuine smile on her face. 'What's been going on, kid? Have I missed anything?'

While Jenny was telling her sister that she had missed a real treat, Mick was back standing next to John who was pulling his leg. 'Got yer eye on Laura, have yer, Mick? Be careful there, mate, she'd eat yer for breakfast.'

'I was only doing what me mam told me to do, looking after the guests.' Mick glanced over to where the two sisters sat. 'I'm waiting for Jenny to grow up.'

'Yer'll have a long wait, mate, she's not thirteen yet.'

'I'm only sixteen meself, so I've plenty of time. I know a lot of water will flow under the bridge before she's old enough, and I also know I might meet someone else before then, or that she might not fancy me anyway. But I've been drawn to her since I first saw her. She was only about three, but I remember thinking the colour of her hair reminded me of a wheatfield back home in Ireland.'

'Blimey, you've got it bad, haven't yer?' John's face gave nothing away as he leaned towards Mick and said softly, 'Yer can get in the queue, mate. I'm before you.'

Mick chuckled. 'We'll continue this conversation in three years' time, when we'll probably both be courting strong and Jenny will be going out with a feller in the next street.'

'Yer could be right,' John said, nodding his head. 'But if not, remember all's fair in love and war.'

So it was, that when the tugs on the Mersey sounded their hooters at the stroke of midnight to herald the arrival of 1934, and all the grown-ups were hugging and kissing each other, Mick and John, armed with a piece of mistletoe, made their way to the sisters. Jenny, not thirteen for another four months, blushed to the roots of her hair and twisted her neck so the kisses landed on her cheek. While Laura puckered her lips, eager and willing.

Chapter Six

'Just look at the time, Stan – ten minutes to eleven and that little faggot still isn't in.' Mary paced the floor, her mood half anger, half worry. 'She knows she's to be in by half ten, and that we'll be waiting up for her.'

'You go to bed, love, I'll wait for her.' Stan rapped his fingers on the arm of his chair. 'And she'll get a piece of my mind.'

'D'yer really think that will make any difference to Laura? She won't take a ha'porth of notice of yer. She treats this place like a hotel, just comes and goes as she pleases, and to hell with anyone else.' Mary glanced at the clock. 'Eleven o'clock. Doesn't it enter her head that we might be worried about her? She's not sixteen yet, and if something awful were to happen to her, we're the ones that would get the blame for letting her stay out till this time of night.'

When the knock came on the door, Mary flew into the tiny hall. 'Where the hell d'yer think you've been, you little madam?' She closed the door and followed her daughter into the room. 'Yer do realise we've been waiting up for yer?'

Stan was standing, his feet astride, his hands locked in front of him. 'Where've yer been until this time of night?'

'If yer let me have me own key, yer wouldn't have to wait up for me.'

'Don't you ever use that tone of voice to me, Laura, I'm warning yer. Push me too far and yer'll find out ye're not too old to get a good hiding. And as for having yer own key, yer can forget that 'cos yer can't be trusted.' Stan unlocked his hands and pointed a finger. 'Now, tell us where yer've been, and I want the truth.'

Laura tossed her head. 'If yer must know, I've been to me grandad's.'

Mary gasped. 'Never! Me dad wouldn't let yer stay until this time, he'd know we'd be worried about yer.'

'Well, that's where I've been.' Out of the three people in the room, Laura was the coolest. She looked bored stiff, as though she just couldn't understand what all the fuss was about. 'Me grandad went to bed early and I stayed talking to Celia. That's all we've been doing, talking. And I can't see any harm in that.'

'She should have more sense than to keep a girl of your age out

73

until this time, knowing that yer'd be walking home alone, in the dark. And *you* should have had more sense, as well. Yer've got eyes in yer head, yer could see the time, and yer knew yer were told to be in by half ten. In future, yer do as ye're told, understand?'

'Dad, I was only keeping Celia company. She said she gets lonely because me grandad goes to bed early every night and she was glad to have someone young to talk to for a change.'

Mary was blazing. How dare that woman talk about her father like that! She was the one who talked him into marriage. If she'd wanted someone younger to talk to, she should have married someone younger. 'She is a married woman and has no right to talk about her husband to a fifteen-year-old girl, who just happens to be his granddaughter, and who is supposed to think the world of him.'

'I'm nearly sixteen, not a baby.'

'Then don't act like one,' Stan said. 'I'm not finished with yer, Laura, not by a long chalk. But we'll leave it for now because it's late and I'm tired. Get to bed now, but be careful yer don't wake Jenny, she's got to get up early for work, too.'

'Yer don't call what she does work, do yer? Sitting on her bottom all day in an office is not my idea of hard work.' Relations between the two sisters had worsened since Jenny left school two months ago, and with excellent references from the headmistress had got herself a job as a clerk in the office of a small toolmaking firm. Laura was so envious she gave her sister a hard time. 'A right stuck-up little snob, she is.'

'It's taking me all me time to keep me hands off yer, Laura.' Mary ground the words out through clenched teeth. 'If yer know what's good for yer, yer'll get up those stairs and out of my sight.'

After Laura flounced out of the room, Mary and Stan looked at each other with sadness and frustration in their eyes. 'I don't know what we're going to do with her,' Mary sighed. 'If she keeps on like this she'll send me to an early grave.'

'It's my fault for not listening to yer.' Stan ran fingers through his thick mop of dark hair. 'They say there's none so blind as they who will not see.' He walked to his wife and took her in his arms, pressing her head against his shoulder. 'Nothing we say has any effect on her, it's in one ear and out the other. We may as well talk to the wall.'

'We'd be better off talking to the wall – at least it wouldn't answer us back.'

Stan held her away from him and kissed her forehead. 'We're both too tired to talk about it now. Let's leave it until tomorrow when we can think straight.' He put an arm across her shoulders and led her to the door. 'I'm absolutely whacked, me brain won't think straight.'

They were cuddled up in bed when Mary said, 'I do love her, yer know, Stan. And I worry about her, wondering what's going to happen to her.'

74

'I know, love, I feel the same way. But she might surprise us all in a year or two, yer never know. Perhaps she'll meet a nice bloke who'll tame her down.'

'I hope so.' Mary kissed his cheek. 'Good night and God bless.' Then she turned on her side and began to pray for her wayward daughter.

'Don't say anything to her,' Mary said next morning as she put her husband's breakfast in front of him. 'I don't want to start the day being upset. Wait until we've had our meal tonight and we'll just sit down and have a quiet word with her.'

'Whatever you say, love.' Stan cut the top off his boiled egg and grinned at her. 'Nice and runny, just the way I like it.'

They both looked up in surprise when Laura came through the door, bright and breezy. It was the first time since she started work that she'd got up without being called half-a-dozen times. 'You're up early,' Mary smiled, determined there would be no angry words exchanged over breakfast, otherwise she'd have a splitting headache all day. 'Pour yerself a cup of tea out while I put yer egg on to boil.' As she was walking to the kitchen, she muttered aloud, 'I may as well put our Jenny's on at the same time.'

'She's on her way down now,' Laura called through. 'Yer know what Miss Prim and Proper's like for being early. She doesn't start work until half eight, but she needs the time to titivate herself up.'

Stan dipped a finger of toast into his egg and kept his head down. That was another thing he wanted to talk to Laura about, the way she treated her sister. Young Jenny had done well for herself, but she'd worked for what she'd got and deserved it. And there'd been no argument over pocket-money, like there had been with Laura. She handed her wage-packet over to Mary and took what she was given with a smile.

'Good morning!' Jenny's bright smile seemed out of place in the room, but she appeared not to notice. 'It looks as though it's going to be a nice day, the sun's trying to shine.'

Mary came to the door and glanced at the clock on the mantelpiece. 'The eggs will only be two minutes, so pour yerself a cup of tea, sunshine. I hope ye're right about the weather because me and Amy are going into town for a couple of hours.'

'Are yer going to buy something nice, Mam?' Jenny put the cosy back on the teapot. 'Yer could do with a new dress.'

'I could do with a lot of things but they'll have to wait. We desperately need pillowcases, the ones we've got are on their last legs.'

'Ooh, would yer let me embroider one, Mam?' Jenny's face was eager. 'I can do it, I learned it at school. Just some flowers and leaves in the corner to make it look nice.'

'Of course yer can, sunshine, but yer need coloured silk thread for that and there's none in the house.'

'You could get some in town, I'll pay for it. I'd only need green and pink to be going on with, until I get me hand in. We only learned a few stitches in school, but when I've had some practise I can try more intricate patterns.'

'More intricate patterns? Oh, how exciting!' Laura's voice was mocking. 'All on a flippin' pillowslip that no one will ever see. Yer'll be making yer own clothes, next.'

Jenny turned and looked her sister straight in the eyes. 'Seeing as ye're so interested, and for your information, I have every intention of learning how to make me own clothes. One of the women in the office makes all hers and yer'd never know they were homemade. She can make a dress for a couple of shillings, and that includes the cotton.'

Mary came through with an eggcup in each hand just as Stan was pushing his chair back. 'Ye're off, are yer, love?'

'Yeah, it's a nice morning so I won't bother with the tram, I'll go on shanks's pony.' Stan reached for his donkey jacket. 'If yer see a dress yer like, love, you get it for yerself. It's about time yer started thinking of yerself, instead of everybody else.'

'I can't afford it, Stan, there's things we badly need for the house.'

'To hell with the house. It'll be here when we're dead and gone,' Stan said gruffly as he picked up his carry-out. 'I'll give yer a bob towards it.'

'And me, too!' Jenny's offer came quickly. 'I don't spend all me pocket-money so I can help towards a new dress for yer.'

'If yer've got money to spare, pass it over here,' Laura said, spooning the yolk of the egg on to a piece of toast. 'I can always find a use for it.'

Mary clamped her lips together as she followed her husband to the door. Why couldn't Laura see for herself how selfish she was? Never once, since she started work, had she bought a sweet for anyone. Mary didn't mind for herself, but she felt for her husband. He'd always been generous with his firstborn, spoiled her rotten, yet she couldn't even buy him five Woodbines. Jenny did. Every Saturday she came home with a packet of ciggies for her dad and a slab of chocolate for her. Laura knew this, but it didn't put her to shame. Every halfpenny she could get her hands on was spent on herself.

Mary stood on the top step and looked down at her husband. 'I'll see yer tonight, love. You take care now.'

'And you get that dress, d'yer hear? I'll be annoyed if I come home and yer tell me yer've got pillowslips but no dress.'

'Ah well, we can't have you getting annoyed, can we?' Mary ran a finger down his cheek. 'If me purse runs to it, I'll mug meself – okay?'

She waited until he reached the end of the street, like she always did, and returned his wave. Then she went back into the living room to find Laura standing in front of the mirror liberally applying bright red lipstick. 'You'd better put a move on if yer don't want to be late. And why yer have to put so much make-up on, I'll never know. Yer look much nicer without it.'

'Ye're old-fashioned, Mam – all the girls wear make-up.'

Mary sighed. She wanted to say that all the girls didn't put it on with a trowel, but what was the use? The only person Laura listened to was herself. 'You get yerself ready, Jenny, while I put the kettle on for a fresh pot of tea. I'm going to park me backside for ten minutes before I start on the beds.'

While she was in the kitchen, Mary heard the front door slam and knew Laura had, as usual, gone off without a word of goodbye. Then she heard Jenny's footsteps running lightly up the stairs. How was it possible for two people like her and Stan, who loved each other dearly, to bring two daughters into the world who were so different in every way? She just couldn't fathom it out, there was no sense nor make in it. If Laura had been badly treated as a child then there could be an excuse for her being so hard. But she hadn't. There'd always been plenty of love and they'd given her everything it was in their power to give her.

Mary carried the fresh pot of tea through just as Jenny came downstairs. 'Sit down, sunshine, and relax for ten minutes.'

Jenny pulled out a chair facing her mother and as she sat down she slid half-a-crown across the table. 'The silk shouldn't come to more than sixpence, Mam, so the other two bob can go towards yer dress.'

'I'm not taking any money off yer. That half-a-crown is yer whole week's pocket-money. Yer haven't exactly got a wardrobe full of clothes yerself, sunshine, so splash out and mug yerself to whatever yer want.'

'I've still got some money left upstairs, Mam, 'cos I don't spend very much. Anyway, I want you to to have it, so take it to please me. As me dad said, it's about time yer started looking after yerself for a change. So take it, as a little gift from me for being the best mam in the world. And because I love the bones of yer.'

Mary swallowed hard. 'Keep that up, sunshine, and there'll be more tears in me cup than there is tea! But to keep you and yer dad happy, I'll buy meself a dress. And I'll have it on when yer come home from work, so yer can see where yer money's gone.' She studied her daughter's face. 'Aren't there any young girls where yer work, someone yer could go to the pictures with?'

Jenny shook her head. 'There's only three of us in the office, and the other two are at least three times my age. They're very nice, and

I get on well with them, but they're too old to make friends with.'

'Yer could do with a friend, sunshine, 'cos a young girl shouldn't be sitting in every night with two oldies like me and yer dad. What about Janet, yer friend from school?'

'I haven't seen her since we started work. I could go around to her house, though, she only lives two streets away.' Jenny glanced at the clock before getting to her feet. 'I'll go round tonight, Mam, and see how she's getting on.'

'Ask her to go to the pictures with yer one night, it'll do you good to get out with someone yer own age. Everybody needs a friend, sunshine.' Mary deliberated as she watched her daughter pick up her bag, then decided quickly. 'Laura was very late getting in last night and although me and yer dad both told her off, we want to sit her down and give her a real good talking to. So if you could go out for an hour after we've had our tea, it would give us the chance. She might pay more attention if you're not here. Yer know how quick she is to flare up and you listening wouldn't help.'

'Yeah, okay, Mam.' Jenny rested her handbag on the table. 'I heard her coming in. I stayed awake because if I'd gone to sleep she'd only have woke me up getting into bed. Where had she been until that time?'

'She went to yer grandad's.'

Jenny's eyebrows lifted in surprise. 'What made her go there? She's never done that before. I'm surprised Grandad didn't chase her home earlier.'

'Aye, well, we didn't go into it last night because it was so late. But we'll have a good talk to her tonight and get to the bottom of it.' Mary put her palms flat on the table and pushed herself up. 'You'd better go, sunshine, or yer'll have to run for it. I'll see yer out.'

Jenny never left the house without giving her mother a kiss and a hug. 'Don't forget the dress, will yer? And get a blue one, 'cos yer don't half look nice in blue.'

'I'll get one, even if it's only to keep you and yer dad happy.'

'Here's the tram, girl, you get on first so I can take me time.' Amy waited until Mary was on the platform, then, with a look of determination on her face, she wrapped her two hands around the steel post and pulled herself up. 'Why the hell they have to make the bleedin' steps so high, I'll never know.' She prodded the driver on his arm. 'Did yer hear that, Mr Tram Driver?'

'Did I hear what, missus?'

'Whoever made those bleedin' steps so high, they must have a wicked streak in them. How is someone with short legs supposed to manage?'

'How should I know? Have you got short legs, missus? If ye're not sure, I could measure them for yer and put in a complaint on your behalf.' The tram driver was delighted by the diversion. It got really boring standing there all day like a lemon, with yer eyes peeled for some stupid bugger who might walk out in front of you. 'I could say that your legs are too short for the tram steps or, if yer'd rather, I could say the tram steps are too high for your short legs. I can put a good letter together when I put me mind to it, even if I do say so meself.'

'Yer cheeky bugger! Did yer hear that, Mary?'

There came the clattering of feet as the conductor descended from the top deck. 'What's the hold-up, Jim? I've rung the ruddy bell six times.'

'Well, it's like this, Tom.' The driver was chuckling. 'This lady wants me to measure her legs for her, so she can put a complaint in. She reckons they're too short, yer see?' He rubbed his chin. 'Or did she say our steps are too high? I'm not sure now.'

The conductor looked at Amy and tutted, 'Oh, it's you, is it? I might have known. Whenever you get on me tram, I may as well throw the timetable away. We'll have people moaning at every flippin' stop now because we're late.'

'So, yer know the lady, do yer, Tom?'

'Know her! She's the bane of me life!' But Tom was smiling. 'If I'd have been downstairs I'd have made yer go past the stop and let the next tram pick her up. Let some other poor bugger put up with her shenanigans.' His grin turned into a full-blown laugh. 'D'yer know why she's got short legs? It's because her mother used to pat her on the head a lot when she was little, and it stunted her growth.'

'Huh! Ye're a fine one to talk, you are. Yer remind me of a flippin' bean stalk, ye're that tall and skinny. While my mother was patting me on the head, yours must have been putting yer through the mangle.'

With the chortling of the men ringing in her ears, Mary put her arm through Amy's and pulled with all her might until she had her in the aisle. Pointing to a seat, she said, 'Sit down, sunshine, for heaven's sake, and let the men get on with their work.'

Amy's friendly grin covered the passengers who were enjoying themselves so much they wouldn't have cared if the tram never took off. 'Do yerself a favour, girl, and you sit by the window. If I get in first there'll be no room on the seat for yer backside, even though the one yer've got is that small it's not worth writing home about.'

'I dunno,' Mary said as she slipped along the seat. 'Coming out with you is becoming a test of endurance. We've only been out of the house five minutes and me nerves are shattered. I hope ye're not going to carry on like that in TJs, I couldn't stand it.' She turned to see her friend gripping the bar that ran across the back of the seat in front with both hands to keep herself from falling off, while half of her backside was suspended in mid-air. And as she clung on like grim death, her face was set and her tongue was sticking out of the side of her mouth. Mary felt a rush of tenderness towards the woman who could bring smiles to a tramfull of people, all because she had short legs. 'Just look at the state of yer,' she said. 'Why don't yer go and sit over there and have a whole seat to yerself?'

'No, I'll stick with you, girl.' Amy just managed to throw herself sideways as the tram lurched around a corner and threatened to unseat her. 'That's the worst of having a backside the size of a rhinoceros – they don't make seats big enough to accommodate it. Mind you, it wouldn't be worth their while when yer come to think of it because they probably don't get many rhinoceroses round here.' The eyes she turned on Mary were full of laughter. 'Except for that Madge Phillips – have yer seen the backside on her? Blimey, she puts me in the meg specks.'

Tom and Jim were talking on the platform when the tram came to a halt in London Road, and they watched with amusement as Amy prepared herself for the step down. 'Close yer eyes, love, and jump for it,' Jim laughed. 'That's the best way.'

'Sod off, the pair of yer.' Amy reached down to where Mary was standing on the pavement with her hand extended ready to help. And when she was safely on the ground, she gave one of her cheeky grins. 'If me prayers are answered, some big bloke is going to give one of yer a black eye for not running on time and making him late for work. Yer'd be laughing the other side of yer faces, then.'

'Amy, will yer knock it off and let's get to the shops? And if yer start acting the goat in TJs I'll pretend ye're not with me.'

'I'll be as good as gold, girl, you wait and see. I'll be that quiet yer won't even know I'm beside yer.'

Jenny was the first home from work and the first to be greeted by her mother wearing her new dress. 'Oh, Mam! Yer look lovely!' Her eyes were bright with pleasure and her heart filled with pride. The pale blue cotton dress was set off by a deep frill around the neck and short sleeves, and it fitted to perfection. 'It really suits yer, and yer look young enough to be me sister. Ooh, wait till me dad sees it, he'll be made up.'

'Yeah, I'm pleased with it meself. It was a bargain, reduced in the sale from seven and eleven to five and eleven.' Holding the skirt out, Mary did a twirl. 'Not bad, eh?'

'It's beautiful. I wouldn't mind one meself. If I nip down on Saturday straight from work, d'yer think they'll have any left?'

'I couldn't tell yer, sunshine. I did think about yer, and if I'd had the money I'd have bought one for yer. But by the time I'd bought two pillowcases and this, I was skint.'

'I know what I can do! I can go in me dinner hour tomorrow! It's only ten minutes on the tram to London Road, and I can eat me sandwiches on the way.' Jenny clapped her hands. 'That's a good idea, isn't it? They won't be sold out by then, will they?'

'You can but try, sunshine, you can but try.'

Laura arrived home then and she eyed her mother up and down. 'Mmm! Not bad!'

Jenny put a hand on her hip and glared at her sister. 'Not bad! It's a beautiful dress and me mam looks lovely in it. I'm going to TJs tomorrow in me dinner hour, to get one for meself. And if I look as nice in mine, I'll be more than happy.'

'How much was it, Mam?' Laura asked.

'Reduced in the sale to five and eleven.'

'I wouldn't mind one meself, in a different style and colour.' Laura put her handbag on the sideboard and pulled out a chair. 'Yer can get me one when yer go down, our kid.'

Jenny glanced at her mother before holding her hand out. 'I'll take the money off yer now, if yer don't mind.'

'I haven't got it now, I'll pay yer on Saturday when I get me wages.'

Jenny saw her mother walk through to the kitchen and knew it was because she didn't want to get involved, didn't want to take sides. Anyway, this row was between her and her sister, and it had been brewing for a long time. 'Some hope you've got! Where d'yer think I'm getting the money from?'

'Yer never go anywhere to spend yer money, and yer said this morning that yer had some saved up. Don't be so flaming miserable, yer'll get it back on Saturday.'

Jenny narrowed her eyes, and although she knew what the answer would be, she asked, 'Give me half of it now, then, and I'll get yer one.'

'I can't give yer half, I haven't got it! I've told yer, I'll give it yer when I get me wages, so stop harping on it, for crying out loud.'

'I'd have to be pretty stupid if I couldn't work out that yer don't get enough pocket-money to pay me back. Don't take me for a sucker, Laura. I choose to save me money, that's my business, nothing to do with you. You choose to spend yours, that's your business and nothing to do with me. So let's leave it that way, eh?'

'You tight-fisted little cow!' Laura's eyes were blazing. She wasn't used to her kid sister refusing her, or answering her back. 'It's no wonder yer never go anywhere. No one would want a misery guts like you for a friend.'

Mary stood in the kitchen, her hands gripping the edge of the sink. She was vexed over Laura calling her sister a little cow, and was in two minds whether to interfere. But Jenny seemed to be holding her own, so perhaps it was better to keep out of it. So she listened, ready to move quickly if things got out of hand.

'I might be a tight-fisted little cow, but I'm the one with the money to buy meself a dress. You've spent all your money, now ye're scrounging off me because yer can't bear to see anyone having something that you can't have.' The main reason Jenny was standing up to Laura had nothing to do with money. She was angry at the thought that her mam very seldom bought anything new for herself, and now the pleasure was being taken out of it by her selfish sister. 'I don't like coming down to your level, Laura, it goes against the grain. But you have asked for it and it's the only language you understand. You are a greedy, selfish little cow who only thinks of herself.'

When Mary heard Laura's cry of anger, followed by the sound of her chair scraping back, she rushed into the room, at the same time as Stan came through from the hall. 'What on earth is all the shouting about?'

Jenny turned. 'It's nothing, Dad, just me and Laura acting soft.'

'No, it's not, yer little liar.' Laura was so angry she didn't realise she was being offered a truce. 'D'yer know what she called me, Dad? She said I was a greedy, selfish little cow.'

Stan looked taken aback. He couldn't imagine Jenny uttering such words. 'Yer didn't, did yer?'

Jenny's eyes never wavered. 'Yes, I did, Dad.'

'What for?'

'Ask Laura.'

'It was for nothing, Dad!' Laura saw her mother watching and listening. She must have heard every word so she couldn't lie herself out of it. 'All I asked was for her to lend me the money to buy a dress like me mam's, that's all. And she took off on me.'

Stan's expression softened when he looked at his wife. 'Yer look very pretty, love.'

'I'm sorry I bothered now, all the fuss it's caused.'

Stan looked from one daughter to the other. 'Yer mam only gets a new dress every blue moon, and you two have to start an argument over it! Jenny, I'm really disappointed in yer, I never thought I'd ever hear yer call anyone a cow, let alone yer own sister. What made yer say such a thing?'

'I'd rather Laura told her herself. Let's see if she can tell the truth.'

Mary banged her fist on the table. 'Enough is enough! While all this is going on, the dinner is in the oven getting ruined. To cut a long story short, the word "cow" came from Laura first, and Jenny retaliated. It's as simple as that. So can we have this table cleared, otherwise the dinner will only be fit for the back of the fire.'

'I'm going round to Janet's, Mam, but I won't be out late.' Jenny kissed her mother's cheek. 'Yer look lovely. I bet me dad will fall for yer all over again.'

There had been tension throughout the meal, but looking at Jenny's open face, Stan knew it had not been caused by his youngest daughter. 'Ye're right there, love, she looks good enough to eat.'

When she heard the front door bang behind her sister, Laura got to her feet, her pretty face marred by a sulky expression. 'I'm going to Cynthia's.'

'Stay where yer are, Laura. Me and yer mam want to talk to you.'

Laura remained standing. 'What about? Can't it wait until I come back?'

'No, it can't! Now sit down.'

Defiant to the last, Laura jerked her head in disgust as she pulled the chair out and sat down heavily. 'Blimey, it'll be time to come home before I get out.'

'Any lip out of you, Laura, and it's up the stairs yer'll be going, not out of the door.' Stan glanced at Mary. 'Do you want to start, love, or shall I?'

'You can do it, but first I'd like Laura to tell yer the truth about the row yer heard when yer came in. Ever since she was a baby Jenny has taken the blame for Laura's wrongdoing, and I think it's time to put the record straight.'

Laura, reluctantly and with a scowl, related what had happened. But because in her selfish mind she couldn't see why her sister wouldn't get the dress for her, her tone was full of self-pity. She ended by saying, 'There was no need for it, Dad. It wouldn't have hurt her to get me one while she's getting one for herself, and I'd have paid her back on Saturday.'

'Where would yer have got the money from?'

'Well,' Laura blustered, 'I could have given her half on Saturday and the rest next week.'

'You get an extra shilling a week pocket-money since yer got yer raise, so yer have more in yer pocket than Jenny does. Don't ever ask her again, d'yer hear? And while we're on the subject, yer whole attitude to her is just not on. God knows, she does her best to make friends with yer, but all she gets back is a load of abuse and sarcasm. Sisters are supposed to be close, and love each other. What's gone wrong in your case, I don't know. But from now on yer treat her with respect and civility, or yer'll have me to answer to.' Stan leaned his arms on the table and laced his fingers. 'Now to last night. Yer'll come in at the time ye're told to, not when it suits yer. I'm not telling you yer can't go to yer grandad's, but whether he goes to bed early or not, ye're to leave in time to get home for half ten. You are not to stay talking to Celia, she's too old for yer. Now, have yer got that straight?'

'I heard yer, Dad, I haven't got doll's ears.' Laura wasn't liking this one little bit. She was nearly sixteen, for heaven's sake, old enough to know what she was doing. 'I don't know what yer've got against Celia, she's nice. At least she doesn't treat me like a child.'

'I'm not going to argue the toss with yer, Laura, so just get it into that big head of yours that I mean every word I say. You'll be more pleasant in the house, nicer to yer sister, and yer'll be in by half-ten every night. It's not much to ask, and it would make life easier for everyone. But keep on as yer are, with an attitude that stinks, then I'll come down hard on yer and yer won't know what's hit yer.'

'Yeah, okay.' Laura would have agreed to anything to get out of the house. She and Cynthia were meeting two boys and she was ten minutes late. 'Is it all right if I go now?'

'Have you listened to a word I've said?'

'Of course I have, Dad.' Laura left her seat, picked up her handbag from the sideboard and made for the door. 'I'll be in by half ten, I promise.'

Stan and Mary watched her flying past the front window, her black hair bouncing on her shoulders. They looked at each other and sighed. 'I may as well have been talking to meself. I don't think it penetrated the first layer, did it, love?'

Mary shook her head. 'No, it didn't, sunshine, but at least yer've made a start. Yer'll have to keep it up, though, otherwise she'll go off the rails altogether. And I'll do my bit, too.'

Stan felt cheered when he saw a smile light up his wife's face. 'I don't know what's brought the smile on, but it suits yer, and it suits the dress.'

'I was thinking of our Jenny. Yer should have seen the way she stood up to Laura. She gave back word for word, and even though I was as mad as hell, I felt like clapping.' Mary cupped her husband's face. 'Yer know, love, it wouldn't surprise me if it's our Jenny who brings Laura to her senses. It may take a while, but I think she started tonight.'

Chapter Seven

'I've a good mind to go up and see that Celia meself.' Mary spoke to the empty room as she walked around the bed tucking the ends of the overhanging blanket under the mattress. 'She has no right to discuss what goes on between her and me dad with our Laura. Fancy talking to a fifteen-year-old like that, and our Laura feeling sorry for her, too! She's old enough in the head as it is, without the bold Celia telling her things that should be private between her and me dad.'

Mary gave the eiderdown a good shake before throwing it over the bed. 'I'd like to tell her to her face exactly what I think about her, the brazen hussy.' She rubbed her temples to ease the headache that had started during the night as she'd tossed and turned, unable to sleep with the worry on her mind. Any idea of friendship between her daughter and the older woman had to be nipped in the bud before it took hold. It was no good telling Laura because she wouldn't take any notice of them. Oh, she'd agree with them, promise them anything they wanted to hear, but she would do as she pleased on the sly. They had no idea where she got to every night because she didn't tell them. And Mary didn't want to involve her father, he must have enough problems with his wayward wife without her adding to them.

She gave a deep sigh. She'd never been back to her old home since her dad had married the girl younger than his own daughter, because she couldn't bear to see her taking the place of her beloved mother. But she would know no peace until she'd voiced her fears. And the only way to do that was to face the woman who was the cause of her headache and upset tummy.

Still talking aloud, Mary made her way downstairs. 'I'll go now and be back in time to go to the shops with Amy.'

Her neighbour's brows shot up when she opened the door. 'In the name of God, girl, has yer clock gone wonky or something? It's not ten o'clock yet.'

'I'm going on a message, but I'll be home to go to the shops with yer.'

A frown crossed Amy's chubby face. 'What d'yer mean, ye're going on a message? Yer never go on a message without me.'

'It's not that sort of message, sunshine, it's personal.' Mary tutted, wondering how she ever, for one moment, thought she'd get away without her mate worming the truth out of her. 'Oh, all right, I'll have to tell yer I suppose, or yer'll plague the flaming life out of me. I'm going to me dad's to have a word with Celia.' Briefly, she told of the reason for her going. 'But yer keep that to yerself, d'yer hear? I'll never speak to yer again if it gets out.'

Amy's answer was prompt. 'I'm coming with yer.'

'You are not! This is something I've got to do by meself.'

'I'm coming with yer in case she thumps yer one.' Amy nodded her head and her chins quivered in agreement. 'You won't be able to thump her back because yer'll be flat out on the floor, so I can do it for yer.'

'I'm quite capable of looking after meself, sunshine, and I'd rather go on me own. But I do appreciate the offer.'

'That's what mates are for, isn't it? To help each other out in times of trouble.'

'I don't know how long I'll be gone because I can't walk past me mam's old neighbour, Mrs Platt, without giving her a knock. So I might be a couple of hours. But don't worry – no matter how long I am, I won't be getting meself into trouble.' Mary turned to walk away. 'I'll try to get back before the shops close for dinner.'

'Don't worry, girl, I'll wait for yer.'

After turning to wave, Mary increased her pace. She wasn't looking forward to this one little bit, so the sooner it was over, the better.

Mary stood outside her childhood home and felt like crying. Her mam used to have the place looking like a little palace, with windows shining, lace curtains as white as snow, front doorstep scrubbed every morning and the red-raddled window sill polished until you could see your face in it. If it hadn't been for the number on the door, Mary would have thought she was at the wrong house. Behind the dirty net curtains the draw curtains were still closed. The windows were filthy, as was the step and window sill. It was as if nothing had been touched since her mam had died. The house was a disgrace, the scruffiest in the street. And as she knocked on the door, Mary thought how ashamed her dad must be, having to come home to this every day. He was a proud man and this must be so humiliating for him.

As she lifted the knocker for the third time, the next door opened and Monica Platt's head appeared. 'Yer'll not get an answer there before twelve.' Then when recognition dawned a wide smile lit up her face and she almost jumped from the top step to embrace the daughter of the woman who'd been her neighbour and best mate for years. 'Mary, sweetheart, it's good to see yer. Me and Phil often talk about yer, and wonder how you and Stan are, and the girls.'

'I came to have a word with Celia, but she must have gone out.'

Monica Platt's smile disappeared. 'Come inside, sweetheart, and I'll make us a cuppa.' With her arm across Mary's shoulders, she led her up the step and into the hall. 'I'm glad yer've come, there's things need saying.'

While Monica put the kettle on, Mary gazed around the room that had been like a second home to her when she was young. Nothing had changed, the same brown chenille cloth covered the table, the same clock ticked away on the mantelpiece, the aspidistra still stood on a small table under the window and the statue of the Whistling Boy had pride of place on the sideboard. The room was homely, comfortable and spotlessly clean. Like her mam had been, Monica Platt was very houseproud.

'There yer are, sweetheart, drink it while it's hot.' Monica set a dainty cup and saucer in front of Mary before sitting down on the opposite side of the table. 'It does me heart good to see yer, and that's the truth.'

Mary sipped on the hot tea, hoping it would chase away the hard lump that had formed in her throat and quell the tears that were threatening to spill. But she was so devastated by what she'd seen of her old home she had no control over her emotions. 'I'm sorry, Auntie Monica, but I'm going to cry.'

'You go ahead, sweetheart. I've cried buckets meself over the last year or so.'

Mary put the cup back on the saucer and the sobs came. 'Me mam must be looking down with sadness at the little house she was so proud of. And she must be disappointed in me for not doing something about it. But I was so hurt and angry when me dad married again so soon after her death, I fell out with him.' Mary sniffed up as she wiped the back of her hand across her eyes. 'I didn't see him for well over a year, but we've made it up now and he calls in every Saturday afternoon and sometimes a night through the week. But he comes alone because I won't have her in my house. I think she only married him so he could keep her and she wouldn't have to work. I can't stand the woman.'

'Did yer come with a message for her? I don't even pass her the time of day if I can help it, but I don't mind passing a message on if it'll save yer hanging around.'

Mary shook her head. 'Our Laura came to see her grandad a few nights ago, and apparently he went to bed early leaving Laura with Celia. Things were said about me dad that I didn't like, so I came to have it out with her. I came early, hoping to catch her before she went to the shops, but she must go to work, does she?'

'Work! Work, did yer say? She couldn't even spell it, never mind do it.' There was disgust on Monica's face. 'She's in bed, sweetheart. She'll have heard yer knocking, but she never surfaces until twelve o'clock. She's the laziest bitch I've ever known. Never does a hand's turn in the house, it's like a tip. If yer think the outside looks bad, yer should see inside, it's like a muck-midden.'

Mary narrowed her eyes. 'Yer mean she's in bed now?'

'Yes, sweetheart, she's in bed now. Twelve o'clock she gets up, not a minute before. And she seldom goes to the shops, except the one on the corner for her ciggies. Yer never see her in the butcher's buying meat, nor have I ever seen her carrying potatoes or veg.'

'Doesn't she ever have a dinner ready for me dad when he comes home from work?'

'I don't want yer to think I'm nosy, sweetheart, but I'd have to be blind, deaf and dumb not to know what's going on next door. There's never any smells coming from the kitchen, never any sign of activity, until your dad comes home. Any cooking done in there is done by him. All she's fit for is making her face up, painting her nails, reading magazines and flirting with every man in the street. Anything in trousers and she's fluttering her eyelashes. Any of the neighbours will tell yer that what I'm saying is true, there's not one has a good word for her.'

Monica leaned her elbows on the table and laced her fingers. 'I don't know whether I should be telling you all this, but me and Phil think a lot of Joe, and we worry about him. He never moans or criticises her, but I've watched him walking up the street on his way home from work, and he looks so unhappy and weary, my heart goes out to him.'

Mary's face was set, her anger boiling over. 'And yer say she's in bed now?'

'Yes, sweetheart, she's in bed now and hasn't got a care in the world.'

Mary pushed her chair back and stood up. 'Right, we'll soon put a stop to that. I'll give her something to care about.' She put her arms around the older woman and gave her a hug. 'Yer did right to tell me, Auntie Monica, so don't worry.'

'She probably won't open the door for yer, 'cos as I said, yer never see sight nor light of her until dinnertime. But if she does, watch out for her, sweetheart, she's got a vile temper. I don't know how Joe puts up with the way she shouts at him – my Phil wouldn't.'

'She'll open the door all right, otherwise I'll put a window in. I'm so angry now I would willingly strangle her with me bare hands. I'm not going to stand by and see a fly turn like her make a fool of my dad.'

'If yer get into trouble, sweetheart, just knock on the wall and I'll come running.'

'The way I feel now, Auntie Monica, if anyone does any running, it'll be the queer one who me dad was soft enough to marry.' Mary was shaking her head as she stepped into the street. 'And by God, he's paying dearly for it now.'

Monica stood on the pavement and watched as Mary banged on the knocker next door. The bangs became louder, but still there was no response from inside. The woman from next door but one came out to see what all the noise was about, but at a sign from Monica she held her tongue and just stood silently watching and wondering what Joe Steadman's daughter was up to. If her face was anything to go by, it boded ill for the lazy so-and-so inside. Perhaps she was going to get her comeuppance, and it wouldn't be before time.

Mary lifted the letter box and bent to put her mouth as near to the opening as she could get. Then, at the top of her voice, she yelled, 'Get out of that bed right now, and open this door! Did yer hear what I said, or shall I start breaking a few windows?' She stood back, looked up at the bedroom and saw the curtains twitch. 'I haven't got all day, so make it snappy.'

Three women from the houses opposite had come to their doors when they heard the shouting and were now standing in a small group with their arms folded. There was a look of pleasant expectancy on their faces that the chit of a girl who'd dragged Joe Steadman down to the gutter, was going to be confronted by his very angry-looking daughter. 'I hope she belts her one,' said Maggie Smith. 'She certainly deserves it.'

'Yer never spoke a truer word, Maggie,' Nellie Mitchell said, hitching up her ample bosom. 'Many's the time I've felt like clocking her one.'

'Aye, poor Ada, God rest her soul.' Lizzie Thompson made the sign of the cross. 'She must be turning in her grave at what's happened to her husband and her little house.'

The door to Joe's house opened slowly and Celia's head appeared. 'What the bleedin' hell are yer making all that racket for? What d'yer want?'

'I came to talk to you. I'm coming in.'

'Like hell yer are!' The door was opened wider and Celia stood on the step, a cigarette dangling from lips that bore traces of yesterday's lipstick. Her hair was tousled and the scrap of nightdress she was wearing looked as though it had never been washed. 'Yer don't live here, this is not your house, so get lost.'

'Just try and keep me out.' Mary acted so quickly the girl was unprepared for what happened. With one hand on the door, and the other on Celia's chest, Mary pushed with all her might. The door crashed back against the hall wall and Celia was sent reeling

89

backwards. 'This is my father's house and I'll enter it whenever I want to.'

To the dismay of the onlookers, who were in the mood for cheering, Mary stepped into the hall and closed the door behind her. Dusting her hands together as though they'd been in contact with something unpleasant, she walked into the living room to find Celia standing by the table, waiting for her, with eyes blazing.

'You can't come barging in here as though yer own the bleedin' place. Just wait until I tell Joe, he'll have plenty to say about it, don't you worry.' Celia took a long drag on the cigarette before throwing it in the direction of the fireplace. 'Now yer can just sod off, I don't want yer in here.'

Mary's eyes followed the flying cigarette and she gasped at what she saw. The grate still held the remains of last night's fire and the hearth was overflowing with ashes, cigarette stubs, sweet papers and an apple core. Then Mary took stock of the room. As Monica Platt had said, it was like a muck-midden. The furniture was thick with dust, curtains and cushion covers were filthy, there were clothes flung everywhere and the floor was strewn with shoes and papers. But it was the overpowering smell of dirt and neglect that had Mary clenching her fists. There was nothing here to remind her of her childhood and her mother. 'You dirty bitch! You dirty, lazy bitch! Lounging in bed all morning, too flaming idle to keep the place clean. Yer should be ashamed of yerself.'

'Don't you come here lecturing me, this is my house and I'll please meself what I do in it.' The brazen look was on Celia's face again as she reached for the cigarette packet on the table. She never took her eyes off Mary as she deliberately took her time selecting a cigarette and then lighting it. Just as deliberately, she drew deeply on it before blowing the smoke into Mary's face. 'Now, get yer skates on and vamoose, before I throw yer out on yer arse.'

'I'll go when I'm good and ready, and not before. And I wouldn't advise yer to lay one finger on me if yer know what's good for yer.' Mary resisted the temptation to take her by the shoulders and give her a good shake. 'Tell me, is this what my father comes home to every night? A lazy good-for-nothing wife and a filthy house?'

'So what if he does? I don't hear him complaining.'

'I'll complain for him then, shall I? And as yer don't seem to know what being a wife's all about, I'll explain that to yer. I'll do it slowly, so yer can't say yer don't understand. When a woman marries a man, she pledges her love and vows to care for him. That means giving him love, warmth and a clean comfortable home. And as you were so keen to marry me dad yer practically threw yerself at him, I believed yer did love him. So I'd like to know why the dirt is meeting him at the door when he comes home from work, why there's no dinner ready for him, and why his wife has turned into a lazy slut? Or would I be right in thinking yer never loved him, yer just wanted a meal ticket? And the real truth is, yer've always been a lazy slut?'

'I'll break yer bleedin' neck, talking to me like that. Who the hell d'yer think yer are?' Celia lunged forward to grab at Mary's hair, but the move was anticipated and Mary pushed her arm away.

'Don't try that again or I'll brain yer.' Mary sighed. She hadn't come with the intention of fighting with her father's wife, just to talk to her. But seeing the way her mam's home had been left to go to rack and ruin, she couldn't help herself. And now she'd probably made things worse for her father. 'I won't tell me dad I've been today because he'd be so ashamed that I'd seen the way he lives. If you want to tell him, that's your business.'

'Oh, I'll be telling him all right, everything yer said. And he'll be straight up to yours to tell yer what he thinks about yer.' There was spite in Celia's eyes. 'There'll be no more Saturday visits from him, that's a dead cert.'

'Please yerself, but when ye're crying down his ear, put a blindfold on him so he can't see that every word I've spoken is the truth. And don't forget about me calling yer a lazy slut, I wouldn't want yer to miss that out.' Mary hoped she was right in thinking Celia wouldn't dare even mention she'd been in case the whole thing backfired on her. 'Anyway, all this is not why I'm here. I came to tell yer not to talk to Laura about intimate details of your life. And yer must never run me dad down to her. The girl isn't sixteen yet, and I'll not have yer putting an old head on young shoulders.'

'I didn't tell her nothing but the truth. He's like an old man, going to bed every night about nine or ten and leaving me on me own. What sort of life is that for me?'

'Perhaps he goes to bed so he won't have to sit in this squalor. Try cleaning the place up and make it comfortable for him, then he won't be going to bed early.'

'Your dad is an old man. He goes to bed because he's tired. But what about me? I'm still young.' Celia's top lip curled. 'And there's no fun in me going to bed with him because all he does is sleep. He's not capable of doing anything else these days.'

As quick as a flash, Mary let swing with her arm, delivering a resounding smack across Celia's cheek. 'How dare you! How dare you talk about my father like that. Your mouth and your thoughts are dirtier than this room, and that's saying something. Cheap, nasty, and as common as muck, that's you. Ye're not fit to wipe my father's shoes. And I can promise you that if I ever hear yer've talked dirty to my daughter, I'll be down here to wash yer mouth out with carbolic soap. Then I'll drag yer out of this house and down the street by yer hair. And don't think I can't, or won't, because when anything

91

threatens my family I'll protect them with me life.'

Mary turned and was halfway down the hall when she felt a blow in the small of her back that knocked the wind out of her. She bent double, and was gasping for breath when she heard soft laughter behind her, and although the movement spread pain right through her body, she straightened up, determined not to give the other woman the satisfaction of seeing she'd been hurt.

Celia was leaning against the wall, an evil smile on her face as she rubbed her knuckles. 'Nobody hits me and gets away with it. And that's only a taste of what yer'll get if yer ever come to this bleedin' house again, with yer preaching and high-falutin', holier-than-thou attitude. To hear yer talk, anyone would think yer were a cut above the rest, but all yer are is a stuck-up bitch. Now get going, and I can say goodbye to bad rubbish.'

Mustering all her courage, Mary walked back and faced her. 'Ye're wrong there. When I go, I'll be leaving the rubbish behind.' She lowered her gaze to Celia's feet, then slowly let her eyes travel the length of the woman until she reached her face. 'You should feel quite at home here with all the muck and rubbish – it's where yer belong. The house could be made clean with the help of some elbow grease, but no one could change you; ye're wicked right through to the core of yer.'

There came a knocking at the door, then Monica's voice. 'Are yer coming, Mary, I've made a pot of tea.'

'Yeah, I'm coming now, I've finished me business in here.' Mary waited for a few seconds to see if Celia had anything more to say, but the woman remained silent, a sneer her only sign of retaliation. So Mary opened the front door and stepped into the street to face the concern in Monica's eyes.

'I've been worried to death about yer, sweetheart, yer've been that long.'

'I'm all right, honest. I said what I wanted to say and got it all off me chest. Actually, I said more than I intended because of the state of the house. She wasn't very happy about it and gave me a load of lip, but it's off me chest now and I feel better for it.'

'Are yer coming in for a cuppa?'

'No, I'll have to get home because me mate's waiting for me. But why don't you come up to ours one day? We could have a good natter and I'd enjoy that.'

'I'll do that, sweetheart. I've got yer address so I'll write and tell yer what day I'm coming. Give my love to Stan and the girls,' Monica hugged her tight, 'and I'll see yer soon.'

Celia stood with her ear pressed against the door and heard every word. And when the talking stopped, she made her way back to the living room, saying softly, 'So yer feel better now, do yer? Protect yer

92

family with yer life, will yer? Well, there's one member of yer family who doesn't think the sun shines out of yer backside. She's the weak link, is Laura, and it's through her I'll get me own back on yer, Mary Nightingale. Yer'll rue the bleedin' day yer ever came here throwing yer weight around because I'm going to make yer pay for it.'

Amy was standing on the doorstep when Mary came up the street. 'My God, girl, I was beginning to think she'd killed yer.'

'Not quite, sunshine, not quite.' Mary had only taken the tram for two stops because every time it swayed she felt like crying out with the pain. So thinking it best to keep her body in motion, she'd walked the rest of the way. She was glad she had now because the pain had eased off a lot. 'Get yer coat and I'll tell yer all about it on the way to the shops.'

'Okay, girl, just give me one minute.' Amy bustled down the hall and was back within seconds, struggling into the sleeves of her coat. 'Let me make sure I've got everything. Me keys, me purse and me basket, all present and accounted for.' She pulled the door behind her and linked her arm through Mary's. 'Right, I'm all ears now, girl. How did yer get on with yer stepmother?'

'Don't call her that, Amy, she's no relation of mine. If she's anyone's stepmother, it's the devil.' As they walked, Mary recounted everything that had happened. And they'd just reached the Maypole when she came to the part where she'd slapped Celia's face.

'Hang on a minute.' Amy pulled her to a halt. 'I can't take all this in so quickly. Yer mean yer really slapped her face?'

'I couldn't help meself, not the way she was talking about me dad. Anyway, she got her own back with a vengeance.' Mary continued her tale right up to where she parted from Monica Platt. 'So, there yer have it. The whole sorry story.'

For once Amy was at a loss for words. Mary was so good at describing things, Amy felt she'd actually been there. In her mind's eye she could see the dirty state of the house and the two women squaring up to each other. 'The hard-faced, brazen bitch! I asked yer to let me go with yer, but yer wouldn't have it. I'd have knocked bleedin' spots off her. In fact, I've a good mind to go up there now and give her a good hiding.' Amy was blazing. She knew what the girl was the first time she'd set eyes on her. She had brazen hussy written all over her. Joe Steadman must have been out of his mind to have got himself involved with the likes of her. 'And yer said some of the neighbours were out?'

'Yeah, me mam's old mates. Women I used to run messages for and played with their children. I didn't get a chance to talk to them, apart from Monica Platt, but I had a feeling they were cheering me on.'

'And to think I missed all this,' Amy said, shaking her head. 'Did yer really threaten to put a window in?'

'Yeah, sunshine, I did. But I can't say I'm pleased with meself, shouting in the street like a common fish-wife.'

'I wonder what yer dad will make of it?'

'I'm not going to say a dickie bird to anyone, Amy, and I'm relying on you to keep it to yerself. I'm not even going to tell Stan.'

'Yer can't keep it a secret, girl, 'cos the queer one is bound to tell yer dad.'

'I doubt it, Amy, I really doubt it. She's not that soft, she knows me dad wouldn't take her part, not now. Yer see, although he's never said anything, I think he wishes he could wake up one morning and find he's been having a nightmare, and there's no such person as Celia. There's no wedded bliss in that house, I can tell yer. There couldn't be, there's no room for it with all the dirt.'

Amy blew out a long, deep sigh. 'Come on, girl, let's get the shopping in. I'll mug us to two cream buns, to have with a cup of tea when we get home. And then yer can go all over it again in slow motion, so I haven't missed anything.'

Mary pushed open the door of the Maypole, but before stepping inside, she turned her head. 'What I've told yer was for your ears only, remember that. Not even a word in Ben's ear when ye're in bed.'

'Ay, girl, when I'm in bed I'm too busy being otherwise engaged to talk. That's for when yer've read all the *Echo* and there's nowt on the wireless worth listening to.'

When Amy saw a smile light up Mary's face, her heart lifted. After a cup of tea and a cream bun, her friend's worries would have all but disappeared. Please God.

Chapter Eight

Janet Porter's smile was wide when she opened the front door. 'Jenny! Oh, am I glad to see you! I've been going to come round to yours a few times, but I was worried that yer might have gone a bit stuck up, now ye're working in an office.'

'Don't be daft, it's just a job, same as any other.' Jenny was pleased with the smile of welcome from the girl who had been her friend all through school. 'D'yer feel like coming for a walk, so we can have a good gab and catch up with our news?'

Janet held the door wide. 'I'm helping me mam wash the dishes, so yer can come in and wait for us, I won't be long. She'll be glad to see yer, she's always asking about yer.'

Jenny followed her friend into the living room where her father and brother were seated at the table. 'Hello, Mr Porter. Hi-ya, Bill.'

'Hello, stranger, long time no see.' Vincent Porter flicked the butt of his cigarette into the fireplace and hooked his thumbs into his braces. 'How's the job going, lass?'

'It's fine, I love it.'

The sounds from the kitchen stopped and Janet's mother came through, drying her hands on her pinny. 'Well, well, a stranger in the camp. It's good to see yer, queen, I thought yer'd fallen out with us.'

Jenny smiled. 'Now as if I would. Me and Janet have never fallen out, have we, Jan?'

'No, not once.' Janet pointed to a chair. 'Sit down, Jenny, while I help me mam finish the dishes, then we can go out.'

Martha Porter shook her head. 'Yer don't have to help, queen, I've nearly finished. But don't be rushing off out, I want to hear about Jenny's job.'

Jenny sat down facing Janet's sixteen-year-old brother, Bill, who had so far not opened his mouth. He couldn't think of anything to say to the girl whose leg he used to pull something terrible. But she wasn't a schoolgirl any more, she was a young lady, and a very attractive one at that.

'I'm only a filing clerk, really,' Jenny told them, the grin never leaving her face and her eyes shining. 'But the manager is letting me practise on one of the typewriters and I'm hoping I make the grade as a typist.' Her familiar infectious giggle brought smiles to the other four faces. 'It'll be years before I get me speed up to match the other women, though. Their fingers just fly over the keys so fast they make yer dizzy. So far I'm only using the one finger on each hand, although I was daring this morning and tried with two.'

'Yer'll get there, queen, don't worry,' Martha said with conviction. 'Yer know what they say about Rome not being built in a day.'

'If they'd only been using two fingers, Mrs Porter, it would never have got built.' Jenny could feel Bill's eyes on her. 'What's the matter with you, Bill Porter? Ye're staring at me as though I've got horns sticking out of me head.'

'I'm trying to make out who yer are.' Like his parents and sister, Bill had rich chestnut-coloured hair, eyes that were constantly changing from brown to hazel, a square chin and a broad nose. 'They keep calling yer Jenny, but the only Jenny I know is one who cadged a bull's-eye off me last time I saw her, and she was wearing a gymslip.'

Her eyes dancing, Jenny leaned closer. 'What's the matter, Bill, d'yer want yer bull's-eye back?'

Janet was getting impatient. 'Ay, come on, Jenny, let's go for a walk.'

'I'll come with yer,' Bill said, bringing a smile to his mother's face. 'A bit of fresh air will do me good.'

'Yer will not!' Janet was indignant. 'Me and Jenny want to talk, and it wouldn't interest you 'cos it's girls' talk.'

'Oh, let him go with yer,' Martha said, thinking to do her son a favour. 'Get him out of our way for an hour.'

'Ah, ay, Mam! I'm not having me brother traipsing around with us! Me and Jenny want to catch up on our news and we won't be able to talk with him there.'

'Just hang on a minute.' Bill sat upright in his chair. 'What about when I used to have to traipse around with *you*? I couldn't go to the Saturday matinée without yer crying to come with me. I couldn't even have a game of footie with me mates without dragging you along. I used to get me leg pulled soft over you. And yer were a proper little pest, always whinging.'

Janet was having a quick change of heart. If he mentioned that she used to wet her knickers she'd die of humiliation. 'What d'yer think, Jenny?'

'I don't mind, honestly. Although I think he'd be bored stiff.'

'No chance of that.' Bill was looking decidedly pleased with himself. 'I've always wondered what girls find to talk about. And yer should be pleased to have a handsome escort, who can see yer both safely home.'

Martha and Vincent exchanged knowing looks. Their son must have taken a shine to young Jenny, that was the only reason they could think of. Wild horses wouldn't have dragged him out of the

96

door to go for a walk with his sister. 'Make sure Jenny's home by ten,' Martha said, 'in case her mother worries where she is.'

When Bill got to his feet, Jenny gaped. 'Good grief, you haven't half got big since the last time I saw yer.'

While Bill grew two inches in stature, his mother did the bragging. 'Five feet ten inches, he is, and still growing. And he takes a size ten shoe.'

'If he keeps on at that rate, Mrs Porter,' Jenny said as she slipped her handbag over her arm, 'yer'll have to be looking for another house.'

After seeing the youngsters out, Martha came back chuckling. 'D'yer know what, love? I think the penny's just dropped with our Bill. He's finally noticed the difference between boys and girls.'

Much to Bill's dismay, the two girls linked arms with Jenny walking on the inside. Wanting to make a good impression, the boy had no option but to act the gentleman and walk on the outside, putting him next to his sister.

Jenny was in a very happy frame of mind. It was lovely to be with her old schoolfriend again. 'How's your job, Janet, d'yer like it?'

'Very hot and very tiring.' Janet was working in the pressing room of a laundry. 'The women are nice, and we have a good laugh, but in the hot weather it's killing. What with the heat from the pressers and the steam, the sweat just pours off yer. I never thought I'd hear meself say this, but I'll be glad when the winter comes.'

'It's a job, our kid, that's the main thing,' Bill said. 'If yer think it's hot in your place, yer should try working with me, in the tannery. But when I get me wage-packet on a Saturday I forget how I've had to sweat to earn it.'

'Ye're sixteen now, aren't yer, Bill?' Jenny leaned forward so she could see him. 'Yer'll be earning more than me, I only get seven and six a week.'

'I started on that, but I've had two rises since. It was me birthday a few weeks ago, and me pay went up to nine and six a week. Not bad, eh?'

'Not bad!' His sister's voice rose. 'It's blooming marvellous! Especially when me mam only takes five bob off yer, the same as she does me.' She squeezed Jenny's arm. 'He's a real mammy's boy, this one. She gives him all his own way, spoils him soft.'

'I pay me own fares out of it, and buy me own shoes.' Bill glared at his sister. Mammy's boy indeed. 'You'll get the same when ye're earning it.'

'I hope you two don't come to blows.' Jenny laughed. 'Yer've both got hot jobs and hot tempers to go with them.'

'It's his fault,' Janet said, as they turned into County Road. 'We should have left him at home.'

It wasn't long before Bill was himself wishing they'd left him at home. Why did they have to look in every shop window? Shoe shops, dress shops, jewellers, even blinking hat shops! And they didn't just glance in the windows, they spent ages pointing out a dress that they'd buy if they had the money. And those high-heeled shoes, well, they'd definitely be getting a pair like that, they were the last word in fashion. Blimey, he thought, it doesn't take much to make girls happy. Men now, they only ventured near shops when something wore out.

'I hate to break it up, girls, but it's starting to get dark and I think we should be making our way back. I don't want Jenny's mam telling me off for keeping her out late.'

There was a wicked glint in Janet's eyes when she turned to him. 'I bet yer've really enjoyed yerself, haven't yer? Think what yer'd have missed if yer'd stayed home.' She was turning her head when she spotted a familiar figure on the opposite side of the road. Giving Jenny a nudge, she pointed. 'Ay, am I seeing things, or is that your Laura over there? Yeah, it is, because she's got that horrible Cynthia with her.'

Jenny clamped her lips together when she saw her sister hanging on to a boy's arm and laughing up into his face. And behind them walked Cynthia, also engrossed in the boy she was linking. They looked like courting couples, but Jenny had never set eyes on the boys before. Her mam would go mad if she knew. She was always telling Laura that if she ever had a date the boy must call for her, so they could see him. And these weren't boys, either, they were men, much older than her sixteen-year-old sister. 'Don't let them see us. Yer know what our Laura's like for showing off.'

'Is she courting?' Janet asked. 'Is that her boyfriend?'

'I couldn't tell yer, she's never mentioned having a boyfriend.'

'If she has, she's two-timing him something rotten,' Bill said. 'I've seen her with loads of fellers, but I've never seen those two blokes before.'

Jenny peeped over her shoulder. 'They won't see us now, so let's go. Wherever our Laura's off to, I hope she keeps her eye on the time because she's got to be in by half ten.'

Bill decided to be daring. 'Let me walk between yer, then yer've got to let me join in the conversation. As long as it's not about dresses, shoes or flaming hats!'

This had the girls laughing and they kept it up all the way home. Funny incidents at work were remembered and exaggerated for maximum effect. And it was a happy trio who stood outside Jenny's front door. 'I've really enjoyed meself, it's been lovely seeing yer again, Jan. And you, Bill, of course.'

'I'll come round here tomorrow night, shall I?' Janet jerked her head at her brother. 'We can talk better without the queer feller with us.'

Jenny cocked an ear when she heard the lock turning. She just had time to whisper, 'Don't mention our Laura, please,' when the door opened.

Mary's face showed her pleasure. 'Janet, it's lovely to see yer again, I've missed that cheeky smile of yours.' Her gaze went to the boy with them. 'My God, Bill Porter, I didn't recognise yer! Ye gods, yer haven't half shot up.'

'It's me mam's dumplings and pies, Mrs Nightingale. I keep telling her I don't want two helpings, but she just keeps piling me plate high. She always makes too much, yer see, and to save her walking down the yard to the midden, she makes me eat it.'

'Well, whatever it is, son, ye're looking well on it. And you, Janet, yer look a treat, a sight for sore eyes.' Mary was happy to see her daughter's smiling face, and in the company of youngsters her own age. 'Has Jenny asked yer if yer'll go to the pictures with her one night?'

'She hasn't asked me yet, Mrs Nightingale, but yer see, we haven't said half what we want to because of big brother here. He's cramped our style something awful.'

'I'll take yer to the pictures, Jenny,' Bill said. 'If yer'll do me the honour.'

Jenny's clear laugh filled the night air. She was used to Bill pulling her leg, he'd done it for as long as she could remember. Many's the time she'd fallen for one of his jokes, but not now, she was wise to him. 'I'm too big for yer to pull me leg now, Billy, and I'm not daft enough to fall for that.'

Where he got the nerve from, Billy would never know, but out came the words he was thinking. 'It's because ye're big I'm asking yer, Jenny. I wouldn't want to take no girl in a gymslip to the pictures.'

'Ooh, er!' Janet started to giggle. 'The state of him and the price of fish! Take no notice of him, Jenny, he's acting the goat. He's always saying he can't stand girls. Oh, what he said was, God slipped up when He gave them mouths. They wouldn't be half bad if they didn't have that hole in their faces.'

Mary looked on with amusement. She wasn't so sure the boy was joking. It was dusk now, too dark to see her daughter's face clearly, but she'd bet any money that Jenny was blushing to the roots of her hair. She was soon to find out how wrong she was.

Far from blushing, Jenny found it so hilarious she couldn't stop giggling. Bill had always made her laugh, the things he came out with. It never entered her head he could be serious. 'If you didn't have that hole in yer face, Bill Porter, yer mam wouldn't have to

99

slave over a hot stove all day. Just think of the money she'd save. And, you wouldn't be able to take the mickey out of people, as yer are now.'

Bill told himself it was best to quit while he was still ahead. After all, he hadn't thought of Jenny Nightingale for ages, until she walked into their house a couple of hours ago. And he'd be seeing a lot of her in future through his sister. 'I keep asking me mam to give me the money instead of the food, but she won't hear of it. I've reached the conclusion she's a sucker for punishment and likes slaving over a hot stove all day.'

'If you weren't so big, I'd hit yer!' Janet shook a fist in his face. 'Will yer keep yer mouth closed long enough for me and me mate to make arrangements to go to the pictures?' She watched as he stood to attention and saluted. She felt more like kissing him than hitting him. He was a good brother, always looking after her when she was little, protecting her when someone older than her picked a fight with her. He made sure she never came to any harm. Even now when she went out, he always asked where she was going and who with. You didn't get many like him in a pound. 'What night were yer thinking of, Jenny?'

'How about Saturday?' Jenny had her hands clasped under her chin. 'We could go to the first house, then yer could come back here and have a game of cards. That's if yer mam will have no objections.'

'She won't mind, the only thing is, she likes me to be in by ten o'clock. She doesn't like me being out in the dark on me own, either.'

Bill saw his opening. 'That's all right. I'll pick yer up at ten and walk yer home.'

Janet voiced her surprise. 'What! You go out every Saturday night! The highlight of yer week, that is. It takes yer ten minutes to flatten yer hair with Brylcreem and another ten minutes to polish yer shoes until yer can see yer face in them.'

Bill roared with laughter. 'A bit of an exaggeration, Jan, but I do have a lot of hair to flatten, and I do have big shoes to shine. Anyway, for your information, me and Johnny had decided not to go anywhere this Saturday because we're saving up to have a day in Blackpool. So as we'll be at a loose end, yer'll have two escorts home.'

'Yer can't ask fairer than that, sunshine,' Mary said. 'Grab the offer while yer can.'

'I'll come tomorrow night and we can see what's on that takes our fancy.' Janet didn't want to arrange things now because she had a feeling her brother was up to something. 'I don't want to go to the Atlas, though, 'cos Herbert Marshall's on and I think he's too old to be a heart-throb.' She linked her brother's arm. 'Come on, Bill, let's get going before yer open yer mouth again and we're here all night.'

Jenny stood on the step with her arm across her mother's

shoulders and waved them off. 'I'm glad I went round, Mam, it was lovely being with Janet again.'

'Bill's grown into a fine-looking boy,' Mary said, closing the door. 'Nice with it, too.'

'Yeah, he's a scream the things he gets up to.' Jenny smiled at her father who was hammering studs into the worn-down heel of one of his shoes. 'Still at it, eh, Dad?'

'Cheaper than taking them to the cobbler's, love. These will keep me going for a few months.' He brought the hammer down one more time before laying it on the floor. 'I bet Janet was glad to see yer.'

'Not half as glad as I was to see her. We're going to the pictures on Saturday night, I'm looking forward to that.' Jenny glanced at the clock. She didn't want to be here when Laura came in, didn't want to listen to her telling lies about where she'd been. 'I think I'll hit the hay, the long walk has tired me out.'

'Yer can sit down for five minutes, sunshine, and tell us about Janet's job and what she's been up to. It's only ten past ten.'

With her eyes keeping watch on the hands of the clock, Jenny gave them a much shortened version of the night's events. She ended with a giggle. 'I think Bill was sorry he signed 'cos he was bored rigid. He couldn't understand how me and Jan got a kick out of window shopping. I bet he never asks to come with us again.'

'He's no different to any other man, sunshine, they all hate shopping.'

'Too true!' Stan laughed. 'I tried it once, but never again. Yer wouldn't get me going to the shops with yer mam for a big clock.'

'I love it. I know I'll never be able to buy half the things, but I still like looking.' Jenny got to her feet. 'Anyway, I'm off to bed, I really am tired.' It was half past ten when she kissed her parents and she was praying her sister wouldn't come in before she got up the stairs. 'I'll see yer in the morning, Mam and Dad. Good night and God bless.'

'What time is it?' Laura had her back to the entry wall and she wasn't very happy with the way Jeff was mauling her. She wished she'd insisted on staying with Cynthia now, but the two lads had worked it so they were split up before the girls realised what was happening.

'Don't be worrying about the time, it's only early.' Jeff pressed his body closer and ran his hand down her back and over her buttocks. 'The night is young, yet.'

'It's not for me,' Laura said, trying to push him away. 'I told me mam I'd be in by half past ten. Yer've got a watch on, tell me what the time is.'

'It's too dark to see.' He had made sure they were at the very bottom of the entry, away from the gas-lamp and prying eyes. 'Anyway, why does a girl of eighteen have to be in at that ungodly hour?'

'Because I told me mam I was only going for a walk with me mate and I'd be in by then. She doesn't mind what time I come in as long as she knows not to wait up for me, but I didn't know I was going to meet you, did I?' Laura's worries were increasing by this time. This bloke was a lot older than her and far more worldly. She could handle young lads, they never wanted anything more than a kiss and a cuddle. And she was always in total control. She had the power to manipulate them, and this pleased and excited her. But Jeff, if that was his real name, was a different kettle of fish. He'd been around and wasn't going to settle for a kiss and a cuddle. 'Come on, Jeff, let go of me. Me mam will be worried stiff, not knowing where I am.'

'Yer weren't worrying about her when we picked yer up, were yer? Or when we took yer to the pub for a drink.' Jeff's mood was turning ugly. 'Me and Larry picked you and yer mate up because yer looked like good-time girls. And good-time girls don't have to go running to mammy at half past ten. Don't take me for a sucker, or I'll get angry, and I'm not nice when I'm angry. I didn't spend money on yer just to hold yer hand . . . understand?'

Laura had never been so frightened in her life. Her heart was thumping like mad, and a voice in her head was screaming that he could beat her up and no one would know. She could shout for help, but what if someone called a policeman? they'd ask questions and her mam and dad would find out. She could only try and talk her way out of it. 'Jeff, I know yer spent yer money on me, and I've really enjoyed meself. I do like yer, Jeff, honest. I could meet yer tomorrow night and make up for it. It wouldn't matter what time I got in, 'cos I can tell me parents I'm going to a dance. I could stay out until midnight, then. But if I'm late home tonight me dad will have the police out looking for me.'

It was the final sentence that had Jeff moving back. The last thing he wanted was to have the police after him. His wife wouldn't take kindly to that, and she was tough enough to beat the living daylights out of him. But if there was a chance of getting something back for his money, he was going to take it. 'Yer'll meet me tomorrow night? Is that a promise, or an excuse to get away?'

'No, I want to meet yer! How does eight o'clock outside the Rotunda suit yer?'

'Make it nine, it's nearly dark then. I've no money to be sitting in a pub for an hour.'

'Nine o'clock it is.' It was the last thing she wanted to do, but Laura kissed his cheek. 'I'll have to fly now.'

And fly she did. She couldn't even feel her feet touching the ground. She wondered briefly where Cynthia was, and if she was suffering the same fate, but her own troubles pushed all thoughts of her friend from her mind. Her chest was paining and she was gasping for breath as she neared her street. She paused by the chip-shop window to look at the time on the large round clock on the wall, and sighed with relief. Thank God, she was only going to be ten minutes late.

Before knocking on the front door, Laura ran her fingers through her untidy hair and straightened her rumpled clothing. She'd get upstairs as quickly as she could, her mother had very sharp eyes. And she'd have to watch her parents didn't get near enough to smell her breath.

'Buy yerself a watch, Laura,' Stan said when he opened the door. 'Then yer'll have no excuse for being late.'

Laura passed him with her lips clamped tight. She didn't speak until she was putting her handbag on the sideboard. 'I've been standing outside Cynthia's, nattering. I'm not that late, anyway.'

The red face and the smudged lipstick didn't go unnoticed by Mary. But she didn't want to upset Stan, so she kept her thoughts to herself. She'd have words with Laura tomorrow, and they'd be harsh words. And she'd keep on having harsh words with her until she got it through her daughter's head that her behaviour wasn't acceptable. 'Jenny's not long gone to bed, so if yer go up now it'll save yer disturbing her later.'

'Yeah, okay.' Laura turned her back on them and pretended to be searching in her handbag until the smile of relief left her face. It had been a close one, but she'd got away with it. And next time Cynthia gave the glad-eye to two passing men, she'd make sure they were young enough to be manipulated. 'I'll see yer in the morning. Good night.'

Stan waited until he heard her footsteps on the stairs, then asked, 'Can we believe a word she says? Or am I being bad-minded?'

'I don't know, love, I really don't. All we can do, as we've said before, is to hope she meets a nice boy and settles down. When she does that, you and I can settle down and enjoy a happy old age.'

Stan grinned. 'Blimey, love, I'm only thirty-nine – not ready for the scrap-heap yet. I've still got a lot of life left in me, and if yer want me to, I'll prove it to yer.'

'Yer'll prove it to me! How soft you are! If you want to make love to me, Stan Nightingale, yer'll do it because yer want to, not to prove ye're capable of it.'

'Playing hard to get, eh?' Stan patted his knee and opened his arms wide. 'Come here and I'll show yer how much I want to.'

* * *

Upstairs, Jenny turned her head on the pillow and sniffed up. 'You've been drinking!'

'Go to sleep like the good little girl yer are, and mind yer own business.'

Jenny turned her body over, dug her fists into the mattress and pushed herself up. She couldn't see her sister, but she could smell her. 'Anything that upsets me mam and dad *is* my business. How did yer get in a pub at your age?'

'Don't be stupid, I haven't been in a pub. I don't know why I'm bothering telling yer, 'cos ye're just a snotty-nosed kid, but I had a glass of sherry at Cynthia's. Now, if yer satisfied, can I go to sleep?'

'Have yer been in Cynthia's all night?'

'Why ye're so interested in what I do, is beyond me. But if it'll shut yer up, yes, I've been in Cynthia's all night. We had a game of cards.'

'Ye're a liar, our Laura, a bare-faced liar. And if I didn't know how much it would upset me mam and dad, I'd go right down and tell them.'

'Don't yer dare call me a liar, or I'll belt yer one. When I say I've been in Cynthia's all night, then that's where I've been. Now shut yer face and let's get some sleep.'

'I saw yer down County Road, Laura, so don't come that with me. You and yer dear friend Cynthia, linking arms with two men who looked old enough to be yer fathers. And I wasn't the only one who saw yer, either.'

There was silence for a while, then Laura said in a low voice, 'I suppose ye're going to snitch on me, are yer? Ye're a miserable little squirt, d'yer know that? Yer think because yer work in an office ye're better than anyone else.'

'I don't care what yer think or say about me, Laura. Yer can call me all the names under the sun if yer like, it won't bother me; it never has done.' Jenny wrapped her arms around her legs. 'I used to feel ashamed to say yer were me sister when yer were telling lies in school, or bullying the younger children into giving yer their sweets or pennies. But then I told meself it wasn't my fault if you were a bad 'un, and I kept away from yer. I don't care what yer do, yer can get yerself a bad name if that's what yer want. Why should I worry, yer've never been a proper sister to me. The only person yer think about is yerself. Yer don't even care about our mam and dad, and they're the best mam and dad in the whole world. But I care about them, and I'll do everything I can to stop yer from hurting them. I won't snitch on yer this time, but if I smell drink on yer again, or see yer picking up strange men, then I will tell them. Because they have every right to know what their daughter is up to.'

Jenny slid down under the clothes, turned on her side, and moved as far away from her sister as the bed would allow. But sleep was a long time in coming. Her mam and dad should know what Laura got up to, but she didn't want to be the one to tell them because she knew how hurt they'd be. What should she do for the best? If only she had someone she could confide in, someone who could advise her on what to do.

She heard Laura's gentle breathing and sighed. Here she was, too troubled to sleep, and the cause of the trouble didn't give a damn.

After seeing Stan out, Mary hovered near the kitchen door waiting for Laura to make a move. She was sitting at the table next to Jenny, and the silence between the sisters hung heavy. Breakfast was never the happiest of meals, but today there seemed more tension than usual. The two girls were acting as though they'd had a row and fallen out, but it couldn't be that because Jenny never rowed with anyone. But where was her smile this morning? What had happened to take it away?

Laura pushed back her chair and stood up. Without a word, she picked up her bag and made for the door. But Mary was quick and caught her as she was stepping into the street. 'Just hang on a minute, I want a word with yer.'

Laura's eyes rolled and she pulled a face. 'Not again! Won't it keep until tonight? I've got a job to go to, or had yer forgot?'

'The job will still be there in five minutes' time.' Mary couldn't believe she'd reared a child who would answer her back with such a brazen look on her face. And it was no use boxing her ears, she was too old for that and it would only make her harder. 'Where were you last night?'

'I told yer, I was at Cynthia's! If yer don't believe me, ask her.'

'Oh, and you and yer friend kiss each other, do yer?'

Laura looked at her mother as though she'd gone mad. 'Of course not! What d'yer think we are!'

'Then how did yer face come to be covered in lipstick?'

Laura was startled, caught offguard. But she quickly regained her composure. 'Oh, that! Well, Cynthia had bought three new lipsticks in different colours, and we were trying them out. We wiped our lips with a piece of rag and it must have gone all over the place. Cynthia didn't mention it, and she would have if she'd seen it. But then she wasn't looking for something to pick on me for, was she?'

'The one thing ye're good at Laura, is telling lies. If yer expect me to believe that load of garbage, yer must be crazy. But yer'll come a cropper one of these days, because liars always trip themselves up.'

Jenny came out and stood next to her mother. 'I poured yer a cup of tea out, Mam, and it'll be stiff if yer leave it much longer. Come in and sit down for five minutes, rest yer legs.'

'Yeah, that's right,' Laura sneered. 'Go and sit down and pull me to pieces.'

Jenny gently turned her mother around and pushed her into the living room. Then she looked down on her sister. 'I've got more to do with me time than pull you to pieces. Besides, I wouldn't waste me breath, ye're not worth it.' With her brows raised, she closed the door.

'How did yer get on last night?' Laura asked, when Cynthia opened the door. 'I had one hell of a time.'

Cynthia put a finger to her lips. 'Not a word,' she whispered, her eyes sending warning signals. 'I'll get me coat and we'll go for a walk.'

Arms linked, they walked down the street. When they reached the corner, Cynthia turned to the right, but Laura pulled her back. 'Let's go this way. I'm keeping clear of County Road, and Scotland Road. I promised to meet that bloke tonight by the Rotunda, but there's no fear of that, not after last night.'

Cynthia laughed. 'Got fresh with yer, did he?'

'He was all over me! I've never been so frightened in me life! I honestly thought he'd kill me if I didn't let him do what he wanted. How I talked me way out of it I'll never know.'

'Oh, I quite liked my feller. His hands were all over me, like yer said, but I don't mind that. I get a kick out of seeing them getting themselves all worked up, and their moaning and groaning excites me.' Cynthia's eyes swivelled sideways. 'I'd rather have an older man than the kids we've been going with, they're more experienced.'

'That's the trouble, they're too experienced. They want more off yer, and yer could end up in trouble.'

'No, Larry said there's no chance of that. He's been around, knows all the tricks.'

Laura gasped. 'Yer didn't let him go all the way, did yer?'

Cynthia laughed. 'I might have done, but some drunken man came down the entry and put Larry off his stroke. But I've promised to meet him tomorrow night.'

'Oh Cyn, he's too old for yer! Yer don't know him from Adam, he could be married with a gang of kids for all you know. Once he got what he wanted off yer, yer'd never see him again, and you could end up in the family way.'

'He said I won't come to no harm, he knows what he's doing.'

'Of course he knows what he's doing, every man knows what to do! He's having yer on, playing yer for a fool. I'm surprised at yer, Cyn, I thought yer had more sense.'

'Ooh, ay, listen who's talking! You've been down every entry in the neighbourhood with every boy in the neighbourhood! Now yer've suddenly gone all straitlaced because I've got meself a man.'

'I won't get meself into trouble with the boys I go with. A kiss, a cuddle, and a bit of groping, that's all. And yer can't get a baby doing that.'

'And yer think those boys are going to be satisfied with that? D'yer think they're not going to want more as they grow older?' Cynthia gave a snort of derision. 'One of these days someone will tire of yer leading them on, getting them all worked up and then leaving them swinging. They'll have yer knickers down before yer know what's happening.'

Laura shrugged her shoulders. 'I can look after meself with the lads we know. But I couldn't have looked after meself with that bloke last night. He made no bones about what he wanted and said he'd get angry if he didn't get it. That's why I had to promise to meet him tonight, but he can go and whistle. I wouldn't go through that again for a big clock.'

'Suit yerself, but I'm seeing Larry tomorrow night. So ye're on yer own, kid.'

'I won't be on me own long, don't worry. I can get plenty of fellers.'

'It's only for tomorrow night, I'll see yer on Thursday. I can't see Larry wanting to take me out every night, he won't have the money.' Cynthia sounded cocky. 'And if he doesn't take me for a few drinks first, there's no way he's getting me down a dark entry. What he wants he'll pay for in advance.'

Laura felt a flicker of envy for her friend's bravado. Cynthia was tough, she was afraid of no one. But with the memory of last night still fresh in her mind, Laura wasn't inclined to put herself in that position again. 'I just hope yer know what ye're doing, that's all. If he's anything like his mate, watch out.'

Chapter Nine

'Me mam said I can come here after the pictures on Saturday.' Janet was seated at the table and as she leaned forward the rich auburn shades in her hair were highlighted in the glow from the overhanging gas-light. 'Our Bill's going to pick me up at ten o'clock.'

'That's nice, sunshine, I'll look forward to it.' Mary smiled, remembering the days when this girl used to hold Jenny's hand as they walked to school. She was glad she was back in her daughter's life, she was a good friend to have. 'We're not playing cards for money, though, we're not gambling. So bring some matchsticks with yer.'

'I'll pinch some off me mam.' Janet's cute, pixie-like face was eager. 'She asked why don't yer come round to ours tonight, Jenny? Her and me dad like a game of cards, although I don't know why me dad does 'cos he never wins.' With her eyes twinkling, she rested her chin on her curled fist. 'I think he cheats, so me mam wins. He'll do anything for a quiet life, will my dad. It must be that, nobody could be as unlucky as he makes out.'

'Oh, yes they can, love.' Stan grinned. 'I don't very often have a flutter on the gee-gees, but yer can bet yer sweet life that when I do, my horse will come in last. In fact, me mate at work says he feels sorry for the horses I bet on, they don't stand a chance. He said I'm a jinx and the bookie's runner must rub his hands in glee when he sees me coming.'

'Yer not unlucky in everything, Dad,' Jenny said. 'Yer were lucky in love.'

Stan looked at Mary and grinned. 'Yeah, the luckiest man alive.'

'Is it all right if I go to Janet's for a game of cards, Mam? I'll be back for ten.'

'Of course it is, sunshine. But don't forget to take some matchsticks with yer.'

Laura, who'd been slouched in a chair filing her nails while wondering how Cynthia was getting on, now looked up with interest. 'I'll come with yer. I wouldn't mind a game of cards and it would get me out of the house.'

There was a stunned silence for a few seconds as glances were exchanged. Then Jenny spoke. 'You will not! You've got yer own friend, go down to hers if yer want to go out. Ye're not coming with us and that's all there is to it.' She stood up and jerked her head towards the door. 'Come on, Jan, let's go.'

Janet was off the chair like a shot. She'd been worried there for a minute because she didn't like Jenny's sister. Her mother didn't either, and she'd have laid a duck egg if Laura had walked in with them. And her mother wasn't one for mincing her words. If she thought it, she said it, and didn't care whether you liked it or not.

'Blimey!' Laura said, with a not very pleasant expression on her face. 'Anyone would think I had the flippin' chickenpox, listening to her.'

Jenny was pushing her friend towards the door. 'Yer can have the chickenpox, Laura, and I wish yer well with it. But yer can't have me friend.'

When they got outside, Janet puckered her lips and whistled. 'Me mam often says that some things improve with age, but your sister's not one of them, is she?'

'She's just a show-off, that's all.' Although Jenny agreed, she didn't want to start running her sister down. She linked her friend's arm. 'Ay, me mam got a lovely dress in the sales, and I was going to go into town in me dinner hour and get one. But I got talking to the women in the office and left it too late. I'm going tomorrow though, definitely.'

'I wouldn't mind one meself, but I spend me money as fast as I get it and I'm stony broke. I could try cadging a shilling off me mam, dad and our Bill, though. They're pretty good at slipping me money now and again.' Janet pressed her friend's arm. 'Ay, if they do, will yer come to town with us on Saturday afternoon?'

'Ooh, yeah! That would be great!' The excitement of going into town, shopping for the first time as grown-ups, thrilled them to the core. And they were so engrossed they failed to notice the two boys walking towards them.

'Good evening, Miss Nightingale.' Mick Moynihan's smile was wide, his dimples deep. 'Enjoying the night air, are yer?'

'Yer gave me the fright of me life, Mick, yer daft beggar. And you, John Hanley, why didn't yer whistle or something?'

'Shall we start all over again, then?' John asked, his face straight. 'Like we used to do in school when we were unlucky enough to be picked to play one of the wise men? Me and Mick will walk back six houses, then come towards yer. And if yer keep yer eyes where they should be, yer'll see us coming.'

'It's too late now, yer daft nit, we've already had the fright.' Jenny shook her head, sending her blonde hair swinging across her face. 'Anyway, yer know me friend, don't yer?'

'If me eyes are not deceiving me,' Mick grinned, 'it's little Janet Porter.'

'Ay, less of the little, if yer don't mind!' Janet managed to give a good impression of being indignant. 'I'm as tall as Jenny, and I'm a working girl, now.'

'Ye're both right, Mick,' John said, nodding as though he'd given the subject some thought. 'It is little Janet Porter, only she's got big, now.'

'And where are you two pretty maidens off to?' Mick asked.

'We're off to London to see the Queen, kind sir.' Jenny tried to keep the smile back, but out it came to light up her face. 'No, we're going to Jan's to have a game of cards with her mam and dad.'

'We'll walk that far with yer,' Mick said, 'and see yer come to no harm.'

'It's only two streets away, silly,' Jenny tutted. 'We're quite capable of walking that far on our own, yer've no need to bother.'

'Oh, it's no bother,' John was quick to say. 'We've got nothing else to do.'

The two girls began to walk, nudging each other and giggling. They didn't see the scuffle behind them as Mick and John fought to be the one to walk next to Jenny. 'I'm the one who said we'd walk them,' Mick said quietly but firmly, 'so it's only fair that I win. You can try yer luck next time, but yer'll have to be quick.'

So it came about that the two girls were being escorted for the first time in their young lives by two strapping young men. They thought it was a huge joke until John's nosy neighbour, Annie Baxter, came walking towards them. Blushing to the roots of their hair, they lowered their eyes, hoping she didn't stop them. But this little scene was just up Annie's street, too good to miss. She stepped in front of John, barring his path and bringing the line to a halt.

'Going out, are yer, John?'

'Oh, I'm not falling for that one, Mrs Baxter, I'm too old to have me leg pulled.'

Annie's beady little eyes almost disappeared. 'What d'yer mean? I only asked if yer were going out.'

'That's it! There's got to be a catch in it, because anyone can see I can't get any more out than I am now.' He looked along the line. 'All take two steps to the right and we're off.'

Annie Baxter scratched her head as she watched their retreating backs. There was something wrong with that lad, there had to be. Mind you, what could you expect? He was a Hanley and they were all tuppence short of a shilling. Especially the mother. Now if ever there was a headcase, it was Amy Hanley. There were people in the loony bin with a damn sight more sense than she had.

By the time they reached Janet's street, Jenny was feeling embarrassed that neither she nor her friend had opened their mouths. The boys must think they were stupid. So she said the first thing that came into her head – and could have bitten her tongue off afterwards. 'Me and Jan are going to the pictures on Saturday. First house, of course, 'cos me mam wouldn't like me to stay out late.' She groaned inwardly. Now they would think her and Jan were a couple of kids.

'Me and John are going dancing,' Mick said, then chortled loudly. 'I should say we're going to a dance, not that we're going dancing. Neither of us can put one foot in front of the other, so we'll be watching rather than taking part.'

'Ay, you speak for yerself.' John began to roll his shoulders. 'I'm pretty nifty on me feet, if I do say so meself. Yer should see me waltzing down our yard with me mam's brush as a partner. Me mam said I look like a crackpot, but she got her words mixed up. She really meant I looked a treat.'

'Don't yer dare bring that brush to the dance with yer on Saturday,' Mick said, 'even if it can do a nifty waltz.'

'Funny yer should say that.' John stuck his hands in his pockets and looked down at his shoes. ' 'Cos I did think about it. I even put a mobcap of me mam's on its head, and tried to tie a cardigan around it. But it was no good, the cardi kept slipping off. Anyway, me mam said I couldn't borrow it. She said it was a sad state of affairs when the only partner a son of hers could get was a yard brush.'

Jenny giggled. 'I always said yer were as daft as a brush, John Hanley.' Then a dreamy look came over her face. 'I'd love to be able to dance. I'm definitely going to learn when me mam says I'm old enough to be out late.'

'Me too!' Janet sighed blissfully at the thought. 'I'll come with yer.'

The boys exchanged glances. John got in first. 'Ask yer mam if yer can come with us one night. We go to Star of the Sea in Seaforth. It's only a church hall, but they get a good crowd there.'

'Yeah,' Mick wasn't going to be left out, 'they've got a feller on the piano and he can fairly make it talk. It's worth going just to hear him.'

Jenny shook her head. 'Me mam wouldn't let me. Don't forget, I'm only fourteen.'

'We're fourteen and five months, Jenny,' Janet reminded her.

Mick grinned. 'I used to count the months when I was your age. Me mam said I was wishing me life away. Now I'm seventeen, I don't even think about it.' His eyes slid sideways to look at Jenny. 'I'll give yer seven of my months, if yer like. That would make yer fifteen, and yer mam might think that's grown-up enough to come to the dance with us.'

They were standing outside Janet's house talking, when the door opened and Martha Porter appeared on the top step. 'Oh, aye!' she said, her hands on her ample hips. 'You two are starting young, aren't yer?'

John gave her a cheeky wink. 'Can yer think of a better time to start, Mrs Porter?'

'No, I can't, lad, but there's young and young. And these two have just come out from under their mother's wing. They're all right with you, I know that, but I didn't recognise yer voices and yer can't be too careful these days.'

'Yer never spoke a truer word, Mrs Porter.' Mick gave her a wide smile. 'We've just been telling the girls the same thing. We said that, if for instance they want to go to the dance at Star of the Sea in Seaforth, then they should go with someone they know, like me and John.'

'You fibber!' Janet said. 'Yer never said any such thing.'

'Well, if he did, he was right.' Martha was quivering with laughter. 'Don't ever go out with strange boys, always get them to call at the house for yer, so the family can give them the once-over.' She looked down as she smoothed the front of her dress so they wouldn't see the smile. 'Mind you, that won't be for a few years yet.'

'Ah, ay, Mam!' Janet was mortified. If her mother had her way, she'd wrap her in cotton wool until she was twenty-one. 'There's girls in work my age, and they go to local hops.'

'Yer live in Kirkdale, queen, and Seaforth's miles away. Yer can't call that a local hop, not by any stretch of the imagination.'

'There's not many places around here, Mrs Porter,' John said. 'Not nice ones, anyway. Unless yer go near town, to the Grafton or the Rialto. And they're more for grown-up experienced dancers. The small hops are better for learners.'

'We'll see when the time comes. Anyway, say good night, girls, or my feller will think I've run off and left him.' Martha Porter gave the boys one of her brightest smiles. 'Thank you for being concerned about the girls' welfare, it's much appreciated. But yer don't have to worry, 'cos the first few dates our Janet goes on, I'll be tagging along to make sure everything is above board.' The wink she gave was so exaggerated it contorted her face and her false teeth became separated from her gums. But Martha didn't mind, she wasn't a vain woman. 'Ta-ra lads, I'll be seeing yer.'

There wasn't a word spoken until she'd passed down the hall and into the living room. Then Mick said, 'I think things look hopeful for yer, Janet. Yer mam wasn't exactly enthusiastic, but she didn't sound dead against the idea.'

'Nah, you don't know me mam. She's frightened of the wind blowing on me. If I sneeze I've got a cold, if I cough I've got pleurisy, and if I say I'm feeling hot then I've definitely got pneumonia and should go to see the doctor.'

'Me mam's the same with our Edna, she doesn't half mollycoddle her. Me and our Eddy don't get a look-in.' John chuckled. 'If I

113

sneezed me mam would tell me to blow me nose. If I coughed she'd tell me to take me germs elsewhere. And the only time I told her I felt hot she poured a cup of cold water all over me.'

Jenny hunched her shoulders as she giggled. 'I can just see your mam doing that. I'll have to remember never to tell her I'm hot.'

Janet pulled on her arm. 'Come on, Jenny, before me mam comes out again.' She smiled at the two boys. 'Ta-ra, we'll see yer.'

'Ta-ra.' Jenny was being tugged up the step. 'See yer soon.'

'Yeah, definitely see yer soon.' The boys waited until the door closed in their faces before walking away. They were quiet for a few minutes, then John said, 'Remember that conversation we had at the party, the Christmas before last?'

'Yer must be a mind-reader,' Mick said. 'I was just thinking about that.'

'Still feel the same about Jenny, do yer?'

'I hate to disappoint yer, John, but my feelings will never change. Jenny's the girl for me, if she'll have me.'

'Well, like I said at the time, all's fair in love and war. So it's a fight to the finish, mate.'

There was a smile on Mick's face when he turned to him. 'Pistols in the park at dawn, is that it? Or would yer prefer swords?'

John returned the smile. 'Words are my choice of weapon, mate. As long as we know where we stand, it's every man for himself.'

'It's not going to stop us being mates, is it?'

'No, of course not. But I've got to tell yer, Mick, I'm a very bad loser.' John punched his friend on the arm and laughed. 'Mind you, I'm not expecting to lose.'

'My God, ye're early this morning, Amy, I'm nowhere near finished me work.' Mary stood aside to let her neighbour in. 'I won't be ready to go to the shops for another hour.'

'I was up before the larks, girl, couldn't sleep. I had me living room done before Ben and the lads got up.' Amy pulled out a chair from the table and sat down heavily. 'I couldn't sit doing nowt until it was time for the shops. Not in that living room of mine – the bleedin' wallpaper gives me the willies. So I thought I'd come and give you the pleasure of me company, and I could sit looking at your wallpaper.'

'Yer'd want something to do to sit and look at that.' Mary waved her arm around the room. 'I can't even remember what the paper was like new, it's been up that long. All I do know is that the background used to be white, not the dirty beige it is now. And the brown flowers used to be a pretty pink.'

'Shall we nag our fellers into decorating, then? They can't moan 'cos it's flaming years since they were done.'

'I don't need to ask Stan, I can decorate meself. I've been using the extra money I get off Jenny to renew me crockery and bedding. And I was going to save up to buy a new fireside chair, that one's on its last legs. But now yer've made me take a good look at the wallpaper, I might do this room first.'

'I'm not as handy as you, I wouldn't know where to start. Anyway, Ben says he wouldn't trust me to put paper up 'cos I'd make a mess of it. He's right, too! Can yer imagine me on the top of a ladder? I'd have more wallpaper stuck to me than was on the wall.'

Mary grinned as she pinched her friend's cheek. 'Let Ben do it, sunshine, I wouldn't rest if I thought yer were perched on top of a ladder without a safety net. Anyway, seeing as yer've made yerself comfortable, I suppose I'd better put the kettle on.'

'I wondered when yer'd get round to it.' Amy followed her friend into the kitchen and leaned against the wall. 'I was just coming out of the door when misery guts came out of hers. I pretended I hadn't seen her, but the nosy cow called me. And yer'll never guess what she was so excited about.' Amy's tummy started to shake, and with it her whole body. 'Hang on till I get meself organised and I'll do the job proper.' She coughed, hunched her shoulders and folded her arms across her chest. Then narrowing her eyes and pressing her lips into a thin line, she put her face close to Mary's. ' "I didn't know your John was courting. He's a bit young for that, isn't he? And the girl only fourteen, that'll lead to trouble, mark my words".'

Mary was chuckling as she poured the boiling water into the teapot. 'That'll be our Jenny she's talking about.'

'Yeah, I saw her passing our window with her mate. And when our John came in he told me him and Mick had met the girls.'

'What did yer say to nosy Annie?'

'Well, I was ready for her, wasn't I, girl? I mean, I'd been pre-warned. So I said I was all in favour of child brides. I said I was hoping our John made me a grandmother by the time he was eighteen.'

Mary's mouth gaped. 'Yer didn't!'

'I bleedin' well did, girl! The nosy cow was asking for it. She wanted some gossip so I gave her some. Made her day, I did – she was over the moon.'

'It'll be all over the neighbourhood by tomorrow.'

'Nah, it won't take her that long. If everyone doesn't know by dinnertime I'll eat me flippin' hat. She couldn't get away from me quick enough. I bet she'd be at Lily Farmer's by the time yer opened the door to me.'

'Which hat will yer eat, sunshine? The one with the big green ostrich feather on, that curls right round under yer chin?'

'No, not that one, girl, I'm hanging on to that.' Amy's face was creased with deep laughter lines. Jokes about this imaginary hat had been going on for years. 'When I'm all on me lonesome, feeling sad and miserable 'cos nobody loves me and I've run out of people to pull to pieces, I put that creation on me head. The ostrich feather tickles me under the chin and in no time at all I'm laughing me bleedin' head off.'

Mary lifted the two cups of tea and nodded towards the door. 'Go on, and I'll bring these through. And I think I've just got two custard creams left.'

'Ay, this is the life, isn't it, girl? Ladies of leisure.' Amy picked up her cup by the handle as though it was delicate porcelain, and stuck her little finger out. 'This is how the posh people hold their cups, girl, did yer know?'

'I'll have to take your word for it, sunshine, 'cos I haven't got any posh friends.'

'Neither have I, girl, but yer know, it's funny how I seem to know how they behave. I think hundreds of years ago my ancestors must have been very rich because I've always felt I was destined for a better life than this.' Amy's chubby fingers were having difficulty holding the handle of the cup so she reverted to curling her hands around it. 'I wouldn't be surprised if they'd been of the nobility.'

'Somebody must have squandered all the money, sunshine, for you to end up in a two-up two-down terrace house in a cobbled street in Kirkdale.'

'I know, girl. Someone's got a lot to answer for, dragging me down from riches to rags. One of me great-great uncles must have been a bugger for wine, women and song, and spent me bleedin' inheritance enjoying himself.'

The two women looked at each other across the table and burst out laughing. 'Ye're two sheets to the wind, Amy Hanley, but if thinking these things keeps yer happy, then you just carry on,' Mary said. 'But can we forget yer fancies for now, and see what we can do to repair the damage yer've caused?'

'What damage, girl? I haven't done no damage.'

'I'm talking about Annie Baxter.'

'Annie Baxter! I didn't do her no damage, I didn't lay a finger on her.'

'Amy, will yer be serious for once? I know most people will take what she says with a pinch of salt, but there's some bad-minded folk around here who'd believe her because they want to.'

'Believe what, girl?'

Mary blew out her breath in frustration. 'What yer told her about yer wanting your John to make yer a grandmother by the time he's eighteen.'

'Is that what the cow is saying? Well, she's a bleedin' liar, and if I get me hands on her I'll break her scrawny neck.'

'But yer told me yer did say it.'

'Yeah, well, I told you 'cos ye're me mate. But I haven't told no one else. And if anyone mentions it, I'll say she's a bleedin' liar and I'll have her up for slander.'

'I give up on yer, I really do. Just don't get me involved, that's all. And don't yer dare mention it to your John, either. You might think it's funny but I don't think he'd appreciate being the butt of one of yer jokes. He's a nice lad and I wouldn't want to see him embarrassed or upset. He'd be frightened of showing his face in the street.'

Amy's face was dead serious. 'Yeah, well, it stands to sense he would be, if it was true.'

Mary stared, unblinking, for several seconds. Then she said, 'It's like leading a lamb to the slaughter, isn't it? Proper muggins, I am. But how was I to know that even you, with all the tricks yer get up to, would make up such a tale?'

'I didn't make it all up, girl.' Amy looked really put out. 'Annie Baxter did stop me, and she did say what I told yer. I only made up the bit about what I said to her to give yer a laugh. But ye're not laughing, are yer, girl?'

'I'll make up me mind when yer tell me what yer really did say to her. And can we have the truth, this time, please?'

'Oh, yeah!'

'Go on, then.'

'Go on what, girl?'

'So help me, Amy, I'll flatten yer in a minute. What did yer say to Annie Baxter?'

'I've just told yer!' Amy was red in the face. ' "Oh, yeah," that's what I said to the nosy bleedin' cow. Yer didn't think I was going to be all matey and hold a conversation with the woman, did yer? I can't stand the sight of her, she gets on me wick.'

'Well, before I split me sides laughing, can I just ask yer never to say anything like that in front of my girls? Or your kids for that matter.'

Amy's cheeks moved upwards and there was a glint of devilment in her eyes. 'Now, as if I would do that, girl.'

Jenny was bursting with excitement as she ran into the kitchen waving a paper bag. 'Mam, wait until yer see me dress, it's out of this world.'

Mary turned the gas low under the frying pan. 'Keep away from here, sunshine, the fat's spurting out all over the place. Let's go in the living room, otherwise yer dress will be ruined before yer've even had it on.'

'I knew as soon as I set eyes on it that it was the one I wanted.'

The words poured out as Jenny took the dress from the bag. 'I didn't look at any other, I really fell for this one.'

'Oh, sweetheart, what a beautiful colour.' Mary's heart filled with love and pride as her daughter held the dress in front of her, her eyes bright with happiness. In a shade of mauve, the dress had three-quarter sleeves, a plain round neck, was shaped to the hips then fell in soft folds. 'It'll go lovely with yer blonde hair.'

'I'm dead chuffed with meself, Mam, honest. The women in work were pulling me leg because I've had a smile on me face all afternoon.'

'That beats having a face on yer like a wet week, sunshine.' Mary smiled, delighted to see her daughter so happy. 'Yer did well, it's a lovely dress.'

'I can't wait to show it to Janet.' Jenny folded the dress carefully and put it back in the bag. 'I asked the woman who served me if they'd still have some on Saturday when we go into town, and she said it was more than likely.'

Laura stood in the hall listening. She'd come through the door Jenny had left open in her haste to show off her dress, and heard every word. Her top lip curled as, under her breath, she mimicked her mother's voice. 'Oh, sweetheart, what a beautiful colour. It'll go lovely with yer blonde hair.' They'd make you sick, fussing over a five and eleven dress. To listen to them talk, anyone would think she'd gone to Lewis's and paid a fortune for it.

Afraid that her father might come in and catch her, Laura pushed the living-room door open and walked through as though she'd just come in. 'Yer want to be careful in future, leaving that front door wide open. Anyone could walk in.'

'I must have forgot, I was in such a hurry.' Jenny smiled at her sister. 'D'yer want to see me new dress, Laura?'

As Jenny bent her head to open the bag, Mary caught the expression on Laura's face and felt a cold hand cup her heart. She'd always known her eldest daughter held no affection for her sister, but what she saw in the brown eyes that were staring at Jenny's bent head frightened her. She doesn't like her, Mary thought. Her own sister and she doesn't even like her.

'Don't bother getting it out,' Laura said, 'I'll see it when yer've got it on.' She ignored the hurt in Jenny's eyes and turned to her mother. 'Will the dinner be long, Mam? I promised to go down to Cynthia's early.'

'I'll put it out when yer dad gets in, and not before.' Mary felt like taking her by the shoulders and giving her a good shake. Why did she always put a damper on things when someone was happy? 'We eat together, not in dribs and drabs.'

Laura tossed her head. 'Well, I hope he puts a move on.'

'Whether he puts a move on or not, we wait for him.' Mary went into the kitchen and vented her sadness, anger and frustration on the pan lid. She'd bent over backwards with Laura to form the same loving bond there was between her and Jenny. Her youngest daughter always showed her love with spontaneous hugs and kisses, both to her and Stan. But Laura didn't welcome, or give, hugs and kisses. She didn't join in the light-hearted conversations that went on around the table when they were having their meals, and when she did smile there was no warmth in it.

Mary heard Stan's voice and reached up to take four plates from the shelf. And as she spooned mashed potato on to the plates, her mind went back to when Laura was a child. She'd been less than eighteen months old when Jenny was born, and although Mary had her hands full she'd always tried to share her time between the two children so Laura wouldn't think her nose was being pushed out. Stan made a great fuss of her for the same reason, but his over-indulgence was a source of worry and caused arguments between man and wife. Still, lots of children were spoilt by doting parents, but they didn't grow up to be surly, impudent and lacking in humour.

Stan came up behind her and put his arms around her waist. 'All right, love?'

She took a deep breath. There was no point in passing her anxiety on to Stan; it wouldn't solve anything and would only worry him needlessly. So when she twisted her head, there was a smile on her face. 'Everything's under control, sunshine.'

He tightened his hold, pulling her closer. Kissing her neck, he murmured, 'When I hold yer like this, I'm not in control.'

Mary slapped his hands which were laced together across her waist. 'Give over, soft lad.' Her eyes darted to the living-room door, afraid the girls might have heard. 'There's a time and place for everything, and this is neither.' She relaxed a little, her body enjoying the nearness of him. She loved him as much now as she had the day she'd walked down the aisle on her father's arm and Stan, standing in the front pew with his best man, had turned his head. His eyes had been full of admiration and love, and she recalled now how that look had chased away the butterflies in her tummy. So when she looked up at him, her eyes were bright and teasing as he nuzzled her neck. 'But if you've got the time, big boy, I know the place.'

He nipped her ear gently before releasing her. 'The girls have said they're going out at half seven. After that I'm all yours.'

Cynthia put a finger to her lips before closing the door behind her. 'Not a word until we're out of earshot.'

Laura linked her arm and contained her curiosity until they turned the corner of the street. 'Well, how did yer get on?'

'What d'yer mean, how did I get on?' Cynthia stared straight ahead. 'I met Larry and we went for a drink.'

'And after that, what did yer do?'

Cynthia shrugged her shoulders. 'Went somewhere dark for a kiss and a cuddle.'

'Oh, come off it, Cyn, yer got more than a kiss and a cuddle. He's not going to spend money on yer just for that. Yer did promise to tell me all.'

'Larry gave me a message for yer, from Jeff. He wants to see yer again. I'm meeting Larry on Friday night, and he's asked me to bring yer along one night to make a foursome.'

Laura pulled her to a halt. 'Not bloomin' likely! I'm not seeing him again, he frightened the life out of me. If I ever set eyes on him I'll run a mile.'

When Cynthia turned to her friend, there was a look of scorn on her face. 'Ye're not half childish, Laura. Yer let young lads kiss yer, but when it comes to a grown man, yer run scared, like a little rabbit.'

'That Jeff was after more than a kiss, and you know it. And that goes for his mate, Larry. Yer can't tell me he didn't try anything.'

'He didn't do anything I didn't want him to do, and that's all I'm telling yer. I'm still here, aren't I, and still in one piece. And if I didn't like it, well, I wouldn't be seeing him again. He's a real man, not like the kids we've been knocking around with.'

'Ay, yer didn't tell him where we lived, did yer?'

Cynthia shook her head. 'No, me dad would have a fit if he turned up on the doorstep. But I'm not stopping seeing him, I don't care what anyone says. And if you had any sense, yer'd come with us and make up a foursome, with Jeff. Start living, kid, instead of messing around with kids. Honest, yer don't know what ye're missing.'

Laura was torn. If she didn't go, she risked losing the only friend she had. But she didn't like the idea of being down a dark entry with Jeff. 'I'm not saying I'll come, like, but if I did, would we stay together? Not split up like we did last time?'

Cynthia turned her head so Laura didn't see the gloating in her eyes. She knew she'd be able to talk her friend round. Like she'd told Larry, Laura wouldn't want to miss out on anything. 'No, we won't split up.'

Still Laura wasn't convinced. 'I will come, but not for a week or two. I'll see how you get on first, and if ye're still seeing Larry in two weeks I'll come with yer. But I'll bet yer any money he's married with a few kids. He's too old to be single.'

'So what? I don't care if he's got dozens of kids, as long as I'm enjoying meself. From now on that's going to be my motto in life. Get as much out of it as I can and to hell with everyone.'

120

'Yeah, I agree with yer,' Laura said. 'That'll be my motto, too. So yer can tell Larry to pass the message on to his friend. I'll come with yer one night the week after next, as long as we all stick together.'

Chapter Ten

'Sixteen tomorrow, eh, Laura?' Stan smiled across the breakfast table. 'Ye're a young lady now.'

'Does that mean I can stay out later?' Laura spread the jam liberally on her toast. 'I'd like to go to second-house pictures, or go dancing, and yer can't do either when yer eyes are on the clock all the time.'

Mary came through from the kitchen with a fresh pot of tea. 'Me and yer dad have talked about this, and yer can stay out until eleven as long as yer tell us where ye're going.'

'Yeah, I'll do that.' Laura wagged her shoulders from side to side, looking very pleased with herself. 'That's the gear, that is.'

'Would yer rather we bought yer a present, or gave yer the money?' Mary sat down next to Stan, facing her daughters. 'It's up to you.'

'Ooh, I'll have the money, please.' Laura's green eyes were shining. 'How much?'

'Half-a-crown off me, half-a-crown off yer dad, and a shilling off Jenny. That's six bob, so yer should be able to buy yerself something nice.'

'Yer could try T.J. Hughes, Laura,' Jenny said, 'they might have some of those dresses left from the sale.'

Laura didn't bother turning her head to look at her sister. 'I'm going to save up for a winter coat. The one I've got is all right to go to work in, but I'd be ashamed to go anywhere nice in it. Cynthia's got a new one, and I look like a tramp next to her.'

Mary had seen Cynthia's mother at the shops yesterday, and if anyone looked like a tramp it was that poor woman. The coat she had on looked as though it had been a dark green at one time, but it was faded with age and frayed at the cuffs and pockets. While Cynthia was forever getting new clothes, her mother always looked shabby and down-at-heel. And she never spoke to a soul, not even to pass the time of day. Most of the neighbours had given up on her and never bothered to let on, but Mary felt sorry for her and never passed her without a nod or a smile of acknowledgement. However now wasn't the time to voice her thoughts on Cynthia's hard-done-by mother. She'd gone out of her way to be nice to Laura over the last week or so, and she didn't want to spoil things by criticising her friend and chance a row developing. 'That's a very sensible idea, sunshine, because the winter is setting in now.'

'And I'm putting all me pocket-money away every week until I've got enough saved up.' Laura piled it on, thinking how easy it was to fool her parents. It would be no hardship to her to save her money, she never went anywhere without a boy paying for her. All she ever bought for herself was make-up, and she wouldn't be doing that for long. Staying out late meant she could go to dances and meet someone with enough money to buy her presents. 'Me and Cynthia are going to stay in every night, playing cards, or perhaps going for walks, so it'll only be a couple of weeks before I have enough saved for a coat.'

Stan raised his brows at Mary as he pushed his chair back, and she knew he was asking if this was the turning point, that their daughter was at last growing up. She answered with a smile, and a shrug which said not to bank on it, because only time would tell.

'I'm on me way, love.' Stan bent to kiss her cheek. 'Don't bother coming to the door with me, finish yer tea. I'll see yer tonight.'

'Don't forget, all three of yer, I want the dinner over as soon as possible tonight. I'm starting to scrape the wallpaper off, and Amy and Mrs Moynihan are coming to give me a hand. All the furniture has to be pulled away from the walls before they come.'

'Me and Janet will give yer a hand, Mam,' Jenny said. 'We're not going anywhere.'

'I'd offer to help,' Laura was thinking of her birthday money, 'but I've promised to see Cynthia and she'll expect me. If yer want me to, though, I could slip down and tell her I can't make it.'

'No, I want yer both out of the way. The place will be crowded as it is.' Habits died hard with Mary, and she couldn't let her husband go without seeing him to the door and waving him off. And as she followed him into the hall, she added, 'I'll have yer dad here, he'll be getting stuck in, same as the rest of us.'

Stan laughed as he stepped into the street. 'Yer don't really want me here, not with three jabbering women, do yer? Why don't I go for a pint with Seamus and I'll be out from under yer feet?'

'How soft you are, Stan Nightingale! Me and me mates slaving away, while you and Seamus Moynihan prop the bar up!'

'Okay, love, but it was worth a try.'

'I was only pulling yer leg, sunshine. Of course yer can go for a pint, as long as yer don't come staggering home, singing at the top of yer voice.'

Stan was chuckling as he walked away. 'That'll be the day.'

'Sure, I'll come and give yer a hand, so I will.' Seamus pushed his plate away and rubbed his tummy. 'That was altogether a fine meal, me darlin', fit for a king and no mistake. Not another bite could I eat, I'm full to the brim.'

'I'll bet if anyone offered yer a pint, yer'd not be too full for that.' Molly gazed with satisfaction at her husband's empty plate. Clean as a whistle, it was. Sure, wasn't he a great man to feed, eating everything you put down before him? 'I'd like to see the day when Seamus Moynihan refused a pint.'

'I'd have to be offered one to refuse it, me darlin', and I don't hear yerself offering.'

'I'm not, no, 'cos I've got better things to do with me money. But Stan Nightingale has offered. According to Mary, he's terrified of being alone with a gang of women.'

'I'll not be blaming the man, for it's a frightening prospect, so it is. And I'll not be letting a mate down in his hour of need.'

Mick, who had been listening with interest, wiped the back of his hand across his mouth. 'That was really tasty, Mam, I didn't half enjoy it.'

'It does me heart good to know that, son.' Molly stood up and began to gather in the plates. 'I'll get these washed and then take meself over the road.'

'I'm not doing anything tonight, Mam, I could give a hand stripping the walls.'

'What! A young lad with a gang of old women? Yer'd be bored stiff in ten minutes, me darlin', so yer would.'

'Jenny's not an old woman, Mam.'

'Jenny! What's Jenny got to do with it?'

When Mick smiled, his eyes twinkled, his teeth shone and his dimples deepened. 'Well, it's like this, Mam. I'm waiting for her to grow up so I can ask her to be me girlfriend. And I just thought that rather than waste me time while I'm waiting, I could put it to good use by getting to know her better.'

Seamus let his head drop back and roared with laughter. 'It's good taste yer have, son, and it's right that yer don't let the grass grow under yer feet.'

Molly plonked herself down again. 'If Mary Nightingale could hear you two, she'd box yer ears for yer. The girl's only fourteen, for heaven's sake!'

'Fourteen and seven months, to be exact, Mam.' Mick's grin didn't falter. Nothing was going to put him off. 'I'm waiting until she's fifteen, then I'll ask her mam and dad if I can take her to the pictures.'

'D'yer not think it would be better to ask the girl herself, first?' Seamus asked, highly amused. 'Unless it's her mother yer want to take to the pictures.'

'Seamus Moynihan, don't yer be putting ideas into the boy's head. Jenny's a lovely girl and I'm very fond of her, but she's only fourteen.'

Molly leaned over and patted her son's hand. 'Bide yer time, sweetheart, let her grow up a bit first.'

'It's a short memory yer have, me darlin',' Seamus said, a loving smile on his face. 'Sure, how old were you when I started calling on yer?'

'I was older than Jenny is,' Molly said, blushing. 'Quite a bit older.'

'It's forgetful ye're getting in yer old age, me darlin', because yer were fourteen when we started walking out together. I remember it as clear as anything. My mother told me to wait, like ye're telling Mick, here. But I wasn't having any of that, indeed I wasn't. Yer were the prettiest girl in the village and I wasn't going to take a chance on another boy coming along and claiming yer for himself.'

Molly had a faraway look in her eyes as memories came flooding back. If the young, handsome Seamus Moynihan hadn't made the first move, sure wouldn't she have thrown all caution to the wind and made it herself? There'd been plenty of lads giving her the eye, right enough, but there was only one she ever wanted. The first time he'd looked into her eyes he'd stolen her heart, and it was still in his possession.

'Haven't yer always said, Mam, that I take after me dad?' Mick took advantage of the situation. 'Well, this proves how right yer were.'

Molly tutted as she pushed herself to her feet. 'So the two men in me life are taking sides against me, eh? Well, I'll have no part of it, me lips stay sealed.'

'Could yer not open them a little bit and put in a good word for me?' Mick grinned. 'Tell Mrs Nightingale I come highly recommended by yerself? Yer could drop little hints, like what a good bloke I am, and how handy I am around the house. I mean, yer could even go as far as to say I'd make someone a good husband.'

Molly was chuckling silently as she made her way to the kitchen door. There she turned, and said, 'Yer've cheek enough for anything, so yer have, Michael Moynihan. I'd not be surprised if yer didn't ask me to propose to Jenny for yer.'

'Oh, I've a long way to go before then, Mam. But I'll certainly bear yer offer in mind 'cos I might just need a bit of help. Especially as John Hanley has his eye on her as well, and he has the advantage of living next door to her.'

Molly put the dishes on the drainboard then stood for a while, deep in thought. They'd been pulling her leg and she'd fallen for it like a ton of bricks. She should have had more sense, knowing Mick was as bad as his father for acting daft. So she walked back into the living room with her hands on her hips. 'I've a good mind to turn the tables on yer, Mick Moynihan, and tell Mary all yer've said.'

'Oh yes, please, Mam! I knew yer wouldn't let me down. Yer see, if I don't pull me socks up, John will get in before me and I won't stand a chance.' Mick's grin was wide. 'For all I know, they might be tapping messages to each other through the bedroom wall.'

Molly shook her head. 'The joke's over now, me darlin', so let it rest. But yer had me going for a while, I have to admit.'

'Mam, it wasn't a joke, I've never been more serious in me life. I want Jenny Nightingale to be me girlfriend, and when we're older, I want her to be me wife.'

Molly looked across at Seamus. 'Is he having me on?'

'I'd say he was very serious, me darlin', and I have to say I'm altogether surprised that yer haven't noticed how often he stands at the window waiting for Jenny to put in an appearance. He's fair smitten with the girl, so he is.'

'He'll get fair smitten if Mary or Stan hear about it. And what's this about John? He's yer best mate!'

'I know he's me best mate, Mam, but not where Jenny's concerned. We've both agreed that it's every man for himself, and may the best man win. And I'm sure yer wouldn't like yer son to be anything but the best, would yer? I mean, there's such a thing as family pride, blood being thicker than water, and all that.'

'I'm fair flummoxed, and that's putting it mildly,' Molly said. 'Are yer telling me that John has his eye on Jenny, and he knows you do, too?'

'Yeah, I told him ages ago. In this very house, in fact.'

'And what did he say to that?'

'Told me to get in the queue.' Mick's laugh ricocheted off the walls. 'But I told him there was no queue, we stood side by side at the starting line.'

'I give up.' Molly glanced at the clock and tutted. 'I'm leaving you two to wash the dishes, I should be over the road by now, they'll think I'm not coming.' She got to the door and hesitated. 'Any boy who needs his mother's help to get a girl, Mick Moynihan, doesn't deserve her, and that's the truth of it.' With those parting words, she banged the front door behind her and hurried across the cobbles chuckling to herself. Sure, wouldn't she be the happiest woman in the world to have Jenny Nightingale for a daughter-in-law?

'Amy, for heaven's sake will yer be careful on that ladder?' Mary's heart was in her mouth as she watched the ladder swaying. 'Come on down and I'll scrape the top half while you do the bottom. I'm not getting anything done for keeping me eyes on you. Yer've got me a nervous wreck.'

'I'm all right, girl, honest!' Pressing a hand against the wall for support, Amy turned. With a broad grin on her chubby face, she winked. 'If I did fall, girl, I'd only bounce back up again.'

Mary screwed her eyes up tight and scratched her nose. 'Molly, will yer just look at the state of this one. Her face is filthy, there's bits of wallpaper stuck in her hair, the top button on her dress has come off and she's showing all she's got. It's a good job the men have gone out otherwise I wouldn't know where to put me face.'

Glad of the break, Molly came to stand next to Mary. 'Sure, if the men knew what they were missing, they'd be home like a shot, so they would. There's not many women got as much to show as Amy has, she's certainly well endowed, right enough.'

When Amy squared her shoulders the ladder swayed precariously and both women ran forward to steady it. 'What d'yer mean, Molly Moynihan, about me being well endowed?'

'She means yer've got a big bust, soft girl, and yer not half showing it.' Mary tugged on Amy's skirt. 'Come down and set me mind at rest.'

'The only thing that'll bring me down this ladder is a cup of tea.' Amy pursed her lips and nodded. 'Ye're a lousy boss, Mary Nightingale, yer don't look after yer workers proper.' Gripping the sides of the ladder like grim death, and testing each rung before putting her full weight on it, she came down slowly. 'Get that bleedin' kettle on, girl, before I clock yer one.'

'A fifteen-minute break, that's all we're having.' Mary wagged a finger in front of her friend's nose. 'Yer don't leave her tonight until all these walls are stripped.'

'Ye're a hard woman, Mary Nightingale,' Amy shouted after her. 'Ye're worse than the priest in Saint Anthony's – at least he only gives yer six Hail Marys. Ten minutes and yer've paid for yer sins and all is forgiven.'

'That's because yer only tell him the little sins. If yer told him what yer really get up to, yer'd still be saying yer prayers when they closed the church and yer'd be locked in.'

'Ay, now, girl, we'll have less of that! I may be big in the bust, but me lies are only ever little white ones.'

'I'll believe yer where thousands wouldn't.' Mary grinned as she made her way to the kitchen. And after striking a match under the kettle, she leaned against the sink and listened to her two neighbours.

'Ay, Molly,' Amy asked, 'does well endowed apply to all women with big breasts?'

'Well, now, me darlin', it doesn't only apply to them. People can be endowed in many ways. With a good figure, nice hair, caring nature and good sense of humour.'

'But it means big, doesn't it? Like my breasts?'

'I suppose yer could say that, me darlin', loosely speaking, of course.'

'Then my Ben is well endowed, too! He's—'

Amy's words were cut off when Mary's hand covered her mouth. She'd had a feeling her friend was going to come out with something outrageous and she'd shot out of the kitchen like a streak of greased lightning. 'Don't you dare, Amy Hanley, don't you dare.'

Amy's eyes were wide and innocent. Brushing her friend's hand away, she asked, in injured tones, 'In the name of God, girl, what's this in aid of? I haven't said nothing wrong.'

'No, but yer were going to. I know you, Amy Hanley, and I wouldn't trust yer as far as I could throw yer. D'yer want to shock Molly to the core?'

'I don't know what ye're on about, girl! All I said was that my Ben is well endowed. I can't see nothing in that to shock Molly – especially to the bleedin' core.'

'Well, just leave it at that, sunshine, 'cos we don't want to know how, when or where, your Ben is well endowed. Keep yer bedroom secrets to yerself.'

Amy's tummy was rumbling with laughter but she managed to keep a straight face. 'Oh, my Ben's not only well endowed in the bedroom, girl, he's the same everywhere he goes. I mean, I can't help it if I've got big breasts, no more than he can help what the Good Lord granted him. And fair's fair, girl, credit where it's due. There's not a man in this street who's got a bigger nose than my Ben.'

Amy's eyes went from Mary to Molly, waiting for their reaction. And when the laughter came it nearly lifted the roof. Mary held her tummy as she doubled up, tears running down her cheeks, while Molly, head back and loud guffaws coming from her open mouth, beat her fists on the arms of the chair. 'Glory be to God,' she gasped, 'have yer ever in yer whole life met a woman like her?'

'Ay, there's nowt wrong with me, Molly Moynihan, me mind's as pure as a baby's. But you two, well . . . yer've got minds like muck-middens. Dirty pair of buggers, that's what yer are. Just wait until I tell my Ben yer were making fun of his nose.'

Mary reached into the pocket of her pinny for a handkerchief. She gave her nose a good blow before saying, 'And just wait until I tell my Stan we couldn't get any work done for you talking the legs off us. We'll never get this room finished tonight.'

'Oh now, have faith, me darlin',' Molly said. 'You see to that pot of tea while me and Amy go at it like the clappers. These walls will be stripped before the men come home, so they will. Even if we die in the attempt.'

'Ooh, ay, I don't like the sound of that,' Amy said. Her lips were pursed as she shook her head, her legs dangling six inches from the floor. 'I don't mind going like the clappers, I'll pull me weight as good as the next one. But I don't fancy this dying in the attempt lark. I knew a woman once who said that, and d'yer know what happened to her? She died, that's what! And she stayed dead, into the bargain.

I don't fancy that happening to me, not when I've just joined the ranks of the well endowed.'

Mary jumped to her feet. 'Oh God, she's off again! Get cracking, Amy Hanley, and not another word out of you until we're finished.'

'Not even to say "thank you" for the cup of tea? If we ever bleedin' get one.' Amy winked. 'Okay, okay, I'm starting. And I'll work that bloody fast yer won't see me arms moving. You just watch, girl, I'll make Buster Keaton look as though he's standing still and the Keystone Cops are closing in on him.'

Cynthia closed the door behind her and linked her arm through Laura's as they set off down the street. 'Where shall we go?'

'*The Prisoner of Zenda* is on at the Atlas, and one of the women in work said it's marvellous. Thrilling, frightening and dead sad. We'd be in time for the big picture if we hurry.'

Cynthia pulled a face. 'I'm not in the mood for crying or sitting with me eyes closed all night. Couldn't we go and see a comedy?'

'It won't make yer cry, soft girl, it's only a picture. Anyway, we could stay on and see the shorts, there's bound to be something on to make yer laugh.'

'Oh, all right.' Cynthia gave in because she had other things on her mind. 'Ye're still coming with me tomorrow night, to meet Larry and Jeff, aren't yer?'

Laura took a deep breath. She'd been dreading this. 'I can't come with yer, not tomorrow, anyway. It's me birthday and me mam's making a little tea for me, just for a couple of the neighbours and John Hanley and Mick Moynihan.'

Cynthia pulled her to a halt. 'Yer gave me yer word that yer'd come! Ye're not backing out now, Laura Nightingale, or I'll never speak to yer again. I'd look a right fool, telling Jeff yer've gone to a kids' tea-party. He'll think we're giving him the round-around, and he won't be very happy – neither will Larry.' Her face like thunder, Cynthia began to walk away. 'If yer don't come with me tomorrow night, then we're finished. Please yerself.'

Laura hesitated for a few seconds before hurrying to catch up with her friend. What was the point of telling a lie to get out of something she didn't want to do, when she was going to have to tell another one next week? 'Cynthia, don't let's fall out over it.'

'You're the one that's falling out, not me,' Cynthia answered, keeping up the fast pace. 'Real friends don't make promises and then break them. And all for the sake of a stupid flaming party! What a lame excuse that is.'

'There is no party, that was a lie.'

The words brought Cynthia to an abrupt halt. 'So, ye're coming tomorrow night, after all?'

Laura shook her head. 'No, not tomorrow night nor any other night. I've tried to talk meself into it because ye're me mate and I didn't want to let yer down. But I don't want to see Jeff again because he scares me. He's too old for me, same as Larry is too old for you. They've both been around and are out for what they can get. A glass of sherry and then down a dark entry with any woman who's daft enough to go with them. On their way home to their wives and kids, they probably laugh themselves sick over how easy some girls are.'

'You speak for yerself, Laura Nightingale. Anyone would think yer were an angel, to hear yer talk. And I'm not just any woman to Larry; he really likes me, so there.'

'If he likes yer that much, he'd have told yer all about his family and where he lives. But I bet he hasn't.' When her friend didn't answer, Laura persisted. 'Well, has he?'

'What's it got to do with you? I don't have to tell you nothing.'

'No, yer don't, Cynthia. You do what yer want to do. If yer want to go out with Larry, then you do that. But don't expect me to go out with someone I don't like, just to please yer. All yer've got to do is to tell Jeff that I've got a boyfriend now. He can't argue with that, can he? And if he does get a cob on, so what? There's plenty of girls about, let him find one for himself instead of pestering me through you. I don't like him, I think he could be dangerous if he didn't get his own way, and he hasn't got a snowball's chance in hell of getting me down an entry ever again.'

'Well, I think ye're dead mean. It wouldn't hurt yer to come with me just this once, to save me looking a fool. I'd never ask yer again. Anyway, yer could tell Jeff yerself that yer've got a boyfriend and that would put a stop to him asking Larry all the time.'

'No, Cynthia,' Laura said, noting the petulant droop of her friend's lips. She was like a baby who couldn't get her own way. 'It's you that's mean, not me. Ye're trying to talk me into something yer know I don't want to do. I told yer how rough and bad-tempered Jeff was, and how he scared the life out of me, but ye're still trying to talk me into seeing him again. That's being selfish, that is, and not something yer'd do if yer were a real friend. So, if yer think more of Larry than yer do of me, then we'd better go our separate ways.' Laura wrapped her coat more tightly around her slim body to keep out the cold wind that was blowing in from the Mersey. 'Yer don't want to see *The Prisoner of Zenda*, so I'll go on me own and you can please yerself.' With that she set off down the street, the click of her high heels on the pavement breaking the silence.

'It's no skin off my nose,' Cynthia shouted after her. 'I don't need you to hold me hand, I'll be better off without yer.' But it was all bravado. She'd thought she could talk Laura around if she kept on at her, but it hadn't worked. And now she'd lost the only girlfriend

131

she'd ever had. It was a stupid thing to fall out over, too! All because of Jeff, whom she didn't much like herself, either! He certainly wasn't worth losing a friend over.

Laura had turned the corner of the street when Cynthia caught up with her. 'It's daft to fall out over a feller, kid, there's none of them worth it.' She linked her arm through her friend's and pulled her close. 'Let's forget it, eh? I'll tell Jeff ye're courting strong and that's the end of the matter. You and me are still best mates, aren't we?'

'Yeah, of course we are.' Laura gave a sigh of relief. Being allowed to stay out until eleven meant she could go to places that were out of bounds to her before, and she'd set her heart on going dancing. But she didn't fancy doing it on her own. 'How about going somewhere exciting on Saturday?'

'Such as where?'

'I'd like to go dancing. Some of the girls in work go, and they don't half enjoy themselves. There's two or three dance halls not that far from here – a couple of stops on the tram, that's all. And it's only a tanner to get in, which includes tea and biscuits.'

'I can't dance for toffee, and neither can you!'

'There's a first time for everything, kiddo, and if we never try we'll never learn.' Laura's voice was filled with excitement. 'We can watch for a while, then have a go ourselves.' She chuckled as she squeezed her friend's arm. 'You can be the man.'

'How soft you are! You look more like a man than I do.' But Laura's excitement was contagious and Cynthia found herself warming to the idea. 'Yeah, we'll give it a whirl, eh? Who knows, we might get two fellers willing to teach us.'

'That is the general idea,' Laura said. 'The fellers will be older than the kids we've been hanging about with. I don't know about you, but I'm hoping for someone who is tall, blond and as handsome as a film star.'

'I want mine to have something more than that, kid. I want a man with loads of money who isn't too mean to spend it. Someone who'll show me a good time and take me places.'

'Yeah, me too.' Laura fished a silver sixpence out of her pocket as they neared the Atlas. 'I won't see yer tomorrow night, with yer meeting Larry, but I'll call the next night and we can talk about what we'll wear and how we'll do our hair.' She held out her hand for Cynthia's money and passed the two sixpences to the girl in the ticket kiosk. 'Two fourpenny ones, please.' As they entered the darkness of the cinema, she handed Cynthia's change over and whispered, 'I can't wait for Saturday to come, me tummy's turning over now, I'm that excited.'

They weren't to know that many tears would be shed before Saturday.

* * *

When Laura parted from Cynthia outside her house, there was a spring in her step as she carried on up the street. Oh boy, what a lot she had to look forward to. But she'd need some new clobber if she was to go dancing, especially silver dance shoes. Even if she couldn't dance, at least she could look the part.

As she neared her front door, she noticed two figures standing outside and the smile dropped from her face. It was their Jenny and Janet's brother, Bill. He always walked her sister home to make sure she arrived safe, but Laura thought it was stupid. What did they think could happen to her in the five-minute walk from the Porters' house? It must be his mother's idea, he certainly wouldn't do it off his own bat. He'd left school before she did, so he must be going on for seventeen, too old to waste his time on a fourteen-year-old. With his looks he could have any girl he took a shine to. Tall, broad, and not a pimple in sight.

Jenny was putting the key in the lock when Laura stopped in front of them. 'Hi-ya, Bill! What have you been up to with my kid sister? Me mam will have yer life, keeping her out until this time of night.'

'Permission for a late pass was requested and granted. Ten thirty yer mam said, and we're right on the dot.'

'I get to stay out later, after tonight. It's me birthday tomorrow, I'm sixteen.'

'Yes, Jenny told us. I hope yer have a happy birthday.'

Completely ignoring her sister, Laura went on, 'Me and Cynthia are going dancing on Saturday night and I'm not half looking forward to it. Do you go dancing, Bill?'

Jenny had had enough. Trust her sister to push herself forward and take over. 'I hate to break this up,' she said, 'but I'm going in. Thanks for walking me home, Bill, and I'll see yer soon. Good night.'

'I'm going meself now, Jenny. Up early for work tomorrow, and I need me beauty sleep.' Bill was too wise to walk into Laura's trap. 'I'll bid you good night, Jenny, and you, too, Laura. Sleep well.' With that he strode away, leaving Laura fuming that he'd given her the brush-off. Raging inside, she pushed Jenny roughly aside and made for the stairs. 'Tell me mam I've gone to bed, I'm tired.'

Using the light from the gas-lamp on the opposite side of the street, Laura began to undress. 'Who the hell does Bill Porter think he is?' she snarled as she pulled her dress over her head. 'God's gift to women, or something? Well, there are plenty more fish in the sea – and I'm going to start catching them at the weekend.'

Chapter Eleven

Laura came out of the factory gates with a huge grin on her face. In her hand she held the six birthday cards she'd got off the women she worked with, plus a pair of rayon stockings they'd clubbed together to buy for her. She was in a very happy frame of mind, declaring this to be the best birthday she'd ever had. There'd been two cards by her plate when she came down for breakfast, one from her mam and dad, and the other from Jenny, and on the top of them were two half-crowns and a shilling. And then the postman had knocked to deliver four more cards, from her grandad, Cynthia, Mrs Hanley and Mrs Moynihan.

'I'll see yer tomorrow, girls, and thanks again for me pressie and cards.' Laura waved before turning to make her way to the tram stop. She'd only taken a few steps when she heard her name called, and looking across to the pavement opposite, she saw Celia beckoning her. Looking both ways to make sure the coast was clear, she hurried over. 'This is a surprise. Are yer going somewhere?'

'No, I've been waiting for you. Yer grandad said it's yer birthday, so I've bought yer a little present.' Celia handed her a small parcel, nicely wrapped in pretty paper and tied with a piece of red ribbon. 'I hope yer like it, but if yer don't I can easy change it.'

Laura's eyes were agog. 'Ooh, that's the gear, Celia, ta very much.' She moved a few steps nearer the gas-lamp. 'Yer've wrapped it proper posh, I must say. I can't wait to see what's inside.'

'Open it and see, unless yer'd rather wait until yer get home.' Celia knew she was on safe ground saying that. She'd had Laura taped all along, knew she was too greedy to wait until she got home. 'Please yerself.'

Laura's mind was working exactly as Celia knew it would. Her mam wouldn't be very happy about this so she'd better keep it to herself. She could always say the girls in work bought it for her. 'I'll open it now, Celia, if yer don't mind. With you and me mam not really getting on, I don't think she'd like me taking a present off yer. So if I tell her I got it off me mates in work, yer wouldn't drop me in it, would yer?'

'Of course not, we're mates, aren't we? It'll be our little secret.' Celia was gloating inside. This was the first step in getting her own back on that stuck-up daughter of her husband. 'I didn't let on to Joe that I was getting it, so there's only me knows, and I won't snitch.'

'Thanks, Celia.' Laura tucked the cards under her arm while she untied the ribbon and opened up the paper. Then she let out a shriek, and worries about her mother were forgotten as she lifted a lilac underskirt from the paper. 'Oh, it's gorgeous!' Fingering the white lace that adorned the bodice, she said, 'It's just what I wanted. Ye're a real pal, Celia, and I'll love yer for ever more.'

'I'm glad yer like it, kid. And don't worry, I won't tell anyone. Anyway, I'll have to scarper now because I left yer grandad's dinner in the oven on a low light.' The lie came easily to Celia; she was well versed in the art. There was no dinner in the oven keeping warm, she'd be buying chips from the local chippy on the way home, and if Joe didn't like it, he could lump it for all she cared. 'Eh, why don't yer come down one night and we could have a good chinwag?' She asked the question casually, as though she'd just thought of it. 'I enjoyed it last time. It was a change to have someone to talk to.'

'Ooh, I don't know.' Laura looked embarrassed. 'I got a good telling off.'

'Forget it then, kid, 'cos I wouldn't like to get yer into trouble.'

Laura looked down at the underskirt in her hand and felt really mean. 'I'd like to, I really would. But Grandad would be there and he'd be bound to tell me mam.'

'Then let's meet one night and go to the flicks! No one would know the difference then. What the eye don't see, the heart don't grieve after.'

Laura felt relieved. 'Yeah, we could do that, and no one would be any the wiser.' Then she frowned. 'But wouldn't Grandad want to know where yer were going?'

Celia shrugged her shoulders. 'I'll tell him I'm going with one of me old girlfriends. He won't think anything of it because I often go out on me own. What night suits you?'

Laura was in a dilemma. She was hoping to get a click at the dance on Saturday, and with a bit of luck the boy might ask her for a date. Much as she would like to please Celia after her buying such a nice present, a date with a boy was more to her taste. 'I'm going to a dance with Cynthia on Saturday, and I've promised to see her tomorrow so we can discuss what we're going to wear. But I could go tonight, if it's not too soon for yer?'

'Suits me, kiddo! Shall we say half seven at Everton Valley and we can decide then where to go?'

Little knowing she was being drawn into a web of deceit, Laura nodded. 'I'll have to put me skates on, but I'll be there. Ta-ra.'

Celia watched her for a while, then spun around and walked in the opposite direction. She was feeling very pleased her plan had worked so well and had a smug smile on her face. It was a pretty face at first sight, until the beholder looked more closely and saw the hardness and malice in her eyes. Especially now, when she was thinking that in the next half hour, Laura would have told her mother two lies. Those two lies, added to the other things she had planned, would one day be used to shatter Mary Nightingale's life. And that day couldn't come soon enough for Celia Steadman.

'Yer've done well, sunshine,' Mary said, having read the cards and been shown the presents. 'The underskirt is very pretty, it must have cost a pretty penny.'

'Ye're lucky, Laura,' Jenny said. 'I wish I had one as nice. Is the girl who bought it a special friend of yours?'

'I told yer, all the girls clubbed together for me presents,' Laura snapped, causing Jenny to widen her eyes at the sharp tone. 'They do it for everyone's birthday.'

'There's no need to bite me head off.' Jenny picked her knife and fork up and went back to the dinner that had been pushed aside when Laura came in. Why was her sister always so hostile towards her? She sometimes looked as though she didn't even like her, and Jenny couldn't understand the reason for it.

Mary's thoughts were also on her eldest daughter. She could read Laura like a book, and the guilty look in her eyes when Jenny had asked about the underskirt had Mary convinced that she was lying. But why lie? If she'd gone to the shops in her dinner hour, and bought the slip out of her birthday money, why didn't she just say so?

Stan finished his sausage and mash, wiped the back of his hand across his lips and pushed the plate away. He could sense a cooling in the atmosphere but couldn't figure out the reason for it. So he tried to lighten the mood. 'Twelve cards, eh, Laura? None of us have ever had that many before. Yer must be a popular girl, eh?'

The smile returned to Laura's face. 'Yeah, they're lovely, too. I was going to stand some on the sideboard and the mantelpiece, but there's not much point with the way the room is, they wouldn't be seen.'

'If yer don't want them to get dirty, yer'd be best putting them in yer bedroom,' Mary told her. 'Amy and Molly will be here in half an hour, we're going to wash the paintwork down, ready for Mr Moynihan and yer dad to start on the ceiling tomorrow night.'

'When are yer getting the wallpaper, Mam?' Jenny asked. 'Are yer getting something light and cheerful?'

Mary smiled. 'Shall I get one with clowns on?'

Jenny giggled. 'There's enough clowns in the house as it is.'

Laura gave her a sharp dig. 'Ay, you speak for yerself. There's only one clown in this house and she's sitting right next to me.'

'Well, it certainly isn't you!' Jenny was stung into saying. 'Clowns are always happy. They laugh and joke and bring smiles to people's faces. You are a far cry from that. I've never seen yer really happy, yer wouldn't know a joke if it jumped up and hit yer in the face, and a smile from you is a rare sight.'

Laura was stunned into silence, but not for long. She curled her fist, and with her weight behind it, she punched Jenny in her ribs. 'Who the hell d'yer think ye're talking to? Don't come that with me or I'll give yer a good hiding.'

Stan banged his fist on the table. 'That's enough of that! Don't you ever raise yer hand again in this house, Laura, 'cos I won't have it.'

Laura's face was sullen. 'She started it, so why don't yer say something to her? Why is it always me what gets picked on?'

'Perhaps it's because yer haven't got a sense of humour,' Mary said. 'Yer don't see the funny side of anything. Jenny didn't mean you when she talked of clowns – it was just a joke.'

'Well, I didn't think it was funny.'

Mary sighed as she pushed her chair back and reached for the plates. Her eldest daughter was hard going, there was no doubt about it. There was just no pleasing her. 'Forget it, I don't want to hear another word on the subject. And both of yer put a move on, I want you out of here before Amy and Molly come.' With the dirty plates in her hand, she looked at Jenny. 'Are yer going round to Janet's sunshine?'

'Yeah, we'll probably have a game of cards.'

'And you, Laura, are yer going anywhere special to celebrate yer birthday?'

Laura lowered her head, appearing to concentrate on her clasped hands, where the thumbs were moving around each other in circles. 'Nowhere exciting, only the pictures with Cynthia.' The lie told, she raised her eyes. 'But we're going dancing on Saturday and I'm not half looking forward to that.'

Jenny saw her mother's shoulders slump as she walked into the kitchen. So for her sake, she tried once more with Laura. 'Which dance hall are yer going to?'

'I haven't got a clue,' Laura said airily, springing to her feet. She pushed her chair back under the table before bending down and whispering in Jenny's ear, 'And if I did, I wouldn't tell yer, smarty pants.'

With a shrug of her shoulders, Jenny went into the kitchen to help her mother with the dishes. 'You wash, Mam, and I'll dry.'

'There's no need, sunshine, I can have them done in no time. You go and get yerself ready to go out.'

'I'm not bothering to get changed, Mam.' Jenny didn't relish the thought of being in the bedroom with her sister because she knew she'd be subject to a load of sarcasm. And it would be a case of standing there and taking it, or answering back and starting a fight. 'I'm only going to Janet's and it's hardly worth it.'

When Laura came downstairs, all dressed up, Jenny took her time putting her coat on so they didn't leave the house at the same time. When she heard the door bang, she smiled at her mother. 'Half ten, Mam, is that all right?'

'Yeah, that's fine, we should be finished by then. Ta-ra, sunshine.'

'Ta-ra, Mam, ta-ra, Dad. Don't work too hard, now.'

Jenny could see her sister further down the street and expected her to stop outside Cynthia's. But Laura kept on walking and Jenny watched until she'd turned the corner of the street and was out of sight. 'What's she up to now?' Jenny asked herself softly. 'She's a mystery all right, yer can't believe a word she says. I don't care what she does, it's nothing to do with me, but I do care that she upsets me mam with her lies.'

Jenny was so deep in thought, she didn't see the two figures until they stood in her path. 'Yer frightened the life out of me, yer daft things.'

'Yer were talking to yerself, Jenny, and that's a bad sign, isn't it, John?'

'Yes, Mick, it's a very bad sign.' John had been walking with his hands deep in his pockets for warmth, but the sight of Jenny was as good as sitting in front of a roaring coal fire. 'They can cart yer off to the loony bin for it.'

'I wasn't talking to meself, I was singing.' They couldn't see properly in the dusk, so didn't see Jenny's blush of embarrassment. 'Anyway, what if I was talking to meself? Is there anyone better I can talk to?'

'Yeah, there's me,' said Mick, his white teeth flashing, 'I'm always available, and yer'll not get a better pair of listening ears than mine.'

'Oh yes, she will,' John chuckled. 'What about me? I can listen for hours without opening me mouth.' He put a hand on Jenny's arm. 'Don't ever take first offer, Jenny, always shop around for the best bargain.'

Not to be outdone, Mick put a hand on Jenny's other arm. 'Now just be careful yer don't end up with shopsoiled goods, Jenny. Yer want nothing but the best.'

John took up a boxing stance. 'Are yer insinuating that I'm shopsoiled, Mick Moynihan? If yer are, I'll set me mam on yer.' Realising his mate had the advantage over him now, with a hand still on Jenny's arm, he quickly relaxed his stance and put his hand where it wanted to be, touching Jenny. 'Yer heard that, didn't yer, Miss

Nightingale? Will yer be me witness when I take him to court?'

'Daft as brushes, both of yer.' Jenny's voice was full of laughter. They hadn't half cheered her up. 'Now, gentlemen, would yer kindly unhand me before *I* become shopsoiled goods? And tell me, pray, what are yer doing down here?'

'It's our night for jazzing and we're going for the tram.' Mick plucked up the courage to take hold of Jenny's arms and held them aloft. With exaggerated movements he spun her around, singing, 'Who's Taking You Home Tonight?'

Ho, ho, John thought, I'm not standing for that! Bare-faced cheek, that is. 'Excuse me,' he tapped Mick on the shoulder. 'Sorry, mate, but this is an Excuse Me waltz.'

Mick stood still but held on tight. 'Only if the young lady is willing.'

'To save any argument,' Jenny said, trying to free her hands, 'John can have three spins, and then ye're even. After that I'm on me way, 'cos Janet will wonder where I've got to.'

As John pushed him aside, Mick whispered, 'I don't wish yer no harm, mate, but I hope yer trip and break a flippin' leg.'

John winked in answer before he reached for Jenny, a look of pure bliss on his face. 'It was five spins he had, so don't be trying to short-change me, Jenny Nightingale.'

Jenny counted aloud and stopped dead on five. 'Now yer can walk down to me mate's with me.'

'I don't suppose, like, that yer could bring Janet out, could yer?' Mick ventured as they walked in line. 'Then we could have a dance in the street, save going all the way to Seaforth.'

'Some hope you've got, Mick Moynihan. Her mam would have yer life.'

'Yer could always ask her mam, too!' John was wishing the Porters lived the other side of Liverpool so the walk would last all night. 'She could chaperone yer, or even join in if she wanted.'

'Yeah, that's a good idea, mate!' Mick felt as though he was walking on air. 'I bet Mrs Porter can do a mean quickstep.'

Jenny was having a fit of the giggles. 'Why not ask the whole street and we could have a party? Mr Porter can knock out a tune on his comb, so we'd have music, as well.'

'And I'm pretty good at whistling,' John said. 'Mind you, yer wouldn't know whether to do a quickstep or a tango, but who cares?'

'I can hum, if that's any good.' Jenny was laughing when they stopped outside the Porters' house. 'And I can click me tongue, as well.'

Mick's laugh was loud. 'All we need is someone on the spoons and we've got a full orchestra. I bags being the conductor.'

'Oh no, matey, I've got yer down as the band's singer.' John's shoulders were shaking with laughter. 'I'll be whistling me head off while I'm dancing with Jenny, and you'll be on the stage belting out a nice smoochy song.'

'What's this about a smoochy song?' No one had heard the door open and they were surprised to see Martha Porter standing on the step, arms folded and a huge grin on her face. 'Come on, tell us about this smoochy song, I like the sound of it.'

'I think yer'd better ask me mate,' John said. 'He's the singer.'

'John Hanley, ye're a coward,' Jenny told him, wagging a finger. 'It was you what said it.'

Mick tilted his head to the side and weighed up Janet's mother, before saying, 'I said I bet yer can do a mean quickstep, Mrs Porter, am I right?'

'I've had me moments, lad, but they were a very long time ago. The best I could manage now would be a slow waltz.' Her laugh was loud and hoarse. 'In fact, it would have to be so bleedin' slow we'd be standing still.'

Janet's head appeared over her mother's shoulder. 'What's going on here?'

Jenny, the unpleasantness with her sister forgotten, was in a playful mood. 'The boys want to invite us to dance in the street, Jan. We've sorted the music out, with yer dad on the comb, you and me humming and clicking our tongues, John whistling and Mick singing. But we haven't got anyone to play the spoons.'

Martha doubled up. 'Oh dear, that's tickled me fancy.' She wiped her eyes and took a deep breath. 'Mr Wilkinson, down the street, he's got a ukulele, shall I go and drag him out?'

Bill towered behind his mother and sister, and when he saw Jenny standing with the two lads, he squeezed between them and joined the trio on the pavement. 'You ain't going anywhere, Jenny Nightingale. I've been waiting for yer so I could win back those ten matchsticks yer cheated me out of the other night.'

'You fibber! I never did no such thing! You're the one who cheats, hiding cards under the tablecloth so we won't see.'

'He's pulling yer leg, queen,' Martha said. 'Take no notice of him.'

'Yeah,' Janet agreed, 'he thinks he's funny but he's a pain in the neck.' She nudged her mother. 'Mam, didn't yer say I could go dancing with Jenny when we're fifteen?'

Martha tutted. 'Don't push yer luck, Janet. I said I'd think about it, as long as yer had someone to walk yer home.'

Mick and John spoke in unison. 'We'll walk them home, Mrs Porter.'

'That's all right,' Bill said. 'I'll go with them and make sure they come to no harm. I can't let me kid sister walk home in the dark.'

Mick and John exchanged glances which said it wasn't his kid sister's interest he had at heart, it was Jenny's. And the look wasn't lost on Martha. 'It's bad luck to plan so far ahead,' she told them. 'Something always turns up to throw a spanner in the works. There's a few months to go yet, so leave it be until then.'

'We'd better scarper,' Mick said, 'otherwise they'll be playing the last waltz by the time we get there.' The lads waved goodbye, then after a few steps, they turned. Mrs Porter and Janet had vanished indoors, and Bill had his hand on Jenny's elbow as she mounted the steps.

'I think we've got some competition there, Mick,' John said, 'and it's going to be stiff competition.'

'Ye're telling me!' If there had been a stone handy, Mick would have kicked it the length of the street. One rival was bad enough, but two? 'And he's got luck on his side being Janet's brother. It's a big plus, that is. We won't be in the meg specks.'

'I'd fight him, if he wasn't so big,' John said, hands dug deep in his pockets. 'But he's built like a flippin' house.'

'Oh, we've got no worries there, 'cos there's two of us. I'll hold him while you batter hell out of him.'

'Oh aye, soft lad! Put muggins here in front of him, while you stand behind, all nice and safe? You are definitely not on, mate! I'm as fond of me teeth as you are,' John chortled. 'Tell yer what, eh? We've got five months before Jenny's birthday, so it's you and me against Bill Porter. But the day she's fifteen, it's every man for himself.'

Celia was waiting at Everton Valley when Laura dashed up, out of breath with running. 'Have yer been waiting long?'

'Only about two minutes.' Celia linked arms. 'Where would yer like to go?'

'I don't mind, it's up to you.' Laura looked sideways and her heart dropped. Celia was dressed up to the nines, as though she was going somewhere special, and here was she in a tattered old coat. 'I don't want to go anywhere posh 'cos I'm not dressed for it. Me frock is all right, but this coat is shabby.'

'Laura, with a face and figure like yours, who the hell is going to look at yer clothes?' Celia gushed, smiling into her face. 'When yer've got the looks and the personality to go with it, kid, clothes don't matter.'

If Laura had been older, with a bit more experience, she might have noticed that the smile wasn't genuine, neither were the words. As it was, she believed what she wanted to believe and preened with pleasure. 'I'm saving up for a new coat, I should have enough in two or three weeks.'

'Anyway, where do yer want to go?' Celia asked. 'The pictures or a dance?'

'Ooh, I'd like to go to a dance, but don't forget, I've got to be home by eleven so I can't go too far away.'

'There's a dance at Spellow Lane, over Burton's, the Thirty Bob Tailor's. It's only a couple of stops on the tram, and if we leave at half ten, yer'll be home in plenty of time.'

'Yeah, okay. But I can't dance so I'll have to sit and watch.' When they had crossed the busy road and stopped by the tram stop, Laura eyed Celia up and down. 'Me grandad must be good to yer with money, yer always have something different on.'

'He's not a bad old stick. He knows I like going out, and as he's always too tired, he gives me the money to go where I want to.' Celia changed the subject. She wasn't going to tell Laura that the money Joe gave her was for housekeeping, but hardly any of it went on the house. She wanted clothes and enjoyment, and it was his own fault for not giving her more when she'd tried to wheedle it out of him. But the less said about that to his granddaughter, the better. She was trying to trap Laura, not the other way around.

When the tram came, Laura got her purse out to pay her fare, but Celia brushed her hand aside. 'This is my treat for yer birthday.' She handed the conductor the coppers and waited for him to turn the handle of the ticket machine which hung from his shoulders by a leather strap. With the tickets in her hand, she turned to Laura and asked casually, 'Would yer like to go for a drink before we go in? There's a pub right facing the dance hall.'

Laura shook her head vigorously. They were in Walton now, not that far from where her grandad lived, and it was too risky. He was the one person in the world she had any feelings for, and she knew in her heart she was doing wrong by seeing his wife behind his back. And if he found out and told her mam, she'd get a hiding. Anyway, look what happened the last time she went in a pub. That experience still gave her shivers when she thought of it. 'No thanks, Celia, I'd rather not.'

'I'm not fussy meself, kid,' lied Celia, who could drink most men under the table. 'Drink gives me a headache.' She felt disappointed that her plan hadn't worked, but there was plenty of time. She'd make a friend of Laura, use her until she had enough on her to shatter the life of the family-loving Mary Nightingale. At first Celia wanted to get her own back on Mary for the row they'd had, and for the slap on the face. But gradually she became obsessed, blaming Mary for everything that was wrong in her life. Like being married to a man more than twice her age who wasn't fun any more. She'd married him for a meal ticket, thinking he would be a soft touch, but the novelty had worn off. And because that man was Mary's father, then Mary was to blame.

'Isn't this our stop?' Laura asked, peering through the window of

143

the tram. 'The conductor has just shouted Spellow Lane.'

Celia, still deep in thought, stared at her blankly for a couple of seconds. Then she remembered where she was, and why, and scrambled to her feet. 'D'yer know, kid, I was miles away! If you hadn't been here I'd have ended up at the terminus in Fazakerly.'

'Me tummy feels as though it's full of butterflies,' Laura said, as they passed through the entrance and began to climb the stairs. 'Yer won't leave me on me own, will yer?'

'Of course I won't! Anyway, how can yer be on yer own in a hall full of people? And I've told yer, with your looks they'll be falling over themselves to dance with yer.'

Once again Celia pushed Laura's hand away when she tried to pay for her own ticket. 'The treat's on me tonight, kid.'

Shaking like a leaf, Laura followed Celia to the cloakroom. After handing their coats over they were given a ticket which Celia told her to hang on to until they were going home.

Then came the moment when Celia pushed open the door to the dance hall. It was crowded with couples dancing to the strains of a slow foxtrot, and some of the tension left Laura as she told herself she wouldn't be noticed in this crowd. She could just sit down and watch, and try to pick up a few points on how it was done. Then tomorrow night her and Cynthia could have a go.

Laura was walking ahead of Celia to where she had spied two empty chairs, when she heard someone saying in a loud voice, 'Hello there, sweetheart, where've yer been hiding yerself? I missed yer last week, it wasn't the same without yer.'

Turning her head out of curiosity, Laura saw a man with his arm around Celia's waist, smiling down at her. He seemed very familiar, as though he'd known her a long time. But he shouldn't be holding her like that, he must know she was a married woman.

Celia could feel herself being watched and waved a hand towards the chairs. 'Go and sit down, kid, I won't be long. Charlie's an old friend of mine.'

Before turning away, Laura glanced at the man's face and decided she didn't like him. Nor did she like the way he was looking down the front of Celia's low-cut dress. But it wasn't any of her business and she was probably being daft. You couldn't tell what a person was like just by looking at them. So Laura took her seat and turned her attention to the dancers. Some of the couples were really good, and it was a pleasure just to sit and admire. One day she'd be able to dance like that and the men would be fighting to dance with her.

The music came to an end and Laura noted how the couples clapped before leaving the floor. Some stayed with their partners, ready for the next dance, while others returned to their friends who were sitting on the chairs minding handbags. There were more girls than boys, and that pleased Laura. Her and Cynthia wouldn't look out of place tomorrow night. But she'd have to buy a pair of proper dance-shoes, all the girls were wearing them. Most of them were silver, with thin straps and very high heels, and they didn't half look nice.

'I'm sorry about that, kid, but Charlie's a very old friend.'

Laura turned to see Celia sitting beside her. 'Yeah, it looked like it too, the way he had his arm around yer.'

'Oh, don't take no notice of that, Charlie's like that with all the girls.' Celia patted Laura's hand. 'He's a real ladies' man, but harmless enough when yer know how to handle him.'

'D'yer come dancing often, Celia, and are yer any good at it?'

'That's two questions in one, Laura. Let's see, which one shall I answer first?' Celia took her time answering, hoping the plan she'd hatched with Charlie worked before the questions got too personal. It was when the band struck up that she answered. 'I don't come very often and I guess me dancing is just about average.'

'Would yer take me for this dance, then? I wouldn't feel so daft about making mistakes if I was with you.'

Celia grinned. 'Yer don't need me, there's a boy making a bee-line for yer.'

Laura looked up in dismay when a male voice asked, 'D'yer want to dance?' The boy was about eighteen and not bad-looking. Any other time Laura would be fluttering her eyelashes, but right now she was worried about standing all over his feet and making a fool of herself. 'I'm sorry,' she croaked, 'but I can't dance.'

'Don't be stupid, kid!' Celia said. 'This is Gary, and he won't mind teaching yer a few steps, will yer, Gary? She's got to learn sometime.'

Gary grinned, showing a set of even white teeth. Charlie had asked him to dance with the girl as a favour, so he could be with Celia. And Gary had reluctantly agreed to have one dance with her. But looking down at her now, he realised he was the one getting the favour. She was a real good-looker, this one, it would be a pleasure teaching her to dance. 'Come on, the floor is crowded, no one will notice. I'll walk yer round until yer get used to it.'

Laura looked up at him and her apprehension began to fade. Tall, slim, blond and blue-eyed, what more could you ask for? She bent to put her handbag under the chair before standing up. 'Don't say yer weren't warned.'

There was a smile on Celia's face as she watched them take the floor, the smile of a victor. Good old Charlie had come up trumps once again. Now she could disappear for a while. But she'd have to be careful or the whole thing could backfire on her. So she waited until Laura's attention was focused on her partner's feet, then hurried out to the foyer where Charlie was waiting. He was holding his overcoat ready to wrap around her shoulders, and grunted, 'I hope she's not with yer next week, this is bloody ridiculous.'

As she was hurried through the entrance door and into the street, Celia's voice was sharp. 'Hey, yer can cut that out. She's here for a purpose, and right now she's more important to me than giving you yer little bit of pleasure. So don't start yer moaning or I'll be back in that dance like a shot.'

'All right, sweetheart, keep yer hair on.' Charlie, hurrying her to the nearest entry, knew what a bitch Celia could be when she wanted, so he kept his voice soft. 'It's just that I want to be with yer as long as I can.'

'Gary said he'd keep her busy for ten minutes, so that's all the time yer've got.' Celia leaned back against the wall. 'So yer'd better get a move on, lover boy, hadn't yer? Otherwise I'll be leaving yer in the middle of the game, and yer wouldn't be a happy man if I did that, would yer?'

Laura didn't think anything of it when Gary asked her to stay on the floor for the next dance. In fact, she didn't think of anything, her head was in the clouds. He'd told her she was getting on really well, that she was a born dancer with natural rhythm and had the body to go with it. And Laura lapped it up. In no time at all she'd be as good as anyone on the floor.

When the music stopped, the singer with the band said there would be a five-minute break before the next dance, which would be a rumba. 'Ooh, I'm not even going to attempt that.' Laura cast her eyes around the room. 'Where's Celia got to?'

'She's probably gone to the toilet,' said Gary, who'd had his eyes peeled for the last five minutes. 'She won't be long, so stay and talk to me.'

When Celia did put in an appearance, quickly followed by Charlie, Laura was too full of her own importance to make a connection. 'I didn't half do well, didn't I, Gary?'

'Yeah, she was brilliant. Took to it like a duck to water.'

Celia smiled. 'Yer'll have to come again next week then, won't yer? Gary comes every Thursday, and now ye're getting on so well with him, ye're best sticking to the same partner.'

'Will yer be here next week, Gary?' There was excitement in Laura's voice. 'I'll come if yer are.'

Gary had taken a shine to her and would have told her that he came three times a week if Celia hadn't been glaring at him. She was the wrong one to make an enemy of, as many people in the hall had found out to their cost. The girls avoided her like the plague, but the men were around her like flies around a honey jar. 'Yeah, I'll be here.'

Gary wasn't the only one doing as he was told. Charlie, who was standing by the main door, had been ordered to keep his distance and he knew better than to disobey. But what he got in return for being a lap-dog was well worth it.

After the interval, Laura had two more dances with Gary, and then Celia said it was time to go. She made a show of being considerate, insisting she saw Laura on the tram so she'd know she got home in time. But she wasn't being considerate, she was being crafty. Laura had had a taste of Gary and would be only too willing to come back for more. And Gary would be ordered to toe the line until Celia gave him the go-ahead.

Chapter Twelve

'This is me very favourite meal, Mam,' Jenny said, gnawing at the bone she was holding between her fingers. 'Spare-ribs and cabbage, yer can't beat it. I could eat it every day and never get fed up with it.'

'Me too,' Stan agreed, 'especially when there's plenty of lean meat on the bones and yer can get yer teeth into it.'

'I'll have you know that sheet of ribs nearly started a war in the butcher's,' Mary told them, smacking her lips.' I noticed it hanging up in the shop window as we passed, and I could see how lean it was. But I didn't crack on to Amy, 'cos I thought she'd beat me to it.' Mary's titter turned into a full-blown laugh. 'Honest to God, that mate of mine will get me hung one of these days with her shenanigans. I asked Wilf for a sheet of ribs and pointed to the one I wanted. As he was hooking it down, Amy asked why that one was so special – what difference was there between that and the other sheets hanging on the iron bar in the window. I told her it was leaner, all the others had too much fat on them. Well, I bet Wilf cursed me up hill and down dale, 'cos she only made him lift every sheet down for inspection. She compared each one with mine and shook her head. "She's right, they are all fatty".'

Mary looked around the table to see Stan leaning on his elbows, his chin resting on his laced fingers, Jenny's eyes were wide with interest and even Laura was waiting for what was to come. 'Can anyone guess what happened then?'

'With Amy, anything could happen, love,' Stan said, 'so yer'd better tell us instead of keeping us in suspense.'

'Right, I'll show yer.' Mary got to her feet and cleared her throat. 'Now, pretend I'm Amy and I'm wearing a scarf around me head that keeps slipping down one side. Here goes.'

She pushed the pretend scarf back into place, folded her arms and sniffed up. ' "Yer've been very kind, Wilf, showing me all those sheets of bleedin' ribs. It's been real interesting. There's not many shopkeepers as obliging as yerself, especially when the customer isn't buying. We're having scouse for our dinner, so will yer cut me a pound of stewing meat up, please. And will yer do me the courtesy of letting me see it before yer take the knife to it, so I can be sure it's bleedin' lean?" ' Mary hitched up her bosom and narrowed her eyes.

' "What are yer standing there with yer mouth open for, Wilf? Yer'll not catch many flies in this weather".'

Stan guffawed and banged his fist on the table. 'She's a bloody hero.'

'I can just picture it, Mam, 'cos yer aren't half good at taking me Auntie Amy off,' Jenny said. 'But I wish I'd been there to see Wilf's face.'

Laura made no comment, but there was a smile on her face. In fact she'd had a smile on her face all day, still on cloud nine after last night. She'd done nothing but talk about it all day, adding little extras to spice it up a bit for the women she worked with. And she couldn't wait to get down to Cynthia's to go over it all again. She'd told the family she'd been to the dance with her friend instead of the cinema so she'd better watch what she said in case she let it slip.

'Come on now, the show's over,' Mary said briskly, knocking Stan's elbows off the table. 'Seamus is coming over to give yer dad a hand painting the ceiling and I want all the furniture covered with some old sheets.'

'Are yer getting the wallpaper tomorrow, Mam?' Jenny asked, following her mother into the kitchen. 'I can't wait to see the room finished, we'll be proper posh.'

'Well, I don't know about being posh, but it'll certainly be an improvement.' Mary grinned as she turned the tap on. 'Amy said she'd help with the papering, but I don't think me heart would stand it. Can yer just imagine the antics out of her? It would be a disaster.'

Laura popped her head in. 'I'm going down to Cynthia's, Mam, but I won't be late.'

'Okay, sunshine, but don't come back before half-ten, give the men a chance to get it all done and dusted.'

When she heard the door bang, Jenny asked, 'Where did our Laura go last night?'

'I couldn't tell yer, sunshine. She just said she'd been to a dance with Cynthia and I never thought to ask where.'

Jenny frowned as she reached for the tea-towel hanging behind the door. She was a dark horse, their Laura; you could never get to the bottom of her. She'd told a lie about last night, she hadn't been out with Cynthia, but why did she think there was a need to lie about it? If she was going out with a boy, their mam wouldn't mind, she'd be made up. In fact, Mary would welcome him with open arms if he was a nice bloke and good for Laura.

Jenny sighed. The best thing she could do was say nothing and hope it all worked out well in the end.

Laura ran down the street with wings on her heels. Wait until she

150

told her friend where she'd been last night, and that she'd danced every dance with a bloke as handsome as any film star. Oh boy, Cynthia wouldn't half be jealous. But best not to tell her who she'd been with, in case it slipped out some time and got back to her mam. She couldn't say she'd been on her own because her friend knew she wouldn't have the nerve, so she'd have to say she'd been with a girl from work.

Cynthia was usually waiting for her and had the door opened before she'd finishing knocking. But that wasn't the case tonight, and Laura's face showed surprise when her mother answered her knock. 'Is Cynthia coming out, Mrs Pennington?'

'No, girl, she's been in bed all day, never went to work.'

Laura's spirits sank. 'What's wrong with her? Is she sick?'

'She said she's got a sore throat, a headache and pains in her tummy.' There was no sympathy in Fanny Pennington's voice. 'At least that's her story and she flatly refuses to get out of bed.'

'Can I go up and see her?' Laura was feeling desperate as her great plans came crumbling around her shoulders. 'I might be able to cheer her up.'

'Suit yerself, girl.' The door was opened wider. 'Yer know where her room is.'

Laura took the stairs two at a time. Cynthia often took a day off when she couldn't be bothered going to work, and her parents let her get away with it. At least her father did, her mother never had a say in it. But she'd never missed coming out at night.

'It's me, Cynthia.' Laura knocked lightly before pushing the door open. In the dim light coming from the candle standing in a saucer on a chest of drawers at the side of the bed, she could see her friend huddled in the middle of the bed, the clothes pulled up to her chin. 'What's wrong with yer, Cynthia? Are yer really sick, or just putting it on?'

'Close the door,' Cynthia's voice was muffled, 'and come and sit on the bed.'

Laura closed the door quietly then did as she was bid. 'Ye're not really sick, are yer?'

Cynthia struggled to sit up, groaning as she did so. 'I'm in agony, Laura, and I don't know what to do.'

'Have yer got pains in yer tummy?'

'I wish that was all it was.' Cynthia rocked back and forth, and when the tears came she covered her face with her hands to stifle the noise of the sobs that racked her body. 'It was terrible, Laura, I thought they were going to kill me.'

'What are yer talking about? Who did yer think was going to kill yer?'

'Larry and Jeff.'

'Larry and Jeff!' Laura's voice rose in surprise. 'What did they do to yer?'

'I can't tell yer. I couldn't tell no one.'

The springs on the bed were squeaking, and afraid that they would be heard downstairs, Laura put an arm around Cynthia's shoulders to try and calm her down. 'Yer mam and dad will be up if yer don't stop, Cynthia. Just take it easy and tell me what happened.'

'I haven't slept a wink, it's like a nightmare. I keep going over it in me mind and I feel like screaming.' She turned a tearstained face to her friend. 'They left me in a dark entry on me own, and I was terrified. All I could hear was them laughing as they walked away.'

'But what the hell were yer doing down a dark entry with the two of them! It was a pretty stupid thing to do, especially as I'd told yer how cruel Jeff was with me.'

'I had no choice, they dragged me. I thought Jeff would leave us when we came out of the pub, but he didn't! I wasn't worried because I was with Larry, and I thought we were walking in the direction of Jeff's home and he'd turn off any minute.' The sobbing started again and Cynthia pushed Laura's arm away. 'I can't tell yer any more, I get too upset and could scream the house down.'

'Shall I go and ask yer mam to make yer a cup of tea? I'll tell her yer throat's not as sore but it's dry.'

Cynthia's head shook vigorously. 'No, I don't want her to come in here, I don't want no one in here.'

'I'll stay down there until she makes the tea, so she won't have to come up. But in case she or yer dad asks if yer were out with me last night, what shall I say?'

'I told them I was going to the flicks with yer.'

'Okay, I won't be long.'

Fanny Pennington made the tea without a word, while Laura chatted with Dick, her husband. But when she passed the cup and saucer over, there was suspicion in her eyes. 'Tell her to drink it while it's hot.'

Walking up the stairs slowly so as not to spill the tea, Laura's mind was whirling. She couldn't imagine what had happened to upset Cynthia so much. She was always so sure of herself, and certainly capable of handling herself. And she had Larry with her, the man who was supposed to be in love with her. 'I just don't understand it,' Laura sighed as she pushed the bedroom door open with her foot. 'But I'll find out, even if I have to sit here all night.'

'Yer mam said to drink it while it's hot.'

Cynthia pointed to the chest of drawers. 'Put it on there for a minute and bring the candle over to the bed.'

Her brow furrowed, Laura held out the candle to her friend. 'Here yer are.'

'No, you hold it and sit on the side of the bed.' Cynthia was unbuttoning the neck of her nightdress. 'That's what they did to me.'

Laura stared in horror at the bruising around Cynthia's throat. It was yellow, blue and black, and it looked very sore. 'Did Jeff do that to yer? Where the hell was Larry when this was going on?'

Cynthia dropped her head in shame. 'Pass me the tea, then I'll tell yer everything.' She took a few sips, then said softly, 'Yer were right all along, Larry is just as bad as Jeff. In fact, he's ten times worse because he'd been leading me on for weeks now and muggins here fell for it hook, line and sinker.'

'I'm all mixed up, Cynthia, it won't sink in. So start at the beginning. Was Jeff with Larry when yer got to where yer were meeting him?'

Cynthia nodded. 'I told them yer couldn't come 'cos yer've got a steady boyfriend, and Jeff winked at Larry and said they weren't surprised, they had an idea yer wouldn't turn up. He said he'd come and have a drink with us and then toddle off home. I didn't think anything about it when we came out of the pub and he started walking with us, I thought he must live near there. Then, when we were passing an entry they each put a hand on me arms and, without any warning, they dragged me down it. That was when I started to get frightened and struggled to get away from them, but they were gripping me arms so tight, they were hurting.' She rolled up a sleeve of her nightdress and lifted her arm to show Laura the deep, angry bruising. 'The other arm's the same.'

'Why didn't yer scream yer head off? Someone might have heard yer, and anyway it would have frightened the fellers, they'd have run like hell.'

Cynthia shook her head. 'I've been thinking about it all night, going over every detail until I thought I was going mad. But I can see now they'd had it planned down to a fine art. They had it all worked out what they'd do if you didn't come. It was all done without one word being passed between them. And as for me screaming, how could I scream when Jeff had his hand over me mouth? They dragged me down to the darkest part of the entry and flung me hard up against the wall. Then Jeff held me there by putting his hand around me throat. I couldn't move or I'd have been choked to death. They were so rough, it was as if they wanted to really hurt me.' Cynthia shuddered as in her mind she relived parts of the nightmare. And when the tears began to flow she wiped them away with a corner of the sheet. 'If I live to be a hundred, I'll never forget last night.'

'I still don't get it,' Laura said. 'What kick would they get out of beating yer up? And why Larry? Yer hadn't done him no harm.'

Plucking nervously at the eiderdown, her eyes looking past Laura to a spot on the wall, Cynthia spoke almost in a whisper. 'If I tell yer

153

something, yer won't breathe a word to a living soul, will yer? I want yer to swear on yer life that yer won't repeat it.'

'Of course I won't tell no one, I swear on me life. I'm yer mate, aren't I, and mates don't clat on each other.'

'While Jeff was holding me against the wall, Larry was pulling me clothes up around me waist and tugging me knickers down.' Cynthia heard Laura's sharp intake of breath and nodded. 'Oh yeah, it sounds terrible, doesn't it? Well, I can assure yer that the reality was far worse than just listening about it. I couldn't speak properly, but I was begging Larry to leave me alone. He didn't seem to hear me because Jeff was egging him on, telling him what to do. And the more he egged him on, the more excited Larry got and I think he'd have killed me if his mate had told him to.'

Laura was shaking her head in disbelief. 'And this is the Larry who was supposed to be in love with yer! What a joke!'

'Oh, he was in love with me all right.' There was venom in Cynthia's voice. 'He loved me that much he wanted his friend to have a share of me.'

Laura's hand flew to her mouth while her eyes widened in horror. 'Not him as well, kid? Yer not saying they both . . . er . . . yer know what I mean?'

'Oh aye, I have good reason to know what yer mean. When Larry had finished, he took over from Jeff in keeping me quiet while his mate had his bit of fun. That's all I was to them, something they could satisfy themselves with, then throw away. And that's just what they did. Used me, then knocked me to the ground, crying me eyes out while they walked away laughing. I could have been dead for all they knew, or cared.'

The horror of it all was slowly sinking in with Laura. If she'd let her friend talk her into going with them last night, the same thing could have happened to her. It didn't bear thinking about. 'I don't know what to say, Cynthia, I've never heard anything like it. They should be sent to prison for what they did.'

'Yer don't know the half of it. The bruises on me throat and arms are nothing compared with the ones at the top of me legs. I walked all the way home because I knew I must have looked a mess, with me clothes all dirty and me eyes red from crying. And every step I took was pure agony.'

'What did yer parents say?'

'They didn't see me. Me mam opened the door and I told her I must be in for a cold 'cos I had a sore throat and a headache. I came straight upstairs and got into bed. Me dad came in to see me this morning before he went to work, but I kept meself well covered and told him I didn't feel well. Yer know how soft me dad is with me, he told me to stay where I was until I felt better.'

154

'And when is that going to be?' Laura asked. 'If yer stay there too long they'll think ye're really sick and send for a doctor.'

'I can't go out looking like this, not with me bruises showing. Anyway, I'm in too much pain to walk.'

'There's only yer throat showing, and a scarf would cover that. We could go for a little walk tomorrow afternoon if yer like. Just around the shops for half an hour, it'll do yer good. Yer'll be in the fresh air and it'll help to get yer legs moving.'

Cynthia eyed her friend through lowered lashes. 'Are yer still going dancing?'

Laura had been so looking forward to tomorrow night and was bitterly disappointed. But she had no one to go with now, and she didn't have the nerve to go on her own. And anyway, Cynthia was her best mate, she couldn't let her down. 'No, I wouldn't go without you. There's always next week.'

'Will yer tell me mam I'm going out with yer tomorrow afternoon, just for a bit of fresh air? I've got a scarf in one of the drawers, so I'll do what yer said.'

'Do yer feel a bit better, now yer've talked about what happened?'

Cynthia nodded. 'Yeah, I do, kid. But I'll never forget it, and I'll get even with them if it's the last thing I do. I've been meeting Larry on a Tuesday and Thursday, so they must be their nights out. I'll haunt Scotland Road on those nights until I come across them. They won't see me but I'll follow them until I find out where they live. And then I'll think of a way to get me own back. They won't get off scot-free, not after what they did to me.'

'Don't do it, Cynthia, yer might get yerself in a load of trouble. They're bad men, I wouldn't tangle with them if I were you.'

'It's easy for you to talk, it didn't happen to you. I'm the one who's in pain, the one who's going to have to live with the memory of it all me life. But I'll live with it easier if I have the satisfaction of knowing they're suffering too.' She saw the apprehension on Laura's face and added, 'Don't worry, I won't involve you. I'll do it all meself and take great satisfaction from it.'

'Did yer say seven rolls of paper, Stan?' Mary sat at the table with a pencil and a scrap of paper. 'Are yer sure that's enough?'

'I say seven, and Seamus and Ben say the same. We can't all be wrong, can we?'

'I didn't say yer were wrong, sweetheart, I was only asking to make sure.' Mary made a note on the paper. 'And don't tear yer hair out when I ask if it was sixteen yards of border?'

Stan grinned. 'I wouldn't tear me hair out no matter what yer said, love, 'cos I haven't got much as it is.' He bent his head so she could see the bald patch at the top. 'That spot seems to be growing bigger every day. If it keeps up at this rate, I'll be as bald as a billiard ball by this time next year.'

When Jenny came through from the kitchen she was giggling helplessly. 'Mam, get an extra roll of paper and do me dad's head. He'd blend in with the walls, then.'

'Don't be so cheeky, young lady.' Stan's smile was wide. 'Anyway, I've got a better idea and it's cheaper. Yer mam can put a tin of black Cherry Blossom shoe polish on her list – that should do the trick. When I'm polishing me shoes I can rub the brush over me bald spot'

'Yer'll not be sleeping on my pillowcases then, sunshine. It'll be the coal-hole for you.'

When the knock came, Jenny made a bee-line for the door. 'This'll be me grandad.'

Mary cocked an ear and grinned across at Stan when they heard Jenny's peal of laughter. 'Grandad, yer haven't had a shave and yer whiskers are tickling me.'

Joe's voice boomed, 'A tickle is better than a slap any day, queen.'

Mary got to her feet to greet her father with a big hug and a kiss. 'Yer cheeks are not half cold, Dad, I didn't think it was that bad out.'

'I think I'd be right in saying it was parky, what do you say, Stan?'

'I'd say we're in for a bad winter, Joe. It's only the end of October and it's bitter.'

Mary studied her father's face. He looked gaunt, but then who wouldn't if they weren't getting the right food inside them. 'Take yer coat off, Dad, and sit by the fire. I've put a dinner in the oven to keep warm for yer. We got ours over early, 'cos I'm going to the shops for wallpaper and paint.'

Joe handed his coat to Jenny before standing in front of the fire with his hands spread out near the flickering flames. 'I'll come with yer, sweetheart, to give yer a hand. Tins of paint can be very heavy.'

'No thanks, Dad, I've got me two mates coming with me. You stay in the warmth and keep Stan company.'

Laura stood at the top of the stairs listening. She'd hoped to be out before her grandad came, and she would have been if he'd come five minutes later. Not that she didn't want to see him, she did. He was always nice to her, and all her life she'd had a sneaking feeling that between her and Jenny, she was his favourite. The only reason she didn't want to see him now was because she was afraid his wife might have mentioned the birthday present or the dance. After all the lies she'd told, she had visions of walking into the room and being asked if she'd liked her present and did she enjoy the dance. She wouldn't know where to put herself, being found out in all those lies in front of the whole family. Celia had promised not to tell, but deep down, Laura didn't quite trust the girl her grandad had married. Oh, she was nice and friendly, fussed over Laura as though she was someone special. And she was generous, no doubt about that. It was just a little niggle, something that didn't quite click with Laura that she couldn't put her finger on.

'I'd better go and get it over with,' she muttered, holding on to the banister for support as she stepped down the narrow, steep stairs. 'It's got to come sometime, I can't keep hiding from me grandad.'

Joe gave her a warm welcome. 'There yer are, sweetheart, I was wondering where yer'd got to. Come and give yer old grandad a big kiss. I'm sorry I missed yer birthday, but I didn't call because I thought yer'd be out celebrating. I did think about yer, though, and there's a slab of chocolate in me pocket for yer.'

Laura was so relieved she rained kisses on his face. 'Thank you, Grandad, ye're a little love, that's what yer are.'

'Being sixteen is an important milestone in yer life, sweetheart, one yer'll look back on when yer get old and grey, like yer grandad. So I hope yer did something that yer enjoyed and will look back on with pleasure.'

Laura knew her mam and dad were looking on with interest and contented smiles on their faces. They'd believe anything she said. But it was the look on Jenny's face that unnerved her. It was almost as if her sister knew everything and was saying, 'Go on, let's see yer lie yerself out of that.'

Deliberately snubbing her sister by turning her back on her, Laura did the only thing she could, she brazened it out. She'd got herself in so deep now there was nothing else for it. 'I got loads of cards and presents, Grandad, they were brilliant. And me and me mate went to our first dance. I would have enjoyed that but Cynthia didn't feel well and we had to leave early.'

'Oh, what's the matter with her?' Mary didn't like Cynthia, but she wouldn't wish the girl any harm. After all, she'd been Laura's friend since they'd started school and as far as Mary knew, they'd never had a quarrel. 'Got a cold, has she?'

'Yeah, she had a sore throat and everything. She stopped off work yesterday and was in bed all day. I'm going down there now to see if she wants to go for a walk for half an hour, then I'll stay in with her.'

'Yer'll stay in all day with her?' Mary's voice was high, showing her surprise. My God, this was a turn-up for the books. Her daughter actually putting herself out for someone . . . it had never been known before. 'Yer mean yer won't go out tonight?'

Laura shook her head. 'I don't mind for one night. We'll listen to the wireless or play cards.' She took her coat down off the hook and shivered as her arms came into contact with the cold lining. 'I won't be in for tea, Mam, I'm having a bite at Cynthia's.' She gave Joe a big hug. 'Ta-ra, Grandad, I'll see yer soon.' With a wave of her hand she was gone.

'That's one out of the way,' Mary said. 'Can't you get yerself an invite somewhere for tea, sunshine, 'cos it'll be pot luck here.'

Jenny shook her head. 'It's too cold to go out just for the sake of it. I'll be going to Janet's about seven, but right now I'll stay in with me dad and Grandad and make a nuisance of meself.' Then her face lit up. 'I've got an idea! Why don't I go and get some meat pies for our tea? They'd be quick, easy, and there'd be no washing up after 'cos we could eat them in our hands.'

'That's a brilliant idea, sunshine. But first, while I'm getting meself ready, will yer fetch Grandad's dinner out of the oven before he starves to death? I can hear his tummy rumbling from here.'

Mary was walking between her two neighbours as they neared the wallpaper shop, and instinctively put her arm out to bar Amy from walking into the shop first. 'Hang on a minute, sunshine, let's get this straight. Just for once, can we go in a shop without you causing ructions and having the place up?'

Amy spread her arms wide and appealed to Molly. 'What would yer do with her? Any stranger listening to her would shy clear of me, thinking I was a troublemaker with a mouth on me yer could hear the other side of the Mersey. Me real friends and neighbours wouldn't think that, like, because they know I'm the quietest, most docile woman in the street. I never raise me voice or finger to anyone.'

'Oh I know, I know, me darlin',' Molly sympathised, 'it's always the wrong ones what get the blame. I've noticed it meself, so I have, and isn't it the same the whole world over?'

'Would you two like to stay out here and pay each other compliments while I go and choose me paper?'

Amy sprang to life and pushed Mary out of the way. 'Not bleedin' likely! I see as much of yer wallpaper as you do, so I think I'm entitled to some say in what I have to feast me eyes on every day.' She huffed with disgust. 'The bloody cheek of yer, Mary Nightingale, thinking about yerself as usual. I've a good mind not to visit yer any more.'

'Amy, sunshine, yer don't visit me, yer practically live with me. Sometimes, without thinking, I even set a place for yer at the table.' Mary gave Molly the nod and they each took an arm of Amy's and frogmarched her into the shop. 'Now behave.'

As soon as Amy was in the shop she came over all sweetness and light. 'Hello, George, how's the world treating yer?'

The man behind the counter scratched his head. 'My God, are me eyes deceiving me, or is it really Amy Hanley?'

Amy smiled, straightening her scarf and throwing her shoulders back. 'In the flesh, George, in the flesh.'

George kept his face straight. 'I must say ye're wearing well, Amy.

I expected yer face to be all wrinkled and yer hair snow-white, by now.'

Amy considered this carefully. She liked the bit about her wearing well, but wrinkled and snow-white hair? That didn't sound like a compliment. 'What the hell are yer on about, wrinkles and snow-white hair? It's not that bleedin' long since I saw yer, only since the last time we decorated.'

'And that's about four years ago!' Still there was no smile on the shopkeeper's face. 'It's a wonder the paper hasn't walked off yer ruddy wall in disgust. Yer've certainly had yer money's worth out of it.' George was warming up to it now. A set-to with Amy Hanley was as good as a pint of bitter any day. 'How d'yer expect men like me to make a living while there's skinflints like you around? Yer'd take the crust out of a baby's mouth, ye're that tight.'

Amy's hackles rose to the occasion. 'Listen to me, yer moaning, miserable sod. I brought me mate here for all the material to decorate her room, and that's a whopping big order. But after what yer've just said, I've a good mind to take her to the shop in Stanley Road and give them the custom.' Hitching her bosom up and giving little nods of her head, she went on: 'I was passing there last week, quite by accident, like, and they had a paper in the window that my friend would love. It was sky blue pink with a finny-haddy border.'

Mary gave Molly a nudge. 'Yer can talk to her until ye're blue in the face, but she never changes.'

'Now would yer be wanting her to change, me darlin'?'

'Would I heckerslike! I know which side me bread's buttered on, Molly. She saves me a fortune in not having to go to the pictures. I've never seen a film yet that can make me laugh as much as my mate can. She saves me money in other ways, too. You just watch her haggle with George. I bet she'll get a ha'penny knocked off a yard of border, a penny off a roll of paper, and if she's in good form I'll get coppers knocked off the tins of paint.'

'Sure, it's crafty yer are, Mary Nightingale.'

'Sure, and don't I know it, Molly Moynihan?'

159

Chapter Thirteen

'Ye're late,' Mary said, wagging a finger at Amy. 'I've been standing with me coat on since yer knocked on the wall, and that's a quarter of an hour ago. I suppose yer've been jangling, as usual?' Her tone changed to one of concern when she noted her friend's red face and heaving chest. 'Yer look all flustered, sunshine, is anything the matter?'

'I've been running and me heart's going fifteen to the dozen.' Amy, her palms flat on the table, inhaled deeply and blew out the breath through puckered lips. 'I'd just closed me front door after me, when I heard a cry. And when I looked to see where the noise came from, I saw old Lizzie lying on the ground outside her house. It gave me a fright, I can tell yer, I thought she'd dropped dead. The poor bugger had fallen down the steps and hurt herself. I tried every which way to pick her up, but every time I touched her she cried in pain. Yer'll have to come with me, girl, and see if we can manage her between us.'

'Oh, dear God, d'yer think she's broken anything? If she has, we shouldn't move her in case we do more harm. Best get an ambulance.'

'Will yer stop thinking the worst until we know for sure? I've got to say, girl, yer can be a right misery guts at times. Yer'll have her dead and buried before we know it. If she does peg out, it'll be from being left to lie on the ground, in freezing weather, and catching pneumonia while we're standing here playing guessing games.' Her wide hips swaying, Amy made for the door. 'Get a move on, girl, or yer'll be too late for the bleedin' funeral.'

As she stepped down on to the pavement, Mary said, 'I'll give Molly a knock, she's usually good at times like this.'

'Okay, but make it snappy.' When Amy looked to where she'd left Lizzie Marshall, who should she see standing over the frail figure, but her nosy neighbour, Annie Baxter. 'Wouldn't yer just know it! There's never a bleedin' show without Punch!' Not bothering to lower her voice, she went on as she hurried along, 'Never misses a trick, the nosy old cow. I bet she's licking her lips at the thought of knocking on every door in the neighbourhood with the news.'

'I'm glad ye're back, queen.' There was pleading in Lizzie's faded

161

blue eyes. Annie Baxter was not a favourite of hers and was the last person in the world she'd want to accept help from. 'Is Mary coming?'

'Yeah, she's knocking for Molly Moynihan. Between us we'll get yer back in the house and make yer comfortable before we see what yer've been and gone and done to yerself.'

'I offered to help her up,' Annie said, fussing as she tried in vain to get in front of Amy. She wanted a ringside seat so she didn't miss anything. 'But she wouldn't let me.'

Amy's eyes travelled the length of her neighbour. 'I see yer haven't got yer jungle drums with yer today, Annie. Or are yer using smoke signals, like Big Chief Sitting Bull?'

'Don't be so bleedin' funny, Amy Hanley. I'm just as concerned about Lizzie as you are, yer sarcastic mare.'

Lizzie stepped in before war was declared and Amy lost her temper and landed one on her neighbour. 'It's very kind of yer to be concerned, Annie, but there's no need. I'll be as right as rain when me friends get me inside.'

But Annie Baxter wasn't going to be dismissed so easily. She had as much right to stand in the street as that fat nosy cow from next door had. And with her thin arms crossed over her thin chest, and her thin lips clamped together, she stood her ground. Even when Mary and Molly came dashing down, she didn't move an inch, even though she was preventing them from seeing to the old lady. Amy stood it for so long, then decided enough was enough and grabbed her arm. She turned her towards the top of the street, saying, 'That's the way to Lily Farmer's. She's usually first on yer list so yer may as well stick to yer routine. And if yer want to spice yer story up a bit, yer can say Lizzie was wearing bright red fleecy-lined knickers with a pocket in. She's not, of course, but yer mate won't know that, and I won't snitch.'

If looks could kill, Amy would have been a dead duck. 'Anyone would think yer owned the bleedin' street, the way yer carry on. But ye're only the monkey, not the organ grinder.'

'Go away, will yer, missus, before I lose me temper. If yer fancy lying beside Lizzie on the bleedin' ground, just say the word because me hands are itching to thump yer one.'

Annie waited until she was far enough away for safety, before calling, 'I'll tell my feller about you, Amy Hanley. He'll be round to see yer.'

'I'll look forward to that, Gabby Annie! Tell him I'm free next Tuesday night.'

While this exchange was going on, Mary had opened Lizzie's front door, while Molly scooped up the old lady and cradled her in her arms like a baby. 'I don't think yer've broken anything, me darlin', or yer'd be screaming in pain, so yer would. But let's get yer inside and give yer the once-over.'

Lizzie Marshall was a spinster. She'd lived in the street since her parents died, many years ago. She'd been forced to move out of the three-bedroomed house that she'd been born in, because with just her wage coming in, she couldn't afford the rent or the upkeep of it. She was small and frail now, with wispy white hair, faded blue eyes and deep wrinkles on her face. Living on a pittance, she managed to keep her house spotlessly clean and there was never a moan out of her.

'Put those two cushions together for her head,' Molly said, laying the old lady down as gently as if she was a piece of Dresden china. 'There yer go, me darlin', we'll soon have yer as snug as a bug in a rug.' She turned to Mary who was standing wringing her hands. 'Nip up and get a blanket off the bed, she's shivering with cold.'

'I'll put the kettle on,' Amy said, springing into action. 'A cup of weak, sweet tea is the best medicine for shock. And yer could do with a few more cobs of coal on the fire.'

'I'm not cold,' Lizzie said quickly. She could only afford one bag of coal a fortnight but was too proud to say so. 'I haven't got much coal until the coalman comes, so I'm having to eke it out.'

Mary came into the room at that moment, and glanced from Molly to Amy. It was only three days since the coalman was round; there was no way Lizzie could have used it all in a couple of days. Unless, of course, the old lady couldn't afford to buy any. 'We'll all lend yer a bucket of coal, Lizzie, so don't be worrying. The main thing is to get you warmed through to the marrow before yer get pneumonia.' She shook the folded blanket she'd brought down with her and tucked it around the shivering woman. 'I'll tell yer what, sunshine, yer house is a credit to yer. Yer put the three of us to shame.'

'You ain't kidding,' Amy said, coming back after putting the kettle on. 'Yer could eat yer bleedin' dinner off the floor out there.'

Lizzie smiled with pleasure, even though every part of her was hurting. 'I do me best. I've never forgotten what my mother used to tell me. "Never let housework get on top of yer. Do a bit every day, then yer'll never have a dirty house".' A look of sadness came to the faded blue eyes. 'It's thirty years since she died, but I've never forgotten her, or me dad. They were wonderful parents.'

'Sure, wouldn't they have to be, to have brought a lovely lady like you into the world?' Molly sat down on the edge of the couch and lifted one of the thin hands. 'Will yer let me run me hand up yer arm, me darlin'? I'll be as gentle as I can, but shout out if I hurt yer.'

Lizzie nodded. 'I trust yer, Molly.'

The kettle began to whistle and Amy jumped to her feet. 'I'll pour the water into the pot and leave it to brew for a while.'

When Lizzie shuddered, Molly quickly took her hand away. 'Does that hurt, me darlin'?'

The old lady nodded. 'It's very painful.'

'Right, we'll have a cup of tea then take yer jumper off to see what's what.' Molly smiled into the lined face. 'Yer haven't broken anything, sweetheart, so that's a blessing.'

Mary glanced towards the kitchen. 'Amy Hanley, have yer gone to China for that ruddy tea? We're all spitting feathers in here.'

'Ay, I'm seeing to the invalid.' Amy appeared, carefully carrying a cup and saucer. 'You can see to yer ruddy self, ye're ugly enough.' She handed the saucer to Molly. 'You hold it, girl, in case Lizzie spills it on herself.'

The old lady looked flustered. 'I've only got a drop of milk, I was on me way to the shops to get some when I fell.'

'That's all right, sunshine, we're not dying of thirst.' Mary felt sorry for the proud old lady who'd never been known to borrow or cadge off anyone. 'We'll see to yer bit of shopping, so don't worry.'

The drink seemed to perk Lizzie up. She licked her lips and said, 'That's the best cup of tea I've ever had.'

Molly took the cup from her and handed it to Amy, who was hovering by the end of the couch. Then she stroked Lizzie's cheek. 'Lean forward, me darlin', and I'll roll yer jumper up from the back. It'll be over yer head in the blink of an eye, so it will.'

Lizzie was covered in bruises, particularly down the right side, where she'd landed. They were only just beginning to colour, but as Molly said, 'Tomorrow they'll be black and blue, me darlin', and very sore. Best if yer stay in and rest for a few days.'

'I wouldn't be able to go out, Molly, 'cos I think I've broke me ankle.'

'I don't think yer'll have broken it, sweetheart, or they'd hear yer screaming down at the Pier Head. But yer may have sprained it when yer fell. Let's take yer shoes and stockings off and have a gander.' Molly sat nursing the painful foot. 'It's not broken, me darlin', or it would be swelled up like a balloon. But yer've sprained it all right and yer won't be able to walk on it for a few days.'

'How's she going to get up the stairs to bed, then?' Amy wanted to know. 'Or down the yard to the lavvy?'

'With our help, that's how,' Mary said. 'We'll make up a bed on the couch so she's nice and comfy, and we'll give her an arm to lean on while she hops down the yard.'

Molly saw the worried frown on Lizzie's face and patted her gently. 'It's only for a few days, me darlin', and won't it be nice to be waited on hand and foot?'

'I'm going to be a nuisance to yer, I'm sorry.'

'Don't be so daft!' Amy felt like picking the old lady up and taking her home, where there was a nice fire roaring up the chimney. 'There's three of us, we'll take turns looking after yer.'

'Then let's start now,' Molly said briskly. 'Mary, if Lizzie doesn't mind, will yer see to the bedding? Oh, and bring a nightdress and something to wrap around her shoulders. And Amy, will you bank the fire up, me darlin', then make Lizzie another cup of tea?' The Irishwoman winked at Amy. 'Sure, I can see in yer eyes what yerself is thinking, Amy me darlin'. So I'll answer yer and save yer the trouble of asking. I'm off home to get a bucket of coal to fill the scuttle and some milk to keep Lizzie in drinks until one of us goes to the shops.'

The small house became a hive of activity and Lizzie began to enjoy herself. It was nice to have people for a change, to hear a human voice instead of just the steady ticking of the clock. She never had visitors and sometimes felt very lonely as each dreary day dragged on to another dreary day. But the house was ringing now with the sound of Mary's laughter and Amy's antics, and although she was in pain, the old lady was thinking her fall was a blessing in disguise.

When Molly came back with the coal and milk, it was to see the old lady looking much brighter and contented. She had a clean nightdress on, with a maroon cardi over her shoulders, and her head was resting on three feather pillows.

'Well, now, don't you look the posh one? Sure 'tis the life of Riley himself yer'll be having for the next few days.' Molly placed a jug of milk on the table before emptying the bucket of coal into the brass coal scuttle at the side of the hearth. 'That should keep yer going until tonight.'

'I'll send our John down with another bucket when he's had his dinner,' Amy said. 'He'll bank the fire up so it lasts all through the night and keeps the room warm.'

'There's no need,' Lizzie said, afraid she'd never be able to pay these women back. 'I don't feel the cold.'

'While ye're lying there, Lizzie Marshall, yer'll do as ye're told. I'll ask our Jenny to come down and sit with yer for an hour, keep yer company. And when it's time for bed, one of us will come and help yer to the lavvy before settling yer down for the night.'

Molly turned her head away so they couldn't see the grin on her face. John and Jenny coming here tonight, eh? Didn't that give Amy's son an unfair advantage? She'd have to pass that bit of information on to Mick, so she would, otherwise he'd be left at the starting post.

'Look, Mary and Amy, you two go and get yer shopping done. I'll stay with Lizzie until dinnertime, then one of you can take over.'

'Are yer sure, Molly?' Mary asked. 'I feel a bit mean, leaving yer.'

'Nonsense!' Molly shooed them out of the room. 'I couldn't pass me time in better company than Lizzie's. We'll have a great time, altogether, pulling everyone to pieces.' But her face became serious when she was showing her neighbours out. 'She seems fine, but I think we should keep our eyes on her for a few days. I'm not worried about the bruises, they'll not kill her. But Lizzie is eighty years of age, so she is, and a fall can be a terrible shock to the system.'

'Yeah, I've been thinking of that meself.' Mary sighed as she linked her arm through Amy's. 'We'll get her a few groceries to keep her going, and go half each with the cost. Is that all right with you, sunshine?'

'Yer've no need to ask, girl, yer know that.' Amy's voice was choked. 'She's a ruddy hero, that old lady, d'yer know that? She keeps her house beautiful, like a little palace. But her cupboards are bare. There's nowt to eat in the kitchen, not even a crumb to give to the birds. It's no wonder she fell, she must be as weak as a kitten and light-headed with hunger.'

'We'll feed her up in the next few days,' Molly said, 'and watch out for her in future. But we'll have to be careful how we do it. She's a proud old lady and would be offended if she thought we were doing it out of pity.' She began to close the door. 'I'll get back to her now and see if she wants to spend a penny.'

In the Nightingale house, the family were seated around the table eating their dinner as Mary told of the day's events. 'Honest to God, there's not a pick on her, she's as thin as a rake. Molly picked her up as though she was a baby. But what a little love she is. I felt like hugging the life out of her.'

'Yeah, she's a nice little thing, always got a pleasant smile for yer,' Stan said. 'And she does well for her age, her windows and step are always the cleanest in the street.'

Jenny's eyes were full of concern. 'I hope she wasn't hurt bad, Mam? I think she's lovely, like a little doll.'

'She's full of bruises, and they must be sore because she's got no flesh on her. But a week's rest, staying in the warmth, should see a great improvement.' Mary pushed her plate back and rested her elbows on the table. 'I want one of yer to sit with her for a few hours tonight, just to keep her company so she's not dwelling on things.'

For the first time, Laura showed interest in the conversation. It was Thursday, her night for Barlow's Lane and Gary. She hadn't seen him since last week and she was going tonight come hell or high water. 'Ah, ay, Mam! I'm going dancing tonight – I've made arrangements! Anyway, I don't want to sit with an old woman, I wouldn't know what to talk about.'

'I'll go, Mam,' Jenny said quickly, before her mother could speak.

'Me and Janet will sit with her – we'd like that.'

Mary sighed as she looked at her eldest daughter. Selfish to the core, as usual. There was only one person she cared about and that was herself. But angry words wouldn't change her so what was the point in getting herself all worked up for nothing? So Mary smiled at Jenny as she thanked God that both sisters were not alike. 'Thanks, sunshine, I might have known yer wouldn't let me down. I've got Miss Marshall's key and I told her someone would be there about seven. So get yerself ready and go round for Janet.'

Jenny's chair scraped back. 'I'll wash the dishes first.'

'No, yer won't,' Stan said, 'Laura will wash the dishes.'

Laura's face was like thunder and a sharp retort was on the tip of her tongue. But it stayed there, because her father's face told her he would brook no argument. So it was with ill-grace she collected the plates and made for the kitchen.

In the house next door sat the Hanley family, and Amy had just finishing telling them the news. Mealtimes in the household were usually lively, with the house ringing with laughter. But tonight was different, as Miss Marshall was well liked by them all. The two boys, John and Eddy, were remembering that when they were younger, never once had the old lady chased them when they were playing footie outside her house. Never shook a clenched fist at them nor threatened to tell their mother like the other neighbours did. And Edna was thinking of the times Miss Marshall had given her a ha'penny for going on a message.

'Is the old girl going to be all right?' Ben asked. 'Shouldn't she have a doctor?'

'We decided to wait and see how she is tomorrow.' Amy cupped her chin in her hand. 'I'll tell yer what, that Molly Moynihan is as good as any doctor. Like Florence Nightingale she was. Me and Mary wouldn't have had a bleedin' clue what to do, but Molly did.' She gave her eldest son a dig in the ribs. 'By the way, I want yer to take a bucketful of coal over and bank the fire up for Lizzie.'

'I'll go now then, 'cos I'm going out later.'

'It's no good going before seven 'cos yer won't get in. Mary took the door key so one of the girls can let themselves in to sit with Lizzie for a couple of hours. It'll probably be Jenny – I can't see the other selfish so-and-so helping out.'

John's spirits lifted. He'd get there for seven and pull a fast one on Mick. 'Okay, I wasn't going anywhere exciting, anyway.'

In the house opposite, the Moynihan family were discussing the same subject. 'So, with one thing and another, it's been quite a day,' Molly said. 'But, thanks be to God, she'd only just fallen when Amy

167

saw her. If she'd been left to lie on the ground for long, in this weather, she'd have died of cold, and that's the truth of it.'

'Is there anything I can do, sweetheart?' Seamus asked. 'Sure, haven't I always had a soft spot for the dear old soul? I bet there's never been an angry word passed her lips, nor a swearword; she's too much of a lady for that.'

'We're sorted out for today, everything's under control. Amy's sending John down with coal and he's going to bank the fire up to last through the night. And Mary's going down last thing to take Lizzie down the yard.' Molly was facing her husband but her eyes were looking sideways to where her son was sitting. 'Oh, and young Jenny is going to sit with Lizzie for a couple of hours to keep her company.'

Mick stopped chewing and his mouth fell open. But he quickly recovered when the implication of what his mother had said hit home. He swallowed the food in his mouth and put down his knife and fork. There were more important things at stake than food. He racked his brain to think of something that would put him on a level pegging with John, but his usually sharp mind was lacking in ideas. 'I'll take her some coal, as well, to save you ladies having to lug it down tomorrow.'

Molly kept her face straight. 'I've told yer, me darlin', John's taking a bucketful. If you turn up with another, the old lady will have a fit, so she will.'

'Well, I'm going down with something, I'm not letting John Hanley have a clear field.' Mick nodded his head for emphasis. 'I bet he's laughing sacks, having it handed to him on a flamin' platter.'

Seamus felt his wife kick him gently on the ankle, and turned to see the laughter in her eyes. 'You could go down tomorrow night, son, that would make it fair. Anyway, aren't yer supposed to be going out with John? So he won't be spending much time there, will he?'

'Huh! Yer don't think he'll be thinking of me, do yer? Not on yer blinking life, he won't. If Jenny's there he'll stay put. Not even Jean Harlow would get him out.' Mick glared at his mother. 'Why didn't yer say I'd take the coal down?'

Molly leaned across the table and gave him a broad wink. 'Well, yer see, me darlin', I thought Miss Marshall would appreciate a homemade custard instead.'

When the words had sunk in, Mick's eyes shone and his dimples appeared. 'D'yer mean yer've made her a custard?'

'I have that, me darlin'. And although I say it as shouldn't, it looks very appetising, so it does. Lovely golden brown, with a pinch of nutmeg on the top.'

'Mam, ye're an angel. And a clever one at that.'

'Perhaps devious would be a better word. But, sure, I couldn't stand back and see me only son and heir left out in the cold.'

Mick jumped to his feet. 'I'm going to get washed and put a clean shirt on.' He got halfway up the stairs, stopped for a second then turned and came down again. Poking his head around the door, a wide smile on his handsome face, he asked, 'Would yer say that a custard was a better present than a bucket of coal?'

Seamus dropped his head back and roared with laughter. 'Sure, now, that would mightily depend upon whether yer were hungry or cold.'

When they were alone, the big Irishman put his arm around his wife's shoulder. ' 'Tis a bit of the divil himself yer have in yer, Molly Moynihan, and that's a fact.'

She met his eyes and the love she had for her husband was there to see. 'I've two men in me life, Seamus Moynihan, and if they need a little help from me, then I'll always do me best. But, sure, I'll not be making friends with the divil to do it.'

Jenny pulled two of the wooden chairs away from the table and set them in front of the couch. 'There now, we won't have to raise our voices to hear each other.'

Lizzie Marshall smiled. 'It's very kind of you to come and sit with an old woman. But young girls should be out enjoying themselves. Haven't yer got boyfriends?'

Jenny got a fit of the giggles. 'We're too young to go out with boys, Miss Marshall.' She turned to her friend, who was blushing to the roots of her hair. 'Anyway, no one will have us, will they, Jan?'

'They will when we're a bit older.' Janet was quite indignant. 'Another few months and me mam said I can go dancing.' She narrowed her eyes. 'Have you asked yer mam yet if you can come with me?'

'Not yet, but I think I could get round her. Especially if I'm going with you.'

Lizzie was visibly startled when there was a loud ran-tan at the door. 'Oh dear, I wonder who this can be at this hour?'

'It'll only be John Hanley, Miss Marshall, don't be frightened. Me mam told me he was coming with some coal. I'll let him in.'

But when Jenny opened the door it was to see Mick standing there with a plate in his hand, covered by a pure white cloth. 'Me mam thought Miss Marshall might fancy this for her supper.'

'Oh, I thought it was John knocking.'

Mick feigned surprise. 'Why, is he coming over?'

Jenny nodded as she held out her hand. 'I'll take it, shall I?'

But Mick wouldn't have parted with the plate for all the tea in China. After all, she wouldn't be asking John to hand a bucket of coal over, it would be too heavy. 'No, I'd like to give it her meself, and ask how she is. It would be bad manners not to pay me respects. And me mam is red-hot on respect. If I went home and said I'd just handed the plate in and didn't see the invalid, I'd get a clip around the ears for not being polite.' His white teeth shone in the darkness. 'And yer wouldn't like me to get a clip around the ears, would yer, Jenny Nightingale?'

Jenny's peal of laughter rang out in the deserted street. 'Mick Moynihan, has anybody ever told yer that yer talk too much?'

John Hanley had just closed the door behind him when he heard Jenny's laughter. A smile came to his face but quickly disappeared when he saw Mick standing outside Miss Marshall's house with a plate in his hand. Then he started to leg it across the cobbles. There was some dirty work at the crossroads going on here – his mam hadn't mentioned anything about Mick. The bucket was banging against his leg, but he didn't slow down, even though he had his best pair of kecks on. The only thing on his mind was to stop his rival from setting foot in that house. But he was too late. Mick was already mounting the step when he reached the pavement opposite. 'Don't close the door, Jenny,' he shouted. 'This bucket is heavy.'

Mick stood in the tiny hall and feigned surprise at the sight of his mate. Jenny had gone inside with the plate, so she wasn't there to hear him tell fibs. 'Well, well! Fancy seeing you here, mate.'

'I'm supposed to be here, you're not!' Although John was none too pleased that things hadn't gone according to plan, he secretly admitted he was being underhanded as well, so he was as guilty as his friend. Changing the bucket over to the other hand, he asked, 'How did yer pull it off, yer devious swine?'

Mick tapped the end of his nose with a finger. 'That's for me to know, and you to find out. But I don't put a foot outside this door until you do. Now, shall we make our presence known, or have yer become attached to that bucket of coal?'

'I feel like throwing it over yer, if yer want to know. I've got me best trousers on and they'll be as black as the hobs of hell.'

Lizzie, who never had a visitor, had seen so many people in her house today she was dizzy. But oh, wasn't it lovely to have company? Particularly in the evening, which was the loneliest time of the day. 'Well, two pretty girls and two handsome lads, aren't I lucky?'

'I can see the two pretty girls, Miss Marshall,' Jenny said, nudging Janet and giggling, 'but where are the handsome lads?'

John was quick to reply. 'She doesn't recognise me, 'cos I'm covered in coaldust.' He took out a hankie and wiped a cheek. 'There yer are, Jenny, it's me.'

'I know it's you, soft lad, but I want to know where the handsome lads are.'

'I'm saying nothing,' Mick said. 'It doesn't do to blow yer own trumpet.'

'Well, I think ye're both very handsome,' said Lizzie, 'and if I wasn't seven times older than yer, I'd be fluttering me eyelashes and going all coy.'

John, still lumbered with the bucket, asked, 'Shall I put this in the kitchen and bank the fire up before I go, Miss Marshall?'

'You've got a date, haven't yer, John?' There was a mischievous twinkle in Mick's eyes. 'So there's no need for you to stay, I'll see to the fire.'

'Over my dead body, mate. When I go, you go.'

'Oh, ye've both got dates, have yer?' Jenny said, before turning to her friend. 'Yer see, Jan, there'll be no fellers left by the time we're fifteen. Just our luck, eh?'

'Neither of us have got dates,' Mick said, turning the corners of his mouth down in an expression of self-pity. 'No girls will have us 'cos we're too ugly.'

'Ah, yer poor things.' Jenny put a hand to her heart in a show of sympathy. 'I don't think ye're that ugly, do you, Jan?'

Janet thought they were two very handsome lads but was enjoying the leg-pull. 'No, not really ugly. I mean, in the dark they could be mistaken for Cary Grant and Gary Cooper.'

'That's where we're going wrong, John,' Mick said. 'We should stay indoors during the day and only come out at night, like Dracula.'

Lizzie was taking all this in and thoroughly enjoying herself. She wasn't missing anything, either. Unless she was very much mistaken, both boys had their eyes on Jenny. It was understandable because she was a lovely girl, in looks and in personality. But both boys couldn't be winners, so it would be interesting to see what happened in the next year or so.

'Can I put this bucket down, Miss Marshall?' John asked. 'Otherwise I'll have one arm a yard longer than the other.'

'Put it in the kitchen, dear, and then you and Mick sit down and keep us company.' Lizzie had a hard time keeping her laughter at bay as she watched Mick take advantage of John's brief absence. Within seconds he had pulled a chair from the table and plonked himself next to Jenny. And John's face when he returned was a study, as he tried to think of a way to usurp his mate. She could almost hear him thinking, and when his face lit up she knew he'd found a solution.

'I know, let's have a game of pass the parcel. And the one what gets left with the parcel, has to do a forfeit.' John thought his idea was brilliant. 'We'll have to spread out, though, so let's put the chairs back around the table.'

Lizzie gave him ten out of ten for initiative. Nevertheless, the idea didn't appeal to her. 'I'm too long in the tooth to be doing forfeits, John.'

'Yer wouldn't have to, Miss Marshall, you could be referee. Yer just turn yer head away, so yer can't see, and clap yer hands when yer want us to stop.'

Mick wasn't about to be moved from his prime position so easily. 'Where are yer going to get a parcel from?'

'It doesn't have to be a proper parcel,' said John, equally determined. 'A piece of coal wrapped in paper will do.'

'Oo, er, what kind of forfeit?' Janet wanted to know. 'I can't sing or dance, and I don't know any jokes.'

'Don't be so miserable, Jan!' Jenny thought it was a good way of entertaining Miss Marshall. 'Yer know nursery rhymes, don't yer?'

Janet looked relieved. 'Is that all I have to do?'

They were being too longwinded for John's liking. At this rate Mick would still be sitting pretty next to Jenny when it was time to go. He took hold of Janet's arm and lifted her from the chair. 'That's all yer have to do, Janet, so sit at the table and Jenny will sit next to yer. Me and Mick will sit the other side.'

For the next two hours, Lizzie Marshall laughed more than she'd ever laughed in her life. The two boys were really comical as they tried to outdo each other. When Mick got caught with the parcel, he chose to sing a song. He had a fine voice, too, but it was drowned out when John decided his whistling would make a fine accompaniment. And when it was John's turn to pay a forfeit, Mick used the table as a set of drums while Jenny and Janet hummed completely out of tune.

The girls didn't get off scot-free, either. While Jenny was reciting *Goldilocks and the Three Bears*, the boys were doing all the actions in such an exaggerated way everyone was reduced to fits of laughter. But Janet's contribution, *Jack and Jill*, had John shaking his head vigorously. 'You can get the pail of water, Mick. I'm not lifting that ruddy bucket again for no one, never mind running up a hill with it.'

Mary had her hand on the knocker when she heard shrieks of laughter. 'In the name of God,' she muttered, 'what's our Jenny thinking about! Lizzie is supposed to be resting, not having a flaming party!' When there was no response to her knock, she rapped on the window and had a sharp rebuke on her tongue when the door opened.

'Mick Moynihan, what the hell's going on here? Just wait until I see our Jenny, she should have more sense.' She brushed the startled boy aside and entered the room, ready to do battle. But when she saw Lizzie wiping tears of laughter from her eyes, and looking happier than she'd ever seen her, Mary had the rug pulled from under her feet. 'Well, I declare!'

'Oh Mary, yer should have been here, yer don't know what yer've missed.'

'Aren't you supposed to be sick, Lizzie Marshall, with pains everywhere?'

'Oh, I've still got the pains, worse than ever.' The faded blue eyes twinkled back at Mary. 'But how can yer lie still when ye're doubled up with laughter? I've got pains now where I didn't have them before. But isn't it better to be in agony when ye're happy, than be in agony when ye're on yer own and feeling miserable? I've had the time of me life tonight, Mary, thanks to these four young people.' She grinned as she added, 'Oh, and a bucket of coal.'

'I've been keeping me eye on her, Mam,' Jenny said. 'I made sure she wasn't doing anything to hurt herself.'

'I've been keeping watch, too!' Mick said.

'I made her a cup of tea, Mrs Nightingale,' came from John.

Mary was beginning to see the funny side of it. She looked at Janet and asked, 'What about you, Janet, what have you got to say for yerself?'

Janet was surprised by the question. 'Er . . . I enjoyed meself, Mrs Nightingale.' And she was even more surprised by the burst of laughter. She didn't think she'd said anything funny, but joined in, anyway.

Mary looked at the clock. 'Right, time yer were on yer way so I can get Miss Marshall settled for the night. Jenny, you and Janet tidy up while John sees to the fire.'

Wanting to curry favour with the woman he hoped would one day be his mother-in-law, Mick asked, 'Have yer got a job for me, Mrs Nightingale?'

Before Mary could answer, John said, 'I have, mate. Yer can get that bucket of ruddy coal. And if yer can manage it, bang it against yer leg a few times so yer kecks are as black as mine.'

When they were leaving, Jenny was the first to kiss Lizzie. The other three looked uncertain, until Mick bent and kissed her cheek, then they all followed suit. The smile on the old lady's face couldn't have been wider. 'Thank you for giving me a lot of pleasure. And seeing as the girls can't get boyfriends because they're too young, and the boys can't get girlfriends because they're too ugly, there'll always be a welcome here if ye're ever at a loose end.'

Mick got in just before John. 'How about tomorrow night?'

'Ay, two nights on the trot is too much, Mick Moynihan.' Mary herded them towards the front door. 'She seems to have enjoyed herself, and I thank yer for that, but let's wait and see how she is tomorrow. It might prove to have been too much for her.' She was about to close the door, when she remembered. 'Oh, and make sure Janet gets home safely.'

'We'll make sure the two girls get home safe and sound, Mrs Nightingale,' Mick said, 'so don't be worrying.'

John thought his mate was getting all the action, so he added his twopennyworth. 'Yer can rely on us.'

Jenny and her friend linked arms and started walking back to Janet's house, unaware of the jostling for position that was going on behind them. Apart from splitting the girls, there was no way they could both walk beside Jenny. So John said, through gritted teeth, 'You go first, but we swop over halfway, d'yer hear?'

'Anything yer say, pal.' Mick's mind was elsewhere. Could he talk his mam into making another custard tomorrow?

And as John fell into step beside Janet, he was telling himself to keep his working trousers on tomorrow night when he took the coal over.

Chapter Fourteen

Laura gave a quick glance at her friend's house as she passed it on the next Thursday evening, wondering if Cynthia was getting ready for one of her twice-weekly visits to the Scotland Road area. Laura never thought for one minute that she'd keep it up, but this was the fourth week and her friend was more bitter and determined than ever. Every Tuesday and Thursday she left the house in flat-heeled shoes, wearing her working coat and with a scarf in her pocket to wrap around her head as soon as she neared her destination. She hadn't seen hide nor hair of Jeff or Larry, but she insisted she'd keep on looking until she spotted them, even if it took her a lifetime.

Laura hopped on to the platform of the tram and made her way to a seat. She missed going out with her mate on a Tuesday night, but not on Thursday, her night for the dance at Spellow Lane. Her dancing had come on in leaps and bounds, thanks to Gary. He partnered her for every dance, was attentive to her, and really seemed to like her. Yet he'd never asked her for a date, and she couldn't understand this. Unless it was because Celia insisted on leaving with her at half-ten – this was enough to put any boy off. He probably thought she wasn't capable of looking after herself. There were times when Laura regretted ever getting involved with her grandad's wife, then she'd remind herself that if she hadn't, she'd never have met Gary.

Her heart beating with anticipation, Laura ran up the flight of stone steps and pushed open the door to the foyer of the dance hall. The first person she saw was Celia, leaning with her back to the wall and deep in conversation with Charlie. But as soon as she saw Laura, she hurried towards her and made a big show of greeting her with a hug and kiss. 'Hi-ya, kid, it's good to see yer.'

This fussing every week was beginning to grate on Laura. There was no need for it; girls didn't kiss each other, it was soppy. She'd known Cynthia all her life, but never once had they kissed each other. Bringing her friend to mind gave Laura an idea: she'd coax Cynthia to come with her next week, then there would be no reason for Celia to stick to her like glue.

'I'll just put me coat in the cloakroom.' Some of the girls folded their coats and put them under chairs, but not Laura. She'd only had this coat two weeks and didn't want it to get creased or dirty. 'You go in, I'll see yer inside.'

Gary claimed her as soon as she walked in the dance hall. 'Just in time for a slow fox, babe, come on.'

Laura scanned the faces around them. 'Where's Celia? She can mind me bag.'

'Hang it over yer arm for now, the dance will be ended soon.' As they were twirling past the stage, Gary took the bag from her and placed it near the pianist. 'Keep yer eye on that for us, Tommy.'

When the dance came to an end, he kept hold of her hand and walked her to the edge of the dance floor. 'There's no point in sitting down, we may as well stay up for the next dance. It should be a waltz or a rumba.'

With a handsome boy holding her hand, Laura was flushed with pleasure. He must like me, she thought, or he wouldn't want to be with me all the time. There's plenty of unattached girls he could take his pick from, but he's only interested in me. Perhaps tonight was the night he'd ask her for a date. They laughed and joked their way through three more dances, then Laura called a halt. 'I'll have to look for Celia, I haven't seen her since I came in. She'll think I'm terrible, not going near her.'

'I wouldn't worry about that,' Gary said. 'Celia is more than capable of looking after herself, believe me.'

Laura thought there was a funny look in his eyes, but it was soon gone and she put it down to her imagination. 'Still, I think I should put in an appearance.'

'Suit yerself. I'll have the next dance with Dorothy then. I've been neglecting her since you came on the scene.'

Laura pulled him back. 'Oh no, yer won't have the next dance with Dorothy, whoever she is. I'll find Celia in the interval. Mind you, I've been keeping an eye out for her and haven't seen sight nor light of her since I came in.'

'She's probably sitting down somewhere, talking to Charlie.'

This gave Laura the opportunity of asking something that had been puzzling her for the last four weeks. 'Is Charlie a very good friend of hers?'

Gary averted his eyes as he shrugged his shoulders. 'Charlie's a friend to everyone, especially if they happen to be female. He's got an eye for the girls.'

It was on the tip of Laura's tongue to ask if that included married women, but she thought better of it. After all, Gary was a friend of Celia and Charlie; he might repeat anything she said. 'Yeah, I gathered he was fond of women.'

'I think there's only one more dance before the interval, and she'll probably come looking for you then.'

176

Gary was right. But then he would be, because he knew full well where Celia was. He'd been given his instructions to keep Laura occupied for at least half an hour. They were walking off the dance floor, hand in hand, when Celia came through the door, followed by Charlie who was straightening his tie. She spotted them right away and made directly for them, leaving Charlie to stand just inside the door where all the men congregated during the interval. 'There's a couple of empty chairs over there, kid, let's grab them quick.'

'You go ahead,' Laura said, 'I want to get me handbag off the stage.' On her way back, skirting the people standing around in groups, her eyes lighted on Gary. He stood out in the crowd because of his light-blond hair. Then she saw him bend towards Celia and the expression on the woman's face halted Laura in her tracks. There was no smile now on the heavily made-up face, and the words pouring from her mouth appeared to be angry ones. I wonder what she's on about, Laura thought. She's giving the pay-out about something.

Laura approached them from the side, hoping to hear something that would give her an inkling about what was going on. But Gary saw her coming and straightened up. 'Yer didn't have to worry about yer bag, babe, Tommy would have kept his eye on it.'

'He'd have a job, seeing as the band have left the stage. All me worldly goods are in this bag. I wouldn't even have the fare home if it got pinched.'

'I wouldn't see yer without, love, yer know that.' Celia patted the seat of the empty chair next to her. 'Come on, park yer carcass.' Smiling sweetly, she took a cigarette out of the packet on her knee. After lighting it, she asked, 'Don't yer smoke, Laura?'

'No, I'm too young,' Laura said, 'and anyway, me mam would kill me.'

'Yer mean yer work in the tobacco works, and yer don't smoke! I thought everyone got an allowance of free ciggies there. What d'yer do with them?'

'I give a packet to me dad and the rest to me mate, Cynthia.' Laura was lying. She sold her free cigarettes to a woman in work whose husband smoked like a chimney. 'Me mate's parents don't mind, but mine would.'

'Well, yer parents are not here, kid, and what the eye don't see, the heart don't grieve.' Celia held the open packet towards her. 'I was younger than you when I started smoking, it's the fashion these days. Go on, be daring.'

Laura could feel Gary's eyes on her, but she didn't look up. If she had, she would have seen the slight shake of his head and acted differently, knowing he was on her side. She didn't want to smoke, but was afraid of being thought old-fashioned. She hesitated, then reached out to take one of the cigarettes and held it awkwardly between her fingers.

There was a gloating expression on Celia's face as she struck a match. But as she was about to hold the flame to the cigarette now dangling between Laura's lips, Gary bent down and stayed her hand. 'Don't breathe in deeply, Laura, or yer'll feel sick and go dizzy. Just take a little puff, and if yer don't like it then don't smoke it.'

'Don't be a misery guts, Gary.' There was a warning in Celia's eyes as she blew out the match which was threatening to burn her fingers. If she could hook Laura on to smoking, it was another thing to add to her list. 'Leave the girl alone and go and amuse yerself elsewhere.'

Gary nodded curtly. 'I'll go to the gents, but I'll be back for the first dance, babe.'

Celia struck another match. 'Gary's right, just a little puff to begin with.'

Laura coughed when the smoke hit the back of her throat and wafted into her eyes, making them water. 'Ooh, I don't like it.'

'Yer haven't given it a chance, kid! Leave it for a minute and then have another go,' Celia coaxed. 'The first cigarette always makes yer feel like that. I remember going down an entry to have my first, with one of me mates. We were only fourteen and we'd bought a packet of five Woodies between us. We had to smoke the five because neither of us would take them home with us in case our mothers found them. I remember we both staggered out of that entry and our faces were green. But next time we tried, it was all right. I don't know about me mate, Sally Greenfield, but I've been smoking ever since. I think a girl looks sophisticated with a cigarette in her hand, particularly if it's in a holder. I've got a long ebony holder and I feel like the pig's ear when I use it.' A sneer crossed her face. 'Mind you, if I used it here they wouldn't know what it was. They haven't a clue about fashion, or how to look glamorous.'

Laura held the cigarette upright between finger and thumb and watched the smoke spiralling upwards. What harm would it do? Most of the women in work smoked, and her dad did too! And after all, she didn't need to have another one after this, not if she didn't want to. So she lifted the cigarette to her lips, but was careful this time not to inhale the smoke. 'I've been thinking, Celia, it's daft you leaving early every week because of me. I'll get Cynthia to come with me next week and we can go home together.'

'No, you mustn't do that!' The words shot from Celia's lips. 'If she lets slip that yer meet me here, yer mam will find out and the sparks will fly. She'll know yer've been telling lies about everything and yer'll land yerself in a load of trouble. So forget the idea, kid, 'cos I don't want to find myself in the middle of a family row.'

Laura was taken aback. 'But Cynthia wouldn't say anything, she's me best mate! And we could always say we'd met yer here by chance.'

'I said nothing doing, kid. You bring yer mate here and I'll find another dance to go to. And Charlie and Gary will come with me.'

Laura was about to blurt out that it wasn't fair! If Cynthia wanted to come here, no one had the right to stop her. But one look at Celia's angry face told her the older woman meant every word she said. And that in turn meant she wouldn't see Gary again. She couldn't care less about Charlie, she'd never exchanged more than a dozen words with him and she didn't like the man anyway. But she did care about Gary. And although she couldn't fathom out why he should do as Celia told him, she knew without doubt that he would. The same as she was going to do. It seemed as though Celia had a hold on each of them. 'Okay, I won't mention it to Cynthia just in case.'

'That's a good girl.' Celia's face relaxed into a smile. 'Yer see, it wouldn't only be you in trouble, but me as well. I don't tell yer grandad about our Thursday nights, and he'd be mad if he found me out in a lie.'

Laura turned her head away. There were a few things her grandad would go mad about, and Charlie was one of them. There was something fishy going on there, but she was best not to get involved. It wouldn't do to cross swords with the woman her grandad had married.

The band were tuning up for a slow foxtrot when Gary reappeared. He held his hand out to Laura. 'Come on, babe, let's be first on the floor.'

'Ooh, I'm not that good yet, I'll make a holy show of meself.'

Celia put a hand in the middle of Laura's back and pushed her forward. 'Go on, kid, ye're as good as most, so get up and enjoy yerself. Ye're prettier than any of them, too.'

As they dipped and twirled, Laura was thinking how suited her and Gary were as dancing partners. They got on so well together on the dance floor, yet she didn't know a thing about him. He didn't mention his family, where he worked, or where he lived. And he knew as little about her because he never asked questions.

Laura was the first to break the silence. 'It's only four weeks to Christmas. Are yer looking forward to it?'

Gary looked down at her and pulled a face. 'Nah, I think it's boring. It's all right for kids, but there's nothing to do for grown-ups. This place doesn't open Christmas week, none of the dance halls do, so it's a case of lounging around the house for two days.'

Laura tried to draw him out. 'I love it. The tree with the surprise presents underneath, and lots to eat. Me mam has a party on Christmas night and invites some of the neighbours. We have a whale of a time. I'm surprised that you don't have any parties to go to.'

'Oh, there's parties I could go to, but I'm not interested.'

Laura took the plunge. 'I'll ask me mam if yer can come to ours, if yer like?'

'I'd rather not, babe, but thanks all the same. I'm not one for mixing with strangers – I never know what to talk about.'

'Yer could talk to me, I'm not a stranger.'

Gary averted his eyes so she wouldn't see the wistful expression in them. 'No, honestly, babe, I'd rather not.'

Laura felt herself blush with shame. She'd practically asked him for a date and he'd turned her down. But why? If he wasn't interested in her, why did he dance every dance with her? Why was he always holding her hand and calling her 'babe'? Then she felt a ray of hope surface. Perhaps he was shy. Yes, that would explain everything. She shouldn't have mentioned the party, she'd jumped the gun. She should have waited until he'd asked her for a date, because he would ask her, she was sure of that. She crossed her fingers, hoping tonight would be the night.

But Laura's heart was heavy when Celia said it was time to go, and the tall blond boy she'd fallen for just squeezed her hand and said, 'I'll see yer next week, babe.'

'Go on, I dare yer,' John said, leaning against the street-lamp almost outside Miss Marshall's house. 'You're the one that suggested it, so go on, show how brave yer are.'

'Ay, pal, I didn't suggest no such thing.' Mick's hands were dug in his pockets and the collar of his coat turned up to keep the icy wind from numbing his ears. 'All I said was, that I'd seen Jenny and Janet going into Miss Marshall's, that's all. I never mentioned doing nothing that would earn me a medal for bravery.'

'Don't yer want to see Jenny, then?'

'Of course I do. And don't forget Janet.' Mick grinned at what he was about to say. 'She's a nice girl is Janet, and anyone can see she's got her eye on yer. She'll make yer a good wife one day, you lucky man.'

'I'll give yer a thick lip if yer keep saying things like that.' John kicked the lamp-post to show he was in earnest. 'And if yer ever say it in front of her, I'll give yer a cauliflower ear to go with yer thick lip.'

'Generous, aren't yer, mate? And what am I going to be doing while ye're bashing me about? Twiddling me ruddy thumbs?'

'We're wasting time here,' John said. 'It'll soon be too late to knock on an old lady's door to ask how she is.'

'Particularly as we know she's been up and about for two weeks now. And more particularly since we asked her the same question last night, and the night before. She'd be telling us to change our tune if she wasn't so polite.'

'I know what we'll do, we'll toss a penny. If it comes down heads, you knock on the door; tails, I knock.'

'I keep telling yer I wasn't born yesterday, why don't yer believe me?' Mick thrust his face nearer until their noses were only an inch apart. 'Have yer forgotten yer showed me the two-headed penny yer had in yer pocket last week?'

John looked equally as fierce. 'So yer think I'm a cheat, eh? Use one of yer own flaming pennies then, if yer don't trust me.'

Inside Miss Marshall's house she was being entertained by Jenny, who was doing a very good impersonation of the woman who came round the factory morning and afternoon, with the tea urn. Suddenly the old lady cocked an ear. 'Shush.' With a finger to her lips, she crossed over to the window and peeped through the side of the drawn curtains. 'Just come and listen to this, but don't let them see yer.'

Jenny stood on tiptoe, looking over the old woman's shoulder, while Janet crouched down to see through the crook of her arm. Jenny suppressed a giggle when she saw the stance of the two boys. 'Yer wouldn't believe they were best mates, would yer? Anyone would think they're about to knock spots off each other.'

'It's very naughty of us to eavesdrop on them,' said Lizzie, with a twinkle in her eye, 'but I'd never sleep tonight if I didn't know the outcome. So let's listen and watch.'

John pushed Mick away. 'Come on, mate, get yer penny out. But I want to inspect it first to make sure it's not a dud one.'

'Everyone knows their own tricks best, pal.' Mick fished in his pocket and brought out a penny coin. 'And in case yer accuse me of cheating, I won't catch it in me hand, I'll let it fall on the ground.'

The coin spun through the air and they heard it hit the ground. 'Where did it go?' John asked. 'I heard it land but didn't see it.'

'Ye've got eyes in yer head, pal, so help me look for it. But whoever finds it, don't touch it. Let's keep it all above board so I don't have to listen to yer moaning.'

The two boys searched for several minutes, but in the dim light of the gas-lamp it wasn't easy. So they bent their knees and squatted, searching while keeping an eye on each other.

'It's like looking for a needle in a blinking haystack,' Mick growled. 'If it wasn't my penny, I'd let yer get on with it.'

John gave a cry of excitement. 'I can see it – it rolled in the gutter.'

'Leave it! I wouldn't trust you as far as I could throw yer.'

They stood looking down at the coin which was now half-covered by a piece of paper, blown there by the breeze. 'I can't see properly,' John said. 'Is it heads or tails?'

'I'm blowed if I know, mate.' Mick stuck his hands back in his pockets. 'But seeing as it's my penny, I think it only fair that I win.'

'Yeah, okay, I'll let you win.' John chuckled, 'I'll let you knock at the door.'

'You can go and take a running jump, mate. That wasn't the bet, and well you know it.' Mick took his hands from his pockets and hunched his shoulders, ready for action. 'The one to pick it up is the winner.' He was off the mark before John had time to think. Holding the penny aloft, he chuckled, 'Behold the winner.'

'Behold the cheat, yer mean. That was below the belt, Mick Moynihan, and I'm surprised at yer. Like kicking a man when he's down, that was.'

'Yeah, it wasn't fair,' Mick agreed. And without further ado, he lifted the knocker.

Jenny wiped her eyes before opening the door. 'Lost the toss, did yer, Mick?'

Both boys stood with their mouths gaping. Mick couldn't think straight because the sight of Jenny, her pretty face alive with humour, chased everything else from his mind. The older she got, the more beautiful she became, and he'd move heaven and earth to win her hand. 'We were only acting daft, Jenny, that's all.'

'Yeah, yer know what we're like,' John said, his thoughts going down the same path as his mate's. 'At least, yer should know by now.'

Jenny opened the door wider and jerked her head. 'Come on in, Auntie Lizzie is expecting yer.'

'Auntie Lizzie!' The boys echoed. 'Since when has she been yer auntie?'

'Since the last half-hour.' Jenny waited until they were squeezed into the tiny hall, then said, 'I can't call her Lizzie, that wouldn't be respectful, and I can't keep on calling her Miss Marshall, it doesn't sound friendly. So she said she'd be thrilled to bits if we call her Auntie Lizzie. Me and Janet are made up.'

The old lady was grinning when they entered the room. 'The same goes for you two, if yer want to.'

'Ooh, yeah, that would be great!' Mick's dimples deepened as his grin spread from ear to ear. 'How are yer today, Auntie Lizzie?'

'I'm fine, thank you. And all the better for seeing my two handsome boyfriends.'

'I'm glad to hear ye're fine, Auntie Lizzie.' John elbowed Mick out of the way, thinking he'd hogged the limelight long enough. 'And it is my sincere wish that you continue to be fine.'

'How come yer never ask me how I am?' Jenny asked.

'We can see how you are, Jenny,' Mick wished he could say what he really thought. 'Ye're always in tip-top form.'

'Yeah.' John was going weak at the knees just looking at her. 'Prettier than a fiddle, but as fit as one.'

Janet coughed. 'Excuse me, but in case yer hadn't noticed, I'm here.'

Mick lifted his hands in mock surprise. 'Ah, Miss Porter! As lovely as ever, I see.'

John decided to go one better. 'It's a delight to see you, Miss Porter. And a sight for sore eyes, as usual.'

Janet's face glowed with pleasure. She was betwixt and between with the two boys. One night she favoured Mick, the next it was John. Perhaps she should wait for her birthday before making up her mind. Her mam had told her she'd have more sense when she was fifteen.

Lizzie gestured to the chairs around the table. 'Sit yerselves down and tell us what yer were up to, out there.'

As they were pulling the chairs out, John and Mick grinned at each other. What excuse were they going to come up with this time? John ran his hands through his hair and pulled a Stan Laurel face. 'Another fine mess yer've got me into, Ollie.'

When the hoots of laughter had died down, Mick said, 'Listen who's talking? You were the one with the bright idea of tossing a coin.' He smiled across at Lizzie. 'Neither of us liked knocking on yer door in case yer were fed up with us, so we dared each other. As yer must have seen, we both ended up on our hands and knees, all over a ruddy penny. Mind you, it was my penny and it had come from a good home.'

'I told yer they were as mad as hatters, didn't I, Auntie Lizzie?' Jenny winked at her. 'One on their own is bad enough, but two together is a recipe for trouble.'

'Well, they don't ever have to worry about knocking on my door – all four of yer will always get a welcome. I've slept soundly every night since yer've been coming and keeping me company, and that's something that never happened before. I used to toss and turn for hours before I could drop off.' Lizzie shook her head to dismiss the memories of all those lonely nights, lonely days, and lonely years. 'Anyway, instead of crawling on the ground in the cold, yer should have come straight in and yer'd have seen Jenny amusing us. She takes after her mam for impersonations, and she had us in stitches.'

Mick leaned back on the wooden chair. 'Come on, Jenny, me and John could do with cheering up.'

'Promise yer won't make fun of me?'

'He won't make fun of yer, Jenny, I won't let him.' John was chuckling inside. 'If he does, I'll break his nose, to go with his thick lip and cauliflower ear. He wouldn't be a pretty sight when I'd finished with him.'

'Oh, aye!' Mick pretended to be angry. 'You and whose army, mate?'

'See what I mean, Auntie Lizzie? They can't be quiet for one minute.'

'I'll be as good as gold,' Mick told her, while John promised to be as quiet as a mouse.

Jenny stood up for effect. 'Well, there's this woman who works in the factory as a cleaner, and she also makes tea for the workers in the morning and afternoon. She comes around with a big tea urn on a trolley and fills the men's mugs. Now if I describe her to yer, it'll give yer an idea of why I think she's so funny.' Jenny brought the actions into play now. Holding her hands out in front of her chest, she said, 'She's out here on top, and her backside's as big as the back of a tram. Her hair is dyed and it's a horrible orange colour. She doesn't talk, she bawls, and she's always got a cigarette dangling out of the side of her mouth. That cigarette is never taken out until it starts to burn her lips, and then she lights another one from it. Sometimes the ash on it is inches long and we all wait with bated breath to see where it lands. Usually it's in the tea urn or in the men's mugs. Honestly, she's like a gangster's moll. The men are terrified of her because she's built like a house and could pick any of them up with one hand.'

Jenny stopped to take a deep breath. 'Have yer all got the idea of what she's like?'

John nodded. 'I can see her as plain as if she was standing next to yer.'

'I'm glad I'm not standing next to her,' Mick said, trying to look solemn. 'She sounds a right nasty piece of work.'

'Why don't the bosses sack her?' Lizzie asked. 'They don't have to put up with that, there's plenty of women who'd be glad of the job.'

'None of them have got the guts.' Jenny laughed at the idea. 'Anyway, I'm coming to that. One day, her whole cigarette fell into one of the men's mugs. She didn't pass him any compliment, just stood there and brazenly lit another one before carrying on to the next man. The poor bloke stood staring down at the cigarette floating on top of his tea, and when she was well out of sight, he called the floorwalker over. "I'm not putting up with this, it's bloody ridiculous. She should have been kicked out on her backside long ago." The floorwalker is a small, slightly built man, and he asked, "Would you like to have the honour of sacking her, Nobby?" ' Jenny bent double as she pictured the scene. 'Nobby's face was a picture. "I don't get paid to sack people, that's your job." The floorwalker thought for a minute then took Nobby's mug from him. "I don't get paid that much, Nobby, but I know a man who does".'

Jenny scanned the faces listening with interest. 'It's a long story.

I'll pack it in if ye're fed up with the sound of me voice.'

'Don't you dare pack it in,' Mick said, 'even if it takes all night.'

There were sounds of approval, so Jenny continued. 'The mug was taken to the office of the manager, Mr Grearson. There's glass windows in his office, and we all stopped work to see what his reaction was. We couldn't hear what was being said, but after what seemed a heated argument, the floorwalker, Phil, went in search of the cleaner. She stood as bold as brass in front of Mr Grearson and as far as we could see, he could hardly get a word in. She stormed out of his office and deliberately stood facing the window and lit up another cigarette!'

'So he did sack her?' Lizzie said. 'Quite right, too.'

Jenny shook her head. 'He didn't sack her, just told her to pull her socks up or the men would mutiny and she'd be out of the door. We had to wait for Phil to tell us what went on in the office, and he said she told Mr Grearson she didn't know what all the fuss was about. After all, she'd only charged Nobby for his tea, she didn't charge him for the cigarette which, after all, was still in his possession.'

Mick was the first to roar with laughter, followed quickly by the others. 'I'm beginning to like her! Mind you, I wouldn't want to share a cup of tea with her.'

'I'll tell yer what I think is the funniest. I've described her to yer, except to say that she's as common as muck and has a filthy mouth on her. But guess what her name is?'

John was first off the mark. 'Mae West?'

'Yer'll never guess, so I'll tell yer. It's Philomena Dorothea Victoria Anastasia Smith.'

They were still laughing about it when the two boys walked the girls round to Janet's to make sure she got home safely. Then on the way back, with Jenny walking between them, their laughter had nothing to do with Philomena Dorothea Victoria Anastasia Smith. It was all to do with Jenny, and their laughter was that of happiness.

Chapter Fifteen

Amy put her arms flat on the table and leaned forward. 'Ay, girl, is it the same as usual this Christmas? Christmas night here, and New Year's Eve over the road at the Moynihans'?'

Mary gasped, or at least pretended to. 'You've got a ruddy cheek, you have, Amy Hanley, the way yer take things for granted. Me and Molly haven't mentioned anything about having no party.'

'I know yer haven't, girl, that's why I'm asking. Ye're that bleedin' slow about it, yer've got me worried. Talk about having no consideration for others, isn't in it! I mean, like, I'll have to make other arrangements if me two best mates are too tight, and too miserable to have a party to celebrate Christmas.'

'Ooh, er! The state of you and the price of fish!' Mary knew how all this was going to end because never a day past without her friend going through some sort of rigmarole. But it always ended up in a laugh and a bit of fun never did no one any harm. So with a look of anticipation on her face, she asked, 'When yer say yer'll have to make other arrangements, does that mean yer might think of having a party in *your* house?' She clapped her hands in glee. 'Oh, I can't wait to tell Molly, she'll be over the moon.'

'Ay, just you hang on a minute, girl, I haven't said nothing about having no party in my house.' Amy was pinching the fat on her arms. 'I only said I'd have to make other arrangements, 'cos yer can't expect me not to celebrate just because you're not in the mood. No, what I mean is, I'll have to go to a party in one of me other friends' houses.'

'Oh, aye, such as?'

'I've got other friends beside you, yer know, girl. I know loads of people who'd be honoured to have me.'

Mary was chuckling silently. 'Name them.'

'Huh! No bleedin' fear! How soft you are! If I tell yer their names yer'll try and wangle an invite for yerself. Find yer own party, Mary Nightingale.'

'I don't need to, I'm all sorted out. But I'll tell Molly what yer said, so she won't expect yer.'

Amy banged on the table with the flat of her hand, her chubby face creased in a wide smile. 'I knew all along yer were having me on, yer know, girl. I just went along with yer for the ride. But I'd better not say what's in me mind in case yer take yer invite back.'

'I haven't given yer an invite, yet! I'll see how yer behave yerself over the next few days, then I'll decide.' Mary narrowed her eyes in suspicion. 'What did yer mean before when yer said yer wouldn't tell me what was in yer mind?'

'I'm not telling yer until I'm certain I've got me invitation and yer won't take it back.'

Mary tutted. 'Yer've got yer invitation, sunshine, so spit it out.'

'Well, I was thinking yer were the world's worst bleedin' liar. Our cat can tell a lie better than you.'

'Yer haven't got a cat, Amy.'

'Ye're right, girl, but I'm saying if I did have one, he'd be a better liar than you.'

'Telling lies is not something to be proud of, sunshine, and it's certainly nothing to go round bragging about. It's one of the Ten Commandments, or have yer forgotten yer Catechism?' Mary saw the gleam of merriment in Amy's eyes and clicked her tongue. 'You'll never go to heaven when yer die, that's for sure.'

'Ay, I've no intention of bleedin' dying, girl!' Amy said, moving her fingers to the dimples in her elbow. 'Not until after the parties, anyway. I'll tell yer what, if I died before then and missed all the fun, I'd ruddy kill meself.'

'Amy Hanley, how you can sleep at night after all the things yer say, I'll never know. If it was me, I'd be seeing the Grim Reaper standing at the foot of me bed, biding his time.'

'Nah! My Ben wouldn't allow another man in the bedroom. Especially since I told him what Molly said about me being well-endowed. He thinks I'm someone special now, treats me with kid gloves.'

'It's boxing gloves he needs, not kid gloves. My Stan would wonder what hit him if he was married to you. He doesn't know he's born, the care I take of him.'

'Ah, but does he have as much fun, girl? That's the question yer've got to ask yerself.'

'I beg your pardon? What makes yer think your Ben has more fun than my Stan?'

Amy closed one eye and squinted at her neighbour. 'Well, from where I'm sitting, ye're not particularly well-endowed, are yer, girl?'

Mary's mouth dropped open. 'That's nice, I enjoy getting insulted in me own house. And if we're on yer favourite subject of bedroom games, I'm going to get on with me washing, which you rudely interrupted.'

Amy held up her two hands in surrender. 'Not another word about bedrooms will pass me lips, Scout's Honour. We'll talk about the parties instead. The only reason I brought it up in the first place is because I want to prepare me costume for my party piece. Like all professional entertainers, girl, I put a lot of thought into me costume.'

'It's a pity yer don't put as much material into them as yer do thought, then. Wear something that covers yer body, sunshine, not one that shows everything yer've got. The kids are getting too old now to see yer half-naked. Don't forget, Mick's just on eighteen and your John's not far off it.'

'Ay, talking about kids, girl, I was worried about our Eddy and Edna. I couldn't leave them on their own on Christmas Day, it wouldn't be right. I didn't mind when they were younger 'cos they went to bed early. I thought of asking yer if they could come, too?'

'Some hope you've got, Amy Hanley! That would be five from your house, three from the Moynihans', four from here, and I've asked Lizzie to come, as well. This room wouldn't hold that many – it would be bursting at the seams.'

'It would if yer scraped yer new wallpaper off.' Amy's face was straight. 'That would give yer a bit more room. We could take it off careful, like, and stick it back on the next day. But yer won't put yerself out for no one, will yer?'

'Don't even think of it, sunshine, I'm not having thirteen people in this house, not for you nor anyone else.'

'Where d'yer get the thirteen people from, girl?'

'Oh, not again! I've just told yer! Four from here, three from the Moynihans', Lizzie and your five.'

'Ye're lousy at adding up, girl. I know yer know a lot of big words, but when it comes to adding up, ye're bleedin' hopeless. There's only three from our house. Me, my Ben and our John. When I went to school, that came to three.'

'What about your Eddy and Edna?'

Amy put on her surprised face. 'Oh, they're not coming. They've both got parties of their own to go to.'

'Holy suffering ducks, Amy, what have we gone all through that for! Yer were even talking of stripping me wallpaper off to make room for them!'

'Ah, ay, now, girl! I only said I *thought* I was going to have to ask yer if they could come. That was before they got fixed up. And as for yer wallpaper, that was only supposing. You know, like, supposing I had to ask yer. But I might have known yer wouldn't strip yer paper off, not for no one. It comes between you and yer bleedin' sleep, that wallpaper. Every time I come in I expect yer to hold yer hand out for me admission fee.'

Mary chuckled. 'Jealousy gets yer nowhere, sunshine. I told yer we'd all give yer a hand to decorate your room if yer wanted, but ye're too ruddy slow to catch cold. Either that or too mean, one or the other.'

'A bit of both, girl, a bit of both.'

There was deep affection in Mary's eyes as she studied her friend. How dull life would have been over the years without her. 'Yer've been a good mate to me, Amy Hanley, and I love the bones of yer.'

The chubby cheeks moved upwards and Amy's eyes almost disappeared. 'Ay, girl, couldn't yer love me fat, instead of me bones? Yer see, in case yer hadn't noticed, I've got a lot more fat than bones.'

Mary turned her head as she laughed, and through the window she saw Molly hurrying across the cobbles. 'Oh, I forgot to mention that Molly would be coming over to see if we felt like going to the pictures with her tonight. She's on her way over now, I'll let her in.'

Molly came in rubbing her arms briskly. 'It's a cold one, today, so it is. Sure, if I had the sense I was born with I'd have slipped me coat on.'

Amy grinned at her. 'Ye're in luck, Molly, we haven't had our cup of tea yet. Mary was just about to put the kettle on, and I'm sure I heard her say she had some custard creams. So yer timed it nicely, girl.'

Mary shouted as she made her way to put the kettle on. 'I haven't got no custard creams. I'm sorry, but would yer like a cracker with cheese on?'

'Oh, my God, it must be someone's birthday!' Amy winked at Molly before calling back, 'Cream crackers and cheese, on a week-day? It's never been known.'

'Not crackers, sunshine, just cracker. Singular.'

Molly saw the frown on Amy's face. 'Mary means ye're only getting one cracker, me darlin'.'

'Yeah, I understood that bit. But what's her singlet got to do with it?'

While Molly's loud guffaw filled the room, Mary came to the kitchen door and doubled up. 'She's priceless, isn't she?'

Amy looked from one to the other. 'Have you two lost yer bleedin' marbles? I'm blowed if I see anything funny in a singlet.'

'I said "singular", sunshine, not singlet. And as Molly rightly said, that means ye're only getting one cracker.'

'You're too bleedin' clever for yer own good, d'yer know that? But yer'll come unstuck one of these days, mark my words.' Amy's chins danced in tune with her nodding head. 'I'm going to root a dictionary out when I go home, and I'll find the longest word in it. Then I'll baffle yer with bleedin' science in the morning.'

'Make sure yer read what it means, sunshine, or it might be you what comes unstuck.' Mary cocked an ear. 'That's the kettle boiling, I'll brew the tea.'

As she reached to take three cups down from the hooks on the shelf, Mary could hear her neighbours talking. 'What picture did yer have in mind, Molly?'

'Charles Laughton's on at the Atlas, he's usually in a good picture.'

'Ah, no, I hate him! He's as ugly as sin! I don't fancy sitting for two hours looking at his ugly mug. I'd be just as well sitting in me own warm house and looking at my feller's ugly mug.'

Mary wet the tea and carried the pot through. Setting it in the middle of the table, she shook her head at Amy. 'That's a terrible thing to say about yer husband. I'm going to tell Ben next time I see him.'

'Oh, yer don't need to bother, girl, 'cos he knows. He sees himself in the mirror every morning when he's getting shaved.' Amy shuffled to the edge of the chair. 'Will yer get the bleedin' cups, girl, 'cos me and Molly are spitting feathers. And when ye're cutting the cheese, let yer hand slip, will yer? Don't be cutting it so thin we can see through it.'

Molly was chuckling as she poured the tea out. 'Sure, haven't I lost interest in going to the pictures, now? Why don't you both come over to ours and we can have a laugh. I'll get Seamus to mug us to a few bottles of stout, then send him to prop the bar up at the pub for a couple of hours.'

'That's the most sensible thing I've heard since I got out of bed, Molly.' Amy's face was beaming when she looked at Mary. 'I'll knock for yer at eight, girl, okay?'

'That's fine, sunshine, and bring yer dictionary with yer, just in case.'

Laura could sense Cynthia's excitement as they linked arms. And the smile that had been missing for weeks, was back on her face. 'You seem in a happy frame of mind. Has something nice happened?'

'I saw them last night, both of them.'

Laura stopped in her tracks. 'Go 'way! Are yer pulling me leg?'

Cynthia tugged on her arm. 'Keep walking in case me dad comes out. He was getting ready to go to the pub when I left.'

When they were well away from their street, Laura could contain her excitement no longer. 'Go on, Cyn, tell us what happened. Did they see yer?'

'I'd been giving it a lot of thought over the weeks while I've been keeping an eye on the pub they took us to. And I began to realise they must have been giving it a wide berth in case I turned up and caused trouble. So last night, I walked back in the direction they were coming from when we met them. I stood in a shop doorway for ages, and it was freezing cold. I was almost giving it up as a bad job when the pair of them came swaggering along on the opposite side of the road.'

'Oo, er, I don't know how yer had the nerve,' Laura said. 'I'd have been shaking in me shoes in case they saw me.'

'Yes, but it didn't happen to you, did it?' Cynthia came to a stop and faced her friend. 'Yer have no idea what I went through, Laura, 'cos I didn't tell yer the half of it. On top of the pain I had, and the raging torment in me mind and the terrible nightmares every single night, I had an even bigger worry that I bet you never even thought of. What if one of them had made me pregnant? For three solid weeks I was out of me mind with fear. I even thought about running away from home, 'cos I couldn't have faced me parents. But I was lucky, and when me period came on, I thanked God from the bottom of my heart.'

Cynthia sighed as she linked arms with Laura and began to walk. She couldn't expect her friend to understand the horror and torment, no one would unless they went through it themselves. 'Anyway, that's why I've been so determined to find them. And now I know which pub they go to, I'll make it me business to find out where they live. And then I'll make them pay heavily for what they did to me.'

'Yer mean to say that yer followed them?' Laura's tummy was churning over as she thought of the risk her friend had taken. 'It's a wonder they didn't spot yer.'

'They wouldn't have recognised me. I had me old clothes on and a scarf pulled low over me forehead. Anyway, if they had spotted me, they'd have been the ones to get a fright. But I don't only want to give them a fright, I want to ruin their lives for them. And I swear, Laura, that's what I'll do. More so, after what I saw last night.'

'Why, what happened after yer followed them?'

'I crossed the road and followed them from behind. When they turned into a pub, I was in two minds whether to wait for them or go home, 'cos I was frozen. I decided to stick it out for a little while, and I was glad I did. They weren't in the pub long, and when they came out they were with two women. Or girls, I should say – they looked about eighteen or so. Jeff and Larry were full of the joys, laughing and joking, and I felt like walking up to them and scratching their eyes out. But I thought, no, I'll bide me time and do the job properly. So I followed them, keeping well into the wall. And guess where they went – down an entry.'

Laura sucked in her breath. 'They want a damn good hiding, they do. Someone should sort them out.'

'Oh, I intend to, believe me. Now I know the pub they go to, and roughly what time they get there, I'll be waiting for them on Thursday. I won't go as early, 'cos it's too cold to hang around, but I'll be there.'

'I still don't see what yer can do to pay them back.' Laura shivered and moved in closer to her friend. 'I mean, we don't know any fellers that would knock the living daylights out of them.'

'I've got a plan in me head, but I'm not telling yer about it in case it doesn't come off. When the time comes, I might get cold feet. I can't see it, not the way I feel, but I'd rather say nowt until I've accomplished what I set out to do.'

'I'll be glad when it's all over and yer get back to normal.' Laura squeezed her arm. 'Yer haven't been the same girl since the night it happened.'

'I'm seeking retribution, Laura, and if I get that I might be able to get on with me life. I don't like being miserable, but what happened that night is in me mind all the time, like a nightmare repeating itself over and over again. The only way to rid meself of it, is by paying them back in some way.'

'I wish I could help yer, Cyn, but I'm not as brave as you. I'm a coward and would run a mile if I set eyes on them.'

'This is my fight, Laura, and one way or another, I'll win it.' Cynthia was well aware that getting even with Larry and Jeff had become an obsession with her, but she couldn't help it. For what they put her through that night, down a dark entry with no one to call to for help, they deserved to be punished. She gave a deep sigh. 'Anyway, kid, how are yer getting on with this Gary feller?'

Laura pretended to have a coughing fit, giving herself time to think of an answer. When her friend was feeling better, she'd want to come to the dance with her, and that was out of the question. But she couldn't tell her that. 'We get on fine together. He's a nice bloke, Cynthia, and not half handsome. He's taught me all the dances, even the tango.'

'Has he asked yer for a date, yet?'

'He's hinted that we should go to the pictures one Thursday, instead of meeting at the dance hall, but I've been too keen to learn how to dance. Perhaps after Christmas we'll go out together.'

'Is there romance in the air, kid?'

Laura laughed it off. 'Ask me again when I've had me first kiss off him.'

'My God, you're slow, aren't yer? All these weeks and he's never even kissed yer?'

'He's not like the boys we used to knock around with, they were only kids. Gary's not the type to kiss a girl when he's only just met her, he's more of a gentleman. And I won't let him bring me home because I have to leave the dance at half ten to be home by eleven, and it wouldn't be fair on him. But it'll be different when we go out on a date and we're on our own.' Laura tittered. 'I only hope he's not a sloppy kisser or I'll go right off him.'

'Ay, don't be so big-headed,' Cynthia said. 'He might go off you!'

'No, he really likes me, Cyn, honest. He dances every dance with me, holds me hand and calls me "babe".'

'I'll have to meet this he-man, and see if I approve.'

'Oh, yer will meet him sometime, Cyn, that's for sure.' Laura crossed her fingers. 'In a couple of weeks, eh?'

'I'm glad we've got the pleasure of yer company again, sweetheart, 'cos we've missed yer.' Martha Porter waited until Jenny had slipped her coat off, then took it from her to hang up. 'But why aren't yer going to sit with the old lady? I asked our Janet, but she didn't seem to know. Did the old girl get fed up with yer?'

Jenny laughed as she took a seat at the table, opposite Bill. 'No, it was me mam that said it was too much for her, four of us there every night. So me and Janet are going one night, and the lads the next.'

No one was more pleased to see Jenny than Bill. 'About time, too! The six matches yer owe me from the last game of cards has gone up to ten. I'm charging yer interest 'cos yer've owed it for so long.'

'Some hope you've got, Bill Porter!' Jenny winked at her friend. 'I didn't know yer brother was a moneylender, Jan.'

'He's tight enough to be one,' Janet said. 'He wouldn't give yer the skin off his rice pudding unless yer paid him for it.'

'Now, now, that's enough.' Her father laid his newspaper down. 'I'm not having two women ganging up on me own son without coming to his aid. What about the time you had the measles, Janet, and yer wouldn't even give him a spot? He cried his eyes out, but yer wouldn't budge. Not one spot would yer part with, even though yer were covered in them.'

'She was generous enough with her colds, though, wasn't she, Dad?' Bill was feeling happier than he'd felt for weeks. It was so good to see Jenny's pretty smiling face sitting opposite to him. 'Remember that time she sneezed all over me, and I had a runny nose for weeks after?'

Martha joined in now. 'That was because yer were bending over her, trying to pinch one of her jelly babies. It served yer right, that did.'

Jenny wagged her head from side to side, her eyes sparkling. 'We never have no rows like this when we're sitting with Auntie Lizzie, do we, Jan? All we do is act daft and laugh and joke the whole time.'

Janet giggled. 'Mick and John act daft, we just sit and laugh at them.'

'Yeah,' Jenny agreed, 'I wonder how they're getting on?'

'Never mind about them.' The last thing Bill wanted to do was talk about the two lads he saw as rivals for Jenny's affection. 'All ye're doing is changing the subject, hoping I'll forget about the matchsticks yer owe me. And the number has gone up to eleven, by the way.'

'I've only got ten with me. I couldn't take any more because the box was nearly empty, and I couldn't leave me mam short or we'd have got no breakfast.'

'Then yer'd better have a winning streak tonight, or yer'll be in debt to me for the rest of yer life.' What a lovely thought, Bill told himself. A whole lifetime of Jenny being in his debt. 'Get the cards out, Janet, there's a good sister, and we'll start.'

'Mr Porter, before we start, can I ask yer to forget ye're a man, and be on my side for a change? I need all the help I can get to make sure yer son doesn't cheat. If we've all got our eyes on him he'd have a job to hide cards on his knee, covered by the tablecloth. He thinks I haven't seen him, but I have, loads of times.'

Vincent roared with laughter. 'Okay, I'll join the girls. In fact, so I look the part, I'll borrow Martha's pinny.'

Bill wagged a finger at Jenny. 'You are one big fibber, Jenny Nightingale. I never hide cards on me knee.' A smile lit up his face. 'I slip them down the side of me shoe.'

By the end of the night, when it was time for her to leave, Jenny had paid the matchsticks back that she owed, and was three in hand. She was over the moon, and holding the matchsticks in an open palm, she held them under Bill's nose. 'How about that, then, old clever clogs?'

'Sheer fluke, that's what it was.' Bill gathered the cards in and slid them back in the packet. 'And the help yer got from me dad did yer no harm. I saw him pass yer the six of diamonds in that last game.' He put the cards in the drawer of the sideboard. 'I'll walk yer home, even though yer cheated and cleared me out.'

'There's no need, Bill, I can be home in five minutes if I run all the way.'

Bill wasn't about to let that happen. 'I'll run all the way with yer, so I should be back home in ten minutes.'

'It's no good arguing with him, Jenny, he'll have his own way if it kills him,' Janet said. 'I'll see yer out and go straight up to bed. I'm up earlier than you, 'cos I don't have a cushy job sitting on me backside all day.'

When the youngsters had left, Martha and Vincent exchanged amused smiles. 'Isn't it funny that our Bill goes out every single night when Jenny's not here?' Martha took the poker from the brass companion set and lifted the coals in the fire, hoping the draught would inject a bit of life back into it. 'Anyone would think he fancied her.'

'I don't only think it, love, I know it! It's sticking out a mile, the way he looks at her.' Vincent chuckled. 'The only one who can't see the cow eyes he makes when he looks at her, is Jenny herself. But yer can understand the lad, 'cos she's a right bonny lass.'

'She'll be bonnier still, in another year or so. Our Bill will have a run for his money, believe me.' Martha hung the poker back in the companion set. For all the good she'd done she might as well not have bothered. The fire was on its last legs and wouldn't be coaxed. 'Our Janet's a pretty girl, too, but we don't notice because we see her every day. She hasn't got Jenny's humour, but there's plenty of time for her to come out of her shell, she's still only a kid.'

Vincent reached for his cigarette packet with one hand, and smacked his wife's bottom with the other. 'The next year or so could be very interesting, love. I'm looking forward to it.'

Mick put the dominoes back in the box and grinned at John. 'That's a tanner yer owe me, pal. But I'll wait until yer get yer wages on Saturday.'

'Yer can wait until the cows come home, mate, 'cos we weren't playing for money, it was only pretend.'

'We'll have no fighting, now, lads,' Lizzie said. 'John's right, it was only pretend. Playing for money is gambling, and I don't hold with it.'

'Don't take anything we say seriously, Auntie Lizzie, we're always having each other on.' Mick swivelled in his chair and placed the domino box on the sideboard. When he turned back, he asked the question he'd been dying to ask for weeks. 'Did yer never think of getting married, Auntie Lizzie? I bet yer had plenty of chances, 'cos I can see yer must have been very pretty when yer were younger.'

John glared at his friend. 'What d'yer mean, when she was younger? That's a back-handed compliment if ever I heard one. Auntie Lizzie is still pretty.'

'Of course she is! Just like Janet is very pretty, but yer don't seem to see that! She hasn't half got her eye on you, pal, so yer'd better watch out.'

'Say that once more, mate, and yer'll be missing two of yer front teeth. If yer'd wear yer glasses, yer'd see it's you she's got her eye on, not me.'

'I didn't know yer wore glasses, Mick,' Lizzie said. 'I've never seen yer in them.'

The two boys looked at each other and burst out laughing. 'I don't wear glasses, Auntie Lizzie, that's John's idea of a joke. The same as when he says he's going to separate me from me two front teeth. It's just wishful thinking on his part.' Mick's eyes were tender as he looked at the old lady. 'Now to me question. Did yer never think of getting married?'

'Oh, yes! I had quite a few boyfriends when I was a girl, but there was only one lad I ever loved enough to marry. He joined the Army in 1914, and before he went away we got engaged. We wrote to each other every day, and he got a week's leave before he was sent overseas. We were going to get married when he came home, and I started buying things for me bottom drawer. But I never saw him again; he was killed in action in 1916.'

When Mick saw a tear glistening in the faded blue eyes, he cursed himself. 'I'm sorry, Auntie Lizzie, I shouldn't have been so nosy. Now I've gone and upset yer.'

'No, yer haven't, son, I'm glad yer asked. I often think about him – his name was Bill Furlong – but I never talk about him because there's no one to talk to. So it's good for me to be able to say his name. I've still got me engagement ring, and every letter he sent me is in me drawer upstairs, tied with blue ribbon.'

John swallowed hard to remove the lump in his throat. 'That's a real love story, Auntie Lizzie. Yer must have loved him very much to have remained true to him.'

'I never looked at another man after he was killed,' Lizzie told them. 'I've lived with me memories all these years.'

'I hope I find a love like that.' Mick rounded the table and hugged her. 'You are one lovely lady. I can see why your Bill fell for yer.'

'I'm a lucky lady, to have young people around me at my age. Yer've brightened my life for me and I do appreciate it.' There was a glint in her eyes as she smiled at him. 'But we've all missed the girls tonight, haven't we?'

'Yeah.' Mick returned her smile. 'I'll have to have words with Mrs Nightingale, see if I can work me charm on her.'

'Yer'd better let me do that,' John said. 'I mean, it's a well-known thing that I've got heaps more charm than you.'

'In yer dreams, pal, in yer dreams. Yer might stand a chance charming a snake, but when it comes to Mrs Nightingale it's a different kettle of fish. A real expert is called for, and that's yours truly.'

'If you two don't stop messing around, yer'll miss Jenny,' Lizzie said. 'She'll be on her way back from Janet's about now.'

John gave his friend a dig in the back. 'Yer talk too much, mate. Move yerself before it's too late.'

'Right, it's all hands to the pump, then.' Mick pointed to the fire. 'You bank that down while I fill Auntie Lizzie's hot-water bottle.'

Five minutes later the boys were standing in the street listening for Auntie Lizzie to shoot the bolt on the door. When they were satisfied she was safe, they turned just in time to see Jenny passing on the opposite side, with Bill by her side. 'Oh,' John groaned, 'she's got that long streak of misery with her.'

'Let's spoil it for him, eh?' Thinking all was fair in love and war, Mick called, 'Hang on a minute, Jenny.'

Jenny was grinning as she watched them cross the cobbles. 'How did it go?'

John got in first. 'We've had a very interesting night, especially the last half-hour.'

Oh, he's not stealing my thunder, Mick thought. I was the one who asked Auntie Lizzie about her life and now he's trying to cash in on it. 'She told us all about herself, when she was young, and it wasn't half sad.'

Jenny looked up at Bill. 'Thanks for walking me home, Bill, but yer may as well go now, it's no good standing here freezing.'

Bill wasn't very happy about that. 'I said I'd see yer home, and that means seeing yer get safely inside yer house. I don't mind waiting.'

'That's daft, that.' Mick couldn't help himself. If this bloke was going to walk Jenny home every other night, they'd be courting in no time. 'This is John's house, Jenny's is next door and I live in that house opposite. We'll see she gets inside safely, so it's no good you getting yer death of cold.'

Bill was now becoming irritated. 'Aren't you frightened that *you* might catch *yer* death of cold? It strikes me that yer stand as much chance as I do.'

'Yes, but you've got that walk ahead of yer, Bill.' Jenny hadn't a clue that there was a fight for supremacy going on under her nose. 'Anyway, I'm freezing meself so I won't be hanging around for long. I'm certainly not standing listening to a long drawn-out tale from these two. So you make tracks, Bill, and tell Janet I'll see her tomorrow night.'

Unless he wanted to make a fool of himself, there was little Bill could do. He knew what he'd like to do, and that was punch these two blokes on the nose for cramping his style. But that wouldn't go down well with Jenny. So with as much sincerity as he could muster, he bade them good night, and with his shoulders hunched, walked away. They'd pulled a fast one on him tonight, but if they tricked him like that again, he'd marmalise them.

Thinking they'd put paid to the enemy, Mick and John were standing with grins on their faces. 'D'yer think yer mam would like to hear about what Auntie Lizzie told us?' John asked, hopefully. 'It's not half sad.'

'Would she heckerslike!' Jenny was thinking her mother would have a fit if these two walked in and she was sitting with dinkie curlers in her hair and a nightdress on. 'It's half-past ten, yer daft nit, yer don't go visiting at this time of night. Anyway, I'm too cold to stand here any longer, I'm going in. Auntie Lizzie can tell me the story herself, tomorrow night.'

Left on their own, the pals looked at each other and shrugged their shoulders. 'The only good thing about that, pal,' Mick said, 'was we put a halt to the queer feller's gallop. I only hope he hasn't put a death wish on us.'

'If he does, the one I'm putting on him will cancel it out.' John felt in his pocket for the front-door key. 'Don't worry, mate, there's always tomorrow. We've got an excuse to call and see Auntie Lizzie, I've made sure of that. I dropped me comb on the floor under her table, accidentally on purpose, like. So who's a genius, eh?'

'I only hope the genius hasn't dropped his comb on top of my handkerchief.'

Inside the Nightingales' house, Mary shook her head when she heard roars of laughter outside. 'Just listen to them! I'm laughing with them, but I haven't a clue what I'm laughing at. I don't know which one of them is the funniest.'

'They're both cracked, Mam,' Jenny said. 'But in a nice way.'

Chapter Sixteen

Cynthia huddled in the shop doorway, stamping her feet to try and get some feeling back in them. They were like blocks of ice and she'd probably get chilblains after this. And for what? If Larry and Jeff didn't put in an appearance she'd have wasted her time and frozen to the death in the process. She folded her arms and stuck her hands under her armpits for warmth. This was the coldest night she'd known, and if the people hurrying by knew why she was there they'd think she had a screw loose. The best place on a night like this was home, in front of a fire roaring up the chimney.

Thinking of home, Cynthia's mind took her to her parents. Her dad never questioned where she was going or who with. All he'd said when he'd seen her going out in the old coat and shoes was, 'What are yer wearing that old coat for? Surely yer've got better than that?' But when she'd told him she was saving her best coat for Christmas, he seemed satisfied. Her mam, though, never said a word, but Cynthia knew she was thinking plenty. She could always tell when her mam knew she was lying, you could see it in her eyes. What a shock they'd both get if they knew what she was up to, and why. Her dad would go stark raving mad and want to find the blokes who had harmed his beloved daughter. He would want to kill them with his bare hands. But her mother would stay silent. Only her eyes would speak, and they would say she wasn't surprised because her daughter was a wayward girl who had probably contributed to what had happened.

Cynthia bent down to press on her toes, which were giving her gyp. And she would have missed the two men passing by on the opposite side of the road if it hadn't been for Jeff's burst of loud laughter. Instantly she was alert, the cold and her pains forgotten as her heart thumped in her breast like a drum. She let them walk a safe distance before crossing the road and following them. And as she pulled her scarf low over her forehead, she vowed she'd stay with them until they made their way home. She was determined that tonight she would find out where they lived, and put a stop to this twice-weekly vigil. Once she had their addresses she would work out how to make the best use of the information. It was only two days to Christmas so there was little she could do before then. What she had

201

in mind had to be planned right down to the last detail if it were to be successful.

There were fewer people on the road now, and Cynthia, afraid of one of them turning, moved in closer to the wall. They wouldn't recognise her as the well made-up, fashionable girl they knew, but if they noticed a lone woman walking behind them for too long, they just might get curious. They'd covered some distance by now, and Cynthia's toes were so sore every step was an effort. It was sheer willpower that kept her going. Then the two men were no longer in front of her, and she hurried to the spot where she'd lost them to find it was a corner pub. That meant she'd have at least half an hour's wait, but even though her nose and eyes were running with the cold, she told herself she couldn't give up now, not after coming so far. So she looked for a safe place to hide, one where she'd be sheltered from the wind. There was a block of shops opposite and she quickly made up her mind that in the shelter of one of the doorways she'd be out of the wind and have a good vantage point.

When Larry and Jeff came out of the pub they were closely followed by a woman. They were all laughing as the woman linked their arms and the trio set off, not in the direction the men had come from, but towards Liverpool centre. Cynthia's instincts told her that if the men ran true to form, they wouldn't be walking very far. As she waited for them to cover a safe distance, she made a mental note of the woman's appearance. Probably about twenty years of age, slim figure, reddish hair, and dressed in a dark green swagger coat. This information would be written down when she got home, under the details of the two girls she'd last seen them with. Times, dates and places were also noted.

When she saw them stop at the top of an entry, Cynthia held back. She was thinking how easy it was for Larry and Jeff to pick girls up, when she heard the woman's raised voice and saw her struggling. Then to her horror, she saw the men pull the same trick they'd pulled on her. She saw them grab the woman's arms, and just before they were lost to view, Jeff's hand was muffling her screams. Cynthia couldn't move, she felt as though she'd been turned to stone. Then memories came flooding back, memories of pain, horror and humiliation. This had the effect of setting her in motion. They'd not get away with putting some other poor woman through what she had suffered. Galvanised into action, Cynthia flew across the road and made for the entry. She didn't know what she could do, but she couldn't stand by and do nothing.

'Oh, thank God,' Cynthia cried with relief when two men rounded the corner of a side street. 'Please mister, will yer help? I've just seen two men dragging a woman down that entry. She was crying and struggling but they wouldn't stop. Yer've got to help her, please.'

The two men didn't even stop to think, they moved like greased lightning. And as they ran down the dark entry, one shouted, 'The bastards, I'll kill them.'

Cynthia knew if she had any sense she'd make herself scarce, but she couldn't go, not until she knew what happened. She moved closer to the entry and could hear roars of anger, then Jeff's voice, shouting, 'What the hell's it got to do with you?'

'I'll show yer what it's got to do with me.' This came from one of the men Cynthia had asked to help. 'Yer dirty buggers, I'll flay yer alive.' There was the sound of scuffling and cries of pain as fists landed on their target. After a minute, the same voice shouted, 'You make a run for it, love. We'll sort these two out, they'll not bother yer again.'

Cynthia flattened herself against the wall as the woman rounded the corner. Her hair and clothes were dishevelled, and her eyes red-rimmed with tears. 'Are yer all right, love?' Cynthia stepped from the shadows. 'I saw what happened and asked those two men to help.'

'Thank God yer did.' The woman ran the back of her hand across her eyes. 'They're beasts, those two are. If you hadn't got help for me, I don't know what they'd have done to me. I honestly thought I was a goner.'

'D'yer know them?' Cynthia asked.

'I've never seen them in me life before.' The woman was shaking like a leaf. 'They came in the pub I go to, and they seemed nice and friendly. So when they asked me if I'd like to go to another pub they know, I didn't think anything of it.'

'I think yer should go on home, love, before they come out.' Cynthia was thinking that she too should put a distance between them and herself. Heaven alone knew what was going on in the entry, there were still sounds of fighting. 'Go on, love, take my advice and scarper.'

The woman took a few steps, then turned. 'I don't know how to thank you; yer saved me life.'

'That's all right, love. I might need help meself some time, yer never know.' As she watched the woman running as quickly as her high-heeled shoes would allow, Cynthia was glad she'd been able to get help for her before she was put through the nightmare she herself had endured. And she was taking great satisfaction from knowing she'd upset the apple-cart for Larry and Jeff. But what was happening in that dark entry? Were Larry and Jeff getting their just deserts, or were the Good Samaritans being punished for their act of kindness? She couldn't go home without knowing.

Ten minutes passed, then the two strange men who would forever be heroes in her mind, came out of the entry dusting their hands as though they'd touched something unpleasant. And Cynthia, huddled in the shop doorway opposite, gave a sigh of relief. They didn't appear to be hurt, in fact just the opposite. She could hear them talking and they seemed in high spirits.

'That sorted the dirty buggers out.'

'Aye, they'll not be going down an entry for a very long time. Serves the sods right.'

'Let's hope it's taught that young woman a lesson. As my old ma used to say, "Never trust a man until yer've met his family".'

Their voices faded as they walked away, and Cynthia was left to consider her position. Nothing would drag her away until she'd seen Larry and Jeff and satisfied herself that they'd been taught a lesson. But after that, what should she do? Go home and put the whole thing out of her mind? Going home would be the sensible thing to do because she was so cold her teeth were chattering. But in the darkness of the doorway, she shook her head. She didn't want to be sensible; she wanted to accomplish what she'd set out to do. Those two evil devils might have got a hammering tonight, but it would be nothing to the terrible things they'd done to her. Acts so terrible, she'd never tell anyone, not even Laura.

Cynthia felt her body stiffen. A man had emerged from the entry and she could tell by the colour of his hair that it was Larry. Her precious Larry, who was forever telling her he loved her. And she'd been fool enough to believe him. He was doubled up, with one arm across his tummy and the hand of his other arm holding his face. And she could hear his groans from where she stood. A grim smile came to her face. It serves you right, she thought, you dirty, wicked, evil monster. I hope you're in agony, and that it lasts a hell of a sight longer than mine will.

Thinking she couldn't be seen, Cynthia had edged herself forward, but when Jeff appeared she stepped back sharply. He too was holding his tummy and his face as he staggered to where his friend was. In the stillness of the night, their voices carried across the road.

'Where the bleedin' hell did they come from?'

'I dunno, but one of them has broke me flaming nose.' This came from Larry. 'I'm in agony and I'm covered in blood.'

'I think my nose is bust, too, I can't bear to touch it. And I feel as though the bastards have kicked the inside out of me. They wouldn't have got away with it if they hadn't taken us by surprise. Someone must have tipped them off.'

'Grow up, will yer, Jeff? The bitch was making enough noise to wake the neighbourhood. The stupid cow.' Larry was a very unhappy man. 'We can't go home like this, so what shall we do?'

'We've got to go home, there's nowhere else we can go. Unless we go to the hospital to get seen to. We can say a gang of drunks set about us and we didn't stand a chance.' Jeff put a hand to his head and groaned. 'I don't know which hurts the most, me nose or me insides.'

'I'm not going to no hospital,' Larry said, 'I'm going home and getting it over with. I'll tell Doreen the one about a gang of drunks. She won't believe me, but she can't prove otherwise.'

'I'll tell Iris the same, and I don't care whether she believes me or not. The way I feel, she can sod off for all I care. We'll walk to the tram stop and catch a twenty-two.'

'Are you crazy? We can't get on a tram looking like this, we're both covered in blood!' When Larry tried to straighten up, he groaned and fell back against the wall. 'Even if I have to crawl home, I'm not getting on no tram.'

'Have it yer own way,' Jeff growled. 'But we'll have to take it easy because I feel as though every bone in me body's been broken.'

Cynthia stepped from the shadows on to the pavement. There went two men who didn't like getting a dose of their own medicine. And if she had her way, there was a worse fate in store for them.

As she was passing a pub, Cynthia glanced at her watch. She was surprised to see it was only ten to ten. So much had happened she thought it was much later. She'd been trailing Larry and Jeff for miles, crossing from one side of the road to the other, so as not to arouse their suspicions. They'd started out in Scotland Road, and were now halfway along County Road. They certainly didn't play in their own neck of the woods, that was for sure. It was no wonder they'd never been caught out; they went far afield for their pleasures. They were walking one in front of the other, with their heads turned towards the shops and pubs so they wouldn't be recognised by passers-by. And it was plain to see they were in great discomfort.

Cynthia pretended to be looking in a shop window when the two men came to a halt. They began talking, looking around furtively as they did so. They must be nearly home, she thought, and were getting their story ready to tell. Her excitement mounted at the thought of being so near her goal. And when the men turned the corner of the next street, her footsteps quickened. It was crucial she didn't lose sight of them at this point. Pretending to be arranging her scarf, she stood at the corner of the street and saw Larry mount the step of a house about five dwellings down, while Jeff crossed to a house opposite. Keeping her eyes fixed on the spot, Cynthia took a chance and began to walk slowly towards it, giving Larry time to let himself in. She appeared to be looking straight ahead, but her eyes swivelled towards the front door and noted the brass plate with the number fifteen outlined in black. Then she calmly turned and walked to the main road, to catch a tram that would take her home.

★　★　★

Jenny opened the door with the key her mother kept in case Lizzie ever took bad and they needed to gain entrance. 'You stay here,' she said to Janet and the two boys, 'while I tell Auntie Lizzie she's got the four of us again.'

However, Lizzie had sharp ears. 'Don't leave them standing in the cold, let them come in. I knew yer were all coming, 'cos yer mam told me.' Her eyes were bright with pleasure when the four of them trooped in, one after the other. 'I've been sitting here waiting for yer.'

Each of them gave her a kiss before making for the fireplace. 'It's not half cold out, Auntie Lizzie,' Mick said, rubbing his hands together in front of the fire. 'I wouldn't be surprised if we had snow.'

'Ooh, I hope so.' Jenny's cheeks were a rosy red, matching the beret she was wearing at a saucy angle on top of her long blonde hair. 'It would be lovely to wake up on Christmas morning and see everywhere white.'

'Yeah, like last Christmas,' John said. 'It was the gear.'

'It's very pretty to look at through the window, son, but not very nice if yer have to walk far in it.'

Mick, warmed through now, moved away from the fire and pulled out a chair. 'If there's snow on the ground on Christmas Day, Auntie Lizzie, I'll give yer a piggy-back over to the Nightingales'.'

John wasn't to be left out. 'And I'll give yer one back. Even if it's not snowing I'll carry yer, just in case yer have too many bottles of stout and yer get a bit tipsy.'

'The day has yet to come when Lizzie Marshall gets tipsy, son.' The old lady giggled at the thought. 'But it's a very kind offer and I'll bear it in mind.'

Mick pouted his lips. 'Wasn't my offer as kind as his?'

'Of course it was, son. Ye're two very kind lads.'

Jenny tutted as she placed her mother's basket on the table. 'Don't start that lark. We came here to make decorations, remember?'

'I was only putting the record straight.' Mick winked at Lizzie. 'It doesn't take much for Jenny to get on her high horse, does it? Best thing to do is humour her, that's what I've found.'

'And I've found the best way to deal with you and John is to ignore yer.' Jenny delved in the basket and brought out some packets of crêpe paper. 'We bought a packet each, Auntie Lizzie, so there's two red and two green. We're going to cut them into strips and make paper chains to go around the picture rail.' Once again her hand went into the basket. 'Me mam mixed some flour and water for us to stick them together with, and she put it in this basin so we can all reach it to dip our fingers in.'

Janet pulled a face. 'I don't fancy putting me fingers in that. Haven't yer got any brushes we can use?'

'No, we haven't, so it's no good yer pulling faces. We used to make them in school and I never heard yer moaning to Miss Harrison about getting yer fingers sticky. If yer had, it would have been three strokes of the cane.'

'I'm not pulling faces, Miss Nightingale, and I don't mind getting me fingers sticky at all.' Even Jenny had to laugh at the look of innocence on John's face as he held his hands out, palms upward. 'I'll do anything yer say, Miss, but I don't want no cane.'

Mick guffawed. 'He used to do that in school. Proper crawler, he was.'

John glared. 'How do you know? Yer weren't in my class.'

'Well, I just happened to be passing your classroom one afternoon and I saw yer on yer knees in front of the teacher's desk, begging for mercy. I remember thinking what a pathetic little creep yer were.'

'Isn't it funny how things come back to yer?' John's face was one big grin. 'I remember that afternoon, I saw yer go past. One of the lads told me afterwards that yer'd been to the headmaster's office for six strokes of the cane. If my memory serves me right, it was for giving cheek to Mr Johnston.'

'No, no, yer've got it all wrong,' Mick said. 'I didn't get the cane for giving Mr Johnston cheek, I got it for tripping him up.'

While the others roared with laughter, Janet's face was serious. 'Did yer trip Mr Johnston up on purpose?'

The laughter increased with her words, until Jenny called a halt. 'Auntie Lizzie wants these decorations for this Christmas, not next.'

'Your word is our command, Jenny,' Mick said. 'Just tell me and John what to do and we'll start.'

'Yer cut the paper in two-inch strips, first. Then yer cut those strips into four inch ones. We've only got two pairs of scissors between us, so I'll cut a couple of strips first and me and Jan can start making the chains.'

Lizzie sat back watching, her cheeks stiff with laughing so much. It was like something out of a comedy picture. The two boys were hilarious, they talked incessantly.

'That's not two inches, mate,' John said. 'More like three.'

'That is dead on two inches, pal,' Mick answered. 'Why didn't yer bring yer flaming specs with yer? If yer had, yer'd know that those strips you're cutting are nowhere near four inches.'

Lizzie's eyes went to the girls. Jenny was quick and efficient. All the time she was geeing the boys up if they kept her waiting. Janet, on the other hand, was taking the job very seriously. With her tongue sticking out of the side of her mouth, she weighed each piece of paper up carefully before linking it through the last piece. And the look of distaste on her face when she stuck her finger in the basin was a picture no artist could paint.

207

'Have yer brought the drawing pins, Mick?' Jenny asked as she eyed the long paper chain she was working on. 'I think this strip will do one of the walls.'

'Now, would I let yer down?' Mick brought a box out of his pocket. Then, with a look of pretend concern on his handsome face, he passed them over the table and said, 'Yer'll have to be careful, Jenny, it's very high.'

'I'm not putting it up, yer daft nit!' Jenny's voice was indignant. 'That's your job, or John's.'

The expression that came to John's face was pure bliss. 'I'll do it for yer, Jenny. As long as you hold the chair and catch me if I fall off.'

Mick pushed his friend down in his chair. 'This is a private conversation, pal, so keep yer nose out before I put it out of joint.'

'I think I'm an inch taller than you, mate, and that inch might make all the difference.'

'Are you heck! Anyway, I can always stand on me toes.'

Janet studied them both before coming out with one of her gems. 'Isn't it funny, I've never noticed yer were an inch taller, John. Yer both look the same height to me. Stand back-to-back and let's see.'

Jenny banged a fist on the table. 'Don't you dare! Don't you flamingwell dare! Ye're both so big-headed it's a wonder yer can get through the door. I bet as soon as yer get home yer'll have a tape-measure out. *And* I bet ye're vain enough to stand in front of a mirror while yer measure yerself. But yer came here to do a job, and if yer don't want to do it, then yer can both scram. Me and Janet will make the chains on our own, and I'll ask Bill if he'll put them up for us tomorrow night.'

That did the trick. Within an hour the chains were made and hanging gaily from the picture rail, brightening the room and making it look Christmassy. The two boys gazed at it with pride, their chests sticking out a mile. 'How about that, Auntie Lizzie?' Mick asked. 'Not a bad job, even if I do say so meself.'

'Yeah,' John said, 'when we put our mind to it, we can go like the clappers.' He punched Mick playfully on the back. 'We make a good team, don't we, mate?'

Lizzie coughed. 'Yer've done a fine job, without a doubt. But what about the girls – don't they get a mention? After all, they had to make the chains for you to put up.'

'Thank you, Auntie Lizzie, I'm glad someone noticed us.' Jenny was feeling very happy inside but wasn't going to let the lads get away with all the glory. 'Listening to these two big-heads, I was beginning to think I'd only dreamt that me and Janet had made all those links. It was the hardest job of the lot, sticking them all together.'

Janet nodded her head. 'Yes, and we've got all our fingers sticky.'

'Ah, yer poor things.' Mick put his arm across Jenny's shoulder. 'You do all the work and we take the credit. I humbly apologise, Miss Nightingale.'

Janet looked at John. 'Aren't you going to apologise? Yer should do, 'cos, as Jenny said, we did all the hard work.'

John gave Mick a dirty look before putting his arm across Janet's shoulder. 'Yes, yer worked very hard, and I do apologise. I'm sorry about yer sticky fingers, as well.'

Jenny clapped her hands. 'Now that's been settled to everyone's satisfaction, let's clear this mess off the table and put the chenille cloth back.' She spied the old lady looking up at the decorations. 'They look nice, don't they, Auntie Lizzie?'

'They look lovely. The room seems bright and cheerful, now.' She caught hold of Jenny's hand. 'You know, lass, it must be all of thirty years since this room saw a Christmas decoration. Yer see, yer don't bother when yer live on yer own, it doesn't seem worth it.'

'Well, ye're not on yer own now, Auntie Lizzie, 'cos yer've got us. We're here to stay whether yer like it or not. We all love the bones of yer.'

Lizzie grinned. Jenny didn't only look like her mother, she had the same sense of humour and had picked up all her sayings.

By the time the foursome were ready to leave, Lizzie was sitting comfortably on the couch with her hands curled around a cup of cocoa. The fire had been damped down and the fireguard put in front for safety. And her bed was being warmed by a hot-water bottle. She was being spoilt in her old age and loving every minute of it. These four youngsters were very considerate and a credit to their parents. She wished things could stay this way until the end of her days, but knew it wasn't possible. They were coming to an age when they would meet someone and start courting. It was surprising the boys didn't have girlfriends already, they were old enough. Even as she thought it, Lizzie knew the answer. It was as plain as the nose on her face that they were both waiting for Jenny, but the girl herself didn't favour one nor the other. They were both mates to her.

'We'll leave yer in peace now, Auntie Lizzie.' Jenny kissed her cheek. 'You go and snuggle up in yer warm bed, and have sweet dreams.'

Lizzie held her face for the other three kisses. 'Yer've been angels, the four of yer. If yer didn't have mams and dads, I'd adopt the lot of yer.'

Mick was the last to wave goodbye and when he heard Jenny's familiar peal of laughter, he hurried down the hall. 'What's going on?' Then he saw her standing on the pavement, her arms outstretched and her head back, catching the snowflakes as they fell. 'Well, yer've got yer wish, Jenny.'

'Oh, I'm so happy!' Jenny was clapping her hands and spinning around. 'I hope it sticks and we have a white Christmas.'

'It's sticking now, and it's coming down thicker,' John said. 'Look at the size of the flakes, they're like big white feathers.'

Laughing with happiness, Jenny bent down to gather a handful of snow from the pavement. It wasn't thick enough to make a decent snowball, but she'd just managed enough to fill her hand as Mick decided she was so pretty he wanted to be by her side. The devil in Jenny couldn't resist, and the snow ended up on Mick's face. Blinking rapidly, he wiped the snow away, growling like an animal. 'Ye're not getting away with that, Jenny Nightingale.' He scooped her up in his arms and laughed as her arms and legs thrashed about. 'Get me some snow, John, and I'll give her a taste of her own medicine.'

This wasn't to John's liking at all. He felt like kicking himself for not thinking of it first. 'Not on yer life, mate. I don't mind holding her for yer, though, so pass her over.'

'Pass me over!' Jenny stopped thrashing about to shake a fist. 'I'm not a sack of flaming spuds, John Hanley. Now let me down from here, if yer know what's good for yer.'

'She means it, mate,' John was happy to say. 'If I were you I'd drop her, quick.'

'I think she's too fragile to drop, so I'll either put her down gently or carry her all the way to Janet's so her feet won't get wet.'

'There yer go, big-head again.' Jenny wasn't struggling now; she'd hit on an idea to take him down a peg or two. Never in a million years did she think he could do it. He might get as far as the corner, but that was all. 'There's no way you could carry me all the way to Janet's.'

'No? Well, just watch me.' Mick began to walk down the street, his back straight and no sign of strain on his smiling face. In fact, he was in his seventh heaven. 'Yer wouldn't like to bet on it, would yer?'

'I'll bet yer don't make it all the way to Janet's. But I'm not betting with money.'

'How about a kiss, then?'

'You cheeky beggar, Mick Moynihan, I'm going to tell yer mam on you.'

'Just a peck on the cheek?'

'Oh, all right.' Jenny thought she was safe in saying that 'cos he'd never make it.

John, walking behind with Janet, was filled with envy. 'If he does manage it, Jenny, I'll have to carry yer back, just to prove I'm as strong as him.'

'You can carry me, if yer like, John,' Janet said. 'That will prove ye're as strong as Mick is. And it'll save me getting me feet wet.'

John was filled with dismay. 'Ah, I can't do that, Janet! I wouldn't have the energy left to carry Jenny home. And it's her we're betting on.' He saw her face fall and felt a heel. But there was a lot at stake here. 'I'll tell yer what, though, I'll carry yer tomorrow night. How does that suit yer?'

Janet nodded, but there was still disappointment showing on her face. 'Yeah, that suits me fine, John. Thank you.'

John felt like crawling under a stone. 'Oh, what the hell, come on, I'll carry yer.'

Janet's face lit up. 'I'll let yer kiss my cheek, John, as long as me mam doesn't see yer do it. If she did, she'd hit yer on the head with the rolling pin, and I wouldn't want yer to get hurt.'

John saw the funny side and his laughter joined Mick's. 'Oh, does it hurt when yer get hit on the head with a rolling pin? I didn't know that.'

Down at the bottom end of the street, Laura was standing on Cynthia's step when they heard the laughter. 'That's our Jenny, the stupid nit. Anyone would think she'd never seen snow before. It's about time she grew up.'

'I could never understand why ye're so against yer sister,' Cynthia said. 'I've always thought she was a nice kid.'

'Nah, you don't have to live with her. She's a real little mummy's girl, never does nothing wrong. She gets on me wick, with that smile pasted on her face all the time. Too flaming good to be true, that's our Jenny.'

Laura could feel the wet of the snow seeping into the thin soles of the high-heeled shoes she was wearing, and she shivered as she wrapped her coat tighter around her body. 'Anyway, it wasn't half exciting listening to what yer did last night. Yer were very brave, Cynthia – I couldn't have done it. Fancy yer catching them in the act and having the nerve to ask those two men for help! I would have wet me knickers and run like hell. But I really hope Larry and Jeff did get their noses broken, it's what they deserve. And fancy you following them all that way. That took some guts, that did.'

'I had to follow them to find out where they lived. Now I know, I can take it from there. The hiding they got last night will be nothing compared to what their wives will do to them when they learn what their husbands get up to every Tuesday and Thursday. I'm going to blow those two sky high, and take great delight in doing it.'

Chapter Seventeen

'Come on, Amy, get a move on, will yer?' Mary sounded impatient. 'The flaming shops will be crowded and there'll be nowt left by the time we get there.'

'Keep yer hair on, girl, I'm being as quick as I can.' Amy waddled into the hall and reached to lift her coat from one of the pegs on the hallstand. 'I don't know what the big rush is for, anyway, seeing as Wilf's put our turkey aside, the greens have been ordered and will be ready for us to pick up, and the Maypole will have our order ready.' She slipped her arms into her coat. 'Ye're a proper bleedin' worry-wart, girl, and yer'll have me nerves wrecked the way ye're going on.'

Mary tutted. 'Who, please, said last night that we'd better get to the shops early so we wouldn't get trampled in the crush?'

Amy grinned as she picked up her basket. 'Aye, well, that was last night. Things look different when ye're lying in bed all nice and warm. It was a real struggle to get me legs over the side of the bed, I can tell yer. They took one look at the snow on the window sill and decided to stay put. I gave them a good talking to, explained that you were coming early, but they wouldn't budge. In the end I had to resort to playing dirty, and I threw the bedclothes back when they weren't looking.' She slipped her keys into her coat pocket and shook her head at her neighbour. 'I don't know why ye're standing there yapping yer head off when we've got stacks to do. Have yer forgotten it's Christmas Eve?'

Mary rolled her eyes before looking down at her neighbour's feet. 'I hope yer've got sturdy shoes on, the snow is inches deep.'

'These are the only shoes I've got, girl, apart from me best ones. They wouldn't be a ha'porth of good in this weather, so it's Hobson's choice, I'm afraid.'

The two friends walked briskly down the street. With each step, Mary was pushed closer to the kerb as Amy clung to her arm in an effort to keep her feet on the slippery ground. 'Careful, Amy,' she said, as a car went past and sprayed her with slush, 'otherwise I'm going to end up in the gutter.'

Amy chuckled. 'Now I wouldn't say it, being yer mate, like. But there are those who would say they weren't surprised that yer ended up in the gutter.'

'Now why would they say that?'

'Well, you know, anyone that's always bragging and swanking, that's where they usually end up,' Amy told her, straightfaced.

'You wouldn't say that, though, would yer, sunshine?'

'Not on yer life, I wouldn't! And I'd flatten anyone that did! I mean, you and me have been mates for nearly twenty years now, and if we ever fell out I wouldn't know what to do with meself.' Amy gave what Mary called one of her dirty laughs. 'Especially on Christmas night.'

'Ye're a corker, Amy Hanley, it's a good job I don't take a blind bit of notice of yer.' Mary pushed her friend into the butcher's shop. 'My God, Wilf's doing some business today. I see he's got his wife in helping.'

'We shouldn't have to wait, we've paid for our bleedin' turkeys. All he's got to do is hand them over the counter.'

'Amy, yer can't expect Wilf to serve yer before all these other people. He'd have a mutiny on his hands if he did.'

'Sod off, girl.' Amy stood on tiptoe to see over the shoulders of the women in front. 'Good morning, Wilf,' she called out. 'I see ye're coining it in as usual. I bet when Father Christmas comes down your chimney, he'll find yer counting yer money. He won't leave yer nothing 'cos he'll think yer've got enough.'

Wilf, red in the face after being on the run since he opened the shop at eight o'clock, looked up and groaned. 'Oh, dear Lord, haven't I got enough trouble without sending me the biggest troublemaker in the neighbourhood?'

Every head in the shop turned. Those who knew Amy smiled; those who didn't tutted impatiently. If the little fat woman thought she was going to jump the queue, she had another think coming. And Wilf's wife, Irene, didn't know whether to laugh or cry. She'd been the butt of Amy's jokes a few times and, not having her husband's sense of humour, she hadn't thought them very funny. She'd make sure she didn't serve her, she'd leave that to Wilf.

Amy, bobbing up and down like a rubber ball, stuck her hand in the air. 'I'm not going to cause no trouble, Wilf, I can see ye're busy. So if yer'll just pass over the turkeys that me and me mate chose and paid for yesterday, we'll leave yer in peace to make yer fortune.'

There was muttering amongst the crowd and dark looks were aimed at the two women 'Yer'll have to wait a while, Amy, I can't serve yer now. I've only got one pair of hands, and some of these ladies have been waiting a long time.'

Mary was beginning to feel uncomfortable, but Amy was undeterred. 'Then they should have done what we did, instead of leaving it until the last minute. This means that me and me mate have got to queue twice for the same bleedin' turkey, and yer can sod that for a lark.'

214

'Yer may as well serve her, Wilf,' said one of the neighbours from their street, 'otherwise she'll carry on something shocking.' The woman said it with a smile on her face, hoping to do Amy a favour, but it didn't go down well with some of those waiting.

'She's not going before me,' said one.

'Let her wait her turn like the rest of us,' said another.

'Ay, missus, I waited me bleedin' turn yesterday. I was stood here so long with me eye on this flaming turkey, that I got real friendly with it. I even gave it a blinking name. I christened it Ben, after my feller, 'cos I always have to wait for him, as well.' Smiles were appearing on faces now, and Amy was encouraged. 'I'll lay odds that when that turkey sees me, it'll run to me shouting "Mammy".'

If Wilf had had the time, he'd have taken his hat off to her. The smiles had turned to titters and even a couple of full-blown laughs. 'Come to think of it, Amy, it does look like you. There's definitely a family resemblance.'

'I'll take that as a compliment, Wilf Burnett, because if I didn't, I'd be round that counter to give yer a fourpenny one. And now, will yer do the gentlemanly thing and reunite me with me baby, so I can take it home and put it to bed in me roasting tin.'

Wilf had served two customers while all this was going on. He'd weighed and wrapped two turkeys which were now lying on the counter. The customers didn't know he was waiting to be paid, they'd turned around to watch Amy. 'Ladies, can I have yer money, please?'

One of the women took a pound from her purse. 'Here yer are, take for both of them and I'll get Lucy's money off her later.' When Wilf came back with her two bob change, she said, 'Give that woman her turkey, she deserves it.'

Wilf gave his wife the eye. 'There's two bags on the floor out there, love, with Hanley and Nightingale on. Pass them over, will yer, so we can have a bit of peace?'

Amy wasn't going to go quietly, though. 'I just want to make sure yer've not pulled a fast one on me and given me the wrong bird.' She pulled the turkey out by its legs and held it high. 'Ay, Wilf, has this bird been on night-shift?'

'Not that I know of, Amy, but then I've been working most of the night and haven't had much time to get acquainted with it. Why?'

'I think yer've been working this poor bleedin' thing all night, too, 'cos it's only a shadow of its former self. Look, it's got no bleeding meat on its legs! I've heard of sparrow legs, but this is ridiculous! And another thing, Wilf Burnett, how could yer notice a family resemblance when it's got no bleeding head?'

'It was while I was cutting its head off, I thought of you. I remember wishing something when I brought the chopper down, but I can't for the life of me think what it was.'

215

Amy's laugh was the loudest as she put the turkey back in the bag. 'Nice one, Wilf. I'll get me own back after Christmas. After all, this is one time of the year it's a slap on the back and goodwill towards all men. So have a nice Christmas, Wilf, and you Irene. Don't be spending all yer time counting yer money, try and enjoy yerself.' Being pulled out of the shop by Mary, she yelled, 'Merry Christmas, ladies. And don't yer be doing anything I wouldn't do if I got half a chance.'

Once outside, Amy turned to Mary, her lips pursed. 'If ye're going to talk that much in every shop we go to, we'll never get finished. So keep yer trap shut, girl, and try and behave yerself.' Waddling ahead, she muttered, 'Honest to God, I've never known anyone like yer for yapping. Yer'd talk the hind legs off a donkey – that's if yer knew a donkey, and providing it had hind legs.'

When they got to the greengrocer's, Mary made Amy stand outside. 'The shop's full, and I'm not putting up with any more shenanigans from you. So you stay right there and I'll bring yer things out to yer.'

Billy Nelson was rushed off his feet, even though he had his wife and son helping. But he still had a smile on his face and a joke on his lips. He spotted Mary as he was weighing potatoes and called, 'Where's the queer one, then?'

Mary jerked her thumb towards the door. 'I've made her wait outside. She's just caused ructions in the butcher's, and I couldn't go through that again.'

'Go 'way, I bet she had them in stitches.' Billy grinned as he emptied the potatoes from the scale into a woman's basket. 'I gave yer good measure, Mrs Gillespie, seeing as it's Christmas.' He put the scale back on the big iron weighing machine that hung from the ceiling. 'I'll be with yer in two shakes of a lamb's tail, love. I just want to show Mrs Nightingale where her order is.'

'Finish serving her, Billy, I can wait.'

'No, these two boxes are your orders, and I'll be glad to get them from under me feet.' He lifted a wooden box and placed it in Mary's outstretched arms. 'That's Amy's, and the bill's inside. If yer take it out to her, I'll follow with yours.'

Amy took one look at the box and shook her head. 'I'll never be able to carry that! Who d'yer think I am, Billy Nelson, King bleedin' Kong?'

'It's what yer ordered, Amy, so don't blame me.'

'Put the turkey on top, Amy, and take the ruddy box off me,' Mary said. 'Billy's got a shop full of people to see to.'

Amy held her arms out and pretended to buckle under the weight. 'If I do meself an injury, Billy Nelson, my Ben will have something to say to yer.'

After passing Mary's order over, Billy bent to smile into Amy's face. 'I've got yer where I want yer now, haven't I? If I wasn't so busy, I could do what I like to yer and yer wouldn't be able to do a thing about it.'

'No, lad, I wouldn't. But whatever yer were doing, yer wouldn't be enjoying it, 'cos I'd have dropped this box on yer bleedin' foot and broke all yer toes.'

Roaring with laughter, Billy made his way through the shop doorway, calling over his shoulder, 'Yer can pass the money in later, ladies.'

Amy looked down at herself with dismay. 'Sod this for a lark, girl, all me well-endowments are getting squashed to blazes.'

Mary didn't want to laugh, but laugh she did. Amy's mountainous bosom was a definite drawback to carring a box in her outstretched arms. If she carried it high, her breasts would be squashed, if she lowered her arms and carried it low, her tummy would suffer the same fate. 'D'yer know what I think, sunshine? Being so well-endowed isn't all it's cracked up to be, is it?'

'Never mind all that now, girl, how am I going to get home? How am I going to carry all this, and me basket?'

'Where is yer basket?'

'Between me bleedin' feet! I suppose I could ask someone to put it over me head, and let everyone have a good laugh at my expense. But somehow I don't fancy that.'

'Well, let's not get excited. I've got my basket on me arm, so if I could pick yours up I could hang it on me other arm.' Very gingerly, Mary bent her legs and lowered herself down. 'Open yer legs, sunshine.'

'Ah, not tonight, Ben, I've got a headache.'

Mary nearly lost her balance with laughing. No matter what the problem, Amy could always find a joke in it. 'If you don't stop making me laugh, Amy Hanley, I'm going to end up on me backside with me turkey and potatoes around me. Now, behave yerself, if yer know how.'

The main road wasn't too bad for walking because the shop-keepers had cleared the snow away. But the side streets were very hazardous, and the friends walked with great care. They were just six houses away from their own homes when Amy said, 'I'm dying to go to the lavvy, girl, I'll have to move. It must be the cold weather.'

'Amy, for heaven's sake be careful or—' Mary watched with horror as Amy's foot slipped on the ice, and unable to use her arms to balance herself, she went flying. She fell on her back and all around her were scattered the contents of the box. Mary could see apples and oranges flying in all directions, but her concern was for the inert figure lying on the ground. 'Oh, dear God, let her be all right.'

Throwing everything down, Mary ran towards her friend. Never very good in an emergency, her heart was pounding in case Amy had really hurt herself and needed the kind of help she didn't know how to give. Taking a deep breath, she looked down.

'I don't need to go to the lavvy now, girl, I've used the public toilet.' Amy's smile turned to a grimace as she tried to move. 'I've certainly come a cropper, haven't I?'

'Don't you try to move, Amy Hanley, it's no joke.'

'Oh, I know that, girl, no one better. But I thought yer might be worried about me wanting to spend a penny. So it's one worry less for yer.'

'I'm going to see if Molly's in, 'cos I'm as much use as that ruddy turkey.' With tears in her eyes, Mary crossed the snow-covered cobbles, praying that Molly would be home. And her prayers were answered when the Irishwoman opened the door.

Molly took one look at Mary's face and her smile vanished. 'What is it, me darlin'?'

'It's Amy, she's fallen over and I don't know what to do.'

Molly put the catch on the door so she wouldn't lock herself out, and hurried after Mary. 'Glory be to God, Amy, what have yer done to yerself?'

'If yer'll give Mary a hand to lift me up, girl, I'll tell yer whether or not I'm still in one piece.' There was much grunting and groaning from Amy as her friends lifted her to a sitting position and dusted the snow from her coat. 'So far, so good, girls – at least there's nowt broke. I'll have a few bruises, but what's a bruise between friends? It's me backside that hurts most, and the bottom of me back. But don't worry, I'll live. Now, if yer can manage it, would yer lift me to me feet?'

It was obvious Amy was in pain when they tried to stand her upright. 'Let me bend for a while, till it eases off.'

Molly nodded to the empty box. 'Mary, me darlin', would yer pick up all the groceries, please? If yer take them inside, sure that'll be a big help, so it will. Amy will move in her own good time, won't yer, me darlin'?'

'It's me own stupid fault, I'm a crackpot. I started to run because I wanted to go to the lavvy, yer see. I don't want to go to the lavvy now, like, but I did then.'

Mary, throwing fruit and vegetables into the box, winked at Molly. 'The woman has no modesty whatsoever.'

Amy tried to stand upright to have her say, but the pain was so sharp she contented herself with raising her voice. 'What the bleedin' hell is the good of trying to be modest when yer've got an orange stuck in yer mouth and there's a ruddy dead turkey lying on yer chest? To hell with modesty, girl, that's what I say.'

When Amy insisted that all the shopping be taken into Mary's house, Molly tried to reason with her. 'But, me darlin', wouldn't it be better altogether if the shopping, and yerself, went straight into yer own house? Sure, wouldn't it save yer the trouble of doing more walking than yer need to? Yer could settle yerself on the couch with a pile of pillows to try and ease the pain. It would make things a heck of a sight easier all round.'

It would have been the sensible thing to do, but then Amy never did anything because it was sensible. It took her all her time to mount the front steps, but grunting and groaning, and using every swear-word she could think of, she finally made it. 'I'd rather get me ease on Mary's couch, it's much more comfortable than mine. Besides, I can lie and look at her nice wallpaper instead of the miserable bleedin' stuff I've got on my walls. It's enough to give yer the willies.'

'I've got to go out again for the rest of our shopping, sunshine, so it means yer being on yer own.' Mary looked at the clock and groaned. There was so much to do and time was marching on. 'Ye're as stubborn as a mule, Amy Hanley; yer'll have yer own way if it kills yer. So don't go blaming me if yer find yer can't walk at all and ye're stuck on my couch all over Christmas.'

'I'll be walking, girl, don't you worry yerself about that. If you think I'm going to let a few aches and pains stop me from coming to yer party, yer've got another think coming. I've spent weeks getting me party piece ready and I'm going to show off come hell or high water.'

Molly shrugged her shoulders at Mary. 'You go and get yer shopping done, me darlin', and I'll stay with her. I'll have a look at her bottom and back, make sure she hasn't done herself any real harm.'

Amy, who was perched on the arm of the couch, looked at Molly as though she'd gone mad. 'Listen here, Florence Nightingale, nobody has seen my backside since the midwife delivered me. Except for my Ben, of course, but then he'd paid seven and six for the marriage certificate, so he was entitled. But I ain't pulling me knickers down for no one else.' Her head and chins wagged. 'The very idea, indeed!'

Molly's body shook with laughter. 'Well, me darlin', I've got to admit I wasn't looking forward to it meself, and that's the truth of it. Not particularly because it's your backside, which I'm sure is exactly the same as me own, but because it's not the most attractive part of the body. But I'll not be criticising the Good Lord for giving us one, 'cos if He hadn't, sure, we'd have nothing to sit on.'

Imitating Molly's Irish accent, Amy said, 'Sure, it's a foine way with words yer have, Mrs Moynihan, and that's a fact. Wouldn't I even go as far as to say that you and I are on a level when it comes to making interesting conversation?'

'Then I'll leave yer to get on with educating each other,' Mary said, 'while I go to the Maypole and pick up our orders. Then there's only the bread to get in.' She shook her head at Amy. 'Yer certainly picked a fine time to take up skating, sunshine, I'll say that for yer. Only the busiest day of the year.'

Amy's face, which had drained of colour from the shock of the fall, was now showing traces of pink in her chubby cheeks. 'Take no notice of her, Molly, she's only jealous 'cos we're more cleverer than she is. Yer see, she doesn't know her arse from her bleedin' elbow.'

'Considering ye're supposed to be in agony, Amy Hanley, it certainly hasn't affected yer mouth, has it? Now, when I come back from the shops I expect to see yer walking around this room. D'yer hear me?'

'The whole bleedin' street can hear yer, girl! Yer've got a mouth on yer like a fog-horn when yer start. But I'll be walking, have no fear, 'cos we're all going to Midnight Mass, aren't we? I promised to go and I'll keep me promise.'

Mary put her basket in the crook of her arm. 'The church will probably fall down when you walk in. I've never known yer go to Midnight Mass before.'

'Well, yer see, girl, it was our John who taught me the error of me ways. He said you and Stan were going with Jenny, and all the Moynihans. He said he was going with yer whether I came or not. So I couldn't let me eldest born think his mother was a heathen, could I?'

Molly turned her face to hide a smile. John and Mick would go to any lengths to spend time with Jenny. Her son had even asked Seamus not to have too many pints because he didn't want to be ashamed of his father smelling of drink in church. And would he kindly refrain from singing at the top of his voice.

'I'll be back in an hour,' Mary said, putting her arm around Amy. 'If it hurts yer to walk, sunshine, then don't walk. Take no notice of me, I was only joking.'

'It's been a right day, I can tell yer. I certainly wouldn't want another one like it.' They were sitting around the table having their meal and Mary had gone over the day's events. 'Yer know what I'm like in an emergency, I'm about as much use as a wet fish. I always think the worst, and when Amy was lying so still, I thought she'd broken her neck.'

'Won't Auntie Amy be coming to church with us?' Jenny asked. 'I was looking forward to all of us going together. Janet and her brother are coming round to walk there with us.'

'I don't know about Auntie Amy, sunshine, we'll just have to wait and see. Me and Molly got her home between us, one holding each of her arms. She said she's coming, and yer know what she's like when she sets her mind to anything. She'll probably get Uncle Ben to give her a piggy-back.'

'I know I shouldn't laugh, love, 'cos it's not funny,' Stan said. 'But I've got this picture in me head of all the potatoes and everything flying in the air and landing all over the place.'

'Oh, when I got back from the shops we all had a laugh over it. And the one that laughed the loudest was Amy! Even though she was in pain, she thought it was hilarious. She said it was a pity no one had a camera because it would have made a good snap.' Mary looked across the table to where Laura sat. Her eldest daughter hadn't opened her mouth since they'd sat down. 'Are you coming to church with us, Laura?'

'No, I'm going down to Cynthia's.' Laura's mind was on Gary. She wouldn't see him for a week, and to her a week was an eternity. 'If she's going, I'll go with her.'

'Before yer go anywhere, yer can help Jenny to finish decorating the tree. I'll wash up and then I've got the turkey to clean and the stuffing to make.'

Jenny collected the empty plates and carried them out to the kitchen. Looking through the window, she could see the snowflakes falling and a smile lit up her face. 'Mam, it's snowing heavy, we're going to have a real white Christmas. Ooh, I'm made up.'

The smile on her face annoyed Laura. She herself had nothing to smile about, and she couldn't bear to see anyone else happy. 'I don't know why ye're getting so excited about snow. It's horrible to walk in, sloshing through it, getting yer feet all wet. I can't see anything nice about it and I think you need yer head testing.'

Mary opened her mouth to say something, but Jenny got in before her. 'It makes everywhere look pretty, but you wouldn't see that, would yer, Laura? I've never yet heard yer say anything was nice. I feel sorry for yer really, but if you want to be miserable, that's your affair. Just don't expect everybody else to be miserable with yer.' All the time she spoke, Jenny kept the smile on her face. 'I'll finish the tree on me own; you hurry out before the snow gets too thick and yer poor feet get wet.'

'Right, that's enough,' Stan said. 'This is supposed to be a happy time, so we'll have no arguments in this house, if yer don't mind.'

Only her father's intervention stopped Laura from striking her sister. She pushed her chair back and glared. 'I'll leave you to the tree, then. They say small things amuse small minds.'

'Is that what they say?' Jenny never batted an eyelid. 'It should follow then, that anyone who is never amused, has no mind at all.'

When Stan saw Laura make a dive towards Jenny, he banged his fist hard on the table and stopped her in her tracks. 'I've warned yer once and I'll not do it again. Any more of this and there'll be no presents under that tree in the morning. And don't make the mistake of thinking I don't mean it, because I damn-well do.'

As the sisters moved in different directions, their emotions were poles apart. Laura was filled with anger as she bounded up the stairs. She'll not get away with making fun of me, the little upstart. One of these days, she vowed, I'll knock that smile off her face.

Jenny was angry, too, but the anger was directed at herself. She should have kept her mouth shut instead of letting Laura get to her. Now, between them, they'd spoilt the night for their parents. But for years she'd put up with her sister's sarcastic remarks and taunts, and there had to come a time when she gave back as good as she got. She wasn't a child any more, nor was she worthless as Laura tried to make out. But she shouldn't have made her stand tonight, in front of her parents. Her mam had had a trying day as it was, without her daughters adding to the pressure.

As Jenny hung a silver ball on the tree, she glanced over at her father, who was reading the *Echo*. He didn't look relaxed, or at ease with himself, and Jenny knew she was partly responsible for putting that look on his face. And it wasn't fair, he was a good father and didn't deserve to be upset. The least she could do was try and make amends. She crossed to where he was sitting and knelt in front of him. 'I'm sorry, Dad, I shouldn't have taken off like that. It was childish of me.'

Stan lowered the paper and put out a hand to stroke the long blonde hair. 'You had reason to, sweetheart. Laura would try the patience of a saint.'

'I know, but I should be used to it now and ignore her. When I stand up to her, it makes matters ten times worse. So I'll take anything she wants to throw at me, at least until after the Christmas holiday.' Jenny scrambled to her feet and kissed his forehead. 'I'll go and say sorry to me mam, then get back to the tree. We can't have Father Christmas coming down the chimney and the place not ready for him. He'd take all our presents back.'

When Mary answered the door to John, he came in rubbing his hands. 'I've come with a message from me mam. Actually she gave me two messages, but I told her one was too cheeky, and I wouldn't pass it on in case yer slapped me face.'

'She's not coming to Midnight Mass?'

'Oh yeah, that's one of the messages.' John nodded to Stan and gave Jenny a wide smile. 'Her and me dad have gone on, so she can take her time walking.'

'She's as stubborn as a mule, your mam,' Mary laughed. 'But I'm glad, because it wouldn't have been the same without her.'

Jenny noticed John was shivering and she pointed to the fire. 'Get a warm, John, yer look like a block of ice. How come yer got so cold coming from next door?'

'I walked down to the bottom of the street with me mam, to make sure she was all right. Me and me dad took an arm each and half carried her. She'll make it, because our Eddy took over from me, and our Edna's with them, as well.'

Mary narrowed her eyes. 'What was the other message, sunshine?'

John's chuckle was loud. 'Promise yer won't hit me?'

'I'll try not to, sunshine, so spit it out.'

'Me mam said will yer leave a decent fire going, and a full kettle on the hob so there'll be a cup of hot tea for everyone when we get back from church.'

Mary's mouth gaped. 'Holy suffering ducks! That's cheek for yer, even by yer mam's standards. D'yer know there'll be about twelve people? I don't have enough cups for that many! Does she think I've got a ruddy cafe?'

John moved to stand beside Stan's chair. 'I'm keeping out of yer way while I pass on the rest of the message.' With his whole body filled with laughter that was yet to come, he went on. 'So help me, Mrs Nightingale, this is word for word. Me mam said if yer moaned about not having enough cups, I was to tell yer she'd lend yer some out of the goodness of her heart. Only ones with cracks and chips in, though, 'cos she knows how rough some of yer friends are and she's not having none of her best china broke by no hoodlums.'

The room filled with laughter. Stan was beating his fists on the arm of his chair, Jenny's arms were holding her tummy as she bent double, and Mary made no attempt to wipe the tears away. Even when she wasn't here, her mate Amy had the knack of filling her heart with happiness. 'She is one corker, your mam.'

'She is that, Mrs Nightingale. The best mother anyone could have, and that's why we all love her to bits.' John suddenly snapped his finger and thumb. 'Oh, I almost forgot. She said something about custard creams.'

'Are we all present and accounted for?' Seamus asked as Mary banged the door behind her. 'I hope ye're all well wrapped up, 'cos it's a night the divil himself wouldn't venture out in.'

'Amy went on early to give herself plenty of time to walk there slowly. But Jenny's friend and her brother haven't arrived yet.'

'It's no good hanging around waiting for them,' Stan said. 'They may have gone straight there with it being so bad underfoot.'

'But I promised them,' Jenny said, 'and I'd feel mean if they came all the way around here and we'd gone without them.'

'If we leave it any longer, sunshine, we'll not get seats.' Mary linked her arm through Stan's. 'I'm not going without yer, and it's their own fault for not being here on time. So come on, grab hold of John and Mick so yer don't slip.'

The boys had always liked Mary, but right now they thought she was wonderful. Taking up positions either side of Jenny, they bent their elbows. 'Stick yer leg in, Jenny,' John said, feeling very grown-up and protective. 'We'll make sure yer stay upright.'

'Yeah.' Mick felt a thrill run through his whole body as Jenny slipped her hand through his arm. This was a mighty step forward in his quest and he wanted to jump for joy. 'Yer've got two escorts tonight and I hope yer know how lucky yer are. There's not a girl in the neighbourhood who wouldn't swap places with yer right this minute.'

John ground his teeth. He's talking too much, he is. If he keeps that up I'll never get a word in edgeways. 'It's true, Jenny, me and me mate are very much sought after by every beauty from here to Glaxton.'

Mick looked over Jenny's head. 'Where's Glaxton when it's out? I've never heard of the flippin' place.'

'Ah well, yer see, that just shows how far our reputation has spread. If yer've never heard of the place it must be hundreds of miles away.'

The grown-ups, walking ahead, were listening to the two lads with smiles on their faces. Now Seamus decided to add his two-pennyworth. 'If I'm not mistaken, John, I've seen the name Glaxton on the map. And if me memory isn't playing tricks on me, it's in South Africa.'

'Oh well, that puts those girls out of the running, doesn't it? I feel sorry for them, 'cos they'll be really heartbroken. But, sadly for them, yer can't get to South Africa on the twenty-two tram for tuppence.'

Mary turned her head. 'Here's Janet and her brother, Jenny.'

'I'm sorry we're late, Jenny,' Janet said breathlessly, 'but the clock was slow.' She smiled at John. 'Can I walk beside me mate?'

By silent, mutual consent, John and Mick put their hand over Jenny's and held it tight. Oh no, this was their night, they'd put a lot of organisation into it. So neither Janet nor her big brother were going to spoil it. 'Ah, not now, Janet,' John said, returning her smile. 'We're just nice and comfortable.'

'Go on, yer big soft nit, let me next to her.' When there was no move made to accommodate her, Janet appealed to her friend. 'Make him move, Jenny.'

But much to Jenny's surprise, she found she was enjoying having a boy either side of her holding her hand. Especially when those two boys were making her laugh. 'Leave it for now, Jan, I'm all nice and warm and these two are making sure I don't slip.'

'You hang on to me, Jan,' Bill said, not liking the situation any more than his sister did. 'We can swap over on the way home.'

Mick's lips were moving as he talked to himself. 'On yer bike, pal, this is definitely not your night.'

While John muttered silently, 'What a hope you've got, mate. This is one night ye're not walking Jenny home. I know it's Christmas, but ye're not getting a present off me!'

Janet, oblivious to the thoughts of the three boys, linked one arm through her brother's and the other through John's. 'There yer are, we'll all be nice and warm now. All pals together, eh, isn't that nice?'

Chapter Eighteen

They'd just finished their dinner when the knock on the door came, and Mary tutted loudly. 'Just look at the state of the place; what a time for visitors to come.' She pushed her chair back. 'Jenny, will you clear the plates away, and you, Laura, pick up all the wrapping paper? Be quick!' As she walked to the door, she muttered, 'I hope it's no one important – the room looks like a pigsty.'

'I don't know what ye're worrying about, love,' Stan called. 'Every house in the country will look the same – it's to be expected.'

When Mary opened the door her misgivings fled. 'Dad! Oh, it's lovely to see yer.' They held each other close and didn't speak for a while. Then, after wishing each other the compliments of the season, she said, 'I expected yer last night, same as usual. We waited until half eleven and then had to leave. I was worried when yer didn't come because it's not like you to miss Midnight Mass. I thought yer were ill or something.'

'No, sweetheart, I went for a few drinks with the men from work and by the time I got home the weather put me off going out again.'

Mary pushed the living-room door open. 'Come in and get a warm.'

Stan jumped to his feet, his face beaming, and shook his father-in-law's hand. 'It's good to see yer, Joe, all the best.'

Jenny ran in from the kitchen and took a flying leap to put her arms around Joe's neck. 'Grandad, a Merry Christmas.' She rained kisses on his cheeks. 'I'm glad yer've made it, 'cos me mam was worried when yer didn't come last night. I told her I'd walk to yours this afternoon to see what was wrong.'

Laura watched with the fear she always felt when her grandad came these days. She wouldn't put it past Celia to let the cat out of the bag if she got in a temper. But today, mixed with the fear of being caught out, was another emotion – one of guilt. She knew the woman he'd married wasn't a nice person, and that Celia was cheating on him.

'What's wrong with yer, sweetheart, have yer fallen out with yer old grandad?' Joe bent to look in Laura's eyes. 'I thought yer'd be glad to see me.'

Laura dropped the papers she'd been picking up and walked into

227

his arms. And as he hugged her tight and kissed her, she kept telling herself it wasn't fair, it just wasn't fair. And she was as much to blame for deceiving him as Celia. In fact, she was more to blame because he was her grandad. He'd always loved her and it would kill him if he knew what she'd been doing behind his back.

'Come on, break it up.' Mary slapped her daughter's bottom. 'Anyone would think yer hadn't seen yer grandad for years.' She plumped a cushion on the fireside chair facing Stan, the one that she usually sat in. 'We've just finished our dinner, Dad, and there's plenty over. So sit yerself down while I rustle a meal up for yer.'

'Give me yer coat, Grandad and I'll hang it up for yer,' Jenny said, smiling up into his face. 'Then yer'll look as though ye're at home.'

'Wait until I empty me pockets, sweetheart, I've got some presents for yer. They're not much, mind, but it shows I was thinking of yer.'

Mary watched him take the badly wrapped packets from his pocket and sighed. Who would have thought her dad would come down to this? He'd lost so much weight his shirt collar was miles too big for him, and the shirt looked as though it had never seen an iron. And she'd noticed when she followed him in from the hall that he had a hole in the heel of his sock.

Joe handed the girls a packet each, gave Stan his, then with a smile that held a tinge of sadness, he offered the last one to Mary. 'As I said, sweetheart, they're not much. I haven't been getting any overtime in, so I haven't been exactly flushed for money.'

'Dad, I wouldn't care if there was only fresh air in this paper, as long as you're here. That's all the present I want.'

Laura was thoughtful as she began to unwrap the paper. No wonder her grandad had no money; his wife spent it all. Celia never seemed short, and she had something new on nearly every week. And Thursday night wasn't the only night she went out, either. Laura had heard Charlie talking to her when they were leaving the dance one night. He'd said, 'I'll see yer tomorrow night, my lovely, and we'll have more time on our own.'

Jenny's shriek of delight brought Laura away from her thoughts. 'Oh Grandad, it's beautiful! Look, Mam, a bracelet with red stones in.' She rushed to her grandfather and knelt in front of his chair. 'It's the best present I ever had and I love it. I love you, too, ye're the best grandad in the whole world.'

Laura looked down at her hand and nestling in the palm was a bracelet identical to the one her sister was holding high, except the stones in hers were blue. The guilt she felt almost brought tears to her eyes. They weren't good bracelets, they probably came from Woolworth's, but he must have left himself skint to buy them. 'Move over, Sis, give someone else a chance.' She pushed Jenny out of the way and took her place. 'Thank you, Grandad, it's lovely. I haven't got any jewellery worth speaking of, so I won't half swank with this on me wrist. Just wait until Cynthia sees it, she'll be green with envy.'

'Yer did well all round, Dad,' Mary said. 'The girls are over the moon, I'm always glad of a pair of stockings and Stan's already opened his packet of ciggies. Now while I see to some dinner for yer, the girls will get your presents off the tree.'

Mary spooned potatoes and carrot and turnip on to a plate, and covering it with another plate, she put it in the oven to heat up. Then she lit the gas under the pan of gravy and gave it a stir before picking up the carving knife. As she cut into the turkey, Mary's sadness turned to anger. Not for one moment did she believe her dad's story about not working overtime. For as long as she could remember, he'd always worked late at least three times a week. He wasn't on a bad wage, so why was he still wearing the same shabby overcoat and shoes that were down-at-heel? She sighed and said softly, 'Do I really have to ask that question? It's that bitch he's married to, she probably bleeds him dry. And if this was a three-bedroomed house, I'd persuade him to leave her and come and live with us. No one would blame him. She's not a proper wife, never has been and never will be.'

Jenny came skipping into the kitchen. 'Me grandad's made up with his presents, Mam. He said they're just what he wanted.'

'They'll come in useful, sunshine, especially in this weather.' When Mary had bought her father the warm scarf, gloves and thick woollen socks, she'd told herself that when he went out to work on these cold mornings, at least parts of him would be warm. 'He needs looking after, he's not getting any younger.'

Jenny held her wrist out and twisted it around. 'Isn't that lovely, Mam? I'm going to wear it at the parties.'

'All the boys will be after yer, sunshine, yer'll be the belle of the ball.'

Jenny giggled. 'All the boys – there's only John and Mick.'

'Well, they're boys, aren't they? If they're not, they shouldn't be wearing trousers.'

'Yeah, but they're me mates, I wouldn't swank in front of them. I'd get me leg pulled soft if I did.'

Mary opened her mouth, then decided not to say what was in her mind. If she told her daughter that she didn't think the two boys thought of her as a mate, she might put Jenny off and she didn't want to do that. Best to let nature takes its course. 'Set the table for yer grandad, sunshine, and I'll bring his dinner through.'

Jenny hesitated as she got to the door. And when she spoke, her voice was low. 'Mam, his wife doesn't look after him proper, does she?'

Mary was surprised, but she kept her voice light. 'What makes yer say that?'

Jenny shrugged her shoulders. 'I don't know, he doesn't look as though anyone cares for him. And sometimes he looks so sad I could cry for him.'

'Yer all know there's no love lost between me and Celia, sunshine, I've never tried to hide it. But it's not up to me to interfere in yer grandad's life, much as I'd like to.'

'Well, I love me grandad, and I hate her for not looking after him proper.'

'Keep that to yerself, sunshine. Don't say anything that will upset him.' Mary picked up a tea-towel to take the plates from the oven. 'Get that table set, there's a good girl.'

While Joe was tucking into his dinner as though he hadn't eaten for a week, Mary said casually, 'We're having the gang here tonight, Dad, for a bit of a party. Why don't yer stay and have a good laugh. That is, of course, if yer haven't got something else on.'

Joe chewed slowly on the food in his mouth, buying himself time. When he'd left the house this morning, Cynthia had still been in bed. But she must have heard him unbolt the front door, and she shouted down to him. 'I'm going to a party at one of me mates' tonight, so don't worry if I don't come home, I might sleep there.' Then, with sarcasm dripping from her words, she added, 'It would be no use you coming, they'll all be young people.'

'I haven't got anything else on, sweetheart, but yer don't want an old man at yer party.'

'Who's the old man, Joe?' Stan asked. 'I hope ye're not referring to me.'

'Go on, Grandad, say yer'll stay,' Jenny pleaded. 'Yer'll be the most handsome man at the party.'

Laura looked up from admiring her bracelet. 'Yeah, go on, Grandad, stay. Yer'll enjoy yerself.'

Mary's brow shot up. 'Don't tell me you're staying in? That would be a change, a real turn-up for the books.'

'I'm going down to Cynthia's to see what presents she got, but I'll be back in time.' Laura lowered her eyes. 'I don't suppose yer'd let her come back with me for an hour, would yer?'

Mary exchanged glances with Stan. This was the first time their eldest daughter had ever asked if she could bring a friend home; they couldn't refuse. 'Of course yer can, sunshine, but warn her that there'll be no room to breathe.'

Laura looked both surprised and pleased. 'She won't mind that, Mam. It'll be better than sitting at home twiddling her thumbs.'

Joe wiped the back of his hand across his mouth, pushed his plate away and rubbed his tummy. 'Well, seeing as there'll be so many lovely girls here, I'll stay meself. But not till too late, mind, 'cos there's no trams running and it's a long walk.'

Amy sat on Mary's couch, cushions beneath her and pillows at her back. 'I must have come a real cropper, 'cos me backside and me back are every colour of the rainbow.'

'How d'yer know that, Mam?' John asked. 'Yer'd need eyes in the back of yer head to see that part of yer body.'

'Don't be looking at me,' Ben said, shaking his head and holding his hands out. 'I did offer to have a look, but was told if I went near her she'd give me a go-along.'

'I should think so, too!' Amy huffed and puffed. 'A girl's got to have a bit of privacy. So yer'll just have to take my word for it, won't yer?'

'Have yer a mirror in yer bedroom, Amy?' Seamus had a grin on his face and a pint glass of beer in his hand. 'Is that how yer did it, me darlin'?'

'Don't yer be so personal, Seamus Moynihan, or I'll set my feller on yer.' Amy turned to Joe, who was sitting next to her on the couch, looking more relaxed and at ease than he'd looked for a long time. 'Wouldn't yer think they'd show a bit of sympathy for someone who nearly broke their neck? They've got no bleedin' hearts, none of them.'

'Ye're telling fibs, Mam,' John said. 'I did tell yer that me heart was bleeding for yer.'

'Yeah, and yer were laughing all over yer bleedin' face when yer said it.' When Amy looked at Joe, her chubby cheeks were almost hiding her eyes. 'I was laughing me own head off, Joe, but because I'm the one with the pains, I'm entitled to that privilege, aren't I? And seeing as I'm the only one in the room with a backside the colours of the rainbow, I'm one up on all of them.'

Joe grinned. 'Take a little bit of advice, Amy. If they ask yer to play truth or dare, just flatly refuse.'

Amy looked puzzled for a few seconds, then the light dawned. 'Oh yeah, I get yer, Joe! That's just what the buggers would do, an' all, the cheeky sods.'

Jenny was standing between John and Mick, looking very pretty in the new jumper and skirt she'd got for Christmas. And her hand kept going to her cheek so she could show off the new bracelet she was so proud of. 'Your mam's a scream, John. I've never yet known her to be down in the dumps.'

'Oh, she has her moments. But if she ever does get in a bad temper, it never lasts long because all me dad's got to do is tell her to look in the mirror and see the gob on her.' He took a deep breath and then said what was in his heart. 'Yer look really pretty tonight, Jenny.'

231

Mick had been all ears, listening to every word. 'Yeah, yer do, Jenny. Yer look good enough to eat. I bet yer'd taste better than me mam's Christmas pudding. And that's saying something, 'cos the pudding was delicious.'

Any other time, Jenny would have told them to stop acting daft, they were making her blush. But last night, as they were holding her hands, she suddenly became aware that what they were doing was flirting with her. It was a new experience for her, and one she enjoyed very much. So now she gave a little curtsy and said, 'I thank you, kind sirs.'

Molly, who had been watching, nudged Seamus. Nodding to where the youngsters were standing, she said softly, 'I wonder what's going to happen there? Sure, there'll be a heart broken somewhere along the line.'

'There's many hearts broken every day, me darlin', but people survive. Isn't it a fact that yer can't put love in anyone's heart; it has to grow and blossom of its own free will.'

'I know, me darlin', but I'll say an extra prayer every night to help it along.'

'As Amy's a friend of yours, wouldn't it be altogether the act of a friend to tell her to say an extra prayer every night, too? After all, the lads have been mates for years and both deserve the same chance. Would yer not be thinking that was right, me darlin'?'

But a knock on the door saved Molly from telling him that he was speaking as a father, not a mother.

Mary was expecting the newcomers to be Laura and Cynthia, and she nearly fell over backwards when she opened the door to find Janet and her brother standing there. Oh my God, she thought, yer can't move in there as it is. But she managed a smile. 'I wasn't expecting you, Janet.'

'We're not staying, Mrs Nightingale.' It was Bill who spoke. 'We only came around to see if Jenny would like to come to our house tomorrow night. Me mam said we could have a bit of a do. Just a few friends, like.'

Mary held the door wide. 'Come in and ask her. That's if yer can get in, the room is pretty crowded.'

'We won't stay.' Even as he was speaking, Bill was ushering his sister into the hall. A few minutes with Jenny was better than nothing. 'We'll have a word with Jenny, then make ourselves scarce.'

Jenny gave a shriek of delight when she saw her friend. 'Janet!' She dashed forward and missed the dark looks John and Mick exchanged when they saw Bill. Mick leaned towards his friend and whispered, 'We'll have to find a way of getting rid of him, he's beginning to get on me nerves.'

'Yeah, I know,' John whispered back. 'I believe arsenic is the best thing for getting rid of people.' His shoulders began to shake and his laugh came out the same time as Mick's. 'It doesn't leave no blood, either, so we wouldn't ruin our kecks.'

'You'll have to have a drink while ye're here, Bill.' Mary was determined to be a good hostess, even though she wasn't sure they had enough glasses. 'After all, it is the festive season. Will yer have a beer, and I'll give Janet a glass of lemonade with a drop of port in?' Her hand went to her head when there was another knock. 'Oh dear, this will be Laura and her friend. I think we've got what yer'd call a full house.'

As Mary walked to the door, Amy shouted after her, 'Ay, girl, have yer been selling bleedin' tickets for this do?'

Mary was smiling as she opened the door. 'Come in, girls, but take a deep breath, the room is at bursting point.'

'We'll put our coats on the bed, Mam,' Laura said, leading the way upstairs. 'We'll be down in a minute.'

Bill tried to get Jenny on her own to invite her to their house the next night, but he hadn't reckoned on his sister. 'John and Mick can come, too, can't they, Bill?' Janet asked in all innocence. 'They're our mates, we can't leave them out.'

Oh, I could leave them out with pleasure, Bill thought. But there was no way he could refuse, so he said grudgingly, 'Yeah, they can come. That's if they want to.'

'Of course they'll come.' Jenny's face was flushed with excitement. And it ran through Mick's mind that she looked better than the Christmas pudding and the Christmas cake put together. 'I'll make them come so they can walk me home.'

John bowed from the waist. 'I'd be honoured.'

Mick did likewise, saying, 'I'd be delighted.'

Bill was grinding his teeth when the door opened and Laura came in, followed by Cynthia. He stopped grinding his teeth and his eyes widened. That couldn't be Cynthia Pennington, surely? The wild girl who, like Laura, was always in trouble when she was young and who had gained a bad reputation since she left school. It must be her, seeing as she was here with Laura, but what a change! She looked very glamorous in a sage-green, soft wool dress which clung to the curves of her body. She was a bobby dazzler, no doubt about that.

'Jenny, d'yer think your Laura would like to come to our party?' The words were out before Bill knew he was going to say them. His mother would go mad because of the reputation the two girls had, but he was willing to risk that. Cynthia had taken his eye and his interest. 'It's only for young ones, me mam's not asking any of the neighbours.'

Jenny shrugged her shoulders. 'I think yer'd better ask her yerself. If I asked, she'd tell me to get lost.'

233

Mick had seen the change come over Bill when Cynthia walked in, and it entered his head that perhaps they wouldn't need to resort to arsenic after all. It just needed a push in the right direction. 'I'm sure she'd come if you asked her, Bill. Go on, she can't eat yer.'

When Bill looked uncertain, John thought it was time he gave a helping hand. After all, the more girls at the party, the more likely it was that they'd have Jenny to themselves. 'Would yer like me to come with yer?'

That was testing Bill's pride and he shook his head. 'I think I'm capable of doing it on my own, thanks.' Without further ado, and with a glass in his hand to boost his courage, he made his way to where the girls were standing. 'Laura, I'm having a party tomorrow night and I wondered if yer'd like to come? And the invitation is extended to yer friend, if she'd be interested.' Without waiting for Laura to reply, he turned his gaze on Cynthia. 'I've been puzzling me brains since yer walked in, and it may sound rude, but aren't you Cynthia Pennington?'

'Yer know damn well I am, Bill Porter, I haven't changed that much.' Cynthia smiled for the first time since she'd entered the room. She knew what most of the neighbours thought of her, and though it wouldn't have worried her at one time, it did now. 'You have, though. Yer've grown into a giant.'

Bill didn't want to take his eyes off her, but knew he was being watched and turned to Laura. 'How about it, Laura? Are you and Cynthia game for a party?'

'What d'yer think, Cyn? D'yer want to go?'

'Yeah, I'd like to. Thanks for the invite, Bill.'

'Right, I'll see you both at ours, about eight o'clock.' Bill pulled a face. 'Me and Janet will have to go now, Mrs Nightingale's got enough on her plate without us gatecrashing her party. But I'll look forward to seeing yer tomorrow.' He handed his now empty glass to Laura. 'Will yer be a pal and take this off me hands?'

By the time Bill and Janet left, enough beer had been drunk to put everyone in a party mood. And Seamus started the revelry with *Phil the Fluters' Ball*. Mick took hold of Jenny's arm and pulled her into the middle of the floor. Then John, having no intention of playing wallflower, joined them. Jenny was embarrassed at first, but when she saw Laura and Cynthia take to the floor, she threw her shyness out of the window and joined in the merriment. But Amy was the one who had the rafters ringing with laughter. She couldn't get up, but wasn't going to be left out. One leg after the other was kicked out and the hem of her skirt was lifted to shake to the tune of the jig. She winced with every movement, and the contortions of her face were enough to send everyone into pleats.

When Seamus stopped singing, Amy sat back and said, 'By, I did enjoy that. It did me more good than the dose of salts I had this morning.'

Laura and Cynthia clung to each other, gasping for breath. 'Oh dear, I've never laughed so much in all me life,' Cynthia said. 'I'm glad yer mam asked me to come.'

'Yeah, it's great, isn't it?' Laura looked over at Amy. 'Yer know, I've always thought me Auntie Amy was crackers. But she's dead funny really, isn't she?'

Stan was standing by the kitchen door, ready to refill glasses, and Mary went to join him. 'Have you ever seen our Laura laugh so hearty before, or let herself go?'

He put his arm around her waist and pulled her close. 'Two great minds think alike, love, I was just thinking the same thing. And that Cynthia's turned out to be a surprise. She's not as forward or hard-faced as I expected.'

'Ay, out,' Mary said, 'Mick is going to sing.'

Mick cleared his throat. 'Yer must be fed up with Irish songs, so I'll do one of Al Jolson's. I'm telling yer it's him I'm doing, 'cos yer won't recognise it otherwise.' He knelt down on one knee and with all the great singer's facial expressions and hand movements, he began to sing 'Mammy'. He did it so well, not even Amy dared to join in. Then he went straight into 'Toot-Toot-Tootsie, Goodbye' and the room erupted.

Cynthia nudged Laura in the ribs. 'Ay, he isn't half handsome, isn't he? Get a load of those eyes and dimples.'

'Yeah, he's not bad I suppose,' Laura said, 'but I prefer blonds.'

'And the other one, John Hanley, he's not to be sneezed at either. It's hard to think of them as the kids who used to play footie in their short trousers. Still, they probably think the same about us. We've all grown up, and changed. I got a shock when I saw Bill Porter – he's grown into a real he-man.'

'Yer can keep them all – for me, I'll stick to my Gary. He knocks spots off any of them for looks.'

'We've only got your word for that, Laura, and everybody has different ideas on what is handsome and what is not. As they say, beauty is in the eye of the beholder.' Cynthia studied her friend's face before saying, 'At the moment I'm off men, I feel uncomfortable with them and wouldn't trust them an inch. That is what those two thugs have done to me. But I'm hoping that when I'm even with them, I'll get back into the swing of things. That's if they haven't put me off men for life.'

'Yer'll be all right, kid, I know yer will,' Laura said. 'All fellers are not the same.'

Cynthia shook herself mentally. It would be a long time before she trusted herself with a man, she knew that. But she was only

235

sixteen, for heaven's sake, so she had to try and put the past behind her and get on with her life. 'When am I going to meet this Mr Wonderful of yours? I can't wait to see if he's all yer've cracked him up to be.'

'Oh, he is, and more. Yer'll meet him soon, Cyn, but I want to get to know him a bit better meself first. After I've been out on a few dates with him, eh?'

Martha Porter faced her son across the table. 'You've what! Have yer lost the run of yer bloody senses? If you think I'm having those two tarts in this house, yer've got another think coming, me lad.'

'Oh, come on, Mam, be reasonable.' Bill had expected opposition but nothing like this. 'You haven't set eyes on them for years, so how can yer talk about them like that?'

Janet's brow was furrowed. She couldn't understand why everything had suddenly gone wrong. Her and Bill had been so happy walking back from the Nightingales', talking and laughing about what games they'd play at the party. And now there was all this shouting. 'What d'yer mean, Mam, about them being tarts?'

'You keep out of it. Your brother knows damn well what I mean.' Martha's face was red and her nostrils flared. 'I will not have those two trollops in my house, and that's the end of it. So yer can just take yerself back there and tell them the party's off.'

'Calm down, Martha,' her husband said, 'before yer burst a blood vessel. If Bill's invited Jenny and the other two girls, yer can't just un-invite them.'

'Oh, can't I? Well, just you wait and see whether I can or not. If he doesn't turn around and go back right this minute, I'll go meself.'

'Martha, I said calm down, and I mean it. Now sit down in that chair and let's talk like reasonable adults, instead of bawling at each other.' When his wife stood her ground, he pointed to the chair. 'I said sit down.'

Martha was taken aback. It was very seldom that her husband raised his voice, never mind used that tone to her. So she turned towards her chair. And when her back was to them, Vincent gave a slight shake of the head, to indicate to his son that he stay out of it.

'Don't think ye're going to change me mind for me, Vincent Porter,' Martha had no intention of giving in, ' 'cos ye're not.'

'Let's talk it through, shall we, just to clear things in me mind.' Vincent leaned forward and rested his elbows on his knees. 'Yer can't go around calling people tarts and trollops, love, unless yer've got good reason to. And as I only know these girls by sight, I'm at a loss as to what yer reason is.'

'Oh, come off it, Vincent Porter! Everybody knows what Laura Nightingale and Cynthia Pennington are like.'

'I don't,' Vincent said quietly. 'So tell me.'

'They're impudent, hard-faced little madams, that's what. And they're a holy terror for the boys. Anything in trousers, they're not fussy.'

'And this is first-hand knowledge, is it, Martha, not gossip? They've given you cheek, and with your own eyes you've seen them fooling around with boys?'

'Well, no, not me personally,' Martha blustered. 'But you ask anyone in their street, they'll tell yer what they're like.'

'So yer'd blacken their names on the word of gossip-mongers? I'm surprised at yer, Martha Porter.'

Bill couldn't let this go on, it wasn't fair to his mother. 'Me mam's not wrong altogether, Dad. The two of them were terrors at school, I know that even though I wasn't in their class. And they did have a bad reputation in their street for giving cheek. But they've grown up now, they've been working for over two years.'

There was suspicion in Martha's eyes. 'Have you been out with either of those girls on the sly?'

'No, I haven't, Mam! In the last year I've seen Laura a couple of times when I've walked Jenny home, but we've hardly exchanged half-a-dozen words. And tonight, in the Nightingales', I saw Cynthia for the first time in years. I only invited them to make the numbers up 'cos we were short of girls. Jenny's coming with Mick and John, and I asked me mate, Gerry. That means two girls and four boys.' In an effort to put a smile on his mother's face, he asked, 'How would you like it, Mam, if yer were playing Postman's Knock, and the chances were fifty-fifty that yer'd get to kiss yer sister?'

When Martha heard her husband chuckle, she knew she'd lost the fight. But she wasn't going to just cave in. 'You haven't had much to say for yerself, Janet. What do you think?'

'Mam, I only wanted a party, I didn't want all this shouting and falling out.'

Martha threw her hands up. 'Okay, okay, you win. But I warn yer, if I see either of those girls messing around with the boys, or snogging, they'll be out of that door so quick they won't know what's hit them.'

'Fair enough, Mam,' Bill said, throwing his father a look of gratitude. 'Now, can me and our kid take our coats off and get a warm by the fire?'

Chapter Nineteen

When John and Mick called for Jenny on Boxing Night, they found Lizzie Marshall sitting in Stan's fireside chair looking warm and happy. They made straight for her, and standing either side of her chair they bent to kiss her cheeks. 'Yer should have come last night, Auntie Lizzie,' John said, 'it was a cracking party.'

'Yeah, yer missed a good night.' Mick's dimples deepened. 'Most of all, and yer'll kill yerself when I tell yer this, yer missed me doing me Al Jolson impersonation.'

Lizzie, her cheeks pink from the warmth of the fire, smiled up at them. 'I did miss a treat then, didn't I? But I knew there were going to be a lot of people here and I'm getting too old now for noisy parties. Tonight will suit me fine, with Amy and Molly and their husbands coming. Seamus has promised to sing *Rose of Tralee* for me, and yer never know, after a glass of port I might even give a song meself.'

'Oh aye, Auntie Lizzie,' John fingered a wisp of the fine white hair, 'yer've got hidden talents, have yer?'

Lizzie tapped her nose. 'Ah now, that would be telling.'

'If yer did happen to have a drink over the eight, Auntie Lizzie,' Mick said, dropping on his haunches so he could look into her face, 'and yer did sing a song, what would it be?'

'My very favourite, son – "Just A Song At Twilight".'

Mary shuffled to the edge of the couch and tapped Mick on the shoulder. 'Do yer know it, sunshine?'

'Mrs Nightingale, there isn't a song I don't know. I've been listening to me mam and dad singing since the day I was born.'

'Would yer sing it for her? Our Jenny and Laura are upstairs getting ready, so yer've got plenty of time.'

Stan leaned forward now. 'Go on, son, it's one of my favourites, too.'

Mick looked up at John. 'If you make fun of me, pal, I'll crack yer one.'

'I won't make fun of yer, mate, not when it's for Auntie Lizzie. If I can get the hang of the tune, I'll whistle along with yer.'

So it was when Jenny opened the door, she heard the pure clear sound of Mick's voice. She stood quietly by the door so as not to disturb them, and wondered at a boy from a small two-up two-down house, having the voice of an angel. And then she saw John curl a hand around his mouth and soon his tuneful whistling joined Mick's voice. The words of the song always made her feel sad, but it was the sight of the two boys that had her sniffing the tears away. They'd been mates all through school and had remained firm friends. Just like her and Janet.

'Oh, that was beautiful.' Lizzie wiped a hand across her eyes. 'I wouldn't have the nerve to sing it after hearing that. Anyway,' she smiled up at John, not wanting to praise one and leave the other out, 'I wouldn't have the marvellous accompaniment that you had.'

Mick straightened himself out. 'We usually charge, yer know, Auntie Lizzie, but not those we love.' He turned to Jenny. 'I knew yer were there. I always know when ye're there, even if I can't see yer.'

Lizzie smiled, while Mary and Stan pulled surprised faces at each other. John, on the other hand, was trying to think of a way to get even. 'The only way yer'd know that, mate, would be if Jenny ponged. And I can't smell nothing.'

Jenny roared with laughter. 'Will you two ever grow up?'

'Not unless we're forced to,' Mick said. 'We like acting daft and yer can't get away with it when ye're grown-up.'

'Well, try and act grown-up tonight, please. Remember, it's me mate's house we're going to.' Jenny slipped into her coat and asked, 'What time d'yer want me in by, Mam?'

'It's work tomorrow, sunshine, so I think eleven is late enough.' Mary cocked an ear. 'Isn't Laura going with yer?'

'Yeah, but she's calling for Cynthia first.' Jenny blew a kiss. 'Enjoy yerselves and don't get too drunk.'

Martha Porter was looking for something to fault the two girls, but so far they hadn't put a foot wrong. They were friendly without being pushy, polite, well-dressed, and their faces weren't caked with make-up. And far from running after the boys, they were sat side-by-side on the couch while Bill and his mate Gerry were doing their damnedest to chat them up. They weren't getting very far, either, from what she could see. It was going to be a very quiet party from the looks of things. If it wasn't for Mick and John, it would be dead boring. They had Jenny and Janet in stitches the whole time. When Mick cracked a joke, John had one ready to throw back at him, and vice versa. They seemed to bounce off each other. And they were keeping Vincent amused, too. Her husband never had a smile off his face.

'Why don't yer put a record on, Bill?' Martha asked. 'Liven the place up a bit.'

Laura showed her interest. 'Ooh, have yer got a gramophone?'

Martha proudly lifted the lid of a wooden cabinet standing next to her chair. 'Yes, and we've got some records.'

'Do yer dance, Cynthia?' Bill asked hopefully.

Cynthia seemed to sink back further on the couch. 'No, I've never been to a dance, but Laura can. I'll be quite happy to sit and watch.'

'What shall I put on, a waltz or a quickstep?'

Gerry, who thought he was God's gift to women, stuck out his chest. 'It doesn't make no difference to me, Bill, I can dance to anything.'

Laura, thinking the night wasn't going to be a complete waste of time, was eager to show off her prowess on the dance floor. It was a pity somebody hadn't told her that Gerry was the biggest liar in Liverpool, and the worst dancer. But she was about to find out the hard way. He couldn't wait for her to stand upright before pulling her into his arms, gripping her left hand tight and thrusting their arms out as far as they would stretch. If anyone had been standing near, they would have either lost a few teeth or been sporting a black eye. He started off with the wrong foot and his size ten shoe landed down hard on Laura's toes. She let out a cry and her face crumpled with the pain, but Gerry soldiered on regardless.

Mick and John looked on with amusement. 'She'll have no feet left by the time this record's over,' Mick spoke out of the side of his mouth. 'He's like a walking plank.'

'Yeah,' John agreed, 'as stiff as a board.'

'Ay, Jenny, d'yer want to have a go? Yer couldn't be any worse than that bloke.'

Jenny shrank back. 'No, thanks, Mick, I've never danced in me life.'

'I'll show yer how, eh? If I excuse yer sister, saving her from a fate worse than death, you could watch what she does with her feet, and then have a go with me when they put the next record on.'

John was certain Mick wouldn't excuse Laura. Even if he liked her, which he didn't, he wouldn't have the nerve. 'Go on, mate, I dare yer. In fact, I double dare yer.'

Mick looked down into eyes as blue as the sky on a summer's day. 'How about it, Jenny, are yer game?'

'Ooh, I don't think so, Mick, I'd be frightened of making a fool of meself.'

'I'll dance with yer, Mick,' said Janet, who was on home territory and didn't care if she did make a fool of herself. 'I'd like that.'

Mick's heart plummeted, but he didn't let it show. 'Okay, Janet, ye're on.' With that he stepped forward and touched Gerry's arm. 'Excuse me, please.'

The relief on Laura's face was obvious. And when Mick began to twirl her around like the experienced dancer he was, she was delighted. 'Thanks, Mick, I owe yer one. That bloke was flaming hopeless.'

Too quickly the record ground to a stop. 'Ah, I was enjoying that,' Laura said. 'Ye're a good dancer, Mick. If I get lumbered again, will yer come to my rescue?'

Mick grinned. 'I've promised the next dance to Janet, but John's a good dancer, better than me. He can come to yer rescue next time.'

Martha turned the record over and the strains of another waltz filled the room. 'Take yer partners for a waltz,' she said, sitting back and folding her arms. Then with a wink at Laura, she added, 'And it's an "excuse me".'

Mick bowed from the waist before extending a hand. 'This is my dance, I believe, Miss Porter.'

Janet was willing and eager. 'Don't twirl me around, though, Mick, not until I've found me dancing feet proper.'

'I'm not that daft, Janet.' Mick led her into the middle of the room. 'I'll put me hands on yer waist, and that way yer can see me feet better.'

Cynthia saw Gerry rub his hands together and look at Laura. Sitting next to her, perched on the arm of the couch, was Bill. She tapped his arm. 'Get Laura up quick, before soft lad gets to her.'

Bill bent towards her ear and whispered, 'Only if yer promise to come out with me one night.'

'We'll talk about that later, now get moving.'

Laura was happy because Bill was a good dancer, and Janet was deliriously happy because, under Mick's tuition, she was mastering the basic steps of the waltz. Her face was animated and she'd never looked so pretty.

'Ye're doing well, sweetheart,' Martha called, 'I'm proud of yer.'

When the dance ended, Mick passed her over to John. 'You can give Janet her second lesson now, while I give Jenny her first.' He saw Jenny was about to object and got in before her. 'Don't forget, I let me mate double dare me so I could dance with yer.' He stood in front of her and put his hands on her waist. 'There's only three basic steps in a waltz, so let's try. You go back with yer left foot, to the side with yer right foot, then bring them together. See, do it again. There yer go, it's as easy as falling off a bike.'

Jenny was feeling quite pleased with herself. At least she'd got over her shyness, and those three steps were easy enough. So when Mick said they should hold each other properly now, she did it without hesitation or thought. And she was too busy keeping tabs on her footwork to notice the strange expression on his face. He was experiencing feelings he'd never felt before, like his spine and legs had turned to jelly, and there were shooting stars in his head. He put his lips close to her hair and whispered, 'Grow up quickly, Jenny.'

She pulled back a little. 'What did yer say, Mick?'

'Oh er, the time's going quick.'

Janet watched them for a while, then looked up at John. 'Mick's holding Jenny different to what we are. Why can't we hold each other proper, like?'

John chuckled. 'What about yer mam and her rolling pin?'

Not for one moment did he think she'd take him seriously. And he blushed to the roots of his hair when she called, loud enough for everyone to hear: 'Mam, if John holds me proper, yer won't hit him on the head with the rolling pin, will yer?'

It was hard to say who laughed the longest, but the loudest definitely came from Mick, with Cynthia a close second. And Martha had to get hers under control before she could answer. 'As long as he leaves a space of three inches between yer.'

'Did yer hear that, John?' Janet lifted a hand and measured with her thumb and forefinger, what she thought was three inches. 'That's about it.' She looked so innocent, he thought, Ah, God bless her, and he felt like hugging her, as he would a baby.

For the rest of the evening, in between having something to eat and drink, the two boys were very fair with each other and swapped partners for every dance. That is, all except for two dances which the girls had with Gerry, who they felt sorry for. The fact that they were beginners didn't make any difference to him; he plodded on in his own way anyhow.

They were enjoying themselves so much, Jenny was sorry when she saw the time was a quarter to eleven. 'I'll have to go, Jan, I promised me mam I'd be home by eleven.'

'Yer don't need me to walk yer home tonight, then Jenny?' Bill asked, thinking she was still the nicest-looking girl he knew. But he was attracted by the mystery and intrigue which Cynthia wore like a cloak. She was very polite, but kept him and Gerry at a distance, as though they held no interest for her. And although his mate might be a lousy dancer, he was a fine figure of a man and had no trouble getting girls. So if this girl sitting on his mam's couch was the real Cynthia, then she certainly hadn't earned her reputation as a man-eater. Either that or she was a ruddy good actress. This was the mystery he wanted to solve.

Mick was holding Jenny's coat when she replied, 'No, I've got two escorts tonight. But the other girls will need to be walked home.' She shook Martha and Vincent by the hand. 'Thank you for a lovely party, I really enjoyed meself.' Her infectious giggle brought a smile to all the faces, even that of her sister. 'And I got free dancing lessons into the bargain, so all in all I'd say I hopped in lucky.'

'Ye're welcome here any time, queen, yer know that,' Vincent said. 'Our door is always open to yer.'

Martha gave her a hug. 'A second daughter to us, that's what yer are.'

Janet showed them to the door. 'Are we going to Auntie Lizzie's tomorrow night?'

She was looking at Jenny, but it was Mick who answered. 'Yeah, we'll all go. We won't stay long, just keep her company for an hour or two.'

'Oh, yeah.' Janet was childlike in her pleasure. 'We can show her how we've learned to do the waltz.'

Jenny put a hand through each of the boys' arms. 'We'll do that, Jan, and give her a good laugh. Thanks for inviting us to yer party, and good night and God bless.'

Back in the living room of the Porters' house, Cynthia and Laura were on their feet. 'We'll be on our way, 'cos it's back to the grind tomorrow.'

'We'll see yer home,' Bill said. 'Just in case there's any drunks around.'

'Yer've no need to, Bill,' Laura said. 'We can look after ourselves.'

'I've no doubt yer can, but we'll still come with yer, even if it's only to stop yer from falling over on the ice.'

'Yeah, it's bad out,' Janet said. 'Yer'd be best linking each other, like Jenny and the two boys.'

They took their leave after thanking the Porters for a lovely evening. And they left Martha looking sheepishly at her husband. 'It just goes to show, doesn't it, that yer can't believe everything yer hear? They seem like two nice girls to me, and if anyone tells me otherwise, I'll clock them one.'

Having been asked to do so as a favour to his workmate, Gerry took Laura's arm and walked in front. 'Do you and yer friend live near each other?'

'In the same street.' Laura was glad of his supporting hand because the slush had hardened and it was very slippery underfoot. 'I live at the top end, and Cynthia at the bottom.'

'How come you can dance and she can't?'

'Because I go dancing with me boyfriend.' Laura thought a little white fib would nip in the bud any ideas he was harbouring. 'He's a smashing dancer.'

Bill allowed the distance between the couples to grow. He wanted to talk to Cynthia without being overheard. 'I asked yer earlier if yer'd come out with me one night, but I never did get an answer.'

Cynthia knew she had nothing to fear from Bill, he was a different breed to Larry and Jeff. But still she couldn't bear the thought of a boy even touching her. Perhaps after next week, when she'd completed the task she'd set herself, she might feel different, be more settled in her mind. And with Bill Porter she'd be as safe as houses. 'I'll come out with yer one night, but it won't be for a couple of weeks.'

'Why is that? Have yer got a boyfriend?'

'No, it's just that I'm tied up for a few weeks, that's all.'

'Yer haven't got a boyfriend, but ye're tied up every night?' Bill raised his eyebrows questioningly. 'And I've got to wait two weeks for a date?'

'That's the way it is, Bill, I'm sorry. I'm not playing hard to get, if that's what yer think. I've got something important on and I can't cancel it. If yer'd rather leave it, then I'll understand. We'll probably bump into each other some time.'

'I'll wait, but give me a date now, so I'll know yer mean it.'

Without hesitation, Cynthia said, 'Two weeks tonight, and yer can call for me.'

With that Bill had to be satisfied. As he had to be satisfied when she would only allow him to give her a good-night peck on the cheek. He kept telling himself to be sensible, she was just another girl and there were plenty of them around. But her very coolness fired his interest in her and he knew the next two weeks were going to be the longest he'd known.

'What are you doing with yerself tonight, sunshine?' Mary asked. 'Are yer coming to the Moynihans'?'

Laura shook her head. 'No, I'm going to the dance. They didn't have one last week with it being Christmas, but it's open tonight. I don't know whether they'll finish at eleven, like they usually do, or if they'll carry on to let the New Year in.'

'Well, if ye're not too late, Mrs Moynihan won't mind if yer call in. Yer don't want to see the New Year in on yer own, do yer?'

'I'll see how it goes.' Laura had big hopes for tonight and wasn't expecting to be going across the street. She'd made up her mind that no matter what Celia said, she was staying until the end. Surely Gary, on this special night, would ask to walk her home. And she should get her first kiss, 'cos at midnight everybody would be kissing everybody else – even strangers. Then a thought entered her head that took some of the pleasure away. Her grandad wouldn't be getting a kiss; he'd be all on his own. Unless, with a bit of luck, his wife stayed in with him. If she did, she'd be doing everyone a favour.

'Is Auntie Lizzie coming to the party, Mam?' Jenny asked. 'Or does she think it'll be too noisy for her?'

Mary chuckled. 'It will be too noisy for her, sunshine, without a doubt. Especially as Auntie Amy's back in fine form and raring to go. I don't know what she's got up her sleeve for us tonight, but she's had a sly smile on her face all day.'

'Oooh, I can't wait.' Jenny's eyes were sparkling with excitement. If there was any dancing tonight, she'd definitely have a go. 'Can I get washed at the sink, Mam, before we start the dishes? Then I can take me time getting ready.'

'I was going to ask that,' Laura said. 'Let me go first, 'cos I've got a long way to go. You've only got to go across the street.'

'Yeah, okay, but don't make a meal of it. There's others in the house beside you.'

When Laura was leaving, her dance shoes tucked under her arm, Mary asked, 'Yer won't be coming home on yer own at that time of night, will yer?'

'No, I'll be with Cynthia.'

'Even so, just take care. There'll be a lot of people out on the street and most of them will be blotto.'

'Mam!' Laura shook her head and rolled her eyes. 'We can take care of ourselves, we're not kids.'

'Yer mam's only warning yer,' Stan said, 'so think on.'

Jenny watched her sister leave the room and she felt worried inside. She didn't know where Laura got to on a Thursday night, but wherever it was, she certainly didn't go with her friend. Jenny had seen Cynthia a few times when she'd been coming back from Janet's, and it was too early for her to have been to a dance. Besides, she was always on her own and wearing her working clothes.

Jenny sighed as she went upstairs for her best shoes. I wish our Laura wouldn't lie to me mam, she thought. And I wish I didn't know she was lying because it makes me feel guilty. If she gets herself into trouble, and me mam and dad find out I knew there was something going on, they'd say I was as bad as her for not letting on. But I just can't bring myself to snitch on my own sister.

'Come on, sunshine,' Mary shouted up the stairs. 'Me and yer dad are ready and waiting.'

'I'm coming, Mam.' Jenny sighed before saying under her breath, 'I'm not going to let our Laura spoil the party for me. She's probably having a whale of a time, wherever she is, so why shouldn't I enjoy meself?'

Laura pelted around the corner of Burton's shop to the side entrance of the dance hall. All the time she was chanting over and over, 'Let him be there, let him be there.' She took the stone steps two at a time, and when she pushed open the door at the top her heart flipped when the first person she saw was Gary. She could tell by the way his face lit up that he was as glad to see her as she was to see him. Even the presence of Celia and Charlie couldn't dim her happiness.

'I've been waiting for yer.' Gary reached for her hand. 'I was worried that yer weren't going to come.'

'Just as if.' Laura nodded to Celia and Charlie. 'Hi-ya. I'll put me coat in the cloakroom, I won't be a tick.'

Celia followed close on her heels. 'Come to the toilets with us, I want a word with yer.'

Looking in the spotted mirror over a sink, Laura wet a finger with her tongue before running it over her eyebrows, making sure every hair was in place. She wanted to look her best tonight. 'What d'yer want to have a word with me over?' she asked Celia's reflection in the mirror. 'I can't wait to get on the dance floor.'

'The dance is going on until twelve o'clock tonight, but it wouldn't be a good idea for you to stay until then. I think eleven is more like it.'

Laura spun round, eyes wide with astonishment. 'What a hope you've got! I'm not leaving at eleven! I've told me mam I'll be late, so it's all right.'

'Have yer told yer mother ye're with me?' There was a sly look on the older woman's face. Her voice was as sweet as honey, but there was a threat in her words. 'I bet yer haven't.'

'No, I told her I was with Cynthia. But what's that got to do with anything? I'm not leaving early, and that's that. I'm staying right to the end.'

Celia leaned against the tiled wall and lit a cigarette. She watched the smoke ring spiral upwards until it broke apart. 'What d'yer think yer mother would do if she knew yer were with me? She wouldn't like it, would she?'

Laura was stung into saying, 'No, she wouldn't like it at all. But seeing as she won't find out, I don't see what it's got to do with anything.'

'She might find out. I might have a row with yer grandad one day and it might all come out in the open. I wouldn't do it on purpose, like, but yer know how it is when yer get in a paddy, yer'll say anything in the heat of the moment.' Celia pushed Laura out of the way so she could stand in front of the mirror. Spitting on a finger and thumb, she took a strand of hair and twisted it into a kiss-curl. 'And I'd have to explain how the Thursday meetings came about, wouldn't I? That means yer mam finding out I gave yer the underskirt for yer birthday.'

Laura sucked in her breath. 'Yer wouldn't be that mean, would yer?'

'Not while we're friends I wouldn't, of course not. And we are friends, aren't we?'

She's blackmailing me, Laura thought, as she stared into eyes that were as cold as steel. And there's nothing I can do about it because she's spiteful enough to carry out her threat. 'I never said we weren't friends, did I? But I still don't see why I have to leave the dance early. What difference does it make to you?'

247

'Well, yer see, kid, I'm going on to a party with Charlie at eleven, and we're taking young Gary with us. So yer'd be all on yer lonesome and I'd worry about yer getting home.'

Would you heckerslike worry about me, Laura said silently. The only person you worry about is yerself. But she knew better than to voice her thoughts. She'd got herself involved with a really bad woman who wouldn't think twice about getting her into serious trouble. 'Why is Gary going to the party with yer? Why can't he stay here with me?'

'I promised me friend I'd bring him 'cos they're a few fellers short. And when I asked Gary, he jumped at the chance.'

Laura's heart slumped as she gazed down at the floor. She'd been looking forward all week to this night, and now it had all gone wrong. But what she couldn't understand was, while Gary's eyes and smile, and his obvious delight at seeing her, told her one thing, his actions told her another. If he had any feelings for her, he wouldn't leave her, not tonight of all nights, to go to a party.

When Laura raised her head, it was to see a gloating expression on Celia's face. And this angered her. 'I'm going to ask Gary to stay with me. I bet he will if I ask him.'

'I wouldn't do that if I were you, kid. He's already said he'd come with us and you'd only put him on the spot if yer asked him to let us down.'

Laura flounced towards the door. 'I'm going into the dance, that's what I came for.'

Gary was waiting and put his hand out to her. 'What the heck have yer been doing? I was beginning to think yer'd flushed yerself down the lavatory.'

She pulled him through the double doors of the dance hall. 'Let's dance.'

'Don't yer want to put yer handbag down?'

'No, I'll do it later.' Laura's tummy was churning over as she followed Gary's steps in a slow foxtrot. 'I've been looking forward to tonight.'

'Yeah, me too, babe. I missed yer last week.'

'Then why have yer promised to go to a party with Celia, leaving me on me own?'

Gary slowed down, a surprised expression on his face. 'What did yer say I've promised to do?'

'Don't come that with me, Gary, yer know what I'm talking about. Celia said she invited yer to a mate's party and yer jumped at the chance.'

Gary kept on dancing, his eyes looking over Laura's shoulder. 'Oh, that? I wasn't fussy, but she talked me into it. She said you'd be leaving early, anyway.'

248

'She had no right to say that, she's not running me life for me. I asked me mam if I could stay till the end, and she said I could. I wouldn't have bothered if I'd known you weren't going to be here.' Laura was near to tears. 'Why d'yer always have to do what Celia tells yer, anyway? She doesn't own yer.'

'I owe Celia a favour and I'm obligated to her.'

'Yer don't have to jump every time she pulls the strings! Can't yer, just for once, tell her to get lost?'

'Can you tell her to get lost?'

'No, I can't,' Laura admitted, 'because she can make trouble for me.'

'Celia can make trouble for a lot of people, babe, believe me. We'll leave it at that for now, but one day I'll tell yer the whole story.'

Laura was thoughtful for a while. And troubled. What had she let herself in for with Celia? Oh, how she wished she'd never seen her outside the factory gates that night. Then none of this would have happened. 'Can I ask yer something, Gary?'

'Go ahead, babe.'

'Do you like me? Yer know, really like me?'

'Of course I like yer.' He pulled her closer. 'I would have thought that was obvious to anyone.'

'And if it wasn't for Celia having some sort of hold over yer, would yer like me more?'

'Listen, babe, this conversation is just between you and me. Don't ever repeat it to anyone. Celia is not a woman to be crossed, she's dangerous. I go along with her because she could bring trouble to me door. One day I'll tell yer the whole sorry story, but just for tonight, for the few hours we've got, let's enjoy ourselves, eh?'

'And you're still going to the party with her and Charlie?'

'If I don't, I won't be the only one in trouble. She'll crucify you and yer family. And don't think I'm exaggerating because I've seen it happen to people who crossed her path.'

Laura pulled a face. 'So I won't get me New Year's kiss after all? That's all I've thought about all week.'

Gary smiled down at her. 'I think we can manage that, babe. When Charlie and Celia go out for their usual half hour, we'll find a dark corner somewhere.'

'Where do they disappear to, Gary?'

'I think I've said enough for tonight, babe, so let's dance.' He lowered his head and spoke into her hair. 'I like you very, very much, babe. And I mean it.'

After the interval, a spot waltz was announced. And with the whole room in darkness except for the light moving over the dancing couples, Gary led Laura to a quiet corner and put his arms around her waist. 'Happy New Year, babe.'

Laura smiled up at him, wishing this moment could last for ever. 'Let's make a wish before we kiss, eh? Let's wish that something happens to Celia and we don't have to see her ever again.'

'I've been wishing that for the last eight months, babe, but me wish hasn't been granted. I keep telling meself she'll come unstuck one day, and she will. She can't go around bossing people and threatening to ruin their lives.' He pulled her close. 'Can I have me kiss now, before the lights go up?'

When his lips came down on hers, Laura felt as though all the breath had gone from her body and her head was spinning. If his arms hadn't been holding her tight, she would have fainted. She had never in all her dreams imagined such a sensation. And when he finally lifted his head, she could hardly speak. 'I think I'm going to pass out.'

'I feel the same, babe, but don't pass out before I have another kiss.'

They broke apart when the lights went up. 'Yer'd better wipe yer lips,' Laura said shakily. 'Ye're covered in lipstick.'

'All these wasted weeks, when I didn't know what I was missing,' Gary grinned as he took a hankie from his pocket. 'I can't wait for the spot waltz next week.'

'Why do we have to wait until next week? Why don't we just tell her to go to hell?'

The smile vanished from Gary's face. 'She wouldn't go to hell, she'd go straight to your mam. From what I've heard, she's got it in for yer mother. She said she's a stuck-up bitch and one day she'll pull her down a peg or two. And you're the one she's going to use to do it. What I can't understand is how she gets away with it with her husband. He must be as soft as a brush to let her gad around the way she does. And it's an uncle of yours she's married to, isn't it?'

'What? No! She's married to me grandad!'

Gary shook his head as he looked at her with disbelief. 'Yer grandad? But yer grandad must be an old man!'

'He's not an old man, he's lovely. And she treats him terrible, gives him a dog's life. I hate her, she's wicked.'

'She's a bigger liar than I thought,' Gary said. 'She tells everybody she's married to this handsome bloke who's got a good job and gives her everything. They both like a good time and have agreed to give each other a lot of freedom. She goes her way, he goes his.'

'Me grandad's a nice-looking man, even though he's nearly sixty. But he doesn't have a lot of money and never goes anywhere except to work or to our house. He doesn't give her everything, she takes it and leaves him skint.'

Gary saw Celia and Charlie come through the door, and he touched Laura's arm. 'That's the end of the conversation for now, babe, the enemy approaches. We'll talk more next week, and there's always the spot waltz.'

'I liked the way yer kissed me, Gary.'

'And I liked the way yer kissed me back, babe. Roll on next week.'

Chapter Twenty

Mary and Stan crossed the slippery cobbles with great care. Mary was carrying a plate of fairy cakes to help out with the food, and Stan was gripping three pint glasses in one hand and three sherry glasses in the other. 'I've got a couple more if they're short, but Seamus said three of each would do.'

'There's not a sound,' Mary said as she knocked at the door. 'We must be the first.'

Stan chuckled, 'If it's quiet, that means Amy hasn't arrived yet.'

'Come on in out of the cold.' Molly opened the door wide. 'Sure, it wouldn't surprise me if we had another fall of snow, the sky's been heavy all day, so it has.'

'I hope not, Molly. This week's been murder trying to get around.' Mary handed the plate over. 'They're not much, sunshine, but they'll help out.'

Seamus greeted them warmly. 'Let me have yer coats, then take a seat near the fire.'

'I'll see if Molly wants any help before I sit down,' Mary told him. 'An extra pair of hands are always welcome.'

'Sure, there's no need, me darlin'. Hasn't my dear wife got everything under control, as usual? And hasn't she had me and Mick running around like blue-arsed flies?'

They heard footsteps clattering down the stairs and then Mick appeared. He was wearing a smile until he saw there were just the two of them. 'Where's Jenny?'

'Her and Janet were upstairs titivating themselves up when we left, but they should be here any minute.' Mary grinned. 'Anyone would think they were going to Buckingham Palace, the time they're spending on themselves.'

'Jenny doesn't need to titivate herself up,' Mick said. 'She always looks pretty.'

Seamus let out a hearty guffaw. 'Keep an eye on yer daughter, Mary, or me son will be stealing her from yer.'

'Not while she's only fourteen he won't, Seamus. I'll be tanning his backside for him if he tries.'

Although Mick smiled at her, his deep blue eyes were serious. 'She'll be fifteen in three and a half months, Mrs Nightingale, and

253

me and John were going to ask yer if she can come to the dance with us? Mrs Porter has already said Janet can come with us.'

'Oh well, if Mrs Porter has already agreed, what can I say?' Mary was shaking inside with laughter. 'If I refused, I'd be the worst mother in the world, wouldn't I? Or like the wicked step-mother in *Cinderella* who wouldn't let her go to the ball, and made her stay home to sweep the floor and wash the pans.'

Mick's dimples appeared. 'I'd go along with that, Mrs Nightingale, as long as I can find out how to get hold of Cinderella's fairy god-mother.'

They heard Amy's loud voice outside. 'Take yer bleedin' hands off it, Ben Hanley. I've carried it this far without your help.'

Then came Ben's voice. 'What's in it, anyway?'

'Mind yer own bleedin' business. And take yer hands off before I brain yer.'

They then heard John. 'Mam, do yer have to shout so loud? The whole flippin' street can hear yer.'

'Sod the whole street, if they've nothing better to do. Now knock on that bleedin' door before I freeze to death.'

Mick, who had been standing behind the door, had it open in a flash. 'I don't know what *it* is, Mrs Hanley, but I promise I won't put me bleedin' hands on it.'

Amy chuckled as she brushed past him. 'You can sod off, too, Mick Moynihan. Ye're as bad as yer old man.' She entered the room with a beaming smile on her face and carrying a battered suitcase in her chubby hand. 'Good evening to yer, Molly, and you, Seamus.' She narrowed her eyes at Mary. 'I might have known yer'd be here first, so yer could have a few sly drinks before anyone else arrived. It's no wonder everyone in the neighbourhood calls yer "those bleedin' scroungers, the Nightingales". They've all got yer taped, girl.'

'I've often wondered what people were saying behind their hands when I pass. Well, I need wonder no more 'cos me mate has solved the mystery.' Mary nodded to the suitcase. 'What have yer got in there, sunshine?'

'Seeing as yer all dying of curiosity, even my feller, I'll tell yer. I am a professional artiste, as yer all have reason to know, and inside here,' she lifted the case that had seen better days, 'is the costume I'll be wearing to entertain my adoring public.'

Ben, as funny as his wife in his own way, put on the downtrodden, henpecked husband face. His hand to his forehead, and looking down at the floor, he said, 'She's wicked is my wife. She lifts yer up one minute, then knocks yer down the next. When she came down with that suitcase, me heart filled with joy. I could even hear birds singing. And that should tell yer how happy I was, when there isn't a tree within miles of us. I really thought she was leaving home.'

When there was a roar of laughter, Ben shook his head sadly. 'No, folks, it's no laughing matter. There I was, floating on air, and she tells me it's her ruddy costume in the case. I came down to earth with a bump, I can tell yer.'

'Ho, ho, very funny, I must say.' Amy's face was set, but everyone could see her tummy shaking. 'Listen to me, buggerlugs, there's only room for one comic in the house and it ain't you. So don't be trying to get in on the act.'

John peeped in the kitchen. 'Where's Jenny?'

'Oh, my God, will yer listen to this son of mine?' Amy was nodding and shaking her head at the same time, which confused her layer of chins. They didn't know whether to sway sideways or go up and down, so they stayed where they were. 'His mam and dad are nearly coming to blows, and he wants to know where Jenny is.'

'It's all right, Amy, we've been through this with Mick. Our Jenny and Janet will be over in a minute, they're dolling themselves up.'

'I don't know why me son and Mick bother.' Amy shifted the suitcase to her other hand. 'Jenny told me she's got her eye on a feller at work.'

When Mary saw the look exchanged between the two boys, she could tell they didn't think it was funny. 'Ye're a lying hound, Amy Hanley. One of these days someone's going to take ye're serious, and then yer'll be in trouble.'

Amy bent down and glared into her face. 'Is it my fault they can't take a bleedin' joke?'

Seamus held out his hand. 'Let me put the case down for yer, me darlin', before yer hit someone with it.'

Amy came over all sweetness and light. 'It's a kind man yer are, Seamus, and I really do appreciate it. But no one gets their bleedin' hands on this case but me, so there.'

'Come with me, me darlin',' Molly said. 'Yer can hide it at the back of the pantry where no one will get at it. Yer have my promise, I'll guard it with me life, so I will.'

The two boys had been eyeing the clock with growing impatience, and when the knock finally came they moved as one. Elbows and feet were being used, and as neither would give way to the other, they ended up getting stuck in the doorway. Ignoring the laughter behind them, Mick said, 'Okay, pal, let's be sensible about this. I'll open the door and you bow them in. Okay?'

'Oh, no yer don't, mate! This might be your house, but fair's fair. I'll open the door and you bow them in.'

Mick knew this would happen and was delighted. When the door was finally opened he was in full view, while John was stuck behind it and all you could see of him was his face.

'Yer look very pretty tonight, Jenny.' Mick didn't care that everyone was listening. He had three months to get in the lead and he didn't intend wasting any time.

John, nearly tripping over his feet, rushed to Mick's side. 'Yes, yer do, Jenny, very pretty indeed.'

Not noticing that all the grown-ups had their hands in their mouths to keep the laughter quiet, Janet tugged on John's arm. 'Don't I look pretty, John?'

John looked into her face and felt ashamed. They shouldn't make such a fuss of Jenny and leave her friend out, no matter how they felt. 'Janet, yer look lovely. Doesn't she, Mick?'

'She certainly does,' Mick agreed. 'Nice enough to be on the lid of a box of Cadbury's chocolates.'

Amy put her hand to her stomach and made a gurgling sound. 'Seamus, if yer don't put a glass in me hand this minute, I'll be sick all over yer floor. And put those four outside, while ye're at it. Sloppy beggars.'

'Now, me darlin', were yer not young yerself once? It's a long time ago, I'll grant yer that, but sure, yer must have some memories of being flattered and courted.'

Amy caught her husband's eye and jerked her head. 'Go on, you tell them how yer flattered and courted me.'

'You tell a better tale than me, love,' Ben said. 'And ye're a better liar than me.'

Amy, her chubby hands around a glass of stout, was in her element. 'Well, when my Ben used to call for me, I'd open the door and he'd say, "Are yer ready, girl?" Then we'd walk down the street with him on the inside and me on the outside near the kerb. I always took me own quarter of wine gums, 'cos I knew he wouldn't dream of buying me sweets. We'd sit in the dark of the picture house, chewing on MY wine gums, without a word being spoken. If James Cagney and Pat O'Brien were on, and it came to an exciting bit, Ben used to close his eyes and I'd have to tell him when it was safe to look. Then when we came out of the pictures, I used to walk him home 'cos his mam didn't like him being out on his own in the dark, and when we got outside his house he'd tap me on the arm and say, "Ta-ra, girl, see yer tomorrow". If I was quick, I'd have a chance to kiss him on the cheek before he had time to put his key in the lock.'

Amy took a long swig of stout before gazing around the rapt faces. 'I knew I'd always have to buy me own wine gums and walk in the gutter, but yer see, although yer wouldn't think so now, he was dead handsome, was Ben. A real he-man, he was, knocked spots off the likes of Clark Gable. Sometimes, when we were walking, our hips would touch and I'd swoon with rapture. He'll tell yer himself the number of times he had to lift me up out of the gutter.'

Ben, who had enjoyed the tale of fantasy more than anyone, cocked an eyebrow. 'Yer were lying in the gutter the first time I set eyes on yer, love. Yer were dead drunk and slobbering. And I remember saying to meself, as I picked yer up, "This is the girl for me".'

Amy grinned. 'There yer are – didn't I tell yer he was dead romantic?'

The laughter increased ten-fold when Janet said, 'I don't think he was dead romantic. Fancy him making yer buy yer own wine gums!'

Amy, the chair creaking beneath her, looked at her son. 'John, spell it out for her, will yer? Or, better still, draw her a picture.'

'Mam, she doesn't know yer well enough yet. How was she to know that every word yer spoke was a lie? Janet's mam's not as daft as you.'

'Ooh, er!' There was a look of amazement on Janet's face. 'Yer mean that was all lies, Mrs Hanley? Well, why was yer husband laughing?'

'Because he's sitting on a feather, girl, and it's tickling his fancy.' Then Amy felt sorry for her. 'It was all a joke, girl, just to make people laugh. I often come out with these weird and wonderful tales, but they're all in fun.'

Janet's face broke into a wide smile. 'In that case, Mrs Hanley, it was very funny. But will yer tell me in future, so I can enjoy the joke?'

'Listen, sunshine,' Mary said, 'just treat everything me mate says as a joke and yer can't go far wrong. She never gives a warning because she doesn't know herself what she's going to come out with.' Mary chuckled. 'Come shopping with us one day, Janet, and yer'll find out what I mean.'

Janet put her hand on John's arm. 'Your mam is very clever, John, to be able to make up stories like that.'

Amy was delighted. 'A girl after me own heart. She'll make someone a good wife.'

'All right, Mam.' John felt it was time to shut his mother up before she said Janet would make a good daughter-in-law. The trouble with his mam was, she didn't expect people to take to heart what she said. 'Yer've hogged the stage for long enough, give someone else a chance.'

'Ye're right, son,' Amy said. 'I should be concentrating on me big performance later on. We artistes are very highly strung and temper – er, tempora –' she glanced at Mary. 'What's the word I'm looking for, girl?'

'Temperamental, sunshine.'

'That's what I am.' Amy nodded. 'So I'll save meself for the big moment.'

257

And the big moment came at half-past eleven, after much beer and port had been drunk, songs sung and jigs and reels danced. Amy made her way into the kitchen and closed the door, telling Molly not to let anyone out there, even if they were desperate for the lavvy. 'Tell them to cross their legs,' she said.

While the adults were engaged in conversation as they waited for the star of the show, Mick said to Jenny, 'Yer mam said yer can come to the dance with us after yer birthday.'

'Did she? Oh, won't that be great!' Jenny's pretty face was animated and flushed with all the laughing. 'I'm really looking forward to it.'

'Yeah, me too.' Mick thought that was putting it mildly. He was counting the days. 'We'll have some fun.'

'You bet,' John said. 'We'll be that good we'll be able to enter in competitions.'

'Will yer teach me to dance proper, John?' Janet asked. 'You know, like they do in the movies?'

Why does she always ask me things, John asked himself. Why doesn't she ask Mick? 'Yeah, me and Mick will both teach yer. We'll take turns apiece with you and Jenny until yer can do all the dances.'

There came a thumping on the kitchen door. 'Molly, as yer've taken over as me manager, it's up to you to introduce me and make sure the audience don't get rowdy. This act I'm doing tonight is a real class act, and I won't put up with any whistling or bawling. So if ye're expecting to get paid for the job, get cracking and give me an introduction worthy of me many and varied talents.'

'Oh dear,' Molly said, 'would somebody else like to be her manager? I'm out of me depths, so I am, and haven't a clue what to do or say.'

There was a lot of pulling of faces and shaking of heads. No one wanted to be Amy's manager when they didn't know what she was going to look like when she came through that door. Oh, it was all in fun, a great big joke to Amy. And the person opening the door for her big entrance could end up in tears of laughter. But they could also end up with a very red face and wishing the floor would open and swallow them up. 'Seamus,' she pleaded, 'will yer not be helping me out?'

Seamus was shaking with laughter. 'With the best will, and all the love in the world, me darlin', I'll not be taking that chance. If Amy comes in here in her birthday suit, wouldn't it be me being chased up the street by yer dear self, with the stiff brush in yer hand?'

Amy was getting impatient. 'What the bleedin' hell is going on in there? I've got me own flippin' legs crossed now, yer've been that long.'

Molly breathed out through her teeth before opening the kitchen door slowly. Then, with a sigh of relief and a smile on her face, she announced, 'Here she comes, for your entertainment, the one and only – *Amy Hanley!*'

When the laughter erupted, it was like an explosion. Amy was wearing her husband's working clothes, right down to the dirty old cap, collarless shirt and braces. Now Ben was a big man, and his wife was swamped in his clothes. The jacket came down to her knees, the trouser legs had been rolled up and secured with large pins, and the waist was tied with a piece of strong string, knotted above Amy's tummy. The sleeves had also been turned up half-a-dozen times to fit. It was the dirty old cap that had everyone rolling about. It came down over her ears and almost covered her eyes. All you could see was her chubby cheeks and the wide smile which told of her delight in the reception.

'In the name of God, love, how did yer do that?' Ben asked. 'I had those clothes on for work today!'

'I know, and I thought I was going to have to drag the bleedin' things off yer, yer were that slow getting changed. Anyway, on with the show. Nobody join in till I tell yer, 'cos some of yer are tone deaf and yer put me off me stroke.' With a thumb hooked each side of the braces, and a swagger to her walk, she began. 'Anytime ye're Lambeth Way . . .' She'd told them not to join in, but the song was so catchy they had to do something, so they clapped their hands and stamped their feet.

What a sight Amy looked, a real scream. And there wasn't a soul in that room who didn't feel like giving her a big hug. One song followed another, all with a Cockney theme. 'Any Old Iron' was followed by 'Maybe It's Because I'm A Londoner'. And as she sang, her legs and feet were never still. Till in the end, with sweat running down her face and her breathing laboured, she called it a day. 'That's all for now folks, I'm all in.'

There were shouts of, 'Encore!' and, 'Bravo!' but Amy shook her head. 'I need two glasses of stout to catch up with the rest of yer. And until I get that, my backside stays on this chair.'

John, his mother's biggest fan, looked across at her and said, 'I don't half love me mam, she's a real corker.'

'I love yer mam, too, John.' Janet nodded her head. 'I think she's brilliant.'

'We all love Auntie Amy,' Jenny said. 'Yer couldn't help but love her.'

Although Mick agreed with their sentiments, he wasn't very happy about it. If Jenny loved his mother, it gave John a head start. 'I love Mrs Hanley, she's great. But doesn't anybody love my mam?'

'Of course we do!' Jenny giggled. 'I always think of my mam, Auntie Amy and Auntie Molly as The Three Musketeers. They're one for all and all for one. If a helping hand is needed, it is quickly offered. They've been friends for as long as I can remember, and I love the bones of the three of them.'

Mick and John were very happy with that statement. But it left Janet wondering whether they lived too far away for her mam to join the friends, so she could be loved by everyone. 'Yer can't have Four Musketeers, can yer?'

'Nah,' John said. 'It doesn't have the same ring to it, somehow.' He looked at Mick and knew his friend was trying to figure out the same thing as him. Was Janet really as daft as she made out, or was she, in her own way, as funny as his mam?

It was a Monday morning, ten days into the New Year, when Cynthia decided to put her plan into action. She left for work as usual, in her old coat, scruffy shoes and a scarf over her head. In her handbag was the letter she'd written and an old pair of her father's reading glasses. She worked through until the dinner break, then asked the supervisor if she could go home as she wasn't feeling very well.

As she walked through the factory gates, Cynthia's nerves were as taut as a violin string. The only thing that kept her going was the knowledge that if the letter had the desired effect, she'd finally get the revenge she sought. Larry and Jeff had made her life a hell, and she hadn't asked for it. She may have been stupid to have taken up with Larry in the first place, but she didn't deserve what he and his friend had done to her. Nobody deserved that. And it wasn't only herself who had suffered at their hands, but others, too. They couldn't be allowed to carry on; they must be punished and have their lives made a hell on earth.

Cynthia could feel sympathy for their wives, for she had no doubt they were married, but they had to know. They were the only ones who could put a stop to it. None of the women they forced into having sex would go to the police, because they'd be too ashamed to put into words what had happened to them. And too ashamed of their families and neighbours finding out. There was always one who would say, 'I bet she asked for it. There's no smoke without fire.'

Cynthia hopped on a tram at Everton Valley and took a seat by the window. And as she swayed with the movement of the tram, the shops and buildings that flashed by were just a blur. She was deep in thought, going over and over her plan. She'd worked it out to the last detail, but would it be as easy in reality? It had to be; she desperately needed it to be successful so her mind would be cleansed and she could put the whole incident behind her. She'd never forget, but it wouldn't be nagging away in her head every day and night. And she wouldn't be looking at every boy with suspicion.

'Walton Church next stop,' the conductor called as he rang the bell.

Cynthia stepped down from the tram and began to walk back to the street with a pub on one corner and a sweet shop on the other. She stopped before she reached the corner and put on her father's glasses before pulling the scarf down to cover her hair. No one would have given her a second glance; she looked like a dowdy, middle-aged housewife. She couldn't see out of the glasses clearly so she bent her head and peered over the rims as she turned the corner of the street. She glanced briefly up at number fifteen as she passed, noting that the house seemed well-kept, with bright windows and clean steps, but kept on walking until she came to number fifty-five. Then, settling the glasses straight on her nose, she lifted the knocker.

The woman who opened the door was middle-aged with a happy face and ginger hair. 'Yes, can I help yer?'

Her eyes squinting, Cynthia asked, 'Is Larry in, please?'

'There's no Larry here, queen, yer've got the wrong house.'

'Oh, I'm sure me dad said fifty-five.' Cynthia held the envelope out. 'He asked me to bring this letter, but he hasn't put the address on. It's just got Larry on the front.'

'I've got it now,' the woman said, smiling. 'It'll be Larry Langton, he's the only Larry I know. He lives up the road at number fifteen. But he won't be in now, he'll be at work.'

'Perhaps his wife will be in?'

'She'll be at work, queen, and the kids are at school. If yer come back tonight, they'll all be in.'

'I couldn't do that, I've come all the way from Bootle.' Cynthia lifted the glasses and pinched the bridge of her nose. 'I've got a splitting headache with these glasses. I need new ones but I can't afford them.'

'Why don't yer pop the letter through their letter box, queen, save anyone having to make that long journey?'

'I don't think me dad would like that. He said to be sure to give it to Larry or his wife. In fact, he thought Larry would be at work, and he told me to give it to his wife. If I tell him I went to the wrong house in the first place, and then put it through a letter box, he'll have me guts for garters.'

'Then give me the letter and I'll nip up with it when Doreen gets in. That's his wife, and she works until three o'clock.' The woman held out her hand. 'My name's June Lawson, by the way, queen. What's yours?'

'Ooh, isn't that funny, my name's June, too!' Cynthia was thinking fast as she passed the letter over. 'June Hardcastle.'

'Right, I'll let Doreen know yer called and she can tell Larry. Yer can promise yer dad he'll definitely have the letter in his hand as soon as he gets home. Is there any other message, queen?'

'No, I don't even know this Larry, it's me dad what knows him.'

Cynthia turned to walk away. 'Thanks very much, yer've saved me life.'

'Think nothing of it, queen, ye're welcome.' June Lawson watched her walk away. A spinster from the looks of her, she thought. And a downtrodden one at that. Seemed her father had the whip hand. She closed the door and gazed down at the envelope. Why the hell couldn't the old man have posted it, save putting his daughter to all that trouble? Whatever was in the ruddy letter couldn't be that important.

When Cynthia heard the door close, she speeded up her steps. The glasses were discarded and thrust in her pocket. The deed was done now and the sooner she got away from here the better. By tonight, Larry's wife, and Jeff's too, with any luck, would know what their husbands got up to. For Doreen was sure to do as Cynthia expected and open the letter as soon as she got in. After all, she wouldn't see any harm in reading a letter that had been hand-delivered, and curiosity would be bound to get the better of her. However, what she would find inside would shake her to the core. First was the date when her husband and his friend had picked up two young girls in a pub and taken them down an entry. The pub was named and a description of the girls given. Then Doreen would read about the woman who was dragged struggling down an entry by her husband and Jeff, and how they were in the act of raping her when two men who were passing came to her aid. This was the night their husbands had come home badly bruised and beaten up. Their injuries had been inflicted by the two men who didn't take kindly to rapists. Again the date was given and the name of the pub.

Cynthia had not given details of her own ordeal for fear of being found out as the writer of the letter. But she had written that the incidents mentioned were only two of many, and that Larry and Jeff were nothing but evil bullies and rapists, unfit to be members of the human race.

While Cynthia was waiting at the tram stop, she told herself it was too early to go home without awkward questions being asked. She'd go into town and have a cup of tea at the Kardomah. She realised with surprise that the tension had left her body and her heart felt lighter than it had done in months. Please God it would stay like that and the dark moods were a thing of the past.

When the tram came and she jumped on board, the conductor was standing on the platform talking to the driver. He held out his hand, asking, 'Where to, love?'

She smiled as she handed him two pennies. 'A single to Church Street, please.'

Doreen Langdon closed the door on June and looked down at the letter in her hand. 'I bet he's been backing the gee-gees and owes the bookie money.' She walked through to the living room and stood the letter up on the mantelpiece. She was alone in the house, the children wouldn't be in from school for another half-hour. 'I'll break his bloody neck for him, if that's the case. What's the point in me going out to work to earn a few bob if he's going to squander it on bloody horses?'

It was anger and curiosity that had her reaching for the letter. 'He's not likely to tell me,' she muttered, her finger slitting the top of the envelope, 'so I'll find out for meself.'

As the words on the paper sunk in, Doreen began to sway and held on to the table for support. Her face drained of colour, she read the letter again to make sure her eyes weren't deceiving her. Then, her voice choked, she cried, 'My God, they could go to prison for this! The bastards! The no-good bleedin' bastards!' Her mind whirled as she gazed around the room. Perhaps it wasn't true. It was someone's idea of a joke. But even as she thought it, she knew it was no joke. Her husband and his mate were selfish swines, they thought only of themselves. Her and Iris, Jeff's wife, could be skint through the week, with no money for food, but the two men made sure they had their beer and ciggie money, and a few bob for the gee-gees.

Doreen looked down at the sheet of paper in her hand. Her husband had pulled some stunts in their married life, but nothing had prepared her for this. If the police found out, he and his mate would spend the rest of their lives in prison. And what shame that would bring on the family. She wouldn't be able to look anyone in the face. The best thing she could do would be to go over and show the letter to Iris before anyone else told her what their husbands got up to.

Iris had a smile on her face when she opened the door. 'This is a surprise, I wasn't expecting yer.'

'I've got a bigger surprise for yer, kid, and it's not a pleasant one.' Doreen brushed past her and walked into the living room. 'Are the kids home yet?'

Iris shook her head. 'Another ten minutes or so.'

There was no time to spare, so Doreen just handed the letter over. 'Take a grip of yerself and read that.'

The silence lasted just a few seconds, then all hell broke loose. 'I'll break his bleedin' neck for him.' Iris was beside herself. 'I won't even bother to ask him if it's true because I know it is. The number of times I've smelt powder or scent on him, and he's always laughed it off. Well he'll not laugh this off, 'cos I'll bleedin' kill the swine.'

'Calm down, Iris, and let's talk before the kids come in. We don't want them to know about things like this.' Doreen put her arm across her friend's shoulder. 'What I'm worried about is that whoever wrote that letter might not be the only one who knows what they get up to. It might only be a matter of time before the police find out. And I'm not staying around to be shamed in front of all the neighbours. So first thing tomorrow I'll be looking for somewhere else to live, well away from here.'

'And what are yer going to do about Larry?' Iris had a quick temper at the best of times and right now it was ready to boil over. 'I'll kill my feller when he gets in.'

'I won't do anything until the kids are in bed. Then I'll give him the hiding of his life to get this hurt and anger out of me system, and to pay him back for what he did to those girls. After that, if he's capable of listening, then I'm going to lay the law down. The Tuesday and Thursday nights out are a thing of the past. I want extra housekeeping money off him. I will not sleep in the same bed as him, I'll sleep with the kids. And if he doesn't want to move to another area, I'll go on me own with the kids. I can get a full-time job to keep us.' Doreen waved the letter under Iris's nose. 'And all the time this letter will be in me hand. I'll put the fear of God into him by saying I'm so disgusted it wouldn't take much for me to go to the police and turn him in.'

They heard children's voices and Doreen quickly folded the piece of paper. 'Keep yer temper in check until the kids are in bed. It wouldn't be fair on them to hear you and Jeff having a slanging match.'

Iris nodded. 'I'll come down with yer tomorrow to the landlord's office and we can ask for a transfer. We shouldn't have any trouble because we've always paid our rent on time. We've been good tenants.'

Three weeks later the two families moved out. And they didn't leave a forwarding address.

Chapter Twenty-One

'Spring is in the air, girl,' Amy said cheerfully as she linked Mary's arm. 'The first day of April, the sky is blue and the sun is doing its best to come out.'

'I'm not sorry to see the back of the bad weather, it's been a hard winter. We needn't light the fire first thing in the morning soon, so we'll save a few bob on coal.'

Amy pretended to smooth down the front of her coat before pulling Mary to a halt. 'Ay, girl, has the elastic gone in yer knickers? They're hanging down.'

Mary's mouth dropped open in horror. She looked down at her legs, front and side, and frowned. 'I can't see nothing.'

Amy's cackle could be heard from one end of the street to the other. 'Ever been had, girl? April fool!'

'Oh God, I fell for it again. Every year yer do it, so wouldn't yer think I'd have learnt by now? The best of it is, I was going to tell yer something when we left our house, but I better not say anything now because yer won't believe me.'

'Why won't I believe yer, girl?'

'Because yer'll think I'm pulling yer leg.'

'Nah, I wouldn't, girl, 'cos ye're not quick enough to catch me out.'

'Well, yer've got a flaming big hole in the heel of yer stocking and it's got about ten ladders running from it, right up yer leg.'

Amy leaned heavily on Mary's arm as she bent one leg backwards, then the other. 'I'm blowed if I can see anything. Yer must be imagining things, girl.'

'I'm not imagining I've just made an April fool of yer, sunshine.'

'Well, I'll be buggered! First time, eh, girl?'

'I'm a bit slow on the uptake, sunshine, but I get there in the end.' Mary pressed on her friend's arm and they carried on walking. 'I hope yer don't start any shenanigans in the shops, with yer April fool. Not everybody appreciates your humour.'

'Stop yer worrying, girl, it gives yer wrinkles and puts years on yer.'

While Mary entered the butcher's shop with trepidation, Amy was full of the joys of spring.

'Good morning, Wilf, I hope we find yer hale and hearty on this lovely day?'

'I'm fine, thank you, ladies. Whether I'll be fine by the time you leave, well, that remains to be seen.'

'Have yer got a pound of beef sausage, Wilf?'

The butcher leaned in the window and lifted a string of sausages. He counted out how many he thought would be the right weight, cut them free from the rest and threw them on the scales.

Mary was growing uneasy. 'Yer told me yer were having brawn tonight,' she whispered in Amy's ear, 'with egg and chips.'

'That's wasn't no lie, girl, that's what we're having.'

'Well, why have yer asked for a pound of beef sausage?'

Wilf heard what was said and his hand hovered over the scale as he waited for the bane of his life to answer.

'I didn't say I *wanted* a pound of beef sausage, girl, I only asked if he *had* a pound of beef sausage. Just taking an interest in his business, like, yer see.'

It was Mary who thought an apology was in order. 'I'm sorry about that, Wilf, but if it's any consolation she caught me out, too.'

'That's all right, Mary.' Wilf threw the sausages back on the tray in the window. 'I wasn't doing anything, anyway. Before you came in I was just standing here catching fleas.'

Amy couldn't speak for laughing. She banged on the counter as she roared her head off. 'Nice one, Wilf. Ooh, I like that! Just standing catching fleas. I'll have to remember that one. Wait until I tell my Ben, he'll laugh his little cotton socks off.'

'I would prefer yer not to repeat that, Amy,' Wilf said. 'Some of my customers wouldn't see the joke and it'd be around the neighbourhood in no time that I had fleas.'

The floorboards began to shake with the weight of Amy's heaving body. Mary and Wilf looked on with smiles on their faces, wondering what she was going to come out with that was so funny she couldn't stop laughing. Eventually she drew herself up to her full four feet ten and a half inches, sniffed up and wiped a hand across her eyes. 'Ooh, it did me a power of good, that. Better than a dose of salts any day.'

'Aren't yer going to let us in on the joke?' Mary asked. 'It's not like you to keep things to yerself, more's the pity.'

Amy looked at the smiling butcher. 'Are yer sure yer want to know, Wilf?'

'If I couldn't take a joke, Amy, I wouldn't last five minutes behind this counter.'

'I was going to say that if yer catch a flea, put it away for us till the weekend. It would probably have more meat on it than that bleeding chicken yer sold me on Saturday. It couldn't have less, that's a dead cert.'

Mary's cheeks were stiff with laughing. 'What would yer do with her, Wilf?'

'Actually, Mary, she comes in very handy for me sometimes. Whenever me missus gets ratty and is moaning her head off, I think of Amy and realise how lucky I am.'

Amy got on her high horse. 'Well, actually, Wilf Burnett, my Ben thinks he's the luckiest man in the world. He wouldn't swap me for all the gold in China.'

'The tea in China, sunshine.'

'What did yer say, girl?'

'I said the tea in China.'

'What about the tea in China, haven't they got none?'

Mary threw out her hands. 'I give up! Wilf, I'll have three-quarters of brawn, please. And when we left the house, me mate was having the same. But if I were you, I'd take her money before yer start weighing it.'

When they got outside the greengrocer's, Mary stood firm. 'You can get me five pound of spuds, I'll wait here for yer. I wouldn't go through another performance for a big clock.'

'I won't do nothing, girl, cross my heart and hope to die.'

'Then go and do nothing on yer own, sunshine, 'cos I ain't going in with yer.'

Amy walked away looking down in the mouth. But it didn't last long. She'd no sooner disappeared inside the shop, when Mary heard her shout: 'Top of the morning to yer, Billy. Have yer got a pound of those soft tomatoes?'

Mary could feel herself cringe inside. How her friend could do it, she didn't know. And she got away with it. Nobody ever fell out with her, only her neighbour, Annie Baxter. But Annie didn't count, 'cos she was as miserable as sin, anyway.

The next thing, Mary heard Billy Nelson roar his head off. 'Yer what! I've a good mind to throw the bleedin' things at yer. In fact, it would be worth losing the tuppence to pelt yer with them.'

Then came a voice Mary didn't recognise. 'She's a big enough target, Billy.'

There was no mistaking the next voice. 'Oh, ye're there, are yer missus? Well, why don't yer try minding yer own business? And when yer get home, if yer've got a mirror that isn't already cracked, take a good look in it and see the gob on yerself.'

That's it, Mary thought, I'll be here all day at this rate. So she marched in the shop, took the basket from Amy and plonked it on the counter. 'We just want two lots of spuds when ye're ready, Billy.' She turned to say something to Amy and saw her friend and another woman eyeing each other up. Oh Lord, she groaned, these two are going to be at each other's throats any minute now. 'I'll wait for the potatoes, sunshine, you go and get our bread.'

Amy's eyes never wavered. 'You get the bread, girl, I'm comfortable where I am.'

Billy weighed five pound of potatoes and threw them in the basket. He'd be best serving them first, for the sake of peace and save his shop from becoming a boxing ring. He covered the potatoes with a newspaper, and weighed out another five pound. Then he had a brainwave. 'Ye're the only one that caught me out today, Amy.'

Amy pricked her ears. Praise was something she never ignored. 'Oh, yeah?'

'Yeah.' Billy passed the basket to Mary and took her four pennies. 'Six of them tried it on, but you were the only one I fell for.'

The woman showed she was curious. 'What did they try on, Billy?'

'It's April Fool's day, Mrs Chambers.'

'Oh.' The woman looked sheepish. 'I didn't know.'

'Well, you wouldn't, would yer, missus? It's just another day to you.' Amy turned when Mary pulled on her arm. 'What is it, girl?'

Mary thrust the basket at her. 'You can carry this, me arm's dropping off.' She waved to the shopkeeper. 'Ta-ra, Billy.'

'Ta-ra, Mary! And you, Amy, my little flower, be careful how yer go.'

When they were outside, Amy said, 'I could have hit that bleedin' woman. Billy took it all in good fun and was laughing his head off until she stuck her nose in. Cheeky cow.'

'All right, sunshine, let's forget about it now, eh? We'll get the bread and then go home for a nice cuppa. If yer can manage to keep yer trap shut in the bakers, I'll mug yer to a cream slice. Is that a deal?'

'It sure is, girl, it sure is.'

Half an hour later the two friends sat facing each other with a cup of tea in front of them and a plate with a cream slice on. The slice had pink icing on the top and cream oozing out of the sides. Amy ran her tongue over her lips. 'I know it's manners to wait until ye're asked, girl, but I haven't got no manners so I ain't waiting.' She picked up the slice and ran her tongue down one side. 'Heaven.' Her eyes were closed as she savoured the luxury. 'Pure, bleedin' heaven.'

'Yeah, yer could get used to being rich, couldn't yer?'

'Sure could, girl, sure could. We should have married men with money, that's where we went wrong.'

'The trouble is, if yer could have them every day, yer wouldn't appreciate them. People who are loaded, they don't have anything to look forward to. They've been everywhere, seen everything and can have anything in the world they want. I wouldn't swap places with them because half the pleasure of getting something yer really want, is the saving up for it, the anticipation. Then yer really appreciate it.'

Amy licked each finger in turn, not missing a speck of cream. 'Changing the subject, girl, have yer any bright ideas on what I could buy Jenny for her birthday?'

'Anything at all, sunshine. She's not expecting anything, so whatever yer buy she'd be over the moon about it.'

'How about an underskirt?'

'Fantastic, she'd be delighted. It's her birthday next Wednesday, and Janet's is on the Friday, so we're having one party for both of them. I'll have to ask the Porters because they offered to have the party, but Jenny said she'd rather have it here.'

'Is Bill Porter going out with that friend of Laura's from down the street? I've seen them together a few times.'

'I couldn't tell yer, sunshine. I know he goes out with Cynthia, but whether they're courting is anyone's guess. Our Laura is not very forthcoming about her friends.'

'I often wonder about your Laura. She seems to have calmed down a bit, but she's still a mystery to me. I mean, with her looks, yer'd think she'd have boys knocking on the door every night.'

'She could have a boyfriend for all we know, she never tells us anything. We don't know where she goes, or who with. I've given up worrying about her, it doesn't get me anywhere.'

'Your Jenny's a different kettle of fish. If she had a boyfriend, she'd bring him home to see yer on the first night. Mind you, she's got two boys right on her own doorstep who are crazy about her. I think it'll be a fight to the death with them two.'

'I suppose ye're talking about John and Mick? I'm keeping out of it, it's up to Jenny who she chooses for a boyfriend. But I've got to say I'd be very happy if she chose one of them. I'm very fond of both of them.' Mary reached for Amy's empty cup. 'Now, missus, will yer go home so I can get on with some work?'

'I'm going round for Janet, Mam.'

'I thought yer were sitting with Lizzie tonight? Surely Janet can find her own way without you walking round there?'

'I enjoy the walk, Mam, after being sat in an office all day. I enjoy stretching me legs and breathing in the fresh air.'

'Are the boys going, so one of them can walk Janet home?'

'We never make arrangements, Mam. They either turn up or they don't.'

'Well, it's not as dark these nights – she'd be all right walking back on her own. Don't stay too late at Lizzie's or yer'll tire her out.' Mary walked to the door with her daughter. 'Will Bill be coming to the party?'

'I've invited all the family, but I'm not sure about Bill. He's been going out with Cynthia off and on, but according to Janet they're always falling out, so yer wouldn't know what was going on. We'll just have to wait and see.'

Jenny walked with her head bent, deep in thought. Laura was still a source of worry to her. Although her sister wasn't as hard-faced as she used to be, she remained aloof and secretive about her life outside her home. She still went out with Cynthia a few nights a week, and it wasn't unusual now for her to have a night in to wash her hair. But there was still a big question mark about what she got up to on Thursdays. She claimed she was going to a dance with Cynthia, and her parents had no reason to doubt her. But Jenny knew it wasn't true and had this terrible nagging feeling that one of these days Laura would be up to her neck in trouble and would bring it home with her.

Janet was waiting for her with the door open. 'Me mam and dad said to tell yer hello and they're looking forward to the party.'

Jenny waited for her friend to fall into step beside her before saying, 'Me mam needs to know the numbers for the party so she'll know how much to get in. So will your Bill be coming, or not? And if he is, will Cynthia be with him?'

'Your guess is as good as mine, Jenny. I would say they're not on speaking terms at the moment because he's sitting in the house with a face on him like a wet week.'

'Oh, well, if he turns up and there's not enough to eat or drink, it'll be his own fault. Me mam's not a mindreader, she can't cater if she doesn't know how many to cater for.'

Janet was eyeing her friend. 'Yer've done yer hair different again, Jenny. I wish I could do mine like you do – I'd have a different style every week.' Then she suddenly reverted back to the babyish voice she'd got into the habit of using. 'I bet John would like to see me hair done different. He wouldn't half get a surprise.'

Jenny put a hand on her friend's arm. 'Jan, this is Jenny – remember me? We used to sit next to each other every day in school. And yer were pretty clever in school, always in the top ten of our class. Can yer remember all that?'

'Of course I can, I'm not daft.'

'Then why do yer act daft? Yer never used to.'

There was a merry glint in Janet's eyes. 'I have me reasons, Jenny, and I'll tell yer them on me birthday. I'm going to grow up that day.'

'I don't get it, Jan, yer've lost me. Why would yer go on letting people think ye're stupid when it's only a game to yer? I don't know what yer hope to gain by it.'

'I might not gain anything by it, but there's a method in me madness. You'll see, on me birthday, I'll be all grown-up and not act daft no more. If I haven't done what I set out to do by that time, then

I never will.' Janet eyed the blonde hair bouncing on Jenny's shoulders. She had it in a page-boy bob tonight, a style that was all the rage, and it suited her. 'On the night of the party, would yer do something with my hair for me?'

'Yeah, of course I will. How would yer like it?'

'I'll leave that to you, whatever yer think suits me. But I would like to look glamorous, Jenny, if yer could manage that.'

'Yer could manage it yerself if yer put yer mind to it! Yer hair's lovely and thick, and the auburn chestnut colour is beautiful. I'll do yer up like a dog's dinner for the party.' Jenny giggled. 'If yer intend growing up that night, yer hair may as well grow up with yer.'

'Is Cynthia in, Mrs Pennington?' Bill shuffled his feet in embarrassment. He'd sworn he wouldn't be the first to give in this time, yet here he was coming cap in hand. He did it every time they had a fall-out, he couldn't help himself. If Cynthia wasn't so indifferent towards him he probably would have lost interest by now, but as it was he was still fascinated by her.

Fanny Pennington smiled at him. She could feel his nervousness and felt sorry for him. He was a nice lad, her daughter could do a lot worse. But then, her daughter was a law unto herself. She pleased herself what she did, regardless of anyone's feelings. Like this lad here; he shouldn't have to come crawling, he was too good for that. 'I'll ask her to come to the door, son, I think that's best.'

Cynthia came along the hall with her arms folded and a slump to her shoulders. 'Hello, Bill. I'm sorry I look a sight, but I'm not in the mood for getting dolled up.' She leaned against the hall wall. 'Did yer want something?'

Bill let out a sigh of exaggeration. 'I want to have a talk to yer. Can't yer slip a coat on and come for a walk?'

'What is there to talk about? Every time I see yer, we fall out.'

'You fall out, not me.' Bill couldn't go through another sleepless night, so his voice was insistent. 'Put a coat on, Cynthia, and let's talk. Yer owe me that much.'

'Wait there, I won't be a minute.' Cynthia took her coat from the hallstand and opened the living-room door. 'I'm going for a walk with Bill, Mam, I won't be long.'

Dick Pennington looked over his newspaper. He'd noticed the difference in his daughter but put it down to her age, and women's trouble. That was why she was on better terms with her mother, he thought, because it was easier for her to talk to a woman than a man. 'Why didn't yer ask the lad in?'

'It's all right, Dad, we'd rather go for a walk.'

Bill cupped her elbow. 'Is there anywhere yer'd like to go? The pictures, perhaps?'

Cynthia shook her head. 'You wanted to talk, so let's talk.'

'I'll get what I've got to say off me chest first, shall I?' Bill looked sideways at her, but her face gave nothing away. 'This has been going on for months now, and I can't understand yer attitude. We seem to be getting on fine one minute, then the next it's as if I'm a stranger to yer. I can't hold yer hand, can't put me arms around you or kiss yer. If that's the way yer feel about me, why don't yer come straight out with it and tell me to get lost, instead of going all quiet and backing off from me. Do yer like me or not, Cynthia?'

'Of course I like yer.' Cynthia's voice was husky. 'But ye're rushing things too much and I don't want to be rushed.'

'Rushing things! Blimey, I've been more patient with you than any other girl I've been out with! Holding hands with a girl ye're out on a date with, or giving her a kiss, that isn't rushing things, Cynthia, that's normal. That's what all young fellers do when they're out with their girlfriend. It's normal and healthy, Cynthia – no harm in it at all.'

It was time for an explanation, Cynthia knew that. She couldn't expect him to put up with her attitude without having a reason for it. She pulled him to a halt by a shop doorway. 'I had a bad experience with a feller, and it scared me. I can't help feeling the way I do, and I'll be all right if I'm given time. It's nothing to do with you, Bill, I swear.'

'What d'yer mean about a bad experience? Who was this bloke, and what in the name of God did he do to yer?'

Wild horses would never drag the truth from her. She'd be ashamed to tell him, and afraid of his reaction. He would probably run a mile on learning how she'd been violated by two men whom she hardly knew. No decent lad would touch her with a barge-pole unless they were like Larry and Jeff. No one would want her for a girlfriend, someone they could take home to meet their parents. So what she told him was; 'I was going out with this bloke for a few weeks, and yes, we did kiss and cuddle. But one night he tried to force himself on me and I was terrified. He was like an animal and I couldn't go through that again for anyone.'

In the dim light of the street-lamp, she could see Bill was thinking deeply. Then he asked, 'What do yer mean by he tried to force himself on yer?'

'He tried to make me do something I didn't want to do, Bill, and don't ask me any more 'cos I've had enough nightmares about it.'

'And ye're afraid I might try the same thing? He was a rotter, Cynthia, and I can't believe yer have so little respect for me that yer think I might turn out to be the same.'

She put a hand on his arm. 'Never for a moment did the thought enter me head, Bill. If it had, I'd never have even looked at yer. I know ye're a nice, decent bloke, and yer deserve better treatment than I've been dishing out to yer. I've told yer now why I've behaved the way I have, and I hope yer understand. If yer don't, then we'll call it a day with no hard feelings on either side.'

Bill spread his arms in a gesture of hopelessness. 'What am I supposed to say or do, Cynthia? I feel like putting me arms around you and comforting yer, but if I were to touch yer, yer'd run a mile. And that's what hurts the most – yer lack of trust in me.'

'I do trust yer, Bill, but can't we take things slowly? Like this.' She put her arms around his waist and rested her head on his shoulder. 'A little comfort and tenderness to start off with.'

Bill held her, but not closely. He was so relieved, and so blissfully happy, he didn't want to spoil things. He'd wait and give her the time she needed. 'I'll do what the song says, eh, Cynthia? I'll Try A Little Tenderness.'

They walked home slowly, arm in arm, relaxed and contented. 'Will yer come to our Janet's birthday party with me?' he asked. 'It's in the Nightingales' 'cos it's Jenny's birthday too, so they're having a party between them.'

'Will your parents be there?'

'Yeah, but what difference does that make? They know I've been going out with yer and me mam will be made up to see us together. She'll tell yer I've been like a bear with a sore head whenever we've had a tiff.'

'Okay, I'd like to come to the party. Shall we buy the girls a present each between us? It would look lousy to turn up at a birthday party without presents.'

'You get them something, will yer? I wouldn't have a clue what to buy for girls.'

'I dunno, that's typical of a man. Talk about act soft and I'll buy yer a coal-yard, isn't in it.'

They stood outside Cynthia's house holding hands. 'Can I call for yer tomorrow night?' Bill asked. And when she nodded, he raised his brows. 'How about a peck on the cheek?'

Cynthia leaned forward and kissed him briefly on the lips. 'I'll look forward to it.'

Fanny Pennington was putting the fireguard in front of the hearth when her daughter came in. 'Yer dad went to bed early, he was feeling tired.'

As Cynthia gazed at her mother, her mind went back over the years. She'd been a bitch to this woman who had brought her into the world. The woman who had kept the house spotlessly clean, did the washing, ironing and cooking, and never been given a word of thanks or kindness. Well, the time had come to try and make amends, and Cynthia hoped she hadn't left it too late. 'I'm going to a party at the Nightingales' on Saturday with Bill, Mam, and I've got to buy presents for the two birthday girls. Have yer any idea what I could get?'

Fanny knew an olive branch was being offered and she grasped it with both hands. She'd been concerned for her daughter over the last few weeks but knew better than to ask what was wrong. Her motherly instinct told her something drastic had happened to change the girl's whole personality, and she worried what it was. When Bill had come on the scene she was delighted because he was a nice lad. But even that friendship seemed to be floundering. 'I wouldn't know what to suggest, love. Why don't we make a list of everything a young girl wears or uses, and pick the one yer fancy most?'

'That's a good idea, Mam, we'll do it now. I'll get a piece of paper.'

So for the very first time, mother and daughter sat together in friendship. Each hoping this closeness would grow into the love that had been missing from their lives. 'Now, let's see,' Cynthia said. 'We'll start on what we wear that nobody can see, and work our way out. Then we'll go on to what they'd use, like lipstick or powder. See if we both pick the same thing.'

'Where's Celia got to?' Laura asked, as Gary spun her around in a foxtrot. 'Apart from seeing her outside when I came in, there hasn't been sight nor sign of her since.'

'Don't worry about her, babe, let's just enjoy ourselves. The less we see of her the better it suits me.'

'I'm not worried about her, I'd be made up if I never clapped eyes on her again.' Laura was trying to pluck up courage to ask something, but the fear of refusal kept the words from being said. 'Just think, if it wasn't for her, me and you could be sitting on the back row of the picture house, holding hands.'

'We're holding hands now, babe, or hadn't yer noticed?' Gary smiled down at her. 'I know I'm holding your hand because I've got that thrill running up and down me spine. The one I get whenever I see or touch yer.'

'I feel the same way about you, Gary, but the difference is, I'm prepared to do something about it, and you're not. I've had enough of Celia telling us what we can or can't do, I'm fed up with it. How long is it going to go on for? For the rest of our lives, until we're old and grey?'

'I've told yer, babe, that if it was only me, I'd tell Celia to sod off. It's me mam I'm frightened for. She's been good to me, me mam. When me dad died, she was left to bring me up on her own, and she had a hard time. I wouldn't burden her with trouble for all the money in the world.'

'I can't imagine yer doing anything so bad that Celia could go running to yer mother telling tales. Ye're not a bad person, Gary.'

'No, babe, I'm not a bad person. And what I did wasn't that bad. Wrong, yes, but not bad. It's what Celia would add to it that makes me afraid. If she ever spills the beans on you, it won't be the truth as you know it, but a pack of lies.'

'I was going to ask yer if, just for once, yer'd take a chance? It's our Jenny's birthday party on Saturday, and I'd love yer to come and meet the family. I know they'd make yer welcome and yer would like them.'

The dance came to an end and Gary cupped her elbow to lead her off the floor. 'Would yer like to go outside for a breath of fresh air?' he asked. 'It's not cold out.'

Laura agreed eagerly. If there was no one else out there, they could steal a few hugs and kisses. Then in her mind, she asked herself was she satisfied with stolen kisses? After months of knowing Gary, caring for him and knowing he cared for her, all she'd had was a few stolen kisses. It was ridiculous to let one woman keep them apart. 'Why don't we both tell our mothers and get it over with – beat Celia to it? She'd have nothing on us then. We could do whatever we wanted, when we wanted.'

'Since I met you, babe, I've thought of doing that many times. Then I picture me mam's face and know I couldn't go through with it. Wouldn't your mam be hurt if she knew yer'd told her lies?'

Laura hung her head. 'I'm all mouth, Gary, all talk. I could no more look my mam in the face and tell her what I've done, than fly.' She looked up at him. 'You know what Celia's got on me, but yer won't tell me why she can wrap you around her little finger. I think yer should tell me – it's only fair.'

Gary gave a deep sigh. 'Yer might be sorry, babe, it might put yer off me.'

'There's no chance of that, unless yer've murdered someone.' Her eyes widened in alarm as a thought entered her head. 'Yer haven't got a girl into trouble, have yer?'

'Certainly not! What d'yer take me for? No, it's nothing like that.' Gary stared up at the stars, too afraid to look her in the eye as he explained the hold Celia had over him. 'When I left school at fourteen, I got a job in a grocery shop. Celia was a customer there, that's how I came to know her. One day she asked me for what shopping she needed, then when I added it up and told her what she owed, she said she was threepence short, and could she pass it in later. I was green, I'd only been there a few days. The manager was serving someone, and as I believed her, I said it would be all right.' This time the sigh came from his very soul. 'I wish I had me time over again, I'd have acted different. She never came back that afternoon and I was a nervous wreck in case me boss found out.

Then when I came out of the shop and started to walk home, she came up to me. She said she was sorry she hadn't made it in time, but she'd definitely be in, in the morning to pay her debt. "This is for yer trouble," she said, slipping a penny in me pocket. And once again I was a fool to believe her. For that was the start of a nightmare. She came in the next day all right, and gave me her order. It came to one and eleven, and I thought she'd give me the threepence she owed from the day before. But she passed one and six over, saying, "We'll stick to our little arrangement, love, and I'll meet yer outside tonight with your cut".'

'The hard-faced bitch!' Laura was beside herself with temper. 'Why didn't yer just call yer boss over?'

'Because I was fourteen, babe, as green as grass. There was a look in her eyes that told me she'd lie through her teeth, and I'd be the one in trouble. I couldn't afford to get the sack because me mam needed me wages to help out with the bit she got from a cleaning job. Celia certainly knew who to pick on; a fourteen-year-old who was too frightened of not being believed and terrified of facing his mam and saying he'd been sacked.'

'Yer don't still work there, do yer?'

Gary shook his head. 'I'd have left the next week if I'd had a job to walk into, but it took me six months to get out of the shop and out of her clutches. One of the neighbours in our street worked in a ship-repairers down at the docks, and he got me a job as an apprentice. That's where I still work.'

'I can't believe anyone is that wicked. Ye're eighteen now, and ye're saying she still has a hold on yer?'

Gary nodded. 'She's quite brazen about it. If she doesn't get her own way she threatens to go and tell me old boss at the shop that I gave her stuff for half price and took some money off her in return, and she'd also tell the firm I work for now. And there's little I can do because it's my word against hers.'

'I could scratch her eyes out for doing that to yer.' Laura felt like crying for him. 'We've got to get away from her, somehow.'

Gary pulled her close and ran a hand up and down her back. 'I'm sorry about not coming to yer sister's party, babe, honestly. And I'd love to meet yer mam and dad. I give me word that I will meet them in the not-too distant future, and that's a promise.' He ran his fingers through her thick mop of rich, dark hair. 'I'm going to tell yer something I shouldn't, until I'm really sure it's true. But I want to take that sad look off yer pretty face and give yer some hope. I want yer to promise not to ask me any questions, and not to breathe a word to a soul. Will yer do that, babe?'

'Of course I will. I've let a lot of people down in my life, but I would never, ever, let you down. I think too much of yer.'

'D'yer remember me saying that Celia would come unstuck one day? Well, if what I've heard tonight is true, that day has arrived. She's come unstuck in a big way. Unfortunately, babe, it might affect your family and there could be hell to play. On the other hand, she might just get away with it, as she's been doing for years. They say the devil looks after his own.' He put a finger on her lips. 'No, don't ask questions because I can't answer them. It'll all come out very soon.'

Chapter Twenty-Two

'Do I look all right, Jenny? They won't laugh at me, will they?'

'Jan, yer look like a million dollars, honest. Yer'll bowl everyone over.'

'I don't want to bowl everyone over.' Janet smiled as though she had a secret and wasn't going to share it. 'Just one or two, perhaps, and I'll be happy.'

Jenny had spent half an hour in the kitchen with her friend, curling her hair with the aid of Laura's curling tongs. There was nobody in the house except her mam and dad, so no one had yet seen the difference the new style had made. They were in the bedroom now and Jenny had just put the finishing touches to it. 'Even if I do say it meself, Jan, I've made a really good job of it. I think I should have taken up hairdressing.' Laughing, she held out her hand. 'That will be one shilling, madam.'

'It's all right for you, Jenny, your hair always looks nice.'

'That's because I look after it, soft girl. And that's what you should do.' Jenny smiled at her friend, who was looking really nervous. 'Come on, everyone's here, they'll wonder what we're doing. After all, it is our party.'

'Yeah.' Janet gave her a big hug. 'We'll always be friends, won't we, Jenny?'

'Of course we will. Now, get going.' Jenny deliberately let Janet go down the stairs before her. She didn't want to spoil her big entrance. The girl walking ahead of her now looked nothing like the girl who had been standing on the step when Jenny had opened the door to her two hours ago. That girl had had her hair parted down the middle with a deep fringe. And although there was a natural curl to it, it hung down to her shoulders looking dull and uncared-for. It was the same style Janet had worn since leaving school – and it didn't do a thing for her appearance. But oh, what a difference now! Her hair had been brushed until it shone before Jenny took the curling tongs to it, bringing out the richness of the colour. And it now looked as if it had been styled by a professional, and was a mass of bouncing curls.

The sound in the room was deafening, as there were half-a-dozen conversations being conducted at top volume from one side of it to the other. The atmosphere was lively, with everyone in the party spirit, when Janet opened the door and stood just inside the room. Nothing happened at first, then slowly the noise died down as all eyes were fixed on the young girl who looked as though she wanted to turn tail and run.

Mary was the first to move. 'Oh, sunshine, don't yer look beautiful! I didn't recognise yer for a minute.'

Every voice was raised in surprise and praise, and Martha and Vincent Porter, sitting next to each other on straight-backed wooden chairs, looked as proud as peacocks. 'By, love, yer look like a flippin' film star,' Martha said with a catch in her throat. 'When yer said Jenny was going to do yer hair, I never expected nothing like this.'

Janet, her courage strengthened by the praise, looked to where Mick and John were standing. Wide-eyed, their mouths agape the boys looked as though they couldn't believe what they were seeing. 'What's the matter with you two, has the cat got yer tongue?' Janet's eyes were dancing with pleasure. 'Don't yer think I look nice?'

John's Adam's apple moved up and down as he swallowed hard. 'I'm trying to think of the words, Janet, but the only ones that spring to mind, are "bobby dazzler".'

'That'll do to be going on with.' Janet turned her attention to Mick. 'You're not usually short of a few hundred words, Mick Moynihan, so what have you got to say?'

'Yer look a real humdinger to me, Janet.'

Bill, standing between Cynthia and Laura, couldn't get over the change in his sister. 'I think yer look a belter, our kid.'

'A little cracker,' was Stan's opinion.

Seamus Moynihan scratched his chin. 'I'm not familiar with any of these new-fangled words, me darlin', so I'll just say yer look as pretty as a picture.'

Jenny stood by the door smiling. She was delighted for her friend. 'Jan, tell them what yer've done today, apart from changing yer hairstyle.'

Jan turned and winked at her before saying, 'I've grown up today. Me mam was always telling me I'd grow up when I was fifteen, so I have. Really, I grew up a few months ago, but I wouldn't like me mam to be wrong, so I waited until today.'

There was a burst of laughter and applause. 'Welcome to the world, girl,' Amy said, before giving her husband a dig in the ribs. 'Go on, slowcoach, tell her how nice she looks.'

Ben raised his eyes to the ceiling, searching for inspiration. Then he sighed. 'This puts me in a bit of a pickle. If I said she looks adorable, which is about the only word that hasn't been used, I'd cop it off you when we got home because I've never said you looked adorable. In me own defence, though, it wasn't that yer never looked adorable, yer understand, but we never used fancy words like that when we were young.'

Amy gave him daggers before saying to Janet, 'D'yer want time to thank him, girl, before I take the poker to him? Huh! Have yer ever heard the likes of it? "Never used fancy words like that when we were young"! What a bleedin' lame excuse that is.'

'Auntie Amy,' Jenny called across, 'we'll have no fighting at my party if yer don't mind. Wait until yer get home.'

'Yeah, okay, girl, I'll do that. I'm better off in me own home when I come to think of it, 'cos I'm used to me own poker. It's all bent, yer see, with me hitting my feller so often, and his head just fits nicely into the bend.'

'Well now, hasn't that just solved a mystery for me?' Seamus shook his head knowingly. 'Haven't I spent many a sleepless night wondering how Ben got that dinge in his head? Sure, I can sleep peacefully now, knowing it was Amy's poker that did it.'

Glasses were replenished and conversations re-started. In another hour the house would be heaving with songs, laughter and dancing. As Molly was heard to say, 'Sure it's a miracle, so it is, what a few bottles of stout will do for yer.'

Jenny and Janet were standing with the boys when Mary came up behind them. 'Are yer going to open yer presents now, so everyone can see what yer got?'

'Where are they, Mam?'

'On the sideboard, sunshine, there's stacks of them.'

'I'll help yer, Jenny,' Mick said. 'I'll open them and you can hold them up for everyone to see.'

'John will help me, won't yer, John?' Janet didn't know there was such a word as coquettish, and even if she did she wouldn't have understood its meaning. But it was the right word to describe the look in her eyes. 'Say yer will, John?'

John was cursing Mick in his head for having stolen Jenny away from him. But when he looked at Janet he realised it was no big deal. It would be a pleasure to help open her presents and see the delight on her face. She was such an easy kid to please. And he'd have Jenny all to himself later, when Mick was singing and they were dancing.

The two girls were like children after Father Christmas has been. They shrieked with delight as each present was unwrapped. And their families and friends had made sure they each got the same gift. Stockings, underskirts, slippers, blouses, and brush and comb sets. There were two presents they particularly liked, but didn't say so for fear of offending. One was the gift off Laura – a tortoiseshell comb, studded with diamond-like stones. This surprised and pleased Jenny so much she felt choked. She hadn't expected anything off her sister. And the last present to be opened had the girls hugging each other in delight. A bottle of Evening In Paris perfume in its famous dark-blue bottle. Well, this showed they really were grown-up now.

There were hugs and kisses all round, and the pleasure on the two pretty faces was enough to lift everyone's heart.

'Clear all the paper away now,' Mary said, 'so we can get on with the party.'

'Me and Janet will take the presents upstairs, Mam, and put them on the bed. Mick and John will clear away, won't yer, fellers?' Jenny got to the door and turned. 'Yer've been good helping us with the presents, thanks.'

'What are yer thanking us for?' Mick asked. 'Yer haven't had our present yet.'

Jenny didn't know how to take this, knowing what jokers the boys were. Then she decided they were having her on. 'Stop acting daft and clear up for us.'

John caught her arm. 'No, Mick's not kidding, we got presents for both of yer.' Still holding on to her tight, he called, 'Mrs Nightingale? Where the heck are yer?'

Mary worked her way round to them. 'What is it, son?'

'They haven't had our presents yet.'

Mary's hand went to her mouth. 'Oh, I'm sorry, boys, I clean forgot with all the running around. I put them in the sideboard cupboard for safety, so Jenny wouldn't see them. I'll get them for yer.'

When Mary came back she was carrying two parcels, and she handed one to each boy. 'I think yer should hand them over yerselves.'

'Which one's which, Mrs Nightingale?' Mick asked. 'We don't want to give the wrong ones.'

Janet dropped her presents on the bottom stair. 'Ooh, isn't it exciting, Jenny? It's the best birthday I ever had.'

Mary looked at the parcels closely. 'That one is for Janet, and this one's Jenny's.'

Amy and Molly had spread the word and the whole gang moved towards the door. 'Go on, girls, open them up.'

Jenny suspected the boys were playing a prank and tried to feel what was inside the parcel. Whatever it was felt hard, and this added to her suspicion. 'You open yours first, Jan.'

Janet didn't need telling twice. She ripped the paper off and was so stunned she couldn't speak. In her hands were a pair of dancing shoes in black patent leather, with a narrow ankle strap and a two-inch heel. Her mouth was moving but no sounds were coming from her.

Jenny looked up to find Mick's eyes on her. 'Go on, Jenny,' he begged. 'Open it up.'

The shoes were the same as Janet's, except for the size, and Jenny was so thrilled she didn't know where to put herself because she felt like bawling her eyes out. She knew she was going to make a fool of herself, so she quickly kissed Mick on the cheek, said, 'I love them,' and fled into the hall. Stepping over Janet's presents she took the stairs two at a time.

When Janet came down to earth it was John she kissed. 'They're the bestest present I've ever had. And when me and Jenny have had a little weep, we'll be down to dance the night away in our new shoes.'

Mary went out to the kitchen to take the cloths off the plates of sandwiches, ready for handing them out, and Stan followed her. 'The girls have done well, haven't they?'

'They certainly have,' Mary smiled. 'They'll be wanting a birthday every week.'

'Our Laura's very quiet.' Stan sneaked one of the sandwiches before leaning against the sink. 'I can't make her out. She's as good-looking as any of them, yet she hasn't got a boyfriend. At least, not one that we know of. Her mate, Cynthia, she seems to be settled with Bill Porter; he can't take his eyes off her.'

'At the moment, Stan, I'm more worried about me dad than I am about anyone else. He should have been here ages ago. He said he was definitely coming and I know he wouldn't miss one of the girls' birthdays unless it was something serious.'

'He might turn up yet, love, it's not that late.'

'I hope so. I do worry about him.'

If Mary had known the real reason for her father's absence, she would have been heartbroken.

Joe Steadman was sitting on the edge of his chair, his elbows on his knees, his hands covering his face. Over the last three years the young woman he'd taken as his wife had humiliated him, shamed him and made him a laughing stock. He was living in a filthy house, slept between sheets that were seldom washed, and wore clothes that were old and shabby. The only decent meal he ever got was when he went to his daughter's, and he seldom had money in his pocket because, as his wife was fond of reminding him, he was an old man who never went anywhere and didn't need good clothes. He'd thought there was nothing more she could do to hurt him, thought it wasn't possible for her to drag him any lower, but how wrong he'd been.

Celia was standing in front of him, her hands planted on her hips, a brazen look on her face and defiance in her eyes. 'Well, haven't yer got anything to say?'

Joe slowly took his hands from his face and forced himself to look at the woman he regretted ever setting eyes on. 'Who's the father?'

Celia's lip curled in scorn. 'You are, of course.'

Joe rolled his hands into a ball. He wasn't a fighting man, had never hit anyone in his life, but right now the urge to knock that sneer off her face was overwhelming. 'I am not yet in my dotage, Celia, so give me the credit of having some intelligence. It is impossible for me to be the father, we both know that. Nor would I want to be. So who is the father?'

'What difference does it make? Yer wouldn't know him if I told yer.'

'Perhaps yer don't know yerself, is that it? Nothing would surprise me about you, Celia, ye're bad through and through.'

'Call me what yer like, it doesn't mean a thing to me. As far as I'm concerned, you are the father of this baby. That's what the neighbours will think, and I can't see yer telling them any different. Nor that precious family of yours. Think how stupid yer'd look if yer told them I had a bun in the oven but yer don't know who put it there?' Celia's smile was unpleasant. 'I'd give anything to see the look on the face of that daughter of yours. My, my, my, how the mighty have fallen.'

'Don't push me too far, Celia, I warn yer. Take that smirk off yer face and sit down. Yer seem to forget this is still my house. Your name was never put on the rent-book, so I'd be in my rights to throw yer out.' He waited until she was seated, then asked, 'The man who is the father, does he want the baby? Yer could always set up house together and we could get a divorce. It would take years, but if the man loves yer he wouldn't mind waiting, I'm sure.'

'Forget it! Ye're not getting rid of me that easy. I'm staying put, whether yer like it or not, so get that through that old head of yours.'

'I wonder why I get the feeling that yer've been very free with yer favours and yer don't know who the father is?' Joe spoke calmly, but inside he was filled with mixed emotions. He was sick in the tummy and worried and angry in his head. 'Well, is that true?'

Celia's hard eyes bored into his. 'You are the father of this baby and I'm sticking to that. If yer tell anyone different, I'll tell them ye're lying because ye're ashamed of fathering a child at your age. I'd get a real kick out of telling yer daughter, and that bleedin' cow next door who looks down her nose every time I see her.'

Joe looked down at his clasped hands. He should be at his granddaughter's birthday party, and he'd been looking forward to it. Instead, fate had dealt him a blow he couldn't see any way out of. Mary and her family were all he had in life, and he'd let them down. If he didn't go along with Celia's story, he'd bring more trouble to their door. Because not for one second did he doubt that his wife would carry out her threats, and take great delight in doing so. The woman he'd married was capable of great wickedness.

Joe pushed himself out of the chair. 'I'm going for a pint and a breath of fresh air. The air in here is putrid.'

Celia knew she'd won, but then she'd never had any doubt. Still, she wasn't satisfied with hurting him, she had to turn the screw tighter. 'What, are yer not going to yer granddaughter's birthday party? I would have thought yer'd like to celebrate with yer mates. It's not every day yer find out ye're become a father.'

Joe looked down at her. 'D'yer know, I feel sorry for the baby. Boy or girl, it's going to have a lousy start in life.' With that he turned on his heel and left, to go down to the pub on the corner. He found a quiet alcove, and with a pint in front of him, he tried to sort out his thoughts. He'd have to go down to Mary's tomorrow, he couldn't let Jenny's birthday go without a word. Besides, he had a present for her and was dying to see her face when he gave her a necklace that matched the bracelet he'd given her for Christmas.

Joe picked up his glass and drank deeply. That would be one solution, to get drunk and forget what he'd been told in the last hour. But although the prospect was appealing, it wasn't the answer. He'd be sober tomorrow with the problems still facing him. Better to sit quietly and get things sorted in his mind now. He had two choices. He could tell Mary and the family, and his neighbours, that he and Celia were expecting a baby, and leave it at that. He'd be embarrassed at his age to admit to it, but it would keep his wife quiet. Or he could tell the truth. That he and his wife hadn't been on intimate terms for eighteen months, so the baby couldn't possibly be his. And let Celia do her damnedest.

When he left the pub, Joe's mind was still in a daze. He didn't know what to do for the best. The best for his family, not for Celia. So he went home to bed, to lie staring at the ceiling for hours while asking God to help him do the right thing.

Celia didn't come home all night, but he no longer cared.

'Grandad's just passed the window, Mam.' Jenny shot out of her chair. 'I'll open the door for him.'

'Good, he's just in time, I'm dishing the dinner out.' Mary was wiping her hands on a towel when she came through to the living room. She grinned when she saw Joe being hugged by Jenny, with Laura waiting for her turn. 'Yer've got a good sense of smell, Dad, the dinner's ready.'

'I could smell it from the top of the street.' Joe smiled as Laura let go of him and Mary's arms came around his neck. 'I felt like one of the Bisto Kids, with me nose following the smell.'

'Where did yer get to last night? Yer had us worried to death.'

'I knew yer would be, sweetheart, but there was no way of letting yer know.' Joe felt the lie sticking in his throat. But what else could

285

he do with the two girls there? 'The boss asked me to stay on until four, to get a job finished. By the time I got home I was whacked.'

Jenny's squeal brought Mary spinning round. 'I don't believe it! I don't believe it! Look, Mam, what Grandad bought me.' Jenny was holding up the necklace and her face couldn't have been happier. 'Yer've got to be the most wonderful grandad in the whole world, and I love you, I love you, I love you!'

Laura held out her hand for a better view. 'I'll be borrowing this.'

Jenny didn't answer at once, then she said, 'Yeah, okay, yer can borrow it if yer take good care of it.'

Mary clapped her hands as she bustled out to the kitchen. 'Come on, set the table before the dinners go cold. Give yer dad a shout, Jenny, he's down the yard.'

Joe was struggling to get his dinner down, for he had no appetite. And Mary watched him anxiously. He looked dreadful, really tired and worn out. But what could you expect when he was working such long hours? He should be letting up a bit now, instead of working all the hours God sends. It wasn't as though yer could see where the money was going; he never looked as smart as he used to. When her mam was alive, she always made sure he was well turned out. Always a pure white collar and shirt, neatly tied tie, shoes so highly polished you could see your face in them, and the creases in his trousers always ironed to perfection. But then her mam had idolised him. She'd have worked her fingers to the bone for him if it had been necessary. What a far cry from the woman he was married to now.

'I couldn't eat any more, sweetheart, I'm bloated.' Joe put his knife and fork down and pushed the plate away. 'I had a lie-in and it's not long since I had me breakfast.'

'That's all right, Dad, at least yer've eaten half of it.' Mary smiled at her daughters who had polished their dinners off in no time. 'Yer dad's nearly finished, so be a pair of angels and start taking the dishes out.'

'We'll wash them for yer, Mam,' Jenny said, touching the necklace which was now her proudest possession. 'I'll wash and our Laura can dry.'

'Come on, Joe, sit yerself by the fire,' Stan said, taking the Sunday paper off the seat of the fireside chair. He couldn't put his finger on it, but there was something not quite right about his father-in-law. He reminded Stan of a little lad who'd broken a neighbour's window playing footie and was terrified of telling his mam. 'Let's leave the work to the women.'

Mary watched with interest as Laura helped clear the table before standing by the side of the sink to dry the dishes as Jenny washed them. That's a change, she thought, not a murmur out of her. And Jenny was doing her best to improve relations between the two of them. Look how she'd offered to lend Laura her new necklace; not many girls would do that for a sister who barely passed her the time of day. That was definitely extending a hand of friendship. I'm not going to knock it either, Mary thought. I just hope it lasts. She cocked her ears when she heard her husband talking to her father.

'How's life treating yer, Joe?' Stan asked. 'Everything okay?'

'Just so-so, Stan, same as everybody else. We all have to muddle along as best we can, I suppose.'

Laura came through rolling her sleeves down. 'I'm going to Cynthia's, Mam, and I might stay there for me tea.'

'She's not seeing Bill, then?'

'No, not tonight. We're having a game of cards with her mam and dad.'

Jenny's head appeared over her sister's shoulder. 'I'm going to Jan's. I promised to comb her hair for her before we take our presents over to Auntie Lizzie. She didn't want to come to the party but she said she'd love to see what we got.'

'Are the boys going, or don't I need to ask?'

'Yeah, they said they were. And I better warn yer, Mam, they're coming to see yer one night to ask if they can take me and Janet to a dance. It's not a big dance hall, just a little place belonging to a church.'

'Do yer want to go?' Stan asked, trying to hide a smile at his daughter's naivety. 'It's no good me and yer mam wasting time spending hours in discussion over this serious matter if yer don't want to go.'

'Oh yes, Dad, I'm dying to go. Especially as I've got those lovely shiny dancing shoes. I've been walking up and down me bedroom in them, to get used to the high heels. I don't want to fall flat on me face in them, do I? Not if I'm dancing with Mick or John, 'cos I'd never hear the end of it. And yer know they'd both take good care of us.'

'Don't worry, sunshine,' Mary laughed. 'Yer wouldn't be allowed to go with them if I wasn't sure about that. I have complete trust in both those lads.'

They could hear Jenny humming as she ran up the stairs, then her voice saying, 'Wait for me, Laura, I'll walk out with yer.'

Joe's nerves were taut; he couldn't sit still. He clasped and unclasped his hands, ran his fingers through his hair and fidgeted with the buttons on his cardi. He'd get it off his chest as soon as the girls went out. He couldn't stand the strain much longer or he'd crack.

Laura gave him a kiss. 'Ta-ra, Grandad. Yer'll be gone by the time I get in, so I'll see yer through the week.'

Jenny kissed him as well, even though she said, 'I'll see yer later,

Grandad, 'cos I'm coming home for me tea.'

Mary and Stan watched the two girls pass the window and smiled when they saw Jenny talking to her sister. Her face was animated and the words were pouring from her mouth fifteen to the dozen. It was a rare sight, but a very welcome one.

'Jenny loves her present, Joe,' Stan said. 'Yer couldn't have chosen anything better.'

'I'm lucky – one of me mates in work has a daughter roughly the same age. It was his wife's idea to get the bracelets at Christmas, and as they went down a treat I asked if she'd help me out again.'

'Are you feeling all right, Dad?' The more Mary looked into her father's face, the more concerned she became. 'Yer don't look yerself today and I think ye're working too hard. Cut down on the overtime – I'm sure there's plenty of fellers would be glad of it. Don't forget, ye're not getting any younger.'

Now is the right time, Joe thought, curling his fists and digging his nails into his palms until he could feel the pain. And with the pain came the courage to speak the words which would devastate his daughter. 'Celia's expecting a baby.'

Mary gripped the narrow wooden arms of her chair and pressed until the skin on her knuckles was stretched to show blue veins standing out in stark relief. She felt as though her heart had stopped beating, and the room was starting to spin around. No, it's not true, a voice in her head kept repeating. My dad wouldn't do that to us! I'm older than his wife, for God's sake, and he's got grown-up granddaughters! We'd all be a laughing stock! And how would she tell the girls? She couldn't, she'd die of shame.

Then Mary looked at her father's face, and the pain etched there. And all thoughts of shame vanished. He looked like an old man who had the troubles of the world on his shoulders. He was her father, she loved him dearly, and he needed her now more than he'd ever needed her. She left her chair to kneel before him and they wrapped their arms around each other. With tears streaming down her face, she sobbed, 'I'm sorry, Dad, I really am, but I've got to be truthful and tell yer I'm not happy about it.'

There were tears in Joe's eyes as he stroked her hair. 'I didn't expect yer to be, sweetheart. I didn't want it meself, but these things happen.'

Stan had had time to recover from the shock, and looking at his father-in-law, he felt heartily sorry for him. He was too old to be starting a new family, especially as his wife couldn't look after him, never mind a new baby. But as Joe said, these things happen and you couldn't do anything about it. It was sad, though, because the old man looked anything but overjoyed about the situation himself.

'Come and sit down, love. It's no good crying, it doesn't solve anything.' Stan cupped his wife's elbows and raised her up. 'What's done is done, and nothing can change things.'

Mary ran the back of her hands across her eyes. 'I'm sorry for upsetting yer, Dad, but I don't think it's right and there's no use pretending otherwise. And I've got to speak me mind. Apart from yer being too old to start again with all the work a baby brings, that wife of yours is not fit to be a mother. The child will never get the love and care it needs.'

Joe felt like blurting the truth out, but knew the consequences would bring more hurt than his daughter was feeling now. Because anger would take over all the other emotions and she'd want to have it out with Celia. And Joe would die rather than see his beloved daughter getting into a fight with a woman who wouldn't fight fair. She was good at biting and scratching was his wife, as he knew from experience. So he had to stick with the lies and the pretence. 'I've had words with Celia, and there's going to be a lot of changes. I'm going to come down hard on her if there isn't.'

Mary sighed, thinking, Aye – and pigs might fly. 'And how d'yer think I'm going to tell the girls, Dad? I don't think I could.'

'Don't tell them yet, sweetheart, it's still early days.' Joe was certain his wife was pregnant, she wouldn't make up a tale like that. But he was hoping against hope that whoever the father was would turn up and take her off his hands. 'And don't forget, I've got to face them, too.'

Stan got to his feet. 'I'll stick the kettle on, we could all do with a cuppa.' And in his mind he added, 'especially Joe.' His father-in-law looked as though he would like nothing better than to curl up and die, leaving his pain and worries behind him.

Jenny steadied herself by holding on to the walls on either side as she tottered along the hall of Lizzie's house in her two-inch heels. Giggling as she went, she called back over her shoulder, 'I can't even walk in them, never mind dance.'

She opened the door to see two beaming, happy faces. 'Yer'll be all right when ye're dancing, Jenny,' Mick said, ' 'cos I'll be keeping tight hold of yer.'

Cheeky beggar, John thought. He's always got to get in first. 'And when he's not, I'll be holding yer tight, Jenny.'

'Close the door after yerselves.' Jenny tried the journey back with just one hand on the wall, and when she reached the living-room door she became daring and walked into the room unaided. 'See, Jan, it's easy when yer know how.' She held her arms slightly away from her body, and much to the amusement of the two boys, swayed over to Auntie Lizzie like a mannequin. 'D'yer think I'll get a feller, Auntie Lizzie?'

The old lady laughed. 'Yer've already got two, how many more d'yer want?'

'No, I've got two mates. I mean a feller of me own. Yer know, like a boyfriend.'

'I'll be yer boyfriend, Jenny,' Mick said. 'I'd be honoured if yer'd have me.'

'And me.' John gave his mate a look to kill. 'I'll be yer boyfriend and I'd be more honoured than Mick would be. He's not very good at being honoured.'

'Excuse me,' Janet said huffily, 'I'd like a boyfriend, too.'

John grinned at her. 'Hello, curly top. I see Jenny's been busy with yer hair again. It doesn't half suit yer.'

'Ooh, er, I've come down in the world, haven't I? I was a bobby dazzler last night, Auntie Lizzie, and now I'm just curly top.'

'Ye're still a bobby dazzler, Janet.' Mick put a finger in one of her curls and smiled when he let go and it bounced back into place. 'And a humdinger.'

Mollified, Janet said, 'I'll let yer off. Anyway, we've shown Auntie Lizzie all our presents, and we're agreed that the shoes were our best present. Except that Jenny's a lucky beggar, she's got two best presents.'

Jenny put her fingers under the necklace and lifted it from her neck. 'Me grandad gave me this, isn't it gorgeous?'

She was fifteen now and Mick was in for the kill. 'It's not half as gorgeous as you.'

John, whose thoughts were running on the same track, was right behind him. 'You put it in the shade, Jenny.'

Jenny stamped her foot. 'Will you two stop acting the goat? If we're going to the dance with yer on Wednesday, I don't want everyone thinking we're raw beginners. So will yer behave yerselves for once, and teach us a few steps?'

'Did yer mam say yer could come with us?' Both boys spoke as one, then turned to grin at each other. Rivalry hadn't spoilt their friendship or their sense of humour. 'That's the gear!'

'Me mam hasn't said I can, but she will when yer ask her.' Jenny raised her brows in a haughty expression. Indeed, with her beautiful necklace and bracelet, and such posh dancing shoes, she was feeling haughty. 'As long as yer ask politely.'

'The boys are always polite, Jenny,' Lizzie said. 'I've never known them to be anything else but polite.'

Jenny turned her head to look at the old lady, and her wink was so broad her whole cheek moved upwards. And there was a mischievous twinkle in her eyes. 'Yes, they are always polite, Auntie Lizzie, when they're not acting the fool. But if me and Janet have got to act like grown-ups now, then these two have, as well.'

'Oh, I am grown-up, Jenny,' Mick said, his dimples beginning to deepen. 'In fact, everyone says I'm old for me age.'

This set Janet thinking. 'How can yer be old for yer age? I mean, like, if I'm fifteen then I'm fifteen, I can't be any older. Same as if I was twenty, I couldn't say I was fifteen.'

'Yer could say yer were young for yer age.' John thought she was hilarious. She reminded him of his mam, but whereas his mam knew she was funny and made the most of it, Janet didn't. 'One of my mates in work is twenty, and he's young for his age.'

'Then he's telling fibs, isn't he?' Janet poked a finger in his chest, her face really serious. 'You should tell him it's a sin to tell lies.'

John took her finger and kissed it. 'D'yer know, Janet, I don't know half the time whether ye're having us on or not. But whatever, yer look very pretty when ye're doing it.'

Jenny giggled. Her friend hadn't stayed grown-up very long. But John was right, she did look very pretty. 'When ye're ready, will one of yer teach me how to dance.'

Mick was by her side in a trice. He picked up her hands, put one on his shoulder and gripped the other. 'Here I am, Jenny – ready, willing and able. Auntie Lizzie can watch and give us points on our performance.'

'Ooh, er,' said Janet, 'yer better dance good, John, so *we* get some points. Don't be relying on me 'cos I'm only a learner.'

Lizzie smiled. Janet might be a learner when it came to dancing, but she had her head screwed on the right way. Although John didn't know it, he was being wooed. Would he succumb, or would his heart stay with Jenny?

Mick sang *Girl of My Dreams* as he took Jenny slowly through the steps. He thought the song was very appropriate because she was, and always would be, the girl of his dreams. To John, the dance was more fun than anything. Every time he looked at Janet's face he doubled up and missed a step. She looked so serious, with her tongue peeping out of the side of her mouth. And when he did miss a step, she'd say, 'Never you mind, John, even I make a mistake sometimes.'

Lizzie awarded the girls ten points each. In her head, Jenny's points were for her ability to learn quickly, and Janet's for her novel way of catching a boy without him knowing.

Chapter Twenty-Three

'I'm all on edge, Mam – me tummy's doing somersaults.' Jenny was pushing a potato around her plate. Her appetite had deserted her tonight, she was far too excited to eat. After all, going to her first dance was a big event in a girl's life. 'I hope me dress doesn't look out of place.'

'Of course it won't, sunshine, yer'll be fine,' Mary assured her. 'Yer'll be with Janet, and her dress is no nicer than yours, is it?'

Laura glanced sideways at her sister. 'It's not a proper dance, yer know.' There was no malice or sarcasm in her voice, as Mary was quick to note – perhaps just a trace of impatience. 'They won't be all dolled up.'

'It's still a dance, though, isn't it?' Jenny said firmly. She wasn't going to let anybody dampen her expectations. 'I mean, it's no use taking our dancing shoes if we're going to spend the night sitting down.'

'It's only a fourpenny hop,' Laura said. 'There won't be a band there, yer dance to gramophone records. It's where beginners go to learn, before they go on to the big dance halls.'

'Oh well, we'll be in good company, won't we? If I fall flat on me face there'll probably be half-a-dozen people stretched out beside me.'

Stan chuckled. 'I learned to dance at a church hop, but it was only tuppence in those days. I can laugh now when I look back, but we didn't half enjoy ourselves. Me and me mate, Ginger Lunt, we really thought we were the bees-knees. We used to swagger down the street with our dance shoes tucked under our arm, without a care in the world. We were seventeen when we went on to the Grafton, and I can tell yer that what we learned at that tuppenny hop stood us in good stead; we could hold our own with anyone.'

Both girls listened with interest. Their dad had never told them he went dancing, and they'd never heard of Ginger Lunt. 'Go on, tell us some more, Dad,' Jenny asked eagerly. 'What happened to yer mate, Ginger?'

'The same as happened to me, love. We were eighteen when we went to the Grafton one night, and I saw this blonde girl dancing with some feller. And could she dance? I'll say she could. It was an "excuse me" quickstep, so I did no more than pinch her off her partner. But she got her own back on me, 'cos she pinched something of mine.' Stan stretched his hand to cover his wife's smaller one. 'Her name was Mary Steadman and she stole my heart.'

Jenny's eyes were bright. 'Oh Dad, that's a lovely story. So romantic! But what happened to Ginger?'

Laura didn't speak, but she was feeling emotional. Gary was eighteen, and she knew he'd fallen for her, like she'd fallen hook, line and sinker for him. Why couldn't they be like her mam and dad? The answer to that was easy: her name was Celia.

'Ginger met a girl the same night; she was called Nancy. We went out as a foursome for a couple of weeks, then we started courting seriously. I wanted yer mam all to meself, yer see, 'cos I loved her so much, and still do.'

Jenny's eyes were moist with tears. 'I hope I find someone who loves me as much as you love me mam.' She turned to her mother and was surprised to see she looked sad. 'What's the matter, Mam, are yer not feeling well? I've noticed yer've not been yerself for a few days. Are yer sickening for something?'

Laura pricked her ears, remembering Gary saying the bubble had burst for Celia, and her family could be involved. There'd been no hint of trouble, but her mam had been quiet and that wasn't like her. She was always happy and joking.

'I'm all right, sunshine – a touch of the blues, that's all. It'll wear off in a day or two, you'll see.' Mary looked at the clock and raised her brows. 'Hadn't yer better start getting yerself ready? It's a special night tonight, yer want to look yer best.'

When Jenny had hot-footed it from the room, Laura said, 'I'm not going out, so I'll wash the dishes for yer. You sit down and rest, Mam, if ye're feeling off-colour.'

'Thanks, sunshine, I'll do that.' Mary hadn't slept well for the last three nights. Even when she did manage to drop off for half an hour, she tossed and turned restlessly. Her father's news had devastated her and she couldn't see her life ever being normal again.

Mick and John looked so happy walking down the street with Jenny between them, anyone would believe they'd come up on the pools. They didn't do the pools, mind, but if they did, and they'd won, they couldn't have looked happier. John carried her dancing shoes so she could link them, and you'd have thought he was carrying the crown jewels.

'Yer look nice, Jenny, and yer smell lovely,' Mick said. 'Yer smell like a rose garden.'

'Yeah, yer do, Jenny, but I think the smell is more like sweet-peas.'

'It's Evening In Paris perfume, I'll have you know.' Jenny tossed her head, sending her blonde hair swishing around her cheeks. 'I put a dab behind each ear, and a tiny little dab on me throat. It's only a little bottle and I don't want to use it up too quick, 'cos one of the women in the office said it's quite expensve.'

'We thought about that, didn't we, Mick?' asked John, whose head the thought had never entered. But Bill Porter wasn't going to go one better than them, even if he did seem to be out of the scene just now. 'Didn't I say "Shall we buy her Evening In Paris?".'

'Yer certainly did, pal! And we were in two minds about it, as well. But after much consideration, we decided Jenny would rather have the dance shoes.'

'You are two of the biggest fibbers in the world.' Jenny giggled and squeezed their arms. 'But if I'd been asked, I would have chosen the shoes.'

Martha Porter answered their knock and her eyes went to the heavens as she said, 'Yer'd better come in, there's been a slight mishap.'

'Is Janet all right?' Jenny asked, mounting the steps. 'She's not done anything silly like catching a cold, has she?'

The smell that met them as they crowded into the hallway was sickly and overpowering. They sniffed up and looked at each other, but no one liked to comment for fear of upsetting Mrs Porter. Janet's mother, however, was forthcoming. 'That smell ye're all afraid to mention is half a bleedin' bottle of Evening In Paris, if yer don't mind. The silly cow doused herself in it and it's stinking the ruddy house down. She couldn't go out like that, they'd smell her a mile away.'

John tried his hardest but he couldn't keep the laughter back. Mick joined him, and then Martha began to see the funny side. Only Jenny managed to keep a straight face. She wasn't going to have a laugh at her best friend's expense.

'Can't she just wash it off, Mrs Porter? The smell would go away then.'

'Where did yer put yours, Jenny?' Martha asked with an amused expression on her face. 'A dab behind the ears, was it?'

Thinking she was helping her friend, Jenny said, 'And a dab on me neck, Mrs Porter. I bet Jan's been a bit heavy with it, that's all.'

'Ah, but my daughter didn't put it on her skin, girl, she put it on her dress. Half a bottle of the bleedin' stuff. She's upstairs now changing her clothes so people won't be fainting all around her. Honest to God, she ponged to high heaven. I had to open the kitchen door to let some fresh air in.'

They all looked up when they heard footsteps on the stairs. And down came Janet, looking so woebegone they all felt sorry for her. 'My mam did the same thing once, curly top,' John said, in an effort to put a smile back on her face. 'Only she couldn't afford an expensive scent so she used Essence of Violets. And yer know me mam, she wouldn't wash it off for anyone. She said she wasn't pouring good money down the plug-hole, and if me dad didn't like it, he could go and sit in Annie Baxter's for a few hours. Well, me dad preferred the smell to sitting in Annie Baxter's.'

'I was stupid,' Janet said, 'and ye're all late now because of me.'

'Who cares?' John asked, while his head was asking him why she always appealed to his soft side. 'We'll be there before the interval.'

'Come on, Jan,' Jenny said, 'yer'll have forgotten all about it once yer get on the dance floor. Yer'll be too busy trying to stop these two from standing all over yer feet.'

'Yeah, come on.' Mick thought the words would choke him, but he managed to get them out. 'I bags the first dance with yer.'

When John said, 'I bags the second,' Janet cheered up considerably and donned her coat. What was the use of worrying about a bottle of scent anyway? She could always get round their Bill to buy her another.

The boys had agreed beforehand to swap partners for every dance. That was the fairest way and would save any arguments. So although it broke his heart, Mick gave way to John when he asked Jenny to dance. And while he was steering Janet around the dance floor, his eyes spent more time watching what John was up to, than they did watching Janet's feet. It was only when the dance was over it struck him that she hadn't done badly at all. 'Yer did well, there, Janet, I'm proud of yer.'

The girl preened. 'Thank you, Mick, and you did well, too.'

Mick looked at her closely to see if she was having him on, but her face was that of an innocent baby. He was an experienced dancer, but she'd managed to reduce him to the status of a beginner. And she'd done it in such a way you couldn't fall out with her.

When the other couple came off the floor, John had his arm across Jenny's shoulder and they were laughing up at each other. This was enough to send Mick's temperature shooting up to boiling point. Just wait, John Hanley, he said to himself, from now on it's no holds barred. Every man for himself and the devil take the hindmost.

After turning the record over and winding up the gramophone, the MC announced a slow waltz. Mick was highly delighted. 'This is you and me, Jenny, and as ye're pretty good at waltzing, we can dance proper.' With a cheeky grin at his friend, he led Jenny on to the dance floor and put his arm around her waist. If this wasn't heaven, it was the nearest he'd ever been to it. 'Just relax, Jenny, and yer'll follow me easy.'

'Ye're not half holding me tight, Mick. I can't see a thing only your chest.'

'If you concentrate on the dancing, I'll give yer a running commentary.' Mick looked down at the top of her blonde head and had to stop himself from planting a kiss on it. He knew she'd clock him one if he did, and besides his mother's words were ringing in his ears. 'Don't yer forget, me darlin', the girl's only fifteen and you're nearly nineteen.' He sighed, wondering how long he was supposed to wait. Hadn't he been wishing his life away for the last ten years?

Jenny pulled herself back and stared up at him. 'I don't think much of yer commentary, Mick Moynihan, yer haven't opened yer mouth yet. There must be something going on, or has everyone gone home?'

Mick grinned and pulled her towards him. 'Well, let's see. John has got hold of Janet's hand and is walking her on to the dance floor. Yes, he's holding her properly and I don't see her complaining. Ay, hang on a minute! He's just kissed her, right in the middle of the floor. Well, that's cheek for yer.'

Jenny jerked herself away and gazed around the dancing couples until she spotted her friend. 'Ye're a lying hound, Mick Moynihan. I've a good mind to tell them.'

'It was wishful thinking, Jenny. Yer know me and John do everything together, and I thought if he'd kissed Janet it was only natural for me to kiss you.'

'You just try it, Mick Moynihan, and yer'll be sorry yer signed.' Jenny went back to staring at his chest so he wouldn't see her eyes dancing with merriment. 'The very idea, indeed.'

'Well, are yer at least prepared to discuss our relationship? That wouldn't do yer no harm, just talking.'

'Our relationship? Well, we're good mates, aren't we?'

'That's what I'm getting at, Jenny.' By this time Mick had given up trying to dance and was walking Jenny around the floor. Still holding her close, though. 'Yer told Auntie Lizzie that yer were looking for a boyfriend, and as I haven't got a girlfriend I thought yer might like to team up with me.'

'Are yer asking me for a date, Mick?'

Mick sighed with relief. After going all around the world, and nearly having a heart attack, Jenny had said the words for him. 'Yes, Jenny, I'm asking yer for a date. Will yer come out with me one night?'

'What about yer mate? I thought you and John went everywhere together.'

'Yer've got eyes in yer head, Jenny, and yer know that me and John both feel the same about yer. We've been rivals for years, even though we're the best of pals. But the time has come, for me at least, to put me claim in before someone else comes along. It's up to John to decide what he wants to do. If he asks yer, and yer would rather have him, then that's the way it is. Me and him will always be pals, no matter what.'

Jenny lapsed into thought. There was no way she would choose between the two boys; it wouldn't be fair. It would ruin their friendship no matter what they thought now. And she didn't want to be the cause of that, even though her heart lay with one of them – and always had. She heard John's familiar laugh and turned her head to see him acting the goat with fancy footwork, and Janet was lapping it up.

'Mick, shall I ask me mam if we can go to the pictures one night as a foursome? I've never had a boyfriend, never even been out with a boy. And I think I should get out and about a bit before I say I'll be someone's girlfriend. Don't yer agree?'

'Yeah, I suppose ye're right.' Mick was disappointed, but at least he'd made a start, put his cards on the table. 'But don't forget, I've got a lot to offer.'

'What have yer got to offer, Mick?'

Mick's dimples appeared. 'Meself, for a kick-off. And I know self-praise is no recommendation, but yer'll not get anyone better. Then there's me mam and dad, they're definitely an asset. Oh, and I almost forgot, there's next door's cat.'

Jenny giggled. 'Mick Moynihan, ye're as daft as a brush.'

'Don't tell yer mam that, or she won't let yer come to the pictures with us.'

'Come on, girl, out with it. What's wrong with yer?' There was concern on Amy's face as she sat across from her friend. 'For the past few days yer've had a face on yer like a wet week. It's a wonder the bleedin' milk isn't curdled.'

Mary sighed. She'd kept her worry bottled up inside her until it was nearly choking her. If she didn't tell someone and get it off her chest, she'd go nuts. And who better to confide in than her best mate? 'Not a word leaves this room, sunshine, okay?'

Amy stiffened a finger and made a cross on her chest. 'Cross my heart and hope to die, if this day I tell a lie.' Hoping to lighten the gloom, she asked, 'Yer haven't got yerself a fancy man, have yer?'

'I'm sorry, Amy, but I haven't got a laugh left in me. I'm drained. I can't eat or sleep, or even think straight.' She came straight to the point. 'Celia's expecting a baby.'

Amy's jaw dropped and she sagged back against the chair. 'Yer what! Christ, girl, yer've got to be joking.'

'I wish I was. I wish to God I was.'

'What's the man thinking of? Has he lost the run of his senses?

Blimey, girl, he must be sixty! And he's got a slut of a wife!' Amy's eyes narrowed. 'Is he sure he's the father? I wouldn't put anything past that one; she's a real trollop if ever there was one.'

'Me dad's not that soft, he'd know if it wasn't his. He's not happy about it, yer can tell, but as he said, what's done is done. He looks terrible and I feel heartily sorry for him. I'm afraid I told him what I thought, and I'm sorry now. He's got enough on his plate without me turning against him.'

'You'd never turn against yer dad, girl, and he knows it. But he couldn't expect yer to welcome news like that, not from a man of his age.'

'Well, he didn't come last night and Wednesday's his usual night to call. I must have really upset him and I'm worried sick.'

'What does Stan have to say about all this?'

'He's not said much because he knows how bad I feel about it. His feelings are that it's done and we can't do anything about it.'

'Do the girls know?'

Mary shook her head. 'I couldn't tell them, I'd be too ashamed. How could I explain that to two young girls? If it was me expecting I'd be too embarrassed to tell them, never mind their grandad. They'll have to know sometime, but me dad said not to say anything to them yet. I think he's dreading the thought of facing them. And I'm such a coward, Amy, I'd rather they never had to know.'

Amy's huge bosom rose and fell as she let out a deep sigh. 'I'm sorry for yer dad, 'cos I think the world of him. But I've got to say, girl, I think he's been a stupid old bugger. Yer'd think, at his age, he'd be past that sort of thing now.'

'Yeah, but don't forget he's got a young wife.' Mary picked nervously at the plush of the chenille tablecloth. 'Whatever I think, I've got to stand by me dad 'cos I love the bones of him. He's been hurt enough, I'll not add to that hurt. So even if it kills me, I'll not upset him any more. But one thing I'm determined on, I'll never visit that house while she's in it, baby or no baby.'

'I dunno, girl, life can be a bugger, can't it? But I know how yer feel about telling the girls because I couldn't tell my kids if I was in your shoes.' Amy stretched her chubby arm across the table and patted her best mate's hand. 'The world keeps on turning, girl, and yer can't stop it. It won't do no good sitting in the house feeling miserable. So come on, get yer coat on and let's get down to the shops. The fresh air will blow the cobwebs away and yer'll feel better. And don't faint when I say the cream slices are on me today.'

Celia was waiting for her as usual. Leaning against the wall, cigarette smouldering between her fingers, she studied Laura's face. 'Ye're a

299

bit late tonight, kid, I was getting worried. I thought there might be trouble at home.'

Laura was in a fighting mood. Last night, when John and Mick had brought her sister home, they'd been full of how much they'd enjoyed themselves. And because of this woman, she wasn't able to bring her boyfriend home. Well, something had to be done about it, she'd had enough. 'I can be late if I want, can't I? And why should there be trouble at home?'

'All right, keep yer hair on, I only asked.' Celia blew the cigarette smoke straight into Laura's face. 'I worry about yer, yer see.'

'Yer must have better things to do than worry about me, Celia. Yer see, I'm quite capable of looking after meself.'

Gary came through the double doors of the dance hall and heard Laura's words. He hesitated just for a second, then walked towards her. 'Come on, babe, don't be standing here nattering when we could be dancing.'

Laura couldn't help her face lighting up when she saw him. 'I'll just stick me coat in the cloakroom, I won't be a tick.'

Putting her cloakroom ticket in her bag, she passed Celia without a glance. One wrong word out of her grandad's wife, and she knew she'd clock her one. So she walked through the doors and into Gary's arms. 'I'll kill her one of these days, Gary, I really will. Who the hell does she think she is?'

Gary put a finger to his lips. 'Yer never know who she's got listening out for her.' He waited for her to put her bag under a chair, then pulled her on to the dance floor. 'Come on, babe, it seems like an eternity since I had me arms around yer.'

'I'm not putting up with it any longer, Gary. I've had a bellyful of this once-a-week lark. Me kid sister can bring her boyfriend home, but not me. So I'm telling yer straight – either yer start taking me out proper, or I'm not coming here any more. And I mean it.'

'Yer might not have to put up with it any longer, babe. I think our Celia has overstepped the mark this time. She's confident she'll get away with it, but I can't see it meself.' His bright blue eyes met her deep brown ones. 'Has there been anything out of the ordinary happened at your house? Any news of anything?'

Laura looked puzzled. 'What's going on? Celia said something about trouble at home, but there's been nothing that I know of.'

'I think you and I are going to have to have a very serious talk tonight.' Gary put his cheek next to hers. 'I want to be yer proper boyfriend. I want to take yer home to meet me mam, and I want to meet your folks. I want to sit on the back row of the pictures with yer, go on the ferry to New Brighton – all the things courting couples do. And I think that between us we can make it happen. All it will take is our sticking together, come what may, and having the guts to tell her to her face to get off our backs. We can turn the tables now, because we've really got something on her.'

'I'll do anything if it means we can see each other as often as we like – but what have we got on her?'

'When Celia and Charlie do their disappearing act, we'll go outside and I'll tell yer what I know. We'll see what yer think, and take it from there.'

They walked a little way from the dance hall so they couldn't be seen or heard, and stood against a wall. Laura shivered. 'I should have got me coat out of the cloakroom, I'm freezing.'

Gary slipped off his navy-blue jacket and draped it across her shoulders. 'That'll keep yer nice and warm.'

Laura snuggled into the jacket and grinned up at him. 'I've never been as close to yer as I am now.' She sniffed up. 'I can even smell yer on it. I think I'll take it home with me so I'll always feel ye're near me.'

'Yer'll be sick of the sight of me pretty soon, if all goes to plan. I'll be knocking on yer door every night.'

'Yer seem very sure of yerself tonight, Gary, and very secretive. What is it that yer've found out about Celia? I hope it's something really bad, so we can tell her to go and jump in the Mersey.'

'She's expecting a baby.'

Laura screwed up her eyes as a dozen thoughts came into her head. And with the thoughts came a picture of her grandad's face. 'Are yer sure?'

'I got it right from the horse's mouth, babe. Celia and Charlie told me themselves. I think I was happier than they were.'

'I don't get it! What's it got to do with Charlie?'

'Well, it's his baby, isn't it? But she was laughing her head off when she said her husband has agreed to let everyone think it's his. She called him all the fools going. But she still never mentioned anything about her husband being yer grandad. Even Charlie hasn't got a clue about that. They're both in for a rude awakening. I can't wait to see their faces when we tell them we'll blow them up if Celia doesn't leave us alone.'

'Maybe I'm thick, Gary, but I don't get it.' Laura's temper was rising. 'D'yer mean yer expect me to let her get away with pulling a stunt like that on me grandad? If yer do, then you're in for a rude awakening, too! I love me grandad, and I'll not go along with her lies just to get me and you off the hook. If I did that I'd be worse than she is – nothing more than a scheming, brazen, lying bitch.'

'What else can we do, babe? If we tell yer grandad, then Celia will get her own back by telling all sorts of lies about us. What we did would be magnified a thousand times to my mam and your family.'

Laura dropped her head. She'd got herself into this mess for the sake of one lousy underskirt. But she knew Gary was right. When Celia told her tale, it wouldn't be just about an underskirt; she'd add a lot more on to it. Like her smoking, even though she'd only ever had that one cigarette. And that she'd lied about going to the dance with Cynthia.

'I'll have to have time to think it over, Gary. After all, it's not your grandad she's lied to and cheated, it's mine. He's a lovely, gentle man, and he doesn't deserve what she's doing to him. If yer could meet him, yer'd know what I mean. I couldn't stand back and let him be made a fool of, just so we get what we want. And me mam would hate me if I let someone hurt him without me lifting a finger to help.'

'What shall we do, then, babe? I'll go along with whatever you decide because, as yer said, it's not my family.'

'I'm not thinking straight, Gary, so I don't want to do anything hasty. I mean, where does Charlie fit into this? He's laughing sacks, isn't he? What sort of a man would get a married woman pregnant and then pass the baby off as someone else's? He's a good match for Celia, they're both rotten.' Laura shook her head as though bewildered by it all. 'Will yer give me until next Thursday to think it over? By that time I'll know exactly what I should do for the best.'

'That suits me, babe, as long as we can sort ourselves out. We need to make the most of what we know because we may never get another chance. You're my girl and I want the whole world to know. If yer think we should throw ourselves on the mercy of our families, then I'll go along with that. But please don't let anything keep us apart for much longer, babe, I couldn't stand it.'

Laura stood on tiptoe to kiss him. 'I won't let anyone keep us apart, Gary, I promise. Especially Celia. Somehow I'll pay her back for laughing at my grandad behind his back.'

Chapter Twenty-Four

Laura was looking in the bedroom mirror as she ran a brush through her hair, but her mind was so occupied she didn't even see her reflection. Nor did she feel the stiff bristles of the brush scraping her scalp as she put her strength behind the strokes. She was trying to cover one pain with another but it wasn't working. Last night had been a nightmare and she was no further forward. For hours she'd lain on her back staring up at the ceiling, seeking a solution that would not only help her grandad, but also her and Gary. She knew she was being selfish, and for the first time in her life wasn't proud of herself. She had the solution in her hands but was too cowardly to use it. All she had to do was go downstairs now and tell her mam and dad everything. But she didn't have the courage to do it because suddenly it mattered to her what her mam and dad thought of her. She couldn't bear the prospect of them turning their heads from her in disgust.

She heard footsteps running up the stairs and quickly slipped the brush into a drawer. She hoped Jenny would get what she wanted and go; the last thing Laura needed was to have to listen to her going on about how good life was. She must have been born under a lucky star, her sister, because everything had always gone her way.

Jenny bounced in, her face wearing a big smile and her whole body exuding happiness. 'Are yer going out tonight, Laura?'

'Only down to Cynthia's for an hour.' Laura cringed inside when she heard the bedsprings creak as her sister sat on the side of the bed. Oh Lord, she wants to be matey and this is the wrong time. 'I'm going to have an early night for a change.'

'Me mam's just said I can go to the pictures with John and Mick on Saturday night, and I'm over the moon. Janet's coming as well, of course – I wouldn't go anywhere without me mate.' Jenny bounced gently on the bed. 'I wonder which picture-house we'll go to?'

Laura snapped. The stupid girl was going to ask her to choose between James Cagney and Cary Grant, when she had so much trouble on her mind. She spun round to face her sister. 'I don't know why yer bother with those two stupid nits. It's about time they grew up. They can't even kiss proper.'

The smile slipped from Jenny's face. 'How would you know that?'

'How d'yer think I'd know? Down the entry, of course.' Laura grabbed her handbag and made for the door. 'Fumbling and sloppy, both of them.' She didn't stay long enough to see her sister's stricken face. With those few words, spoken without thought or truth, she'd stripped Jenny of her happiness and her belief in the two people she'd have trusted with her life.

'Can we go up to yer bedroom to talk?' Laura whispered anxiously when Cynthia opened the door. 'I've got something terrible to tell yer.'

'Yeah, you go on up, I'll tell me mam.' Cynthia poked her head around the living-room door. 'I'm going to me bedroom with Laura, Mam.' She winked when her father's eyes appeared over the top of the *Echo*. 'Girls' talk, Dad, yer wouldn't be interested.'

When her head disappeared from view, her father looked across the room. 'She seems to have got over whatever was ailing her.'

Fanny lowered her eyes to the sock she was darning. 'Yes, she's a lot better.'

Cynthia bounded up the stairs and closed the bedroom door behind her. 'Well, what's this terrible thing I'm about to hear?'

'Sit down and I'll tell yer.' Laura moved along and patted the eiderdown. 'Don't say anything until I've finished, Cynthia – just listen.'

Laura hesitated, wondering where to start. The incident with the underskirt was the beginning, so her tale began on the night she'd walked out of the factory gates to find Celia waiting for her. She didn't leave anything out, as the words came tumbling from her mouth. The lies she'd told, the way she'd deceived her parents, how she'd met and fallen for Gary, and how Celia had manipulated them both. It was when she came to last night, and what she'd heard about the way her grandad was being made a fool of, that her voice faltered and tears sprang to her eyes. 'I'm at the end of me tether, Cynthia. I just don't know what to do for the best.'

'Of course yer know what yer've got to do, otherwise yer'd take the easy way out and you and Gary would be laughing sacks. But yer know damn well that's not what yer should do, or yer wouldn't be here telling me. Ye're feeling guilty, and ye're hoping I'll tell yer what yer want to hear. But I'm not going to.' Cynthia put a finger under Laura's chin and raised her face. 'I've listened to you, now it's your turn to listen to me. Yer might not like what I'm going to say, but it's the truth. When me and you were at school, we were horrible. We bullied the younger kids, and we cheated and told lies. And we kept on like that even after we'd left school. We did exactly what we wanted to do, and it was to hell with everyone else. We didn't care about hurting our parents, as long as we got our own way. We've been bitches, Laura, and there's no other word for it. I gave my mam a dog's life, treated her like a skivvy. But I've tried to make it up to her in the last few months, and we're getting on fine. It's a bit late in the day for me to find out, but I know now that a mother can be yer best friend.'

'I've noticed that ye're nicer with yer mother, and she looks a lot happier.' Laura wrung her hands. 'What am I going to do, Cyn?'

'Stop telling lies for a kick-off. Yer mam has the right to know about this Charlie, and she'll know best how to handle it.'

'But Celia will tell her everything, and more. And she'll get Gary into trouble.'

'Don't give her the chance – beat her to it. Own up to everything, tell yer mam and dad the lot. And ask Gary to do the same. That way yer'll take the wind out of her sails and she'll be left high and dry.'

'But you don't know what she's like.' Once again Laura was finding that her friend was a much stronger person than she was. 'And what about me grandad? She'd take it out on him and she can be really wicked.'

'Laura Nightingale, I'm surprised at you! Fancy even thinking of letting this person, this Celia, get away with it! If I was in your shoes I'd be up there right now, giving her the bloody good hiding she deserves.' Cynthia felt like shaking some sense into her friend. 'This feller, Charlie, is he married?'

Laura shook her head slowly. 'I don't know. I was that confused last night, I never thought to ask. Why?'

'His baby, his problem. Blow the whole thing sky-high, Laura, and get yer grandad off the hook. Yer can't let him be lumbered with another man's baby, not at his age. And from what I've heard, he's sorry he ever married her in the first place, so yer'd be doing him a favour. If yer don't, and yer go on letting him carry the can while you and Gary waltz off into the sunset, then I'll never speak to yer again, Laura – and I mean it. We've done some lousy things in our lives, but never anything as bad as this. If yer don't do the right thing by yer family, then I wouldn't want yer as a friend.'

No one could have got through to Laura as her childhood friend did. Every word struck a chord. 'I know ye're right, Cyn, I've known all along that's what I should do. I just didn't have the courage. But I have now – you've given it to me. I'll see Gary next Thursday and I'm sure he'll go along with what I say.' Laura sighed. 'I don't know why I have to lie all the time. I even lied to our Jenny, just before I came out. She was telling me she was going to the pictures on Saturday night with Mick and John, and she looked so happy I had to spoil it. So I told her I'd been down the entry with them and they're sloppy kissers.'

'Oh Laura, that was wrong. She's a nice kid, your Jenny, and she's been mates with the two boys all her life. If you've spoiled that friendship, then ye're not worth having for a sister. Yer've got to tell her the truth.'

'I will, Cynthia, I promise. And I'll tell me mam and dad everything next Thursday. I won't go in the dance, I'll get there early and wait outside for Gary. He might come home with me so we can tell me mam and dad together, but if he doesn't, I'll do it on me own.'

Jenny pushed her plate away. 'I couldn't eat that, Mam. I'm sorry after all the trouble yer've gone to, cooking it, but I don't feel well.'

'Yer've probably got a cold coming on,' Laura said, mopping gravy up with a piece of bread. 'Take a Beecham's Powder.'

Mary rounded the table in a flash. Kneeling by her daughter's chair, she felt her head to see if she was running a temperature. 'Have yer got a headache, sunshine, or any pains?'

'I just don't feel well, Mam, me tummy's upset.'

'Yer must be sickening for something,' Stan said. 'I'd go and lie down for an hour if I were you.'

'I think I will.' Jenny pushed her chair back. 'And I think I'll stay in bed, 'cos I feel faint and dead tired.'

'See how yer feel after a couple of hours,' Mary suggested, ' 'cos ye're supposed to be going to the pictures with Janet and the boys.'

'It won't matter if I don't go, the boys will take Janet.' Jenny looked through her sister as though she wasn't there. 'I'll go up to bed.'

'You do that, sunshine, and I'll bring yer a hot drink up.'

Laura put her dirty plate on the draining board. 'I'm just nipping upstairs,' she told her mother. 'I'll help yer with the dishes when I come down.'

Jenny was slipping between the sheets when her sister entered the room. She didn't even turn her head. In fact, Laura was the last person on earth she wanted to see or be near.

'Look, our kid, what I said last night isn't true. So if that's got anything to do with yer not feeling well, I'm sorry. I don't even know why I said it.'

Jenny laid her head on the pillow and pulled the blankets up to her chin. 'Yer wouldn't have thought of saying it, if it wasn't true. And I'll tell yer why yer said it, it was because yer wanted to spoil things for me. Like yer've always spoilt things for me.'

'It was a lie, Jenny.' Laura heard the stairs creak and knew her mother was on her way up. 'Honestly, kid, it was a lie.'

'Yer said it, and yer can't un-say it. So go away and leave me alone.'

Laura was leaving as her mother came through the door with a cup of hot, weak tea. 'I'll make a start on the dishes, Mam, so take yer time.'

Mary put the saucer on top of the chest of drawers before sitting her daughter forward while she plumped the pillows. 'Get the tea down while it's hot, sunshine, and I'll nip to the corner shop for a Beecham's for yer.'

Jenny heard the knock and the sound of Janet's voice. 'Is Jenny ready, Mrs Nightingale?'

'I'm sorry, kids, but Jenny's not well, she's in bed.'

'Ah, isn't she coming with us?'

'What's wrong with her?' John asked. 'It's nothing serious, is it?'

'No, she'll probably be as right as rain tomorrow. But it's not like our Jenny to take to her bed, especially as she'd been looking forward to going out with yer. So she must really be feeling under the weather.'

Mick was looking down in the mouth. 'I don't suppose we could see her for a minute, could we? Just to say hello, like?'

'I don't think so, Mick, she was asleep the last time I looked in on her. Perhaps tomorrow, eh? Anyway, she said to enjoy yerselves and make sure Janet's well looked after.'

'Don't worry, Mrs Nightingale, Janet will make sure she's well looked after.' John chuckled. 'It's me and Mick that Jenny should be worrying about. Anyway, I'll give a knock in the morning, see how she is.'

'Yeah, me too,' Mick said. 'Give her my love and tell her I'll miss her.'

Jenny pulled the bedclothes over her head so she couldn't hear any more. She felt sick all right, but it wasn't a sickness that could be cured by a Beecham's Powder. It was in her heart and mind she felt sick. She'd never feel the same towards John and Mick now. Not when she knew they'd been kissing her sister down an entry. She felt betrayed by them, but knew that was stupid. They were both old enough to have been out with girls and kissed them. She could forgive them that, but not when one of the girls was a fly turn like her sister.

Mary opened the bedroom door and popped her head in. 'They've gone, sunshine, and Janet looks as proud as Punch with her arms through theirs. It's a pity yer couldn't go, yer'd have enjoyed it. The boys were disappointed, especially Mick. He looked as though he'd lost his wage-packet down a grid.'

'He'll get over it.'

'Of course he will. Anyway, if ye're feeling better, yer'll all meet up tomorrow night at yer Auntie Lizzie's.'

When her mother had gone, Jenny lay on her back. She knew she'd have to see the boys again, it couldn't be avoided. But she didn't want to go out with them ever again, and didn't want them to touch her. They'd been part of her life for as long as she could remember – good mates who had looked out for her since she was able to toddle. But the thought of them kissing her sister was more than she could stomach. She wouldn't tell Janet, that wouldn't be fair, but she wouldn't be so friendly with them in future. And losing them from her life was all down to Laura. At that moment Jenny wished she'd never had a sister.

Sighing, Jenny curled up and tried to sleep. But although she could close her eyes and shut out anything she didn't want to see, she couldn't close her mind or her heart. And pictures of a boy with raven-black hair, the deepest of blue eyes and dimples in his cheeks, kept popping up in her head. She could hear him speaking as clearly as if he was standing next to her. 'As I haven't got a girlfriend, I thought yer might like to team up with me.'

And with the words and the pictures came the tears.

Mary opened the door on Monday morning to Lizzie Marshall. 'Well, this is a surprise. It's not often we get honoured with your company. Come on in, Lizzie, me mate's here for her usual cuppa and natter.'

Lizzie didn't look too sure. 'Perhaps I'd be better coming back when yer haven't got any visitors. I don't like to intrude.'

'Visitors, did yer say, Lizzie?' Mary leaned forward and pulled on the old lady's arm. 'Come on in and don't be daft. I haven't got no visitor, but me lodger's here.'

'Ay, I heard that, buggerlugs,' Amy grinned. 'But I ain't no lodger, 'cos lodgers have to pay for what they get. I get mine for nowt.'

'Ye're telling me.' Mary pulled a chair out for her visitor and saw her settled before going on. 'Proper skinflint you are, if there ever was one.'

Amy combined an expression of surprise and hurt. 'How can yer say that, girl? Have yer forgotten those cream slices already?'

'Oh my God, am I going to get that thrown up at me for the rest of me life?' Mary winked at Lizzie. 'She mugs me to a cake once – just the once, mind yer – and never a day goes by that she doesn't remind me of it.'

'Only 'cos ye're getting absent-minded, girl.' Amy shuffled to the edge of her chair, cupped a hand around her mouth and wagged a podgy finger at Lizzie to move nearer. 'She's going a bit senile. Terrible thing to happen to a woman of her age, but there yer go, that's life for yer. So I remind her of me generosity every day, just to keep her mind active.'

'Lizzie, sorry to change the subject, sunshine, but would yer like a cuppa?'

'No, thanks, Mary, I've not long had one. I just came over to see how Jenny was. I didn't think she was herself last night at all. Usually she's always laughing and joking, but last night she was very quiet.'

'Oh yeah, our John mentioned something like that before he went to work this morning,' Amy said. 'In fact, he said every time Mick spoke to her, she nearly bit his head off.'

'That's not like our Jenny, I've never known her be in a temper with anyone. She was quiet this morning before she went out, but that's all. I'll have a good talk to her tonight, make sure she's telling me the truth. I wouldn't like the girl to go to work if she's sick, just because she doesn't want to worry me.'

'I'm going on without yer, Dad,' Mick said as they came out of work. 'I want to catch Jenny on her way home, and I can run faster on me own.'

'Is true love not running smoothly, son?'

'No, it's not, Dad, and I want to find out why. Ask me mam to put me dinner between two plates, will yer?' With that, Mick took to his heels and ran like the wind. He had to know what was wrong with Jenny, because he didn't believe it had anything to do with her not feeling well. And he wanted to be alone when he asked her.

His heart flipped when he saw her walking towards him, shoulders hunched and head down. 'Jenny,' he spoke her name softly so as not to startle her, 'can I have a word with yer, please?'

'Mick, what are you doing here?'

'I want to ask yer what's happened in the last few days to change yer so much? Yer looked at me last night as though I was something the cat had dragged in. I could tell yer didn't want to talk to me, or even be in the same room. And I want to know why, Jenny, 'cos I would never do anything to hurt you.'

'There's nothing wrong, Mick, I just wasn't feeling well. But now ye're here, and we're on our own, I may as well tell yer I've been thinking about what yer said about me being yer girlfriend. I don't think it's a good idea because I'm too young, really, to start courting proper. I haven't been anywhere yet, and never met any other boys.' Jenny saw the hurt on his face and hated herself for putting it there. But she was hurting, too, and it was his fault. She felt like shouting out loud, asking him why he'd kissed her sister. But that would be childish.

'I only asked yer to be me girlfriend, Jenny, I didn't ask yer to marry me. Yer'd have been free to end it any time yer wanted, if yer met another bloke yer liked better.' Looking the picture of dejection, Mick dug his hands in his pockets. 'And where does John fit into your plans?'

'John's never asked me to be his girlfriend, but if he did, I'd tell him the same as I'm telling you. I want to get out and about on me own for a while, do a little growing up.'

'So me and John are not even on yer list of friends? No more going to the dance, or even a game of cards?'

Jenny turned her head away from those deep blue eyes that could make her go weak at the knees. 'Of course we're still friends, we'll always be that. It's just that I don't want to get serious, that's all.'

'All right, Jenny, I've got the message, I'll not bother yer any more.' As he turned away, he said, 'I'll tell John so he won't have to listen to the price yer put on our friendship.'

'I'll be seeing yer around, like at Auntie Lizzie's.'

Mick turned back and looked down at her. 'Yer intend taking our ten years of being mates and tearing it up into little pieces. But yer want to keep some of the pieces that suit yer. Well, it doesn't work like that, Jenny. I have loved you for as long as I can remember. I've never even tried to find anybody else because I've always known you were the one I wanted. But I'll not hang around just in case I bump into yer, like, as yer said, "at Auntie Lizzie's".'

This time when Mick walked away he kept on walking. Slowing down only long enough to say, 'Goodbye, Jenny. I hope yer find what ye're looking for.'

'What's gone wrong in this house, love?' Stan asked Mary. 'We always managed a laugh when we were having our dinner, but lately I can't even raise a titter. I know what your worries are, and I can understand, but what's up with the girls? Our Laura looks as though she's sitting on a time bomb and yer hardly get a word out of Jenny.'

'We'll start with me, shall we?' Mary shrugged her shoulders. 'I'm worried sick about me dad. He didn't come Sunday and this is the second Wednesday he's missed. But I can't bring meself to go to his house 'cos I know once I set eyes on Celia I'd clock her one. I'll give it until Sunday, and if he doesn't come then – well, someone will have to go and see what's wrong.'

'I can take a hint, love – I'll go. If he doesn't turn up Sunday, I'll be there the next night.'

'As for our Laura, I haven't a clue. She comes and goes as she pleases, as she's always done. Never a dickie bird out of her. And I'm not going to ask because I wouldn't believe what she told me anyway.' Mary sighed as she bent to straighten the rug in front of the hearth. 'Our Jenny is a little more complicated. For some unknown reason, she's fallen out with John and Mick. She says she hasn't, she just doesn't want to go out with them like courting couples. Janet's gone to the dance with the boys, but she couldn't persuade Jenny no matter how hard she tried. Molly was over today and she said Mick is devastated. He can't understand why they're the best of mates one day, then out of the blue she told him straight to his face that she wanted to meet other people.'

310

'What about John?'

'Well, apparently our Jenny, who wouldn't say boo to a goose, told Mick she felt the same about John and the message was passed on. Something must have happened to make Jenny the way she is; she thought the world of those boys and would never hurt them for no good reason. But whatever the reason is, she's not saying. Even Lizzie can't get it out of her.'

'I'm surprised about that,' Stan said. 'I always thought she'd end up marrying one of those boys. I'd have bet a pound to a pinch of snuff on it.'

'Oh, I think John's been out of the race for weeks now,' Mary smiled. 'Janet pulled him off the starting line. She set her sights on him from the beginning and yer've got to hand it to her, she's never given up. Amy thinks it's hilarious. She said the lad doesn't know he's been caught yet, but he will when he tries to wriggle out of the fishing net.' She sat back in her chair and rapped her fingers on the wooden arms. 'Before me dad hit me with his troubles, I used to often think how nice it would be if the two boy mates married the two girl mates. I'd be made up to have Mick for me son-in-law.'

Stan chuckled. 'How does Amy feel about having Janet as her daughter-in-law? Mind you, it's Janet we should feel sorry for.'

'Amy seems quite delighted. She said the girl's either a genius or as thick as two short planks. It doesn't matter to her which, because she's a bit of both herself.'

'I'm sorry about Mick, our Jenny couldn't have got a better bloke,' Stan said. 'And we get on well with his family.'

'Yeah, but what we want and what Jenny wants, are two different things. She's a very level-headed girl and she must know what she's doing. You and me, sunshine, will just have to stand by and watch, hoping for the best.'

The card game was over and Fanny Pennington was putting the cards back in the box when Cynthia took hold of Laura's arm. 'Come up to me bedroom, I've got a new lipstick to show yer.'

Laura sat on the bed and was surprised when her friend plonked herself down beside her. 'Where's the new lipstick?'

'That was only an excuse. I've got something to tell yer.'

'I hope it's something nice,' Laura said, pulling a face. 'I'm dreading tomorrow night, I just hope I can go through with it.'

'Of course yer can go through with it, don't be stupid. Just remember how many people yer'd be letting down if yer didn't. Particularly yerself, Laura. For once in yer life do something that counts. Neither of us can look back on the good things we did, because there aren't any. If yer want to make yer family happy, then do this for them. I've changed a lot, kid, since I met Bill. He's been good for me. I told him at the beginning that I'd lost me trust in men, and not to rush me. And I'll always remember what he said to me: "I'll try a little tenderness." Do the same, Laura. Forget the tough girl who lied and cheated, be more caring for those who love yer, and remember – a little tenderness will go a long way.'

Laura took a deep breath and squared her shoulders. 'I will, Cynthia, even if it kills me, I'll do it. And now, what's this news of yours?'

Cynthia hugged herself. 'Bill's asked me to get engaged on me seventeenth birthday.'

Laura's mouth opened wide. 'Go 'way! Ooh, isn't that marvellous!'

'I don't know whether I'm on me head or me heels, I'm that excited. I haven't told me mam and dad yet, I'll wait until Bill's with me and we can do it together. And when we've told my parents, we'll go round and tell his. I think they'll be pleased because we all get on so well together.'

'I'm going to start being the new me right away,' Laura decided. 'No more lies, no more cheating. So I'll be honest and say that when yer said yer were getting engaged, I was as jealous as hell. But it's made me more determined to sort meself out, so me and Gary can get engaged. Then he can take me to meet his mam, who he loves the bones of, and he can meet my family.' Laura closed her eyes. 'I just hope I don't make a hash of the whole lot.'

'Ay, look at me, kid. You are not going to make a hash of it, or I personally will kill yer. All yer have to do is tell yer mam and let her take over. But tell her everything, don't leave a thing out for Celia to latch on to.' Cynthia gave her a hug. 'Come down on Friday and let me know how yer got on. If it's possible, bring Gary with yer. I can't wait to see this blond's answer to a maiden's prayer.'

Laura stood up. 'I'd better be going. Are yer seeing Bill tomorrow night?'

Cynthia's smile was her answer. 'He's the best thing that ever happened to me.'

Chapter Twenty-Five

Gary was startled when he saw Laura walking towards him, his first thought being that she was in trouble. He ran to meet her and took both of her hands in his. 'What's wrong, babe? Has something happened?'

Laura shook her head. 'Not yet.' Her whole body was tingling, as it always did when he touched her. She loved him so much, she'd go through hell, fire and water for him. 'I came to meet yer 'cos there's something I want yer to do. Something that will get us out of this mess once and for all.'

Gary grinned as he squeezed her hands. 'I'm already out of it, my dearest, darling Laura. I've been and gone and done it: I told me mam everything. So Celia can do what the hell she likes, she can't hurt me now.'

Laura was dumbstruck. She'd imagined having to talk him into going along with her, and had even prepared herself for him refusing. But here he was, with a big smile and a clear conscience. 'What did yer mam say?'

'She called me for all the silly buggers under the sun, said I should have told her right from the start and none of this would have happened. If she ever meets Celia, she'll skin her alive, or so she says.'

'But didn't Celia say she'd go and tell yer old boss, and the place where yer work now? She could still do that.'

'Me mam's sorted it all out. She went to see Mr Brown, he's the owner of the shop, and he was disgusted. Apparently she'd tried it with one of the older workers, but she had the sense to tell her to scram. So she tried me, soft lad, and I fell for it. Anyway, me mam gave Mr Brown five shillings, to help towards what she'd fiddled. He didn't want to take it but me mam made him. Her motto is, out of debt, out of danger. And guess what? He even offered me a job! I wouldn't go back, though, even though he's a smashing feller, because I'm on better wages where I am.'

Laura thought suddenly of Celia, who would be along this way any minute. She pulled on Gary's hands. 'We'd better move. I want yer to come home with me, while I tell me mam and dad. If yer think anything of me, Gary, yer won't let me down.'

'Think anything of yer! Babe, I love yer and adore yer.' His laugh rang out. 'Oh, it feels good to say it at last. I'll be only too happy to come with yer to hold yer hand and give yer support. And to see that worried look disappear from yer eyes.'

As they walked arm in arm, Laura said, 'I'm glad yer've told yer mam, and she was all right about it. I hope my parents are the same.' She glanced up at him and thought how lucky she was to have met him. He wasn't half handsome, and nice with it. 'Your mam must have some guts to do what she did.'

Gary chortled. 'She's not the size of sixpenn'orth of copper, but when she gets her dander up, she can be a real spitfire. When she knew what Celia had done to her lovely son, she went haywire. Mind you, I came in for it. She couldn't believe I'd been stupid enough to let meself be blackmailed without telling her. She knows some choice words, my mam, and I got called every one of them when she was telling me how dumb I'd been. So I'm warning yer what to expect.'

'My Auntie Amy's like that, she's always swearing. She once said that if the King came to her house for tea, she'd still tell him to wipe his bleedin' feet before she'd let him in. And if he pulled a face because his cup had no handle, she'd tell him to bugger off back to his palace.'

'My mam would get on well with your Auntie Amy. The air would be blue if the two of them got together.'

'She'd get on with me mam, as well. Me mam doesn't swear much, but she's full of fun and always laughing.' Laura shuddered. 'I hope she's able to laugh after what I've got to tell her tonight.'

They came to the end of her street. 'Would yer mind waiting outside by the entry, Gary? I think I'd be better doing it on me own; I'd be too embarrassed if you were there. I'll come for yer when it's over, if she hasn't thrown me out before then.'

'Okay, babe. I'll walk up and down in case someone thinks I'm up to no good and thumps me one.'

Laura took a deep breath. 'Here goes.' Before she had time to change her mind, she covered the few yards with purpose in her step. He'd told her he loved her, and she clung to those words.

'I thought yer were going to the dance?' Mary looked up in surprise when her daughter walked in. 'Don't tell me you're not feeling well.'

Laura pulled a chair from the table and sat down next to Jenny, who was reading. 'I want to have a talk to you and me dad. Ye're going to be shocked, but I want yer to hear me out before saying anything.'

Jenny closed her book and stood up. 'I'll go upstairs.'

'No, I want yer to stay.' Laura held on to her arm. 'Please, Jenny?'

Jenny pulled her arm free and looked down at her sister. Harsh words were on her lips but there was something in Laura's eyes that held them back. She put her book on the table and sat down.

'What's all the mystery?' Stan asked. 'Yer sound very melodramatic.'

Laura's tongue flicked over her dry lips. She'd have given anything for a drink, but that would take time and she was eager now to get it over with. 'I haven't been a good daughter, I know that now. I've lied and cheated all me life, and led me mam a merry dance. But lately I've been a bigger liar than even you could imagine. I'm not proud of it, and I only hope yer don't all hate me when I've said what I've got to say.'

Mary and Stan looked at each other with apprehension. The last thing they wanted to hear was that their wayward daughter had got herself into trouble. But they stayed silent and listened to the story unfolding. Several times Mary shook her head and closed her eyes, signs of the disgust she felt at the string of lies her eldest daughter had told. But she never spoke until Laura came to the baby Celia was expecting.

'How d'yer know this?' Mary was red in the face with anger. 'Did the cheeky bitch tell yer herself?'

'No.' Laura felt faint with worry. Her family were going to despise her after this. 'I told yer about the boy I met at the dance, Gary, and the way Celia has been blackmailing him, too. Well, he told me. She doesn't know I know yet. And Gary also told me something else.' The tears she could no longer control, started to roll down her cheeks. 'I know I've been bad, and I'm sorry, 'cos I want yer to love me, not hate me. But I've got to tell yer what Gary found out. The baby isn't me grandad's baby. The father is a bloke called Charlie, and he goes to the dance. I'm pretty sure Celia goes out with him a lot.'

Stan looked at his wife and saw the colour drain from her face. 'Are you all right, love?'

'I can't take it in!' Mary looked dazed. 'How does this Gary know?'

'Celia and Charlie told him. He said they were having a good laugh because she said her husband had agreed to let people think it was his. And she hasn't told them that she's married to me grandad, she said she'd married me uncle, and that's how she knows me.'

Stan asked, 'How long have yer known all this?'

'Only since last week, Dad. I was frightened to say anything right away 'cos Celia's always hinting that she's going to tell yer about me lying. And she'd make up worse tales about me, to get me into trouble with me mam. That's why she started all this, just to get back at me mam, she's so spiteful.'

'And where does this Gary feller fit in to all this?' Mary asked. 'Is he a crony of theirs? He must be pretty thick with them to know all this.'

315

'Oh no, Mam, he doesn't even like them. I only ever see him every Thursday at the dance, but I really like him. So would you, if yer'd let me bring him in. He's waiting outside for me. He's told his mother what's been going on, and she called him a stupid bugger for letting someone blackmail him. But Gary was only fourteen, Mam, and yer know how wicked Celia is. He was terrified of her 'cos he didn't want his mam to find out. He hasn't got a dad, he died when Gary was very young, so there's only him and his mam.'

'I don't want yer to bring him in,' Mary said. 'Not tonight, anyway. I want to get things straight in me head first. If what ye're saying is true, I'll have to think about what to do about yer grandad.'

'Hang on a minute, love, don't be so hasty.' Stan stroked his chin thoughtfully. 'I'd like to ask the lad a few questions, see whether it is true or whether he's made it all up.'

'He hasn't made it all up, Stan, 'cos we know Celia's pregnant. And if this Charlie is the father, me dad has a right to know.'

'Bring the lad in, Laura,' Stan said. 'Let's see if he can answer some questions.'

'Yer won't take off on him, will yer? It's not his fault I've told yer lies. He's lovely, and I like him better than any boy I've ever met.'

'We'll see about that.' Stan's face was stern. 'Just bring him in.'

Jenny hadn't opened her mouth, even though everything surprised and shocked her. Now she knew why her mother hadn't been herself for over a week now. She'd been worried about Grandad. She looked across and met Mary's eyes. 'Our Laura's done a lot of things to hurt all of us, but I think she's been very brave doing what she's done tonight.'

'I know that, sunshine, and even though she's been very naughty, I admire her speaking up. But we've got to get at the truth now, for everyone's sake.'

All eyes went to the door when Laura came in, hand-in-hand with a tall blond boy who looked nervous at first, until he smiled. 'I've wanted to meet yer for a long time,' he said, 'and I'm sorry it has to be like this.'

Mary studied his face for a few seconds, and knew she was going to like him. His handsome face was as honest and open as could be. 'Sit down, son.'

Jenny moved to another chair, making room for Gary to sit next to Laura. She noticed that their hands stayed gripped, as though they didn't want to be parted.

Stan was more reasonable than he thought he'd be. If he was any judge of character, there wasn't much wrong with this boy. 'We're finding it hard to believe all that Laura's told us, son, so can yer shed some light on it?'

'I don't know where to start, Mr Nightingale, but I suppose

Laura's told yer how stupid we've both been for letting Celia get her claws into us?'

'I understand that, and believe it,' Mary said. 'She's as evil as they come. But what's this about the baby she's expecting? I'll be truthful with yer, me dad told us she was expecting, but never gave a hint that the baby might not be his. I've been out of me mind with worry, 'cos he's too old to be starting a family. And I can't stand his wife, I won't have her in the house.'

Stan held up his hand. 'Leave all that for now, love. I would like Gary to answer a few questions for me. Will yer do that, son?'

'If I know the answers, Mr Nightingale, I'll be glad to answer them.'

'Tell me about this bloke called Charlie, and why yer think he's the one got Celia in the family way?'

'I don't think it, I know it! They told me themselves and they thought it was funny! She's been knocking around with Charlie for ages and makes no secret of it. I honestly didn't know that she was married to yer dad, Mrs Nightingale, not until Laura told me a week or so ago.'

'And is Charlie a married man?' Stan asked. 'Or don't yer know?'

'No, he's definitely not married, he lives with his mam. I'm certain of this 'cos he only lives a few streets away from me. He doesn't half fancy his chances, does Charlie, he's a real ladies' man.'

'Is he now?' Stan stroked his chin. 'I wonder if he fancies being a family man?'

'What are yer thinking of, Stan?' Mary asked. 'I don't want me dad getting into a fight with a younger man, it would kill him.'

'Yer dad doesn't need to know anything, love, if we play our cards right.' Stan looked at the young couple still holding hands. 'Are yer willing to help me put Celia and this Charlie in their place? And help Grandad to be happy again – give him his life back?'

'Oh yes, Dad, I'd do anything to help me grandad,' Laura said. 'And I know Gary will too, after what she's done to us.'

Gary grinned. 'It would give me great pleasure to see them squirm. And the thought of Charlie pushing a pram down Walton Road – well, it's a sight I'd like to see.'

There was hope springing in Mary's heart. She'd often said to Stan that if Laura met a nice boy he might be the makings of her. Well, from what she could see, the boy sitting opposite to her was a nice boy, and he'd certainly changed her daughter.

'Jenny, will yer put the kettle on for us, sunshine?' Mary smiled at the daughter who had never caused her a moment's anxiety. Please God she'd now have two daughters to be proud of. 'We'll have a cuppa while yer dad tells us what he's got in his mind.'

Laura followed her sister out to the kitchen. 'Seeing as I'm getting all me sins off me chest, kid, I can't leave you out because I've made you suffer more than anybody. I've been a lousy sister to yer, and I am so sorry. Yer see, I've always been jealous of yer.'

Jenny raised her brows. 'Jealous of me! Why?'

'I know it sounds daft, but it's the truth, and I feel so guilty. I was jealous of yer blonde hair because yer looked like me mam, and I didn't. Jealous because yer were always laughing and happy, and everybody loved yer. Jealous because yer were good at school and I was a dunce. Yer were too good, and I walked all over yer. I can't tell yer how sorry I am and I want yer to forgive me. Give me a chance and I'll prove I want to be a real sister to yer. To share things, like sisters should do. I want yer to believe I mean all that from the bottom of my heart. I also want yer to believe me when I tell yer again, I was lying about John and Mick. I have never been down an entry with either of them, or kissed them. They wouldn't have touched me with a barge-pole. Please believe that, and then I'll have a clear conscience.'

Jenny didn't answer for a while, then a slow smile spread across her face. 'You make the tea, big sister, I'm going on a message.'

Molly opened the door and her eyes widened in surprise. 'Yes, me darlin'?'

'If Mick's in, Mrs Moynihan, can I have a word with him?' Jenny knew he was in, she'd seen him through the window. Although she would never admit it, she'd been keeping tabs on him since Monday night. He hadn't been out any night, and she was glad he was as miserable as she was. 'If he's not, it doesn't matter, I'll come back tomorrow.'

Molly felt herself being pulled backwards. 'It's all right, Mam, I'll see what Jenny wants. You go in.' He waited until his mother had closed the living-room door. 'What can I do for yer, Jenny?'

'Would yer like to be me boyfriend, Mick?'

There was no smile on Mick's face. There hadn't been for three days and four nights. 'If this is yer idea of a joke, Jenny, I don't think it's funny.'

'It isn't a joke, Mick. I've never been more serious in me life.'

Mick's heart wanted to beat faster with hope, but he wouldn't let it. 'Yer were dead serious on Monday, Jenny, when yer told me, in no uncertain terms, that yer wanted to get out and about on yer own. So I decided I'd do the same thing.'

'But yer haven't been out, have yer?' Jenny wasn't going to be put off. 'I know yer've been in every night 'cos I've watched yer through the window.'

'You haven't been out, either.'

'How d'yer know?'

'Because I've seen yer through your window.' Mick realised how childish it sounded and almost laughed out loud. But he didn't. Jenny had hurt him so much, he wasn't about to let her hurt him more. 'Anyway, what have yer come over for?'

'To ask if I can be yer girlfriend. I know yer haven't found another one, 'cos yer haven't been anywhere to meet one.'

'Yer've changed yer tune, haven't yer? What about all those things yer said to me about meeting other boys?'

Jenny thought if Laura could admit to lying, so could she. 'It was all lies, Mick, I didn't mean a word of it. I've wanted to be your girlfriend for as long as I can remember. I don't want no one else. But I'll not crawl to yer, Mick Moynihan, so either yer close the door in me face or yer get yer coat and come out with me. Which is it to be?'

'Yer do know that if I'm yer boyfriend, I'm entitled to kiss yer?'

'I can't wait, Mick. In fact, if yer come down off that step we can have our first kiss in the street and give the neighbours something to talk about.'

'Don't tempt me, Jenny.'

'I'm not tempting, Mick, I'm offering.'

When Mick stepped on to the pavement, he expected Jenny to back up, but she didn't. 'Yer mean it, don't yer?'

'Of course I mean it! Now, when a girl gets her first kiss, it's a big day in her life. One she can look back on with happiness. So will yer put a smile on yer face, just for me?'

It was a brief kiss, but lasted long enough for Mick to see stars and Jenny's knees to buckle. 'This is for keeps, isn't it, Jenny?' His voice was husky.

'For ever and ever, Mick.'

'Hang on, I'll get me coat and we'll go down to Auntie Lizzie's. John and Janet are there and I want them to be the first to know.'

Molly was standing inside the living-room door with his coat in her hand. May God forgive her, but hadn't she been listening to every word that was said? 'Romance back on track, is it, me darlin'?'

His dimples deep holes in his smiling face, he kissed his mother's cheek. 'On track and it's full steam ahead, Mam.'

Seamus chortled. 'Sure, now, isn't it meself yer take after? It's a one-woman man yer are, right enough.'

'We're only going to Auntie Lizzie's, Mam, so I won't be late.'

'Will John not be thinking he's had his nose pushed out of joint? Yer know he's always had a soft spot for Jenny.'

'That's why I want to be the first one to tell him. But somehow I don't think he'll be that upset. Janet seems to have found favour with him. Anyway, I'll see yer later. Ta-ra.'

* * *

319

Lizzie Marshall's face lit up when she saw Jenny. 'Oh, it's good to see yer, love, I was beginning to think yer'd fallen out with me.'

Jenny kissed her and lightly pinched her cheek. 'I fell out with everyone, Auntie Lizzie – I was a real misery guts. Even me mam couldn't get a smile out of me.' She would never tell anyone how Laura had lied to her. 'I can only put it down to feeling under the weather.'

'Well, let's hope it doesn't happen often,' John said, 'otherwise none of us will have heads left. Yer'll have bitten them all off.'

'Ay, don't you talk to my friend like that.' Janet wagged a finger at him. 'She can't help it if she's not well.'

John grinned at her. 'If yer don't put that finger away, I'll bite it.'

'You do that and see what'll happen. Either I get me mam to come after yer with the rolling pin, or yer kiss me finger better.'

'I'll give both options my consideration and let yer know.' John turned his eyes to Jenny. 'How come you and Mick have both turned up?'

'I called for him. I wanted to say I was sorry for being nasty the last time I saw him. I'm glad to say he accepted my apology.'

'I've asked her to be me girlfriend, John.' Mick put his arm across Jenny's shoulders. 'I finally plucked up the courage.'

It was difficult to read anything from John's face. 'I gather, seeing as ye're both grinning like Cheshire cats, that Jenny's answer was the one yer wanted to hear?'

Mick nodded. 'We've come to see if yer approve, or whether yer want to throw down the gauntlet and challenge me to a duel, at dawn, in the North Park.'

John searched Jenny's face, and a feeling came over him that he couldn't put a name to. He'd loved her for so long he couldn't imagine stopping loving her. But he now knew that though he would always love her, it would be the love of a brother for a special sister. He turned to Mick, and grinned. 'What d'yer mean, the North Park? That's flipping miles away! What's wrong with Walton Park?'

Relief flooded Mick's body. He wasn't going to lose his best mate after all. 'Well, it's like this, yer see, pal. Knowing what a lazy begger yer are, I knew yer wouldn't travel all that way just to kill me.'

'So after years of rivalry, it's you who's won the fair maiden's hand? Well, I don't think ye're good enough for her, she deserves better.' John put his arms around Jenny and held her close. 'I'm cut to the quick, I really am. Me poor heart is bleeding.'

'I'll bet it is,' Jenny laughed, hugging him back. 'But we'll always be mates, won't we, John? Nothing will change that.'

'We'll always be that, Jenny, and I'll always be there for yer.' His arms dropped to his side. 'At least, I will when me bleeding heart is mended.'

'Ah, yer poor thing.' Janet sidled up to him, and in her childish voice, asked, 'Shall I kiss it better for yer?'

'Not as long as yer mam's got a rolling pin and you talk like a parrot. I like the shape of me head as it is, thank you.'

Janet patted his head as she would a child, then moved close to her friend. 'So is it all settled, Jenny? Mick is officially yer boyfriend?'

'Yeah, I think so.'

'Yer think so! Hasn't he asked yer yet?'

'No, I asked him, Janet.'

'Ooh, er!' Janet pursed her lips. 'You asked him, eh?'

John bent his elbow and gave Mick such a hard dig in the ribs, he caught his breath. 'Just watch this, Mick. Can yer hear her head ticking over? Let's see what gem she comes up with this time. Honest to God, she comes out with some corkers.'

While this was going on, Lizzie was drinking it all in. She needed to go down the yard but she didn't want to miss a single word. Mind you, she might have to if they didn't hurry up. At her age, she'd die of humiliation if she disgraced herself.

Janet wanted a bit more information before she decided. 'What did yer say to him, Jenny? Did yer come right out with it, or did yer go all round the world?'

Jenny giggled. 'There wasn't much point in going around the world, Jan, so I just said, "Will yer be me boyfriend?" '

Janet tapped her lips with a finger. Then, her mind made up, she walked over to John, stood in front of him and looked him straight in the eyes. 'Will yer be me boyfriend, John Hanley?'

'Ooh, I'd have to think about that, Janet. After all, it's not only you I'd be taking on, but yer mother and her rolling pin.'

'Me mam doesn't hit members of the family, she only hits people who do things she doesn't like. And she wouldn't like it if you turned me down, so there. It would be in yer own interest to say I can be yer girlfriend.'

'Oh dear.' John couldn't look at her because he knew he'd burst out laughing. 'Are yer listening to this, Auntie Lizzie? I've got a choice between a duel to the death with Mick, or Mrs Porter's rolling pin. And I'm not a strong lad, as yer know, so for either one I'd have to get a stuntman to stand in for me.'

'Ye're not palming me off with any stuntman, John Hanley. If yer won't be me boyfriend, I'll have to pinch Mick off Jenny.'

'I can't let yer do that, curly top, 'cos they're me two best mates. It looks as though yer've got me over a barrel and I'll have to give in to yer.'

Lizzie could no longer resist the call of nature. She struggled to her feet, and on her way to the door, she said, 'I'll be gone a couple of minutes, that's plenty of time to seal yer relationship with a kiss.

321

But for heaven's sake don't tell yer mam I suggested that, Janet. I've never been partial to rolling pins.'

As she hastened down the yard, Lizzie could hear the laughter, and she knew that John and Mick would be doubled up, while the girls waited for their kiss.

'Yer are sure this is Charlie's address, aren't yer, Gary?' Stan asked as he made notes on a notepad. 'And that his mother's name is Hettie?'

'That's definitely his address, and he calls his mam by her first name. I've heard it hundreds of times. Their surname is Owens.'

'What do yer intend doing with all this information, now yer've got it?' Mary asked. 'I'm not going to call on the woman, if that's what yer've got in mind.'

'We're all in this, love, so I don't expect any one person to do what needs to be done. We mustn't forget that Charlie's mother is not to blame for what he does. It could come as a terrible shock to her.'

'She's quite a nice lady, actually,' Gary said, 'keeps her house like a little palace. And she dotes on Charlie, waits on him hand and foot. But unless she's blind, she must know what he's like for the ladies. Everyone else does, he's got quite a reputation.'

'I'd go with yer to see her, Mam,' Laura said, 'if yer wanted.'

Stan brushed the offer aside. 'This will take some working out, so yer grandad doesn't know anything about it until it's over.' He glanced at Mary. 'Yer did say that none of the women in the street liked Celia, didn't yer?'

Mary nodded. 'They can't stand the sight of her. Especially the near neighbours, who were me mam's friends. I know they wouldn't need asking twice if we wanted them to help. But what they could do, I don't know.'

'I do,' said her husband, 'but we need to work from two sides. Someone, who they won't know from Adam, has to go and see Charlie's mother with the news that she's to become a grandmother. And at the same time – and this is the tricky part – we need to get Celia out of that house for good. That's where I think yer mam's old neighbours would come in – they could drive her out.' He saw the look on Mary's face and reached for her hand. 'Strong measures are needed, love, to keep her away from yer dad. Otherwise she'll be pestering him for money and we don't want that. It has to be a clean break. And if she knows the neighbours are gunning for her, and that they mean business, she'll think twice about setting foot in the street again.'

There was a look of concern on Laura's face. 'Dad, she'll know something's up with me and Gary not being at the dance. Whatever ye're thinking of doing, it'll have to be soon.'

Mary conjured up her father's face to give her the strength she

322

needed. 'We'll do it tomorrow and get it over with. Laura, you take a day off work and come with me. If she sees us together, she'll know her little game hasn't worked.'

Stan raised his brows. 'Who's going to see to Charlie and his mother?'

'Just leave it to me, Stan. I'll get Amy and Molly over first thing and I'll enlist their help. They're me best mates, and I know they'll get stuck in and help because they think the world of me dad. If we're going to do it, let's do it properly, with our own army.' Mary jerked her head and rolled her eyes. 'I'll never hear the last of it off Amy, 'cos she didn't believe it was me dad's baby from the start.'

All eyes turned to the door when Jenny walked in with Mick. And Mary was quick to note that for the second time that night, one of her daughters had come in holding the hand of a boy.

Jenny was all smiles. 'We've made it up, Mam, and Mick's come to ask if he can start taking me out. And me dad, of course, he'll have to ask me dad. I'm going to be his girlfriend and I'm very happy about that.'

For the first time that night, there was laughter in the room. But the tears that rolled down Mary's face weren't all from laughter. They were emotional and sentimental. 'Oh sunshine, that's the second surprise we've had tonight.' She smiled across at Gary. 'And both pleasant surprises.'

Mick's grin couldn't be wider. 'Is it all right then, Mr and Mrs Nightingale, if I come courting yer daughter? I know I'm older than her, but that doesn't matter, because I'm young for me age and Jenny's old for hers. And yer know I'll always look after her and she'll not come to any harm from me.'

'I know that, sunshine, and I couldn't be happier.' Mary turned to her husband. 'They've got my permission, have they got yours?'

'If I don't give it, I won't get invited to any parties over there. And the Moynihans give the best parties in Liverpool. So, permission granted.' Stan suddenly remembered his manners. 'Oh, this is Gary, a friend of Laura's. I'm afraid I don't know yer second name, son.'

'It's Stevens, Mr Nightingale.' Gary stood up to shake Mick's hand. 'It's nice to meet yer, Mick, and I think yer've got a very pretty girlfriend.'

The two boys liked each other on sight. 'Ay, keep yer eyes off her, Gary, I've only just got her – she's brand new. If I ever get tired of her, I'll give yer a shout.'

'You won't ever get tired of me, I won't let yer.' Jenny leaned against him as she grinned at her mother. 'And guess what, Mam? Janet's going to be John's girlfriend. She's absolutely over the moon. Mind you, I'm not quite sure that John knows it yet.'

'Oh, he knows it all right,' Mick said. 'It started to dawn on him a few weeks back. He wouldn't have it though, when I told him.'

Mary's heart felt lighter than it had done in days. 'So the four mates have become two two's eh? I'm delighted for yer.' Her attention was caught by Laura pulling on Gary's arm. And she saw her daughter mouth the words, 'Go on!'

Gary cleared his throat. 'I'm the new boy in the camp and I'm embarrassed and blushing like mad. But have I your permission, Mr and Mrs Nightingale, to call for Laura tomorrow night? And the next night, and every other night after that?'

Mary saw the way her daughter was looking up at this handsome blond boy, and knew he was the one for her. She also knew he'd keep her on the straight and narrow. 'As long as yer promise to look after Laura, like Mick did over Jenny. Yer see, me and Stan, we love both our daughters dearly.'

Chapter Twenty-Six

'Don't get yerself involved in any fighting, d'yer hear?' Stan looked up at his wife as he pulled his cap lower on his forehead. 'Any sign of trouble and you get out of there quick.'

'Don't worry, love, I won't be on me own. Anyway, last night was such a lovely night I'm convinced everything is going to go fine for us from now on. I'm made up over Mick, I really am, he's a smashing lad. And although it was the first time I'd clapped eyes on Gary, I can feel it in me bones that he's going to be good for Laura.' Mary unfolded her arms and shooed him away. 'If yer don't hurry, yer'll be late clocking in.'

'Will yer be here when I get home?'

'I don't know, love, we'll have to take things as they come. I'm hoping for big things, all in one day, and perhaps I'm hoping for too much. If all me dreaming and scheming comes true, I'll be the happiest woman in Liverpool and I'll greet yer with a smile on me face. But anyway, if I'm a bit late, Jenny will do yer beans on toast or something – it won't kill yer to do without a cooked dinner for one day.' Once again she shooed him away. 'Get going, love, 'cos I can't afford to stand gossiping, I've got a busy day ahead of me.'

Mary closed the door and paused in the hallway for a while when she heard her daughters talking. It was a sound seldom heard and was like music to her ears. It was with hope in her heart she entered the room. 'Laura, will you see to the beds while I tidy up in here? I don't want it looking like a muck-midden when Amy and Molly come. As soon as I think Seamus and Ben have gone to work I'm going to give them a knock.'

Amy opened the door rubbing the sleep out of her eyes. 'Christ, girl, fancy calling on anyone at this ungodly hour! The bleedin' streets haven't been aired off yet.'

'It's an emergency, sunshine – I need yer help.'

The hour was early, but not too early for Amy's brain to look for humour in any situation. 'Ay, girl, ye're not going into labour, are yer?'

Mary tutted. What would you do with her? 'Me dad's in trouble and I want yer in our house in half an hour – fully awake.'

Amy's face showed concern. 'Serious, is it, girl?'

Mary nodded. 'Very.'

'Right, half an hour it is.'

When Molly opened her door, she agreed without question. Except to ask, 'D'yer need me to bring anything, me darlin'?'

'Only yerself, Molly, thanks.' Mary hurried across the cobbles to make sure the house was tidy. She didn't worry about Amy because her best mate didn't give a continental what her place looked like. But Molly was a different kettle of fish. As soon as her husband and Mick left for work, she got stuck in and the whole house was spick and span by nine o'clock. That's unless it was the day for changing bedclothes, then she finished a little later.

'Laura, yer've got five minutes to get yerself washed, then I can get to the sink.' Mary caught her daughter's arm as she passed. 'There's no need to come out with the whole story. Yer just went to a dance and Celia happened to be there. Yer met Gary, fell for him and started going to the dance every week. From that point, we tell the truth. Okay, sunshine?'

Laura felt choked. Her mam and dad had been great, and she knew it was more than she deserved. She gave Mary a big hug. 'Thanks, Mam, for everything.'

Jenny popped the last piece of toast in her mouth and stood up to take her plate out. 'I was saying to Laura, Mam, that she's got a good-looking boyfriend. And he seems to be nice inside as well as out.' Her body still feeling the effects of the excitement of last night, and her heart singing with happiness, she laughed. 'Mind yer, he's not as handsome as my Mick – no one is.' Then she added, 'Except for me grandad – he's the most handsome man in the whole wide world.'

After Jenny had left for work, mother and daughter rushed around like mad to get everything done before Amy and Molly arrived. And Laura had just finished the last job of wiping the hearth over when the knock came.

'This emergency had better be good, girl.' Amy waddled in, followed closely by Molly. 'Every bleedin' bone in me body is complaining about the way it's been rushed this morning. Me face doesn't even know it's been washed yet.' Her brow rose when Laura walked in from the kitchen. 'What are you doing at home this time of the day? Did yer sleep in?'

'No, she didn't, I kept her off work.' Mary pulled the chairs from under the table. 'Thanks for coming over this time of the morning, both of yer. Sit yerselves down and when yer've heard what I've got to say, I'm hoping yer'll help me out. It's about me dad.'

'I'll make meself scarce, Mam,' Laura said, knowing she'd be embarrassed to listen to them talking about someone having a baby, especially her grandad. 'I'll go upstairs and dust the bedrooms, shall I?'

'You do that, sunshine, there's a good girl.' Mary understood and was relieved because she didn't think it was a fit subject for young girls. 'It'll save me having to do them tomorrow.' She waited until her daughter was out of the way, then with her head bent and a finger running along the plush of the chenille tablecloth, she began to speak.

Amy opened her mouth several times, her face red with anger and disgust, but Mary silenced her with a shake of her head. However, keeping silent didn't sit well with the big woman and she could be heard muttering under her breath, 'The bleedin' bitch, she deserves to be skinned alive.'

Molly, who didn't know anything about a baby, listened with mounting horror. And when Mary had finished, the Irishwoman made the sign of the cross and said, 'In the name of God, what sort of a person is she?'

'A very wicked woman, Molly.'

Amy had so much to say she spluttered. 'What did I tell yer, girl? Didn't I say it might not be yer dad's baby? It was the first thing I thought of when yer told me. But yer wouldn't have it, would yer?'

'Me dad didn't give a hint that it wasn't his, so why would I think different? He probably thought it was the easiest way out. But that bitch has ruined his life. He didn't look his age until she got her claws into him, now he's old and haggard. He looks so unhappy, as if he's got the troubles of the world on his shoulders.'

'So he doesn't know what yer've found out?' Amy asked. And when Mary shook her head, her neighbour tutted. 'What are yer going to do about it? If I was in your shoes, and it was my dad, I'd break her bleedin' neck for her.'

'Stan thinks we should get her out of me dad's house without him knowing anything about it until it's all over. So I've got a plan in me head, which might work, but I'd need the help of me friends. That's why I asked yer over.'

Amy lifted her ample bosom and laid it on the table so she could lean forward. 'If yer want someone to kick her out, I'll be more than willing to do the job. It's what yer dad should have done ages ago, when he first found out what she was really like.'

'Me dad hasn't got the strength to argue, never mind throw her out. But I'll do that, with the help of me mam's old neighbours. That's why I kept Laura off, for some moral support. What I'm short of, is someone who'll go and see Charlie's mother and tell her she's going to be a grandmother. Her son's got this girl in the family way, her parents are throwing her out and she's nowhere to go. Under no circumstances is me dad's name to be mentioned, or our real names.'

'I'll do that,' Amy said, with a look of relish. 'I'm good at that sort of thing. What did yer say her name was, Hettie Owens? Well, I'm

327

sure me and Hettie will get on like a house on fire. I'll have her feeling heartily sorry for the girl and the unborn baby what her son is the father of. What I won't tell her, is that the girl in question is the devil in disguise.'

'Yer'd have to be diplomatic, Amy. She wouldn't have to know who yer are in case it gets back to me dad. He'd never show his face around here again if he thought everyone knew his business.'

Molly read the misgiving on Mary's face and was quick to reassure her. 'Don't you worry, me darlin', I'll go with Amy and we'll be discretion itself.'

Amy's eyes flew sideways. 'What did yer say we'll be, Molly?'

'Discreet, me darlin'. We'll be careful what we say.'

'Oh aye, we'll be that. I'm good at being careful, I am.'

Mary wrote the address down and they discussed how the two women should go about it. Then she told them of her plans to get her mam's old friends to rally round and help her put the frighteners on Celia. 'I know things don't always go to plan, but I hope these do. I said so many prayers last night, God must surely have heard them.'

'When we've done our bit, d'yer want us to go up to yer dad's?' Amy asked. 'To let yer know how we got on?'

'Call in to Monica Platt's first, see how the land lies. Celia isn't going to take this without putting up a fight, I can tell yer.'

'Yer'll have Laura with yer, so it's two against one.' Amy showed her serious side. 'Just keep thinking of yer dad and what she's done to him. And what she's done to the home yer mam was so proud of. That should give yer enough courage to belt merry hell out of her.'

Molly pushed her chair back. 'Let's go and get dressed properly, Amy, and make a start. We need to get there early before the woman goes to the shops.'

Mary waved them off, then called Laura. 'Ten minutes, sunshine, then we're on our way.'

Amy put on her brightest smile when the door opened. 'Hello, are you Hettie Owens?'

The woman smiled back. She was quite tall, ramrod straight, with steel-grey hair plaited into a bun at the nape of her neck. 'That's me, queen, can I help yer?'

'We'd like a word with yer, if yer don't mind. It's about your Charlie.'

The door was opened wider and the woman stepped back. 'Come in.'

The hallway and living room were spotlessly clean. Furniture highly polished, grate rubbed until you could see your face in it, and the brass companion set gleaming. 'Yer've got a nice house, Mrs

Owens,' Molly said, trying to hide her Irish accent which would be a dead giveaway. 'It's a credit to yer.'

'Thank yer, queen. And the name's Hettie, that's what everybody calls me.' Hettie gestured towards the couch. 'Sit down and take the weight off yer feet.' She sat in a rocking chair at the side of the fireplace. 'Did yer want to leave a message for Charlie?'

'Well, no, not really.' Amy pulled a face. 'I don't know whether this will be good news for yer, or bad. But your Charlie's been a naughty boy, and he's put a girl in the family way. Well, she's not a girl really, she's in her thirties. But her family are up in arms about it and they're going to throw her out. She'll be on the streets today, with nowhere to go. Being a mother meself, I didn't think yer'd want that to happen, not when your Charlie has admitted to everyone that he's the father.'

The rocking chair stopped and Hettie looked shocked to the core. 'I don't know nothing about this, Charlie hasn't said a word. Does he know this woman's being thrown out?'

'That I couldn't tell yer, Hettie. It's just that I know the family and they're very religious. They're mortified with the shame their daughter's brought on the house. So I just thought yer should know, seeing as the baby will be your grandchild. If it was me, I'd take the girl in, rather than see her roaming the streets looking for somewhere to lay her head. I'd feel it was my Christian duty.'

'What's this girl's name?' Hettie asked, some colour returning to her cheeks. 'And where does she live?'

'Her name's Celia, but that's all I'm going to tell yer. After all, it's got nothing to do with me, except I couldn't live with meself if I hadn't tried to do something. I'm not so worried about the girl, it's the baby I'm thinking of. And I can tell just by looking at yer, Hettie, that yer've got a kind heart. So ask Charlie when he comes in, he'll tell yer all yer want to know.' It took three attempts before Amy could push herself up off the low couch. 'I know yer'll see yer son does the right thing and I'm glad me and – er – and Margaret came. My name's Olive, by the way.'

Hettie looked shell-shocked as she followed them down the hall. 'How can I get in touch with yer, if I need to?'

'I've done what I thought I had to, Hettie. I don't want to get involved any more. Have a word with yer son 'cos, after all, it *is* his baby.'

Amy linked her arm through Molly's and the two women set off down the street, leaving Charlie's mother with very unChristian feelings towards her son. But as the day wore on, and the shock wore off, she began to think it might be nice to be a grandmother. A baby would certainly put a halt to her son's gallivanting. It was about time he settled down.

329

Halfway down the street, Amy asked in a muffled voice, 'How d'yer think it went, Molly? Did I do all right?'

Molly squeezed her arm. 'I'm proud of yer, me darlin', so I am. Yer were that convincing I got carried away and almost offered to take the girl in meself, so I did. It's an actress yer should have been, Amy.'

'And did yer notice, girl, I did it all without using one swearword? That's a record for me. If I told my Ben, he wouldn't believe me.'

'Yer could hardly swear when yer were doing yer Christian duty, Amy. Sure, wouldn't that have been very unChristian of yer? And wouldn't yer have had the Good Lord frowning?'

'D'yer think it worked, though? Or have I given the performance of me life for nothing? I should have had an audience – I was wasted there.' Then came her mischievous chuckle. 'I know, I'll go over it again tonight for my Ben. He can take the part of Hettie, 'cos she didn't have much to say for herself, did she?'

'Sure, the poor woman didn't have much chance, not when you were in full flow. She was flabbergasted, and that's putting it mild. I'll bet a pound to a penny she's sitting in that rocking chair wondering whether she imagined it all.'

'I hope not, Molly, I hope it sunk in. Otherwise Mary will have me guts for garters.'

'Oh, it sunk in, right enough. Charlie might be in for an ear-bashing when he comes home, but I doubt if she'd turn Celia away. It was the use of the words "religious" and "Christian" that did it. Did yerself not notice the statue of Our Lady on the sideboard? Sure, the woman's a Catholic and she'll not be tempting the wrath of God.'

'I wonder how Mary's getting on?' Feeling as though her mission had been accomplished and successful, Amy's thoughts went to her best friend. 'We got the easy bit – she'll have a fight on her hands. Celia is one tough cookie; she won't leave like a lamb, all meek and mild.'

'Then let's get to her side as quick as we can.' Molly tugged on her arm. 'We're in luck – there's a tram coming.'

'It's a fine how-d'yer-do, isn't it?' Monica Platt had thought nothing that Celia did would surprise her any more, but this latest news had knocked the stuffing out of her. 'All the neighbours thought yer dad was mad at the time for marrying a woman half his age, but if it had worked out, we'd have been glad for him. But the queer one didn't even try, she wrapped him around her little finger from day one. And he's too much the gentleman, he let her get away with it. But this latest trick goes beyond the pale. He wants his head testing if he doesn't throw her out, bag and baggage.'

'I don't want to give him the option – I don't think he could stand up to it. So I want to do it for him, and I was hoping you, and some of me mam's other old mates, would help me.'

'I will, queen, I wouldn't hesitate. And I know three or four others who would rub their hands in glee if they were asked.'

'The thing is, I want to do it today, before she can get her hands on him. I've seen marks on his face that couldn't have got there by accident, and I'll swear it was her that put them there. Yer see, if she went for him, he wouldn't fight back because he thinks any man who lifts his hand to a woman is a bully and a coward.'

Monica looked at her with sympathy and understanding. 'Yer don't need to tell me anything about yer dad, Mary – I've known him since before you were born. And as for Celia, yes, she would have put the marks on his face. These walls are very thin and we've heard her carrying on. She shouts and yells at the top of her voice, and her language, for a woman, is terrible. Sure enough, the next day we'd see Joe with scratches on his cheeks, or bruises.'

Laura hadn't said much, but now she ground her words out. 'If I get my hands on her, I'll give her a good hiding for doing that to my grandad.'

Mary patted her hand. 'Let's be content if we can get her out of me dad's house and out of his life.' She appealed to the woman who'd been her mam's best friend. 'How about it, Monica, will yer help?'

'With the greatest of pleasure.' The older woman smiled. 'Besides, I've got nothing on today, so it'll fill in me time and I'll consider it time well spent.'

Mary explained what she had in mind, and also what Amy and Molly were doing right this minute. And while she was speaking, Monica was nodding her head in agreement. 'Good planning, queen, yer'd make a good army captain. Now if you'll put the kettle on and see to a pot of tea for yerselves, I'll go and make a few calls.'

It was half an hour before Monica came back, but she didn't come back alone. With her were four neighbours whom Mary had known all her life. Maggie Smith, Nellie Mitchell, Lizzie Thompson and Ada Bullen. Tears came to her eyes when they stood in a line facing her across the table. They spoke as one. 'Hello, queen.'

Remembering the laughs her mother had had with these women who, when times were bad, would help each other out with half a loaf, a shovel of coal or a cup of sugar, Mary had to speak through the lump in her throat. 'If me mam's looking down on yer now, she'll be smiling and saying "thank you".'

'Ay, girl, we're doing it for yer dad,' Maggie Smith said, folding her black knitted shawl across her chest. 'But we'll be doing ourselves a favour at the same time.'

'Ye're not kidding, we'll be glad to see the back of her.' Nellie Mitchell turned her head to make sure her neighbours were nodding in agreement. 'Have yer seen the state of her bleedin' house?'

'Bloody disgrace it is,' Lizzie Thompson said. 'Spoils the whole street.'

'Aye, and that's what we see when we look out of our window,' Ada Bullen complained, playing with the long hairs that grew from a mole on her chin. 'It'll be good riddance to bad rubbish.'

'*If* we can pull it off. Still, we can but try.' Mary sighed. 'Has Monica told yer what's happened, and what I'm trying to do?'

'Yeah, girl, we know about the baby and what yer friends are doing.' Maggie Smith took it upon herself to be the spokeswoman. 'I hate to say this, but the woman yer dad married is no more than a whore. Am I right, Monica?'

'I'm afraid so. I don't want to pile the agony on, Mary, but the more yer know, the more determined yer'll be. Many a night me and Phil have heard her in the entry with a bloke. And we could tell from the noises that they weren't just having a friendly conversation.'

'Right, that does it.' Mary stood up so quickly the chair would have toppled over if Laura hadn't caught it in time. 'Me temper's on the boil now, I'm just in the mood for her.'

'She'll still be in bed queen.'

'She was in bed last time I came, but I got her up. If you ladies will give me fifteen minutes after I get in, then will yer stand in a group outside her window?' Mary waited for their nods, before tapping her daughter on the shoulder. 'Come on, sunshine, let's go.'

Celia heard the banging on the door and pulled the bedclothes up to her chin. 'Whoever it is can sod off, I'm not getting up for no one.' The banging became louder but she still ignored it. 'Bleedin' cheek knocking like that, I've a good mind to go down and belt them one.'

But the sound of breaking glass had her slipping her legs out of bed and struggling into a scruffy dressing gown. 'Just wait, whoever yer are. Yer'll be sorry yer signed by the time I've finished with yer.'

Celia was prepared for a slanging match, but she was not prepared for the two people who confronted her when she opened the door. Her surprise showed briefly, then an evil smile crossed a face that still bore the traces of yesterday's make-up. 'Well, if it isn't the stuck-up bitch herself, and her lying daughter.' Her laugh was scornful. 'I don't know which window yer broke, but it doesn't worry me 'cos yer old feller will pay for it. Now, yer can just bugger off to where yer came from, 'cos this time ye're not getting in.'

Laura moved before her mother. She was in the hall before Celia had time to stop her. 'Come in, Mam, it's me grandad's house, not hers.'

'Oh, you'll be sorry, yer little bitch. Wait until I tell yer dear mother what you've been up to.'

Mary squeezed between them and went straight to the living room. She shut her eyes at the sight that met her, but she couldn't stop the smell of dirt from invading her nostrils. And her beloved father had to live in this pigsty. She shook her head; not any more he didn't, not after today.

Celia crossed to the mantelpiece and picked up a packet of cigarettes. She lit one and took a few puffs before brazenly staring at her husband's daughter and granddaughter. 'I don't know why ye're here, but seeing as yer are, yer may as well listen to a few home truths about this daughter of yours. Perhaps yer won't be so high-and-mighty when I've finished.' She moved to stand in front of Laura and pushed her sneering face close. 'I wonder where I should start?'

Laura put her hand in the middle of Celia's chest and pushed with all her might, sending the woman reeling backwards. 'Don't come near me, yer smell dirty.'

Mary stood in front of her daughter when, mad with rage, Celia went to grab her. 'Take yer filthy hands off her. And I know about the underskirt, the lies, the smoking and Gary. So that leaves yer with little to say to me. But I have a lot to say to *you*. We'll start off with the baby ye're carrying, and its father, Charlie.' She heard Celia gasp and smiled. 'Oh, there's much we know about you. Down the back entry with every Tom, Dick and Harry, like a woman of the streets. Well, yer heydays are over, at least from this house. It's up to Charlie to look after yer now, ye're his responsibility. So I want you out of here now. And I mean within the next half-hour.'

Celia's lip curled. 'Some hope you've got, yer stupid bitch. I'm not going anywhere so yer can forget it and bugger off.'

'Ye're leaving, Celia, if I have to kick yer out.'

'Just you try it, yer bleedin' cow! Wait until Joe hears about this.'

Laura lunged forward. 'Don't yer call my mother names.' She smacked Celia across the face. 'Ye're not fit to be in the same room as her.'

Mary pulled her daughter back. 'She's not worth it, sunshine, just leave her. She's got half an hour to pack her things and get out. Then we can clean this place up before yer grandad gets home.'

'Are yer deaf or something?' Celia asked. 'I'm not going anywhere, and you can't make me.'

Mary's eyes went to the window. 'The neighbours can make you.'

'Neighbours! They're not going to chase me, why should they?'

'Because they don't like yer. And they can chase yer, don't worry. They'll be glad to see the back of yer.' Mary jerked her thumb. 'Look out of the window, Celia – can yer see them? They know all about yer baby, and Charlie, and what ye're trying to do to me dad.'

Celia saw five women, all with their arms folded across the handles of stiff brushes. And she no longer felt sure of her ground. 'They can't throw me out, it's my home.'

'Shall we invite them in and yer can ask them? But I'd take my word for it if I were you, 'cos they don't think very kindly of yer at the moment and I wouldn't vouch for yer safety. If I don't go out there in the next five minutes and tell them yer've agreed to leave, then heaven help yer. And if ye're wondering why they're doing it, it's because they know ye're an out-and-out rotter, not fit to lick me dad's shoes.'

'I'd better go and tell them what's happening, Mam,' Laura said. 'Otherwise they might break the door down.'

'Yes, okay, sunshine. Tell them to give me another five minutes.'

As soon as Laura was out of the room, Mary turned on Celia. 'If yer know what's good for yer, yer'll leave without fuss. And yer won't show yer face in this street again.'

'How the hell can I leave? I've got nowhere to go.'

'Oh yes, yer have! Yer can make a home with the father of yer baby. In fact, Hettie Owens will probably be expecting yer any time.'

The colour drained from Celia's face. 'You cow. You bleedin', stuck-up, toffee-nosed cow. One of these days I'll meet yer when ye're on yer own and I'll scratch yer bleedin' eyes out.'

'I'll give yer two bits of advice before yer go upstairs to pack yer things. Don't even think of retaliating 'cos yer'd come off worse, I promise. And secondly, keep away from my father. Don't be waiting for him outside work to wheedle money off him, because I'll find out and yer'll live to regret it. From this day, you and the baby are Charlie's responsibility. He's had his fun, now let him pay for it.'

Laura came running in. 'Mam, the neighbours said they're coming over.'

'Go and tell them to wait, Celia's just going upstairs to pack her things.'

Mary and Laura got home five minutes before Stan was due. Jenny was already there and had set the table. 'I didn't know what yer had in for tea, Mam, otherwise I'd have got it ready.'

'That's all right, sunshine, we'll have to make do with egg and chips. Yer can start peeling the spuds if yer will, to give me time to get me breath back.'

'Tell me how yer got on first, I'm dying to know. I've been a bundle of nerves all day, I couldn't settle to work.'

'Can yer wait until yer dad gets in? He'll be here any minute. If I start telling you, it would mean me starting all over again with him.

334

And it's a long story, sunshine, I can't tell it in five minutes.'

Stan popped his head around the door. 'I'm here now, and I'll have a heart attack if I have to wait much longer to hear how it went.'

Mary looked surprised. 'I didn't hear yer coming in!'

'One of yer had left the door open.' Stan slung his cap on the couch and sat down. 'Ye're all in one piece, so yer didn't have a fight on yer hands, thank God. Now tell us, is Celia still at yer dad's house?'

'I don't want to tell it in dribs and drabs, so wouldn't yer like yer dinner first? Not that ye're getting anything to write home about, I'm afraid, just egg and chips. But if it's any consolation, Ben and Seamus are having the same, 'cos Amy and Molly have only just got home.'

'Me dinner can wait, I want to know what happened.'

'Okay, let's all sit around the table and I'll start from half seven this morning, when I knocked on Amy's door.'

It took well over half an hour, and in that time Stan smoked three cigarettes. He wasn't normally a heavy smoker, but his nerves were on edge. He did raise a smile when Amy's and Molly's part in the operation was told. But although he had many question flying around in his head, he never spoke. And Jenny felt as though she was sitting in the pictures watching a sad but exciting film.

Mary was coming to the end of the saga. 'So the last I saw of Celia, she was walking down the street carrying a suitcase with all her belongings in. And behind her marched five women clutching stiff sweeping brushes. Amy and Molly had arrived by then, and they helped me clean me dad's house. We sent Laura to the shops for everything we needed because there was no Aunt Sally, no dusters or floorcloths. In fact, there was nothing – she must never have done any housework. Anyway, I left me mates to it and went down to me dad's works when I knew he'd be on his dinner break. That was the hardest part, because I didn't know how he'd take it. But he seemed relieved, although ashamed that we'd done what he couldn't bring himself to do. And he did no more than ask his boss for the rest of the day off, saying there was a problem at home. On our way back, I did some shopping and made a big pan of scouse for him.'

'I can't take it all in, yer've done so much in one day.' Stan gazed at his wife with love and admiration. 'I take me hat off to yer.'

'I didn't do it on me own, love. I had all my friends to help, and also me mam's. I could never have done it without them.'

'And all without a fight! I thought she'd be like a raving banshee!'

'Ah, well, I was saving that until the last.' Mary gazed across the table at her eldest daughter. 'There wasn't a fight, but there was a

335

hand raised. Celia called me a not very nice name and Laura gave her a really hard slap across the face.'

Jenny looked at her sister in awe. Then she put an arm across her shoulders and squeezed. 'I'm glad yer did that, sis. I'm proud of yer.'

'And me, too, love,' Stan said. 'Thanks for sticking up for yer mam.'

Mary was dog-tired, but it was a pleasant tiredness. 'Me dad's coming here straight from work tomorrow dinnertime, and he's staying for dinner and tea. And talking of food, I'd better get cracking on feeding yer, 'cos Amy and Molly are coming over later to go over it all again.'

She stretched her arms above her head. 'I'll sleep without rocking tonight, with no worries on me mind. Oh, peace, perfect peace.'

Chapter Twenty-Seven

They were just finishing their meal when Laura saw a figure pass the window. She was off her chair like a shot. 'I'll open the door – it's Gary.'

'It looks like he's the one for her,' Stan said, smiling at his wife. 'He seems to have done wonders for her.'

'He'll do for me, he's a nice boy,' Mary said. 'And we've got him to thank for what we've achieved today.'

Gary was laughing as he was pulled into the room. 'Nice to see yer again, Mr and Mrs Nightingale – and you, Jenny. I've only heard a few garbled words, but it sounded as though yer've had a good day.'

'A brilliant day, son, thanks to you. But I'll leave Laura to tell yer the part we played, and Amy and Molly will be here soon to tell yer theirs. I must warn yer though, that me best mate, Amy, has a wicked sense of humour and a vocabulary that includes quite a few words yer won't find in no dictionary. So I hope ye're not easily offended.'

'Laura's told me about her Auntie Amy, and I can't wait to meet her. She sounds like a barrel of fun.'

Stan grinned. 'She's the funniest thing on two legs, son, and as sound as a pound.' He'd only just finished speaking when there was a knock on the window that had the pane of glass quivering in its frame. 'Yer didn't have to wait long, this is her.'

'Oh Lord, look at the state of the place.' Mary tucked a stray lock of hair behind her ear. 'Dirty dishes still on the table and me without the energy to move.'

'I'll clear the table, Mam.' Jenny was already collecting the plates. 'Laura can open the front door.'

Amy waddled in, followed by Molly. 'Is your Laura stuck to that feller? Silly buggers, they shouldn't mess around with glue, their hands are stuck together now. We had to flamingwell squeeze past them.'

'This is me boyfriend, Auntie Amy,' Laura looked so proud as she said it, 'and his name's Gary. I told him all about yer and he said he was dying to meet yer.'

Amy stretched to her full height, which was up to Gary's chest. 'Me reputation has gone before me, has it? Anyway, lad, it's nice to meet yer.' Amy pumped his hand before saying, 'This is me partner in crime, Molly Moynihan.'

Molly held out her hand. 'It's a pleasure, so it is. Mary has told us about yer.'

'Will yer all sit down,' Mary said, 'yer make the place look untidy.' She noticed Laura was still gripping Gary's hand. 'If ye're not going to let go, you two had better sit on the couch.'

Amy gave Stan a dig in the arm before plonking herself on one of the wooden chairs. 'Eh, Stan, have yer heard I've added another string to me bow? I'm in the acting lark now, and if I do say so meself, Ethel Barrymore's got nothing on me.' She leaned forward to seek confirmation from Molly, and being top heavy, nearly overbalanced. Everyone held their breath as she steadied herself, and laughed when she muttered, 'God strewth, I nearly went arse over elbow.' She covered them all with her cheeky grin. 'Anyway, Molly, me darlin', am I right about me acting, or am I right?'

'Yer were so convincing, me darlin', didn't meself get carried along? I felt so sorry for the pregnant girl who was being thrown out by her family, I only just stopped meself in time from saying I had a spare room she could have. And didn't poor Hettie Owens look as though she'd been struck by lightning?'

'Amy has that effect on people, Molly,' Mary said. 'I often feel I've been struck by a thunderbolt.'

'It's what yer need, girl.' Amy's chins did a quickstep as she nodded her head. 'Ye're that bleedin' slow on the uptake, sometimes I feel like sticking a firework up a certain part of yer – er – yer atemy.'

'The word is anatomy, Amy,' Mary told her, biting on the inside of her cheek to keep a smile at bay, 'and I'd prefer yer not to mention my unmentionables in mixed company, if yer don't mind.'

The chair seat was hidden under Amy's rather large bottom, but it creaked its protest when she shook with laughter. 'Ay, girl, if I had to go through life without mentioning the unmentionables, I'd never open me bleedin' gob! And, anyway, God gave us everything we've got, and He wouldn't have done if we couldn't mention them.' There was more than a hint of mischief in the look she gave Mary. 'Or make good use of them. I can't speak for you lot, but me and Ben make good use of what the Lord gave us.'

Mary capitulated and chuckled when she said, 'This is only the second time Gary's been in this house, and the poor lad must be wondering what sort of family and friends Laura's got. I only hope he knows that ye're just a one-off, there's no more like you.'

Gary was in a state of bliss. Holding the hand of the girl he was head over heels in love with, and being made welcome in a home full of warmth and friendliness – well, his cup of happiness was overflowing. 'I'm not easily offended, Mrs Nightingale, and I'm really

338

enjoying meself. I just wish me mam was here, she'd be in her apple-cart.'

'You bring her to me, son,' Amy said, 'I'll teach her a thing or two.'

Gary burst out laughing. 'Yer don't know me mam – there's not much she doesn't know. In fact, she could probably teach you a thing or two.'

Amy studied him for a while before turning to Mary. 'Ay, girl, he's all right. Your Laura has her Auntie Amy's permission to court him.'

Laura finally let go of Gary's hand and jumped up. She gave Amy a big hug and said, 'I'm glad ye're me auntie.' Then she turned to her mother. 'Me and Gary will wash the dishes, Mam, and I can tell him what we did today. Then I want to take him to meet Cynthia.'

'Is it all right if I go and get changed, Mam?' Jenny asked. 'I'm going down to Auntie Lizzie's with Mick.'

'Yes, to both of yer. But remember, Grandad's business is his own and that's the way it stays. It is not a subject for discussion.' She gazed at her two daughters who seemed to have changed overnight from young girls to young ladies. 'Anyway, I'm sure yer've got more important things to talk about.'

Cynthia weighed Gary up as they shook hands. He was certainly everything that Laura had said he was. 'Well, we meet at last. I was beginning to think yer were a figment of me mate's imagination.'

'No, I am real, I can assure yer. And I hope we'll be seeing a lot of each other from now on. Laura tells me yer've been friends since yer started school.'

'Yeah, a real pair of horrors we were. Anyway, come and meet me mam and dad. I'm expecting Bill any minute – perhaps we can go for a walk and get to know each other?'

'Ooh, yeah, I'd like that,' Laura said. 'I want us all to be friends. Is that all right with you, Gary?'

'Anything you want, babe, suits me. As long as you're happy, I'm happy.'

Cynthia's parents made him welcome and were soon engaged in an easygoing conversation. Fanny Pennington was finding a peace in her home she had not experienced since her daughter was old enough to know she could get her own way if she played up to her father. But those bad days were behind them now, never to return. Her husband treated her with affection and respect, and her daughter with a love that grew stronger every day.

When Bill arrived, Gary noticed he greeted Cynthia with a kiss, and he promised himself he'd do the same next time he called for Laura. After all, he was nearly nineteen; he wasn't a kid.

'D'yer feel like a walk, Bill?' Cynthia asked, after introductions were made. 'Just for an hour or so.'

'Yeah, that's fine.'

'I'll go up and get me coat, then. Come up with me, Laura – I've got something I want to show yer.'

Cynthia closed the bedroom door behind her and leaned back against it. 'Well, did yer do it, kid?'

Laura nodded. 'Celia's out of me dad's house now, and although we're not sure, we think she may have gone to Charlie's. Gary will find out 'cos he knows people who know Charlie and his mam. I haven't got time to tell yer now 'cos it would take too long. I'll come down tomorrow afternoon and we can have a good chinwag. But it would never have happened if you hadn't told me straight what a bitch I've been.'

'We've both been, kid, not just you. Anyway, I'm happy for yer mam and yer grandad. And I've got to say, I think Gary's smashing. We've both done well – better, I suppose, than we deserve. I for one know how lucky I am, with Bill.'

'Me too! I love the bones of Gary, and me mam, dad and Jenny. They've been really brilliant with me. I'm going to make it up to them, I've promised meself that.'

'Going out with Gary will help yer. When yer love someone, it doesn't half change yer. I was as hard as nails before Bill came along, now I'm as sentimental as anyone can get.'

Laura smiled. 'I know, don't tell me: "Try a little tenderness".'

'That's it, kiddo! Keep singing the song.' Cynthia opened the wardrobe and took out her best coat. 'Wouldn't it be smashing if we both got engaged on the same day?'

'It would be more than smashing, it would be heaven.'

'Janet's late,' Jenny said as they sat in Lizzie's. 'Didn't she say she'd meet us here, John?'

John looked at the clock and nodded. 'I think I'll take a walk round there, see what's keeping her. I won't be long.'

'If Mrs Porter opens the door, and she's got a rolling pin in her hand, run like hell.' Mick chortled. 'I've heard she's got a good aim.' As John was opening the front door, his mate yelled, 'Ay, yer didn't kiss Janet good-night last night, did yer? If yer did, then I'd start running now if I were you.'

John set off with a grin on his face. He'd only ever kissed Janet on the cheek – surely that didn't warrant a bash on the head? As he turned into the side street, he told himself it didn't seem the same in Auntie Lizzie's without her.

Martha Porter opened the door. 'Come in, son, she's upstairs putting the finishing touches to herself. She's been that long getting ready, anyone would think she was going to a ball.'

'I heard that, Mam.' Janet came slowly down the stairs. 'I haven't been that long, only an hour.' When she reached the bottom stair, she patted her hair, which was a mass of shining curls. 'Me mam bought me some curling tongs and it took me ages to get the hang of them. I hope I look all right.' She stared at John. 'Well, John Hanley, have I made a mess of meself?'

With her mother looking on, John blushed. 'No, it looks great.'

'Right, then, we'll be off. I won't be late, Mam.'

They reached the top of her street and when she hadn't spoken one word, John asked, 'It's not like you to be so quiet, curly top. What's wrong?'

'I was thinking. In fact, John, I've been doing a lot of thinking these last few days. The last few months, really, but it's only the last few days that are important.'

'That's a lot of thinking for you, Jan, what's on yer mind?'

Janet sighed. 'Can we stand here, on the corner, while I tell yer? I don't want to say anything in front of the others.'

John cupped her elbow and led her to stand against a high wall. 'Don't look so serious, curly top, I don't like to see yer with a frown on yer face. So come on, get whatever it is off yer chest.'

'Well, I know you and Mick both wanted Jenny to be yer girlfriend, I've always known it. And now she's definitely promised to be Mick's, I don't want yer to say yer'll be me boyfriend just because of that. Yer see, I'd be second choice then, and I don't want to be yer second choice, John.'

John closed his eyes and let his head drop back for a second. 'I wouldn't do that to yer, Janet. I wouldn't want to spend me life with someone who was me second choice.' His forehead creased as he sought the right words. 'I've lived next door to Jenny since she was born and she's always been special to me – always will be. And she was twelve and a half when Mick told me he was waiting for her to grow up, then he'd ask her to be his girl. He said he'd loved her since he was six years of age and she was a toddler. I was jealous and told him to get in the queue. And over the years, we've acted out the part of rivals. We've had a lot of fun doing it, 'cos he is me best mate and we like to clown around. I've gone along with it without really giving it any thought.' He reached for Janet's hand. 'Then you came on the scene and it was nice being with yer 'cos yer made me laugh.'

'Yer mean yer thought I was daft.'

'Yes, to be honest, I did! But I know now there's nothing daft about yer. Yer've wormed yer way into my affections, and woven a spell around me heart. I didn't know this was happening until the night of yer birthday party. And even then I wouldn't believe it because me and Mick were still acting as rivals and it had become a habit. The test came the other night when Mick said Jenny had agreed to be his girlfriend. I expected to feel angry, or sad, but I

341

didn't. It was the end of a chapter in me life, but not the end of the story. I love Mick as much as I love Jenny, and nothing will ever change that.'

'Ye're talking a lot, John Hanley, but yer not saying what I want to hear. So will yer get on with it, please?'

John grinned, thinking life would never be dull with her. Placing his hands on her shoulders, he bent to put his face on a level with hers. 'If I'd had any doubts, they disappeared when I was sitting waiting for yer in Auntie Lizzie's. It wasn't the same without yer, and I got this terrible thought that yer might have dumped me. Because if yer won't be me girlfriend I don't know what I'll do – probably join the Foreign Legion.'

'Then for heaven's sake, ask me!'

'Janet, curly top, darling, will yer be me girlfriend?'

'Yes, John Hanley, I will.' There was a twinkle in her eyes. 'If I remember rightly, Jenny got a kiss from Mick.'

John feigned a look of horror. 'Oh no, not without asking yer mam first!'

'I don't tell me mam everything.'

'Yer mean right here on the street?'

Janet pulled his head down, and when their lips met John didn't see the woman who nearly walked into a lamp-post because she was watching them instead of where she was going. And all thoughts of rolling pins fled. He was experiencing a sensation he'd never felt before, and loving it. 'Wow! Even me toes have curled up.'

'Yer can have another one when yer walk me home.'

'Oh no, curly top, not until I've asked yer mam and dad if I can start taking yer out.'

'Yer don't need to do that – I'll tell them.'

'I'll do the job properly, so until then, don't act daft.'

She pulled on his coat-sleeve as they started to walk. 'I'm not daft, John Hanley. I've got you, and I think that's very clever of me.'

'Where the heck have yer been?' Jenny asked as she let them in. 'We were getting very worried about yer.'

Janet's face was one big smile. 'I'm sorry if yer've been worried, Auntie Lizzie, but I've just been proposed to and had me first kiss.'

John doubled up, his laughter louder than anyone's. 'I haven't proposed to yer, curly top!' He spluttered. 'Yer only do that when yer want to get engaged or married.'

But Janet had her own ideas on that. 'Yer can't get engaged or married without courting first, can yer? I mean, yer've got to start somewhere, and you've just proposed that I be yer girlfriend. If yer hadn't done that, we'd never be able to get engaged or married 'cos I'd be a stranger to yer.'

Jenny hugged her friend. 'There's logic in there somewhere, Jan, and when I'm in bed tonight I'll try and figure it out.'

Lizzie wiped her eyes. 'Oh dear, you'll never know what joy you children have brought me. In all me eighty odd years I've never laughed as much as I have since I fell off the front step. It was the best thing I ever did.'

Mick said, 'She's got me thinking now. I think I'd better go over it all again 'cos I'd hate it if I could never get engaged or married to yer, Jenny.' He went down on one knee and took her hand. 'Jenny Nightingale, will yer be my girlfriend?'

Jenny's infectious giggle rang out and her pretty face was a joy to behold. 'Yes I will, Mick Moynihan, with the greatest of pleasure.'

Lizzie was saying a little prayer, asking God to leave her on this earth long enough to see these two couples happily married and settled down.

Mick and Jenny stood with their arms around each other's waists and watched their best friends walking down the street. Janet had a habit of moving her head when she spoke, so they knew she was talking fifteen to the dozen. Then they saw John pull her to him as his laughter filled the night air.

'They were made for each other, them two,' Mick said. 'I've been telling him for ages that she was the one for him, but he wouldn't have it.' He gave a quick glance around before planting a kiss on her cheek. 'Just like we were made for each other.'

They were so engrossed in their own little world, high on excitement and emotion, they didn't see the courting couple until they nearly stumbled over them.

'Sorry, pal,' Mick said. 'We weren't looking where we were going.'

Laura and Gary broke apart, but it was with reluctance. 'I'm afraid we weren't looking either,' Gary laughed. 'We were otherwise engaged.'

'Ay, our kid, I'm older than you so I'm pulling rank on yer.' Laura's white teeth flashed when she smiled. 'This is our spot.'

Mick didn't like the sound of that. 'And I suppose yer'll be seeing each other every night, will yer?'

Laura put her arms around Gary's waist and her voice was husky. 'Every night, even Sunday.'

'Then we'll have to come to some arrangement,' Mick said. 'You stay this side of the window, and me and Jenny will take the other. And they'll be reserved places.'

'Suits me fine.' Gary moved Laura the yard needed to make it fair. 'It's best we know where we stand.'

'Right, pal.' Mick pulled Jenny into his arms, then looked across at the other couple. 'And no peeking, right?'

It was Jenny's giggle which alerted Mary. She left her chair and crossed to the window. Moving the draw curtain just a little, she looked out and smiled. Both her daughters were in safe hands, they'd never come to any harm from the boys they had chosen.

'Ay, Stan, come and see this. Things have moved faster this week than I thought. Yer two daughters are standing outside, in their boyfriends' arms being kissed very soundly.'

Stan joined her at the window. 'We shouldn't be doing this, yer know – they'd go mad if they knew.' But wrong or not, he couldn't resist a peep. 'It takes yer back, doesn't it, love? Twenty years ago, we were doing the same thing.' He took her hand from the curtain and let it fall back into place. 'I don't see why they should have all the fun. We're not too old to enjoy a kiss and a cuddle.'

Mary walked into his arms, tilted her head back and waited for the kiss that could still send tingles down her spine. 'This has got to be the happiest day of my life, Stan Nightingale.'